# Book III
# Brothers
## of
# Darkness
## and Light

# Jeff Thomson

ISBN: 978-0-6459286-5-5

Published by Jeff Thomson

RACK & RUNE
publishing

Typsetting by Rack and Rune Publishing
rackandrune.com
email: info@rackandrune.com

# Contents

# CHAPTER I

# WILLOWEN AND DARKMOR

Willowen's eyes fluttered open. She gazed into darkness. Slowly her vision adjusted to the gloom, and she made out what seemed to be a rocky ceiling above her. Was she in a cave? What had happened? She felt groggy, and her head ached. The Princess felt about herself. She seemed to be lying on a cold stone floor. She sat up, and peered about. Everything was dim. She couldn't make out where she was. Willowen rose to her feet, and groped about cautiously. She seemed to be in some sort of stone room; no stick of furniture or even a rug met her gaze. It was empty and cold. As her eyesight adjusted to the darkness, she could see that the room was completely barren. The Princess held her throbbing head in her hands. Had someone struck her? Where was she, and where was –

In a sudden flash of memory, everything that had happened burst upon her mind. Willowen saw the events that had occurred as though she watched them in action again. She staggered, and went to her knees. Darkmor had come to the Goblin-King's hall! He had taken the talisman from Silveron, and had thrown him aside like a rag doll. She moaned; a piteous sound that echoed hollowly in the dark space that surrounded her.

"*Silveron!*" she cried agonizingly. "My love!" The image of him flying through the air and smashing into the table burst before her. Willowen gasped, as the sight of his body lying in the wreckage came back to her. Surely he had been slain by such a devastating impact. No one could live after such a collision.

The Princess bowed her head and wept. Then she raised her head, and howled like an animal, all of her Elven control lost in a burst of pent up emotion that rushed through her like a whirlwind. Her eyes blazed with hatred, and she clenched her fists until her nails bit into her palm and drew blood.

A sound came to her in the darkness. What was that? It sounded like bolts being drawn in a door. A moment later, a portal opened in the shadows, and a flood of light stung her tear-filled eyes. Willowen shrank away from the blinding light, and cowered on the floor.

"Oh, my dear. I'm sorry; I forgot to provide you with a bed." The voice was silken, mocking her dishevelled state.

Blocking the blinding light with her hand, the Princess peered at the speaker. She could only see a vague shape, silhouetted against the light. "Who are you?" she asked. "Why have you brought me here?"

The figure came forwards. It snapped its fingers, and the brightness from the open door lessened as the portal began to close. The door closed with a thud. The darkness of the room faded away, and was replaced by a glowing light that came from the ceiling and dispelled the gloom. Willowen stared, and then rose to her feet. "*You!*" she hissed.

Darkmor bowed mockingly. "At your service, Your Highness."

Willowen groped for the amulet that focussed her power. It was gone! Her eyes burned with hate as she regarded her enemy. Had he taken it from her when she was unconscious?

"Is *this* what you want?" he said. He held up the amulet, which dangled from his fist. He smiled.

The Princess screamed and hurled herself at her tormentor. With an electric flash, and a bone-numbing shock, she hit Darkmor's shield, and was thrown back across the floor. Willowen scrambled to her feet, and fixed Darkmor with a freezing gaze.

The sorcerer clicked his tongue. "That's no way for an Elven Princess to act, My Lady." He shook his head.

"You animal! You *killed* Silveron!" She glared at him, hatred emanating from her every pore. She wanted to throw herself upon him, and kill him with her bare hands, but she knew that the sorcerer's shield protected him from such desperate attacks. Willowen forced herself to manage her fury, and look for a better opportunity.

Darkmor shrugged. "He opposed me. I had to deal with him."

Willowen shivered with the force of her loathing. "I will destroy you," she said coldly. Her hands clenched and unclenched in fury.

"Not today," Darkmor said. He placed her amulet inside his robe. He advanced towards her. "I want you to do something for me. I want you to unlock the power of the Starstone."

*"Never!"* Willowen said icily.

"No?"

"I would rather die." She folded her arms.

Darkmor raised his left hand. The jewel eyes on the snake bracelet glowed with fire. Willowen rose into the air, her hands went to her throat, and she made choking sounds. The Princess tried desperately to breathe, but Darkmor's spell negated any effort she made.

The sorcerer watched her struggles coolly. The Princess gasped, unable to get any air. She gaped at Darkmor, her heart pounded in her chest, and her lungs struggled to breathe. Just as she was about to black out, her enemy lowered his hand to his side. She dropped to the floor, gasping for breath. She regarded him with eyes filled with hate.

"I suggest you co-operate with me, Willowen. I can destroy you any time I want to." His voice lowered, became cajoling. "Why not join me? I can show you wonders that even the Elves have never dreamed of. You could become my Queen, and rule all of Erathyn with me. For I *will* rule it, none can oppose me. Silveron is dead, and I have the talisman. Amberon is my puppet, and there are no other wizards who will dare to defy me. If your father leads his army against me, I will crush it." His eyes flashed with fire.

Willowen glared at him. "I will *never* join with you. Kill me now, for if you do not, I *will* find a way to kill you."

Darkmor laughed. "I don't think so. You won't get the opportunity. You will stay here in this cell, and if you don't do as I ask, I'll leave you here to rot."

The Princess smiled. "No, you will not. You need me to give you the power of the Starstone. I wonder if you are strong enough to stand against the Army of Light without its power." She gave him a mock concerned look. "You look tired. Is the effort of controlling the Elf within you wearing you out?"

Darkmor sneered. "No. I am in complete control. He can do nothing. He cannot take back his body. It is mine for all time."

"Are you sure?" Willowen rose to her feet. "He was a powerful wizard. Can you not feel him fighting you? Is he not even now trying to break through, and cast you out?"

Darkmor's eyes thinned to slits. "It is impossible. The spell cannot be broken." Anger suffused his voice.

"I think you lie. I think he *is* trying to regain control. You are using a lot of your power just to –"

"*Enough!*" Darkmor snarled. He regarded her coldly. "I know what you're trying to do. It's hopeless. The Elf is gone. I am the master of this body. You will help me, or I will leave you here to die. I wonder how long that would take? Centuries, perhaps?"

Willowen laughed scornfully. "You are so predictable. Do you think I care if I live or die, now that Silveron is dead? You cannot force me to help you, nor can you threaten me with death." She folded her arms and stared at him haughtily.

A retort was about to burst from Darkmor's lips, but at that same moment, the door reverberated to heavy pounding. As the sorcerer spun about, furious at the interruption, the door was flung wide, and a man rushed in.

"Master!" he gasped. He glanced at the Princess, and hurried to Darkmor's side. He put his lips next to the sorcerer's ear, and whispered urgently.

Darkmor's eyes widened. His mouth fell open in astonishment. The servant stood back, and stared at Darkmor fearfully.

"Is this true?" Darkmor said coldly.

"Yes, Master." He nodded. "He lives." He glanced at Willowen again, and she saw him swallow nervously.

"Silveron lives," she said, guessing the import of the servant's whispered words. "You could not kill him." She gave Darkmor a withering stare. "Now he will come for me. You will see that he is much more powerful than you thought. He will destroy you."

The sorcerer returned her stare. "I don't think so." He reached into his robe, and took out the talisman from where it hung about his neck, and showed it to her. "He needs this. Goldwen himself knew he was no match for me. He realised too late what I'd done when I created the child that gave me this body." He returned the talisman to his robe. "Now, with the knowledge of the Black Circle, and this immortal body, I am invincible."

The Princess laughed again. "No, you are only a foolish Man, who knows nothing of immortality. You are not invincible. Silveron will defeat you, and your army will fall to the Army of Light."

Darkmor smirked. "Do you think so? I have allies that your father and all of those other fools have never even seen. They will crush the Army of Light, and bring Anarys to me, to serve me as my slave. All the others will be wiped out."

Willowen gave him a cynical look.

"You don't believe me?"

She shook her head. "No. You *have* no allies. You stand alone against the might of the combined strength of all the races of Erathyn."

The sorcerer smiled. "You think so?" He turned from her, and gestured at the wall. A light began to glow there, and dim shapes were seen in its heart. As Willowen looked on, the light spread over the wall, and a picture formed before her, as though she gazed upon a tapestry, a tapestry that became filled with movement. A vast army of uncounted numbers appeared, Cobrans, evil Men, and as she looked, thousands of O'skaa riders and their hideous mounts joined them, led by a huge spider, upon which rode the Queen of the Schaaka.

Darkmor turned to her. "Well?"

"It is only an image conjured by you in an attempt to fool me. No such army exists. Even if it did, the Schaaka would be of no use to you; they cannot face the sun, and if they only came out of the Underworld at night, they would not be much use to you."

"What if there *was* no sun?"

"What do you mean, 'no sun'?"

The sorcerer eyes glittered. "What if I could cast a spell, one that could make an eternal night fall upon Erathyn? The Schaaka would be able to move about without fear of the sunlight. They would cover all the lands, and none could stand before them."

"No such spell exists," Willowen said scornfully. "What you are saying is merely fantasy."

"Is it?" He turned his attention back to the image. With a wave of his hand, the army disappeared, to be replaced by the astonishing sight of the moon covering the sun. The light that fell upon everything was blood red. The vision showed them the Overworld soaked in the ruddy light; trees, grassland, mountains, rivers, all were red.

"It is not real," Willowen said. "You have conjured it to try and intimidate me."

He looked at her condescendingly. "You still don't believe what your own eyes show you. Shar."

The man bowed. "Master?"

"Bring her." Darkmor snapped his fingers, and the vision winked out. He paced over to the door, and with a wave of his hand, the portal opened wide. He paused on the threshold, and looked back at his servant. "*Now*, Shar."

Shar grabbed Willowen by the upper arm. She shrugged him off, and walked imperiously over to join Darkmor. Shar followed sheepishly. The three of them came out into the corridor, and the sorcerer led the way to a door that opened onto a flight of stairs. Without pause, he started to climb. Willowen followed, with Shar bringing up the rear. They ascended for several minutes, passing other doors. Willowen guessed that her prison lay deep underground. Several Goblin guards were stationed at some of the doors, and they grinned evilly as the Princess passed by. After an interminable climb, they came to a door. Darkmor halted. He turned and gave Willowen a superior smile. He waved his hand theatrically, and behind him the door opened wide.

Blood-red light flooded in. He stepped aside, and Willowen, gasping in shock at the vision that met her eyes, stepped forward, walking out onto a platform at the very top of the tower. A stone railing surrounded its edge, and above was only the reddened sky. She walked out into the middle of the platform, gazing in amazement at the impossible sight of the moon occluding the sun. She looked down, and everywhere her gaze went, only the colour of blood met her eyes. The Princess stared in disbelief at the awful scene below her. The vision that Darkmor had shown her *was* true.

"*Now* do you believe?" Darkmor's voice came from behind, mockingly.

She spun about and faced him. "How have you done this?" she said, incredulously. "Not even the combined powers of the Council of Light could do such a thing. It is impossible."

He spread his arms wide. "And yet, here you see it before you."

She stared at him in horror. He was much more powerful than she had first thought. Suddenly, the realisation of how he had accomplished such a feat of magic exploded in her mind. "The Starstone!" she gasped.

"Yes." He smiled. "But I only used a fragment of its power. This is the result." He came closer. "Just think what could be done if the full power of the Starstone were unlocked?" He gazed up into the heavens. "I could move *worlds*!" Darkmor raised his arms triumphantly. "I could remake the universe as I see fit." He regarded her, his eyes burning with fervour. "I would become a *god.*" He lowered his arms and stepped towards her. Willowen shuddered as his multi-coloured eyes bore into her. Darkmor placed his hands on her shivering shoulders. "And I would make you a goddess. You would be worshipped by all of the races of Erathyn. They would bow down to us, or be destroyed. All would become our slaves. Think of the wondrous things we could create with such power." His face was flushed with passion. "All you need do is help me."

Willowen stared at him, sickened. Her skin crawling, she shrugged his hands off and backed away from him. She came up against the railing, having nowhere to go. Or was there?

"I will never join you," she said icily. The wind whipped through her hair as it howled up from the valley. Her eyes blazed with hatred. "I would rather die." She turned and looked over her shoulder; her gaze was drawn down, down from the dizzying height to the hard rocks far below. Willowen turned back to face him defiantly.

"You wouldn't do it," he said, folding his arms.

"No?" she said. The Princess leapt up onto the railing. She fixed him with a freezing gaze. "You think not?"

A strange expression crossed the sorcerer's face. The many-coloured fires in his eyes went out, to be replaced by dark eyes that regarded her in terror. He gasped and unfolded his arms.

"Willowen!" he begged, and his voice was not the sneer of a moment ago. "Do not do it!" He stretched out his hands imploringly.

Willowen stared in disbelief. "Darkmor? Is it you?"

His face twisted in agony. "Y-yes...." He rasped. He doubled over, clutching his stomach as he groaned in agony. The sorcerer bowed his head upon his chest, and his groans increased.

Shar stepped forward. "Master? Are you ill?" the unusual change in the sorcerer's demeanour had unnerved his servant. Shar approached his master warily, glancing between him and Willowen. *What was going on?* He thought wildly.

*"Fight him, Darkmor!"* Willowen cried. She watched as the sorcerer fell to his knees, his body shaking with the struggle of the two souls within it that were attempting to take control.

The Princess made to step down from the railing as Shar came to his master's side. Tremblingly, the servant reached out tentatively, to touch the sorcerer's quivering shoulder. *"Master?"* he whispered nervously.

With an inarticulate cry, the sorcerer's head came up, and he glared at the one who had dared to touch him. Darkmor's hand shot out, and he took Shar by the neck. The sorcerer slowly rose to his feet, his hand clenched about the man's throat. He stared at Shar with maddened eyes. Then he raised him high above his head, and hurled the hapless servant away from him with a powerful throw.

*"Master!"* Shar's scream dwindled as he went over the railing and hurtled down towards the unforgiving rocks. Willowen watched his fatal plunge, turning away at the last instant as Shar smashed into the ground.

She turned her shocked gaze upon his destroyer.

The Princess flinched away from the fires that had returned to the sorcerer's eyes. "Step down!" he ordered her, pointing imperiously at the platform at her feet.

Willowen saw that the sorcerer had regained full control of the Elf's body. Was there any way to help Darkmor gain the upper hand, and cast the mortal out? She *must* try.

"Darkmor," she said in beseeching tones, "I know you can hear me. Fight! Fight and drive him out!"

The sorcerer sneered. "No. He will not return. For a moment only, I lost control. It won't happen again. Step down. You have no choice, but to help me."

Willowen shook her head. "Never."

Darkmor glared at her. "You will change your mind when you've spent more time in your little cell."

The Princess's heart fell. There was no escape. She was at his mercy. He had taken her amulet, so that she couldn't focus her Stone Shaping magic. Her one hope had been lost. For a brief instant, she had thought that the Elf who's body the sorcerer had taken could have wrested that control from him, and regained the use of that body. Surely she could have reasoned with him. Now, it seemed hopeless. She would be forced to do his will, betraying her father, her race, and all of Erathyn. Once again, she looked back over her shoulder. Far below, a group of men were clustered about Shar's shattered corpse. She turned back and faced her enemy. Her decision was made.

Willowen smiled at him. She closed her eyes.

And allowed herself to fall backward.

# CHAPTER II

# THE KHARDEN MOUNTAINS

The Elven-King shuddered. He blinked furiously, as though to rid his eyes of some foreign matter. Everything seemed to spin around him. There was a brief flash of Willowen's face in his mind, an image of walls and flights of steps. She stood somewhere high above the ground, and looked out upon the blood-red landscape. The Princess turned and then everything spun, becoming a kaleidoscope of whirling images. For a moment more, the vision lasted, and then suddenly it was gone. He felt a chill. *Something has happened,* he thought. *Something terrible.* He brought his mount to a halt. The riders around him also reined in. Slowly, the Army of Light came to a stop. He put his hands up, and massaged his temples.

"What is it, Sire?"

Anarys turned to his left, where Lord Nildoron sat his horse. The Elf-lord regarded his king with concern.

"A vision. It was Willowen." He had sensed something, but *what* it was he had sensed, he didn't know. There had been walls of stone, and steps…. No, he could not remember. But he somehow knew that his daughter was in desperate danger.

He looked about himself, and saw the concerned faces that surrounded him. "I saw her. She was somewhere high above the ground. She looked out upon the red light that hangs over all of Erathyn." He concentrated on the fading vision, but it was waning quickly. "No. It is gone. I cannot see anything more. I fear she is in great peril. Lord Merys."

"Your Majesty?" Lord Merys was in charge of the Army of Light.

"We will camp here for the day." Anarys looked up, into the reddened sky. It was hard to tell if it *was* still day.

"As you wish, Sire." He bowed in his saddle. Then the Elf-Lord turned his mount, and rode down the line, giving the order to prepare the camp.

There was a musical jingling. Nomayon the Seer rode forward. He raised his staff.

"The Elven-King has had a powerful vision," he said. "Nomayon has seen it, too." His eyes pierced Anarys. "The enemy makes her suffer."

Anarys nodded. "That was what I felt, too."

"The dog!" Brador rasped out. "At *our* hands, he will suffer, for harming one hair upon her head!" The Dwarf-Lord shook his fist. He sat upon a hill-pony that they had convinced him to ride. He looked uncomfortable. The Dwarven army had marched with the main force.

Anarys smiled. "Thank you, Brador. I fear that we cannot do anything to help her. We must continue on, and attack his stronghold."

Nildoron leaned forward. "Surely the enemy would want to keep the Princess alive? We know now it was his purpose to take her, and force her to unlock the secrets of this Starstone. It is in his own interest to ensure she lives."

"Perhaps he's already made her do that, and this darkness is the result," said Egon. "Maybe she's already dead." The agent's face turned white. "My apologies, Your Majesty. I didn't mean to imply..." Egon trailed off, embarrassed.

"I am not offended, Egon," Anarys said. "We simply do not know if she is unharmed. We must have faith that she is not."

"She lives, Your Majesty."

The Elven-King turned to his right.

Silveron sat there on a grey horse. He looked drained, and pale. His eyes were half-closed. He nodded to himself. "Yes. She lives."

"Are you certain?' Nildoron asked.

"No, My Lord, I cannot be certain." He turned to face Nildoron, his eyes opening. "But my heart tells me she lives. As His Majesty has said, we must have faith."

"What is this unnatural darkness, then?" said Egon. "Is it the work of the Dark One?"

"Of that, I have no doubt," said Anarys.

"Why has he done this?" Egon frowned. "I don't understand. What can blocking out the sun do for him?"

"The Schaaka," Brador said grimly. "And the O'skaa, too. With the Overworld in shadow, come crawling up from the Underworld, they can."

"That is true," Jhara Shin added. King Sirlyk had sent him with one thousand chokhutai to assist the Army of Light. He and his warriors had marched on foot. Unlike the Schaaka, they did not ride beasts; but they were swift and their endurance was legendary among all the races of Erathyn. "They are terrible in battle. The O'skaa are difficult to kill, and are savage opponents."

"Not foes that we would wish to face," Anarys said. He remembered the last battle, two thousand years ago, when they had met and finally beaten the Schaaka. The O'skaa were savage opponents. They had lost many of their finest warriors that night. But eventually, they had won, and the remnants of the Goblin army had slunk back into the shadows, never to be seen again.

"Sire?"

Anarys came out of his reverie. "Yes?"

"Look, Sire," said Lord Nildoron, pointing into the sky above them.

Coming swiftly towards them were two large winged shapes, hurtling through the air. As they watched, they came closer, becoming two winged figures. It was F'Leet and his wingman. They landed in front of the group and came forward and bowed.

"Greetings, Your Majesty, My Lords," F'leet rumbled.

"Well met, F'Leet," replied Anarys. "What can you see ahead?"

"Something strange, Sire. At the pass that leads to Stonebridge, there are many bodies. Both Goblins and Men lie there in death. We flew over the fortress, but there seemed to be no one there. If the enemy is here, where is he? He cannot be found nearby. For many miles, there are abandoned cottages and villages. It is as though the Schaaka have returned to the Underworld."

"Doubt that, I do," Brador said. "Come to destroy and slay, they have. Close by, they must be."

"I agree, Brador. We must know where they are." Anarys wondered where the enemy lay. It was certain that they were somewhere in hiding, waiting for the chance to attack.

"It seems you need someone who can track, Your Majesty."

The Elven-King turned. Ervin urged his horse forward.

"I can find them for you." The Kandaran grinned.

"I know you could. But I will not allow you to go alone."

"It'd be better that way. I can go quietly, and none will see me."

"I will join you, Chakh-Mekh," Lord Shin said. "I will bring ten of my best chokhutai."

"Thank you, My Lord," Ervin said.

"*I* can go quietly," said Nilda, urging her own mount forward. "Your Majesty, I will go with the Kandaran too."

Anarys smiled to himself. Nildoron had told him of his daughter's love for the Forester, but so much had happened, it had been driven from his mind. He could see how much in love with the Man she was. But he could not afford to consider their problem at the moment.

"No. It is too dangerous. I will send Lord Nildoron and thirty of his best warriors with them. Lord Nildoron."

Nildoron bowed. "Sire?"

"Go with Ervin and Lord Shin. Do not engage the enemy," Anarys said. "Find him, and report back his whereabouts. Your force is too small for battle."

"Very well, Your Majesty," Nildoron replied.

Nilda glanced quickly at her father, and then looked away and fixed her eyes on the ground, embarrassed at being humiliated in front of her lover.

"That's not necessary, Your Majesty." The Kandaran looked insulted. "We won't be caught. It's better to have a small group seek out the enemy than to send a larger force. The more numbers there are in a scouting party, the greater the risk of being discovered. Lord Shin and his chokhutai are fine trackers, and can move about unseen."

Anarys nodded, and raised his hand in a placatory gesture. "I know, Ervin. It is a risk. But it is one that we must take. We must find them. I know that you are a fine scout, and I can trust you when you say that Lord Shin and his warriors are experienced. But we cannot afford to lose you both. Please take Nildoron and his warriors with you." He smiled.

Mollified, Ervin returned his smile. "All right, Sire."

"Thank you, Your Majesty," Jhara Shin said. "I will go and choose my chokhutai." He bowed to the Elven-King. As he straightened, he winked at the Kandaran and went over to where the Goblin contingent had halted.

Anarys looked at Nilda. She was downcast, and obviously her mind was filled with anxiety for Ervin's safety. Anarys thought for a moment. What would *he* do if he wanted to ensure Willowen's safety? *Anything.*

Against his own better judgement, he made a decision.

"You may go too, Captain."

She looked up and beamed. "Thank you, Your Majesty." She and Ervin bowed in their saddles.

"Perhaps one of us should go with them, Your Majesty?" F'Leet said.

Anarys shook his head. "No, F'Leet. If the enemy is here, we will not find him by searching from the air. The Schaaka are dwellers of the Underworld. If they are hiding, they are only to be found by searching the caves and the fortress at Stonebridge. You have already sent your other wingmen to your people and the Felininn. Only the two of you remain. The army needs your eyes in the air."

"But what if a message has to be sent to you in haste?" The Winglord said. "If they are discovered, and need assistance, I would reach you far quicker than one of the warriors on his steed. My companion can remain with the army."

"Hmmm. Right he is," rumbled Brador. "F'Leet *would* get to us swifter."

The Elven-King considered. It *would* make sense to have F'Leet go with them. If the scouting party were to be surrounded, the quickest way they could send for help was by using the Winglord. The other Avianinn could be the aerial scout for the army.

"Very well," he said. "Join them, F'Leet. Lord Nildoron, if by any chance you are discovered by the enemy, and need our help, you will send him to us."

"I understand, Sire. It will be as you say."

"Good. Go and choose your party."

Nildoron, Ervin and Nilda bowed to the Elven-King, and then they rode off to choose their warriors. Anarys watched them go, a sense of foreboding filling him, as though he were seeing them for the very last time.

"None can see all ends," Nomayon said.

"True," Anarys replied. "Well, my friends. Let us camp and rest and enjoy a brief respite before the last march."

"Serve His Majesty while I am gone," F'Leet ordered his Wingman. The Avianinn bowed.

They all watched as Nildoron, Nilda, and Ervin, followed by thirty of the Elven warriors the Elf-Lord had chosen; rode past. Jhara Shin and his chokhutai ran behind them. He nodded to Anarys. The Elves bowed in the saddle to their king. F'Leet bowed to the Elven-King, and took to the air. The Forester waved in farewell. They moved away up the track, and disappeared from sight. For a few minutes, they could see the Avianinn as he flew over the party, and then he too vanished.

"Good luck to them," Brador said.

"May they find the enemy, and return safely," Anarys added. Then he turned his horse to join the camp that was being set up. The others followed.

High above them, a Goblin scout sat upon an O'Skaa. The Schaaka and his mount had watched everything. He smiled to himself. The group that had ridden off was headed towards Stonebridge, which was now in the Schaaka's hands. The Men who were supposed to defend it had fled, and had been struck down as they ran. The Goblin had a puckered scar on his face. It ran from one cheek and ran down his neck. It told the tale of a horrific wound that he had sustained in battle. *In battle with the Bright Ones*, he thought, subconsciously running a finger down his ruined face.

"We must report this to Ragnak," he said to the spider. "You will feast on the flesh of the Bright Ones." He stroked the arachnid's fur.

*Yesss*, it sent to his mind. *Give them to uss.*

He pulled on the reins, turning the monster away. They hurried towards Stonebridge.

The group advanced along the trail. In the lead rode Nildoron, Nilda, and Ervin. The Kandaran searched the ground for tracks. The Elves rode silently behind them. Shin and his chokhutai brought up the rear. They entered a long tunnel formed of the intertwining branches of overhanging trees. The ruddy light was even dimmer here. The Elves scanned their surroundings, wary of attack.

*A perfect place for an ambush,* Nildoron thought to himself. He glanced at his daughter. *She should not have come.* He frowned.

Feeling his scrutiny, Nilda turned and regarded him. "Is anything wrong, Father?" she asked softly.

"Yes," he replied. "Many things are. But unfortunately most of them are out of our control." His gaze went to the Forester.

She followed his look, and then returned her attention to him. "I have made my choice, Father."

He nodded. "I know."

*"Hold,"* Ervin whispered.

The column of riders halted. Bows were strung, and swords whispered stealthily from sheaths as the Kandaran rode forwards. The chokhutai armed themselves, and peered into the trees that surrounded them. Ahead of them, the tunnel of trees opened out, and the blood red light seeped in. They could see a path of stones ahead that led to a bridge which spanned a river flowing through a valley. Strewn upon the path were the bodies that F'Leet had told them about. As Ervin advanced, Nildoron made a sign to his warriors to hold their position, and then he and Nilda followed Ervin. Jhara Shin came and joined them.

They rode out of the tree-covered trail, and came to the path. Ervin dismounted, and knelt by the side of one of the bodies. Looking around themselves, Nilda and the Elf-Lord could see that it was as they had been told; Goblin and Man lay there, sprawled where they had fallen. Forty or fifty bodies were there, lying under the ruddy sky.

"All are dead."

The Winglord sat upon the post of the bridge like a great bird of prey. He leapt down, and came over to them. The Kandaran rose to his feet. His horse shied, and he stroked its neck to calm it.

"Go and tell the others to advance," Nildoron said to his daughter.

"Yes, Father." She wheeled her horse, and rode back to the trail.

"This is strange," Ervin said. He shook his head. "I don't understand it."

"What do you mean?" Nildoron asked.

"The Schaaka advanced to here, killed all of these men they were pursuing, and then they just retreated. Why would they do that? They should have kept advancing. There was no one to oppose them. It makes no sense."

"I agree," Shin said. "Why would they retreat?"

"Who knows why those filth do anything?" F'Leet said.

"Perhaps they were ordered to retreat," Nildoron said.

"I don't think so. Why would they do that?" The Kandaran gazed about. "My Lord, there's something very wrong about this. You should go back, and let me go on alone."

Nildoron regarded him. "My King has charged me to find the enemy. That is what I will do. If you are afraid, you may return to our camp."

Ervin's eyes blazed. "I'm *not* afraid. I'll happily face Goblins or O'skaa or whatever we meet, but I sense that this is somehow wrong. It could be a trap. I can't shake the feeling that this has been staged for our benefit. It would be better if I carried on, and you returned to the camp."

"You will not go alone, Ervin," Lord Shin said. "I and my chokhutai will go with you."

Nilda and the others rode up.

The Elf-Lord stared at the Forester, his gaze steely. "I will not say this again, Kandaran. King Anarys has ordered me to find where the enemy is. This I *will* do, despite your misgivings. You may accompany us if you wish. *Endoi!*" He rode off, and his warriors followed him onto the bridge. Their mount's hooves thundered on the planks, setting off echoes that reverberated in the valley.

The others left behind watched them go. Ervin clenched his fist.

"How can he be so blind?" he gritted.

"Are you sure that this has been staged somehow?" F'Leet said.

"No," Ervin said, "but I don't like it. It feels wrong."

"That is my thought also," Shin said.

"We should go after them," Nilda said.

The Kandaran leapt onto his horse, and spurred it forward. Nilda followed him, and they hurried across the bridge, and went in pursuit of Nildoron and his warriors. Jhara Shin made a sign to his chokhutai, and the hardy Goblins ran after the pair. The Winglord watched them for a moment, and then threw himself into the air, and flew after them.


At Stonebridge, the O'skaa rider and his mount arrived, and were admitted. He rode up to the front door of the main hall, and straight in. The spider's claws clicked across the stone floor, until they had reached the far side of the hall, where a company of O'skaa sat eating at a large table, presided over by a huge Goblin who sat on a throne at the head of the table. He was drinking from a flagon, and at his side was a small table that groaned under a plate that was piled high with bread and meat. He was very fat, and his tunic was stretched over his protruding stomach. He looked with distaste at the new arrival. All talk at the table ceased as the rider urged his mount up to the throne.

The O'skaa rider bowed in his saddle, and the spider lowered its foreparts to the floor in salute.

"Well?" The fat Goblin said brusquely. He was obviously displeased with this interruption of his meal. He put the flagon down on the table with a thud. "Why do you disturb me?"

"My Lord Ragnak, there is a group of Bright Ones coming."

"Bright Ones?" Ragnak echoed. He waved his hand dismissively. "Slay them."

"But we were told not to show ourselves," said a voice to his left.

Ragnak's piggy eyes narrowed in anger, as he turned to the speaker. "Do you question my order, Gorlik?" He wiped his mouth with his greasy hand.

"No, My Lord. But we were ordered to take this outpost, and then let the Army of Light advance, and pass us by. We were to remain hidden." Gorlik was Ragnak's lieutenant, and he often had to remind him of his orders. Ragnak drank so much; it was a miracle that he could think at all.

Ragnak's lip curled. "Are you sure that was what the order was?"

Gorlik nodded. "Yes, My Lord. I heard it from Toh-Tuh-Masikh myself. I was with you when he gave you the order."

Ragnak frowned. "Huh! *That* white devil. Why the Master allows *him* to control us, I'll never know." He scratched his head.

"The Master said that we were to follow his orders," Gorlik added.

The huge Goblin peered at him blearily. "Well then," he said in disgust, "what did he say we should do if the Bright Ones were to come seeking us?"

"We were to remain hidden," Gorlik repeated slowly, his voice sounding as if he were explaining something to a little child, or an idiot.

The Goblin lord's brow furrowed in concentration as he considered Gorlik's words. His drink sodden brain was slowly working it through.

All through this dialogue the O'skaa rider had sat his mount, bemused by the befuddled condition he'd found Ragnak in. The Goblin was enjoying the exchange between the drunken Ragnak and his lieutenant. The others at the table were also hiding their mirth; he noticed several of them grinning. He suddenly straightened up as the Goblin lord turned to him.

*"Don't just sit there!"* Ragnak bellowed, slamming his fist down on the table. "Go and pass the order to get out of sight! *Now!*"

"At once, My Lord!" The O'skaa rider bowed in the saddle, and wheeled his mount. They raced out of the hall.

*"All of you!"* Ragnak roared. *"Get out! Get out and watch the bridge!"*

The Schaaka leapt to their feet, and ran towards the main door. They enjoyed watching their lord's drunken antics, but when his anger arose, none of them dared to ignore his orders. As they clattered out Gorlik rose from his chair.

"You take charge, Gorlik. You know what is to be done." Ragnak picked up his flagon, and drank deeply.

Gorlik bowed. "Yes, My Lord." He walked towards the door. *And leave you to wallow in your wine, you fat pig,* he thought. As he reached the main door, Ragnak called out to him.

*"Gorlik!"*

The lieutenant turned in the doorway. "Yes, My Lord?"

"If these Bright Ones discover we are here, shoot them down like dogs. Let none escape."

"It shall be as you say, My Lord." He went out of the door.

Ragnak smiled, and grabbed up a choice cut of meat. He washed it down with another deep swig of wine. *Life is good,* he thought as he smacked his lips with relish.

Silveron stared into the bleak mountains that lay ahead. How much further did they have to march? He was fretting. The Army of Light moved at a snail's pace. At this rate it would take days, perhaps weeks to reach Willowen. Would she still live? Would Darkmor force her to assist him, and then kill her out of spite? Darkmor knew Silveron was in love with her. She had returned that love, and now his heart ached at their forced separation. *Does she even know I am alive?* He wondered. The last time he had seen her was at the Goblin-King's banquet. Anarys had told him about how she had been taken by the Dark One after he had been struck down. Did she believe him to be dead? She saw what had happened. What did the Elven-King's vision mean? The wizard had seen something himself, but he couldn't make sense of it. He hadn't seen it in the same way Anarys had. That was logical. As her sire, the Elven-King had a much stronger connection with her. Even though Silveron loved Willowen with all his being, he couldn't enjoy such a bond.

"The Princess lives."

Silveron turned. Nomayon was there.

"Nomayon has seen her too," he said. "The Dark One must not kill her. He needs her." He strode up to join Silveron.

"That is what I feel too, Nomayon," the Elf said.

They stood at the edge of the camp. People moved to and fro behind them, setting up tents and making fires to prepare food. Horses were being fed and rested. A mild wind blew, but the scene was peaceful. It was in stark contrast to the fear and doubt which plagued the wizard's mind.

"Do not worry," the Seer said. He squatted down, and took up a fistful of dust from the ground beneath their feet. Nomayon rose to his feet. He closed his eyes, and chanted in a deep voice. Then he opened his eyes, and tossed the dust high. As it blew away in the wind, he peered deeply into the shapes it formed. He nodded in satisfaction.

"It is good. The Princess lives. She defies her enemy." He met Silveron's gaze. "But he grows impatient. He knows the Army of Light comes. He wants to crush us. A great shadow comes to meet us."

Silveron sighed. "We are moving far too slowly."

"Yes," the Seer agreed. "An army is a great beast; in battle it is worthy." He looked deeply into the Elf's eyes. "But swift it is not. Perhaps a smaller group would move more quickly, and save the Princess?"

The wizard looked away. "The King wished me to do this. We met with Vairon and Vandaron, and discussed the idea of me taking the talisman into the Dark One's stronghold, and facing him." He turned back to the Seer. "But now King Anarys is doubtful. My defeat at the hands of the enemy weighs upon his mind. I think he does not trust me to complete that task."

"He does not think that you are strong enough to defeat the Dark One?"

The Elf shook his head. "I do not know. He told me to rest and regain my strength. He said we will march closer, and then he will decide what to do."

"That is foolish," Nomayon said. "It will be too late then. Too late for the Princess, and perhaps too late for all of us as well." He stepped closer, and spoke emphatically. "Silveron must speak to him, and convince him that his original plan is the only way to succeed."

"I do not know if he will listen to me –"

"My Lord Silveron."

They regarded the newcomer. It was an Elf warrior. He bowed to them.

"Please excuse me, My Lord. His Majesty wishes to speak to you."

"Very well, I will come." He nodded to the Seer, who bowed to him.

"All will be well," Nomayon said.

"That is my hope," the wizard replied.

As they left him, Nomayon stared out at the mountains. *Pitiless, the Kharden mountains are*, he thought. *But the enemy is even more* remorseless. "The Darkness comes," he said softly. He stood there for a moment longer, and then he turned towards the camp and food.

Silveron followed the warrior back through the camp, until they came to the Elven-King's tent. The guards saluted Silveron with their spears. Then one of them opened the tent-flap and announced him. Anarys bade him enter.

The wizard came into the tent, and saw Anarys sitting in a simple camp chair. Another was set beside it. The Elven-King gestured for him to sit. As Silveron began to bow, Anarys waved the motion away.

"Do not bother with that, Silveron. Here we are just two friends. Please sit."

"Thank you, Your Majesty."

Anarys thought for a moment. Silveron waited for him to speak. What was on the King's mind?

"I miss Goldwen," Anarys said.

"As do I, Sire. I wish we had had more time together."

The Elven-King nodded. "So do I." He reached out to a table that sat to one side. On it were a carafe filled with wine, and two goblets. Anarys filled them both, and offered one to the wizard.

"Thank you, Sire."

They both took a drink. Anarys took a deep breath.

"Silveron."

"Sire?"

"I miss Goldwen's counsel. For many years, during which we saw many battles, I would always consult him about the correct course to follow. Now that he is gone, I find myself wishing that there were another to advise me in the way he did."

"I would not presume to take his place, Your Majesty. His knowledge was far beyond mine, especially when it comes to warfare and tactics. I am not well versed in such things."

The Elven-King shook his head. "It is not of tactics on the battlefield that I wish to speak. Once, we sat here and talked of a plan that would see you and a small group infiltrate the enemy's lair."

"I recall the meeting, Your Majesty."

Anarys rose, and paced the tent. The wizard waited again. He knew something weighed heavily on the Elven-King's mind. He watched him walk back and forth.

Finally, Anarys stopped pacing and looked him in the eye.

"Your fight with Darkmor has been in my thoughts. He proved to be much more powerful than you. Goldwen and I –" He faltered to a stop.

"I know what you wish to say, Sire."

"Do you?" Anarys said. He went on. "Goldwen and I placed so much trust in your power. He assured me that you would defeat the Dark One." He sat down again. "The reality was different. Not only did Darkmor beat you, he took the talisman from you." He picked up his goblet, and drank. He put the goblet down on the table. "The talisman was supposed to be the only weapon that could destroy him."

Silveron listened in silence.

Anarys stood again. He was clearly agitated. He began pacing again.

"*Willowen,*" he whispered to himself. "Are you still alive? What has he done to you?" His eyes shone with tears.

Silveron put his goblet on the table. He rose to his feet and came to him.

"I do not know if I am strong enough to defeat him, Your Majesty, but I beg you to let me try. Let me go and face him, as we decided once before."

Anarys regarded him. "Can you save her? Can you bring her back to me? Do you think you can destroy him?"

"I will succeed or die, Sire."

The Elven-King put his hand on the wizard's shoulder. He smiled.

"There is no doubting your courage. We thought you dead after the fight in Sirlyk's hall. There is much strength in you, Silveron. May it prove to be more than a match for the enemy." He took his hand from the wizard's shoulder and held it out. Silveron took it and they shook hands in the way of Men. "Do you know who you want to take with you?"

"I think I would choose Ervin first. He knows these mountains. As a guide, he is unsurpassed."

"That is true. Who else?"

"Lord Brador? He is a staunch ally, and if we have to go into the mountain, who better than a Dwarf-Lord to show us the way underground?"

"Very good. Who are the others?"

"I must think, Your Majesty. Please let me consider the matter, and make my choice."

"Yes, that is the best thing to do. Of course, each of these companions must make up their own minds. It is their decision to accompany you on this mission or not."

"I agree, Sire."

Anarys turned to the table. He refilled both goblets, and handed one to the wizard.

"You have calmed my troubled mind, Silveron," Anarys said. "Consider your choices well. Now come and enjoy this fine wine with me."

"I hear and obey, Your Majesty." He smiled.

They sat together and drank in fellowship.


Several hours later, Silveron left the Elven-King's tent. He was replete with honey wine, and felt good. The wine coursed through his veins and warmed him. The air had turned colder, and a chill wind blew down from the mountains. The camp had settled down. Warriors sat around camp fires eating and drinking. Sentries patrolled the perimeter of the camp, alert for any sign of the enemy. The wizard walked towards his tent. He was satisfied that he had convinced Anarys that he would be victorious in his mission. He would retrieve the talisman, defeat Darkmor, and rescue Willowen. All would be well.

*Or would it?* He thought. He had convinced the Elven-King, but now he had to convince himself. Could he really hope to defeat Darkmor? If Darkmor had the power to move a world, what chance did he have of winning in a confrontation with someone as powerful as he? *If he unlocks the power in the Starstone,* he thought, *he will be unconquerable.*

Silveron came to a stop. His mind roiled with thoughts. What would Willowen's fate be, if he could not succeed? Would Darkmor slay her, or keep her, to satisfy his lust? Silveron thought back to that day in the forest outside Algol. He remembered how Darkmor and his master had tried to turn him. He recalled how they had said that there was no such thing as love, only desire. Those dark desires had filled Darkmor. Silveron knew that his master had promised him Willowen to use as he wished. But now, Malkaar had tricked the Elf, and had taken possession of his body. Now it was he that lusted after Willowen. An image of them together exploded in Silveron's mind. He clenched his fists angrily.

"No!" he said fiercely, "I *must* defeat him!"

"Silveron? Are you well?"

The Elf regarded the speaker. It was Toran-en.

"Yes," he replied.

The Felininn stared at him. His tail twitched behind him.

"I am sorry," the wizard said. "My mind is filled with a problem."

"You think of the Dark One."

Silveron nodded.

"I have been speaking to the King about a plan."

"You mean the plan to sneak into the Dark One's stronghold, and rescue the Princess Willowen?" His amber eyes stared into Silveron.

"How do you know this?" The wizard asked, shocked.

Toran-en's eyes closed for a moment. Silveron knew that this was how the catmen smiled.

"My father and I were speaking of it. It seems to be the logical thing to do. Some of your friends think so too."

"Friends?" Silveron echoed. "What do you mean?"

"Will you not join us at our fire? Come and eat and talk with us." He beckoned to Silveron and then turned and pointed.

The Elf looked in the direction that Toran-en had indicated. A group sat around a fire at the edge of the camp.

"Very well, lead on."

They walked through the camp until they came to the fire. Yosh-en was there, as were Brador, Egon, Nomayon, M'Shaan, K'taal, and F'leet's Wingman. His name was K'Reel.

Yosh-en came to his feet as they arrived.

"Silveron. Well met. Join us."

A joint of beef roasted above the fire. All of them had goblets, except for Brador. A large mug of ale was in his brawny fist. He saluted the wizard with it.

"Aye! Join us, lad. Good food and drink there are here."

The Elf came and sat on a camp chair they had prepared for him. Toran-en sat in another as Brador held out a goblet to Silveron.

"No, thank you, Brador," he said. "I have had my fill in the King's tent."

"One more will not hurt you," the Dwarf-Lord said.

The wizard looked at the goblet.

"Go on, lad," Brador said. "Fine honey wine it is."

Silveron smiled. "Very well. But just one."

Brador laughed, and gave him the goblet. Silveron took a drink. His gaze swept them.

"Now, tell me what you were speaking of."

"Why, your mission, of course," Egon said.

"How did you know of it? It is supposed to be a secret. Only the King and I were supposed to know. Have you been spying on us?"

Brador waved his beefy hand in negation.

"No, no. Spying on you we were not. Guessed the purpose of the meeting, we did." He grinned broadly.

"Nomayon sees what is on Silveron's mind," the Seer said. "Has he convinced the Elven-King to attempt this task?"

"I have," the wizard said. "He wishes me to proceed with the original plan."

"But Silveron is doubtful," Nomayon said. "He doubts himself."

The Elf nodded. "I *do* doubt myself. Do I have power enough to defeat the enemy? I do not know."

"If the King believes that you can accomplish it, you should trust his judgement," said Egon. "But you should not go on your own."

"We want to help you, Silveron," added Yosh-en. "Let us come with you."

"Yes," said K'Reel. "Surely the Elven-King does not wish you to enter the Dark One's domain alone?"

"No," the wizard admitted. "He told me to choose some companions to join me."

"Well, here we are then!" Brador said, opening his arms wide. "Take us you must. Alone you should not be."

Silveron smiled.

"I was going to ask Ervin to come with me. His knowledge of this area would be useful. I must wait for him to return."

"If you take the Kandaran, then go Captain Nilda must also," Brador said.

"Why?"

"Lad, have you not seen how they are together?" Brador said. "Know you not how the Elf loves him?"

"Yes, but it is forbidden. The King himself will deal with the matter."

All the time they had been speaking, Egon had been carving some beef from the roast. Now he came to Silveron and offered him a plate full of the steaming meat.

"Here. It's very good." He handed the plate to him.

"Thank you."

Brador offered him a small dagger. The Elf accepted it and stabbed a piece of meat and brought it to his mouth.

"It is delicious. Thank you."

"Only the best for the wizard and his companions," Toran-en said.

They laughed.

"The King is concerned that the scouting party has not returned," Silveron said. "If they have not shown up by morning, a search party will be sent to find them."

A murmur of disquiet followed this. Where were they? Surely they had had enough time to go to Stonebridge and investigate the fortress?

"I hope they haven't met with any trouble," Egon said.

"I hope so too," Silveron said. "Their loss would be a blow to the King."

"Well," said Yosh-en, "Lord Kitar-en and his riders should be here in two days. They are hardy warriors. Perhaps they could go and search for them?"

"I do not think the King will want to wait for two days to find them," the wizard said. "He wishes to be on the march again as soon as possible."

K'Reel rose to his feet. "Then I shall go and search for them at first light. The Winglord T'Kaan will be here tomorrow. I will inform him of the situation, and he will set a detachment of warriors to provide the army with cover and to scout from the air."

"Thank you, K'Reel," Silveron said. "I am sure King Anarys will be grateful for their support."

The Avianinn bowed and resumed his perch upon the camp chair.

"Well then," Silveron said, "it appears that I have chosen my companions. Or have they chosen me?"

Laughter met his words.

"Friends we are, Silveron," Brador said. "Come with you, we will, and bring back the pretty Princess." He raised his mug. "As for the Dark One, deal with him you will."

A chorus of assent arose. Goblets were raised in salute.

"There is another matter to consider," Silveron said.

"Silveron speaks of the talisman," The Seer said.

"Yes," Silveron said. "Much of the power of the Council was sent into it. Darkmor took it from me, as you know." He considered the faces that surrounded him.

"Worried you are," Brador said, reading his face. "Is it so powerful?"

The Elf nodded. "The wizards that gave it their power believed so. Especially Goldwen. They thought that it was the only way to destroy him."

"Wasn't it a spell of banishment that was put on it?" Egon asked.

"That is correct," the wizard replied. "Now that Goldwen is gone, it is our only hope of defeating him."

"Surely there's another way?" Egon said. "He isn't immortal." He saw Silveron's doubt. "Is he?"

"I do not know," the Elf said. "When he was a mere Man, perhaps..." His voice trailed off, and he stared into the fire.

"But now?" prompted K'Reel.

"But now he has possessed an Elf's body. If we are not slain in accident or combat, we *are* immortal." He looked up and met their concerned gazes. "This was his plan all along. This is why my brother was created; so that the Dark One would have an immortal body, and the evil knowledge of the Black Circle together. He fooled my brother, allowing him to believe that he was going to make him his apprentice. Instead, he took possession of him."

"So there are no other weapons we could use to defeat him?" Yosh-en asked.

"None." Silveron took up another piece of the meat. It was getting cold.

Brador stood up. "Then take this talisman, lad. Use it, and rid the world of his evil you will." He indicated the group sitting around the fire. "Some small part in this your friends will have." He raised his mug, and drained it.

They toasted the wizard again.

Silveron met Nomayon's gaze.

"All will be well," Nomayon said.

# CHAPTER III

## BETRAYAL AT ALGOL

Telewen looked out of the window of his tower. Blood-red light lit the land below him, covering everything with its unnatural ruddiness. The Council had met when the eldritch magic had occurred, and had agreed that it was the work of the Dark One. A heated debate had broken out; some of the wizards wanted to go and join the Army of Light, and assist the Elven-King in the Dark One's destruction. Other Council members had disagreed, and had insisted that they should stay and protect Algol. It was obvious which groups had made the differing suggestions. Those who had wanted to go and join the fight were Telewen and Vairon, Goldwen's old companions. Naturally, Amberon and his confederates were the other group. However, since Vandaron was already with Anarys and the army, there could not be a vote, and Goldwen's allies were told that they were to stay in the city of the wizards. The Eldest made it an order, and had set his companions to watch them both closely to ensure that they obeyed it.

The Keeper of Records stared at the reddened landscape, his mind whirling. He had told Anarys of his suspicions of Amberon's duplicity, and the King had charged him to keep watch on the Eldest, even as he himself was under Amberon's scrutiny. *What would Amberon do now?* He wondered. *What has the enemy told* him *to do?* He turned away from the window as someone knocked on his door. He slowly walked across the room, still not quite fully healed from his encounter with Darkmor.

He opened the door. Narwen stood there. The Master of Earth Magic smiled.

"How do you fare today, Telewen?" He asked solicitously.

"Well enough," he replied.

"I *am* pleased," Narwen said. "Do you think you could come and help the Eldest?"

"In what way?"

"He is trying to decipher a scroll that was delivered to him."

"A scroll that was delivered to him?" Telewen echoed. "Who brought it? Where did it come from?" His face became serious. "It could be something sent from the Dark One, something dangerous."

Narwen shook his head. "No, no," he said. "It was examined, and was clean. No spells were hidden in it to harm anyone."

Telewen frowned. "And the messenger?"

"A mortal Man. He is frightened." Narwen smiled ruefully. "He stood there sweating as The Eldest looked over the scroll. We have tried to make him comfortable; giving him some wine, and bread, but it is clear that he is afraid of us."

"He is still here?"

Narwen nodded. "Oh, yes. The Eldest will not let him leave until you come and look at the scroll. None of us can understand the writing upon it."

"I see. Did this Man say who had sent it?"

"No. He can hardly speak for his fear. Will you come?"

Telewen regarded him closely. Narwen was not known for his

considerate attitude towards Men; in fact, he had spoken against them many times, arguing that the Elves had shown Men far too much, and only thought of them in much the same way he considered the animals upon Erathyn. For him to show such a difference in attitude was unsettling. Was Amberon planning something? Telewen kept his face neutral, and hid his thought, lest Narwen see his discomfort.

"Very well," Telewen said. He walked over to his staff, and taking it up, he rejoined Narwen at the door.

Narwen smiled again. "You will not need that. You only have to read the scroll, not cast any spells."

Telewen saw something flicker deep within the other's eyes. He gave Narwen a smile in return. "I am not very steady on my feet. I will need it to help me walk."

The Master of Earth Magic's smile began to fade. "I can help you walk, my friend. Take my arm, and leave your staff here." He held out his hand.

*My friend?* Telewen now became alarmed. Narwen had *never* addressed him as such. In fact, he and Korwen and Amberon considered Telewen the most useless member of the Council. Even though he also held the position of Master of Fire Magic, they only thought of him as the librarian, someone far below their status.

"Thank you, but I will use it as a prop. Lead on." Telewen saw Narwen's smile leave his face.

"As you wish," he said, the former caring tones gone from his voice. He dropped his hand and turned and walked down the corridor. Telewen followed behind, his staff beating out a cadence on the stone floor. *I must be careful,* he thought, watching Narwen closely as they continued down the corridor. He cautiously sent out feelers of thought to try and sense if there was anything amiss. Nothing came to him. *Still, Narwen is acting oddly. It is better to be on guard.* They continued on until they came to a stairway. Narwen halted and turned at the railing.

"Let me help you," he said thoughtfully. He held out his hand for Telewen to take. The smile had returned to his face.

The Master of Fire Magic looked at him doubtfully, and then peered down the stairs. *Can I trust him? Does he plan to throw me down the stairs?* Telewen slowly advanced, watching the other for the slightest move that would show Narwen to be planning his death. He reached out to take Narwen's hand. He met his gaze, and saw that Narwen's eyes glittered, and his smile was one of triumph. He stepped back, and brought his staff up in a defensive move. He spoke a Word of Power, and a ball of flame ignited at the head of the staff. He brandished it at Narwen.

"Telewen!" Narwen gasped. "I am not your enemy. What are you doing?" He backed away, his hands held up spread open, to show Telewen he was not armed.

Doubt entered Telewen's mind. He gazed at the Master of Earth Magic. *Did I imagine that look in his eyes?* He thought. He lowered the staff.

A sharp pain tore through him. He gasped, and dropped his staff. Telewen looked down, and saw an Elven longknife protruding from his chest. Even as he stared at it, it was pulled out with a horrible sucking sound. He staggered, and turned to see his attacker. Korwen stood there, a sneer written on his face. Telewen slumped down, and clutched the railing with trembling hands. He gathered the last of his strength. *Silveron!* He sent, and fell to the floor. His murderers stood over his body, gloating.

Far away, sitting in the pavilion of the Elven-King, Silveron suddenly rose to his feet. His face was white. Anarys and the others were sitting around a table that was in the middle of the pavilion, eating their meal. All eyes turned to the wizard.

"Silveron," Anarys said, "is something wrong? What is it?"

Silveron regarded his king. "I sensed Telewen making a Sending to me in Mind-Speech. He was desperate." The wizard's face clouded. "And he was in great pain." He stood as though he were listening to something. "I cannot sense him now."

"Has something happened to him?" Anarys said.

Silveron's brow knitted. "I do not know, Sire. But I fear he is in danger."

"Danger?" Brador echoed. "What danger?"

"I do not know, My Lord."

"What can we do?" Egon said.

"Did you sense anything, Vandaron?" asked the Elven-King.

"No, Your Majesty," replied the Master of Birds. He looked at Silveron. The young wizard read his eyes, and knew that Vandaron doubted his word.

"I *did* feel something," he said firmly. "I did not imagine it."

"Perhaps you did," Vandaron said casually. He drank some wine from his goblet.

Silveron knew that the older wizard did not believe him. Vandaron had always regarded him as one who had not fully mastered his powers, and had even been condescending at times during the army's march.

"Do you wish me to send some warriors to find out what has happened, Sire?" Lord Merys asked.

Anarys shook his head. "No. We are too far away. It would take too long for them to reach Algol. If something has happened to Telewen, we cannot do anything." His face was grim. "Perhaps Amberon's treachery is now revealed."

"I could fly to Algol to find out if there is any danger to Telewen, Sire," Vandaron offered. The Master of Birds gave Silveron a patronizing smile as he rose to his feet.

The Elven-King turned to him. "No, Vandaron. I want you to stay here with the army."

"As you wish, Sire." Vandaron sat back down, and took another pull at his wine.

"Murdered Telewen he has, you think, Your Majesty?" Brador said.

"I do not know, Brador." The Elven-King addressed Silveron: "Do you think you can Send to Vairon to find out what has happened? If Telewen has been slain, you would be also warning him."

"I will try, Sire. I have never made a Sending over such a long distance before." He bowed to Anarys. "Please excuse me, Your Majesty. My Lords." He walked to the opening in the pavilion and left them.

He strode away from the pavilion, his mind filled with worry. Had Telewen been killed? How? Had Amberon somehow taken the Master of Fire Magic off-guard? Silveron walked away from the camp, until he reached a small hill that looked back down the trail that the Army of Light had followed into the Kharden Mountains. He looked about; no one was around. He closed his eyes, centred himself, and concentrated. The wizard sent his thought out upon the wind, imagining it flying through the air. At the same time, he pictured Vairon's face in his mind.

*Vairon*, he sent.

He felt a tingling in his head. Was that a response? Goldwen had not taught him how to make a Sending over such a great distance. He hoped he could reach Vairon before Amberon could make a move against the Master of Beasts.

*Silveron?* Vairon's face came clearly to his inner vision. *What is it? Is something wrong?*

*It may be nothing, Vairon. I thought I received a Sending from Telewen, and then there was emptiness. I could not sense him again. Is everything well?*

Vairon smiled. *Yes. He is resting. Perhaps you sensed him dreaming. I saw him not an hour ago, and he was tired; we had been speaking together for a long time, and he had sought his pallet. When I left him, he was sleeping peacefully.*

Silveron frowned. *Why would I sense that there was something wrong?*

*Maybe you should go and look in on him.*

*There is no need. I told you, he is sleeping. Let him rest.*

Silveron shook his head. *I cannot shake this feeling that there is something wrong. I know I sensed his thoughts, and he was distressed. It was as though he had cried out to me for help.*

The Master of Beast's image seemed to grow in Silveron's mind. *Do you not think it strange that I have not felt such a call, especially since I am closer to him than you are? Why would he think to contact you, when I am in Algol, and you are far away?* Varion paused for a moment, and then sent: *You do not have the control of your powers that he and I possess. I assure you, he is well. There is nothing to concern yourself with. I tell you I would have sensed any danger, and would have gone to his assistance.*

Silveron felt the admonishing tone in Vairon's thoughts. Even though it had been expressed in the nicest possible way, here he could again sense the same condescension in Vairon that Vandaron showed him.

*Very well,* he finally sent, *if you are sure all is well, I will trust your judgement. I will report to the King that there is nothing to worry about.*

Vairon's image smiled. *Yes, that is good. How goes the march?*

*Slowly. We have sent scouts ahead, and have camped for the night. We will continue on in the morning.*

*Excellent. Please tell His Majesty that I have not sensed any disloyalty in the Eldest. I do not believe that he is in league with the enemy. Perhaps Goldwen and Telewen's suspicions were groundless.*

Silveron frowned. *Are you certain? Telewen was adamant that Amberon was somehow involved in the Dark One's designs.*

The Master of Beasts shook his head. *I have seen nothing to make me think that is so. Rest assured, I will keep my eyes on Amberon and his confederates, and will alert you if anything occurs. Farewell.*

*Farewell.*

Vairon's image faded from his mind. There was still something not quite right; something that Silveron felt deeply. However, if Vairon said that all was well in Algol, he must accept that, and report it to Anarys. He turned and walked back towards the camp.

Many miles away, in Algol, Amberon smiled to himself. That had gone very well. He picked up a goblet of wine from a small table at his side, and drank deeply. His confederates sat at a larger table. All had goblets in their hands. They were sitting in the Eldest's dining chamber, congratulating themselves on how easily Telewen had been slain.

"Do you think he believed your Sending was actually Vairon?" Korwen asked.

The Eldest regarded Korwen. "Of course he did. He suspected nothing." He sneered. "He believed he conversed with Vairon, and was told what I wanted him to hear. He will report back to Anarys that there is no need to concern himself about Telewen and Algol. *'All is well',*" he said mockingly, using Vairon's tone of voice. He sat in his chair and drank from his goblet.

"He is a fool," Candreen said.

"No," said Narwen. "He has great powers, but he is easily fooled. That does not make him a *fool*. We are lucky that Goldwen did not teach him more."

"It does not matter," Amberon said. He poured himself another wine, and took a deep draught. He lowered the goblet, and ran a finger around its lip. "Now we will deal with Vairon. Korwen, did you dispose of Telewen's body?"

"Yes. There is nothing left. It is as if he had never existed."

"And you left no trace that can point to us?" Candreen asked.

The Master of Air Magic gave him a withering stare.

"Of course you did not," Candreen said. "Forgive me." Even though he had become the Master of Void Magic, and was now part of Amberon's entourage, Candreen knew that both Korwen and Narwen regarded him as well beneath their station. He changed the subject. "How will you deal with Vairon, Eldest? He is not as weak as Telewen was."

"Indeed," Narwen said, "Candreen speaks truly. We cannot hope to sneak up on Vairon as we did Telewen; he is like a beast himself, his senses are finely honed. He would hear the slightest noise, or sense a hidden assailant, and be alert instantly."

"He would even sense an archer from a distance," added Korwen. "We must try something else."

Amberon put his empty goblet on his table. As he went to fill it, he stared at the bottle from which the wine poured. He smiled, and turned to look at them all.

"Vairon likes wine, does he not? If his senses are so finely honed, it would be better for us if they were dulled." He poured his wine. "Perhaps we can add something – *special* – to his wine?" His smile became wolfish.

The others all smiled at his meaning.

Hours later, there was a knock on Vairon's door. He got up from the table, and walked towards the door, grumbling. He'd spent the entire day attempting to master an unusual animal's shape, but it had eluded him. The Master of Beasts didn't like to fail. And now, some fool wanted him. He threw open the door with a swift wrench.

Candreen stood there. He bowed. "Good evening."

Vairon regarded Candreen with an impatient glare. "What do you want? I am busy."

Candreen smiled. "The Eldest has invited us all to join him for the evening meal."

"I told you, I am busy. Please tell the Eldest that I must decline his offer."

The Master of Void Magic's smile faded. "I am afraid that just will not do. He was very insistent that you join us."

"Master Candreen. I have spent the entire day trying to master a spell, and I have not the time to sit and eat at leisure. I must decline the Eldest's offer."

"The Eldest will be very disappointed if you do not come." Candreen thought for a moment. "Perhaps you should have a rest. If you have been working all day, it would do you the world of good."

"No. I am sorry. Please give the Eldest my thanks for the invitation, but I must succeed with this spell."

"That is your final answer?" Candreen said.

"Yes. Goodbye." Vairon started to close the door.

"The Eldest has obtained several bottles of Corlan spiced wine," Candreen said, watching Vairon's face.

The Master of Beasts paused. The door was half-opened. His face became thoughtful. Candreen knew that he had awakened Vairon's appetite for the wine that he loved.

"He knows of your fondness for this wine. Will you not reconsider?"

Vairon opened the door all the way. A slow smile came to his lips. "Perhaps I *could* do with a brief respite." He stepped out into the corridor, and closed the door behind him. "I believe I *will* join you. Lead on."

Candreen bowed, and walked down the corridor. Vairon followed.

They left Vairon's tower, and continued on towards the Eldest's tower. They strode through the blood-red gloom. The Dark One's spell still held the sun in the moon's shadow. Vairon had wanted to go to join the Army of Light, but Amberon had refused his request. The Master of Beasts had retired to his tower, and worked fruitlessly on his spell. *I wonder how Telewen is doing?* Vairon thought. He addressed Candreen: "Have you been to see Telewen? He should be invited also."

The Master of Void Magic gave him a quick glance, and then looked away. "I believe he is still sleeping. We should not disturb him." He quickened his pace.

Vairon stopped. "Nonsense. Telewen likes a fine wine as much as I do. It would lift his spirits. We should go and bring him along."

Candreen came to a stop, and turned and smiled. "I understand that the healers said that he should be allowed to rest."

"Surely a goblet or two would not hurt him." Vairon made to retrace his steps. "I will go and fetch him. Go and tell the Eldest we will join you soon."

"*No!*"

Vairon came to a halt, and turned. He regarded Candreen with a puzzled look.

"I – I mean, we should not disturb him. The healers were adamant that he must have complete rest."

The Master of Beasts frowned. What was this? He himself had visited Telewen earlier in the day, and the Master of Fire Magic hadn't seemed exhausted; indeed, he had talked and talked. The healers had allowed him to return to his tower. If he was in such poor condition as Candreen intimated, they would never have allowed him to do that. What was the meaning for Candreen's outburst? He regarded the other, puzzled at Candreen's demeanour. The Master of Void Magic's smile seemed to be forced. As Vairon watched, beads of sweat appeared on Candreen's brow.

Vairon smiled, thinking that he knew the reason for Candreen's discomfort. "Do not worry; you will not get in trouble with the Eldest. I will take the blame."

"No, it is not that –"

"Candreen! Vairon!"

Korwen appeared on the path, and hurried towards them. "Where have you been? The Eldest is waiting."

"There is no need to rush," Vairon said. "I was just going to get Telewen. He likes a fine wine also."

Korwen and Candreen shared a quick glance. "I am afraid that Melandor has forbidden Telewen to drink anything other than water," Korwen said.

"I was unaware of this," Vairon said. "We drank some honey wine this morning. It did not seem to affect him adversely. Are you certain?"

Korwen nodded. "Yes. Melandor told Telewen himself. He must have been disobeying the healer's strict instructions. I should report this to the Eldest."

"There is no need to do that," Vairon said. "He only drank one or two goblets."

Korwen seemed to consider this. "Very well," he said. "I will overlook this transgression this time, as long as you can promise me he will not do it again."

"I will vouch for him."

"Good," Korwen said. "We must ensure that he regains his health. Come, the Eldest is not very patient."

"That is true," Vairon said. "Go on then."

They continued on towards the Eldest's tower.

"Ah, Vairon. Come in, come in," the Eldest exclaimed, as a few minutes later, the trio entered his dining chamber. He went forward and grasped Varion's hand in the way of Men. "How are you this fine evening?" Amberon's smile was bright. "I have obtained some fine Corlan wine. Come and join us." He gestured at the table, which was laden with meat and drink, and Vairon saw the promised wine sitting there ready for him.

The Master of Beasts shook his hand. "I am well, Eldest. Thank you." Vairon was puzzled. Amberon had never seemed so solicitous before. In fact, when he and Telewen had supported Goldwen, Amberon had been infuriated. He had not spoken to Vairon at all while Goldwen had been Eldest. He went to the table, and sat at the place that Amberon had indicated. The others came in and sat down.

"How is your spell casting proceeding?" Amberon asked, reaching for some bread and breaking off a large piece. He gestured to the servant that stood behind him. It was Ari, the boy who had served Goldwen before him. He came forward, took up the bottle of wine, and poured it into Amberon's goblet. With a motion of his head, the Eldest indicated that he should do the same for Vairon. Ari went to Vairon's side, and filled his goblet. He bowed, placed the bottle on the table, and stepped back.

"It is very difficult, Eldest," Vairon replied. "I cannot master the shape. I do not understand why I have failed."

"Perhaps you are only fatigued," Amberon said.

The Master of Beasts nodded. "Perhaps."

"Drink, Vairon. Eat, rest. You can attempt your spell tomorrow." Amberon smiled, and raised his goblet.

"Yes," added Korwen, "there is no hurry. Take your ease." He picked up his own goblet, and took a deep draught.

Narwen and Candreen, sitting opposite him, did the same. Vairon reached for his drink, unaware that all eyes were on him. He drank deeply, and sighed.

"Ah. This is excellent." He saluted Amberon with his goblet. "I must congratulate you on finding such an exceptional vintage, Eldest." He took another drink.

"Only the best will suffice for the Council," Amberon said. He waved Ari forward, and the Elf boy came and refilled both his and Vairon's goblets.

They all selected from the various dishes that were heaped upon the table. Vairon was still unaware of their scrutiny.

"How is Telewen?" asked Narwen. The other three gave him withering glances, but Vairon did not notice.

"He is resting. I understand Melandor has forbidden him to drink anything but water." He turned to Amberon. "I must tell you, Eldest; I was unaware of this instruction. When I saw Telewen today, he and I had some honey-wine. Please do not punish him, as it was I who brought it to him."

The Eldest smiled and waved his hand magnanimously. "It is of no matter. I will not punish him. But I must ask you not to take him any more." He took up a small dagger that was at his side, and with it he placed several cuts of meat on his plate.

Vairon inclined his head in a bow. "I thank you, Eldest. I will do as you say."

Amberon gestured to Ari, and the boy came and filled Vairon's goblet. The Master of Beasts emptied it and put it on the table. His face was flushed.

"More wine?" Amberon said.

"Please." Vairon said.

"Master," Ari said, "the bottle is empty."

Amberon turned and addressed him: "Go and fetch another."

"I do not know where they are, Master. Master Candreen gave me this one." Ari was shamefaced.

"I will go and show you," Candreen said. He rose from his seat.

"Good, Candreen. Go with him, Ari."

"Yes, Master." He bowed and followed Candreen out of the chamber.

"Have you heard from Silveron, Eldest?" Vairon enquired.

Amberon nodded. "Yes, only an hour ago. He said that the army was advancing, and had met with no opposition." He skewered a choice piece of meat with his dagger, and brought it to his mouth. He ate it with relish.

"I see." The Master of Beasts frowned. "Is that not strange?"

"Strange?" echoed Narwen. "What do you mean?" He shared a glance with Amberon and Korwen.

Vairon sat back in his chair. His eyes were glazing with the effect of the wine. "Do you not think that they would have met with the enemy by now?"

"Why?" Korwen said.

Vairon turned his bleary gaze upon the Master of Air Magic. "Because every report told of the Dark One's army advancing like a wave, and destroying everything in its path. Surely they would have met them in battle by now."

"Not necessarily," Amberon said. "You know yourself, Vairon, that even in the midst of a war, there are calm spells where nothing seems to be happening. This is probably the case at this time." He smiled, and picked up his goblet. He looked at Vairon searchingly as he drank.

The Master of Beasts listened, his face ruddy. They could tell that the wine was having an effect on him. He seemed to be deep in thought. Suddenly, he rose unsteadily. "Perhaps I should contact Silveron, and see how they are faring." His voice was beginning to slur. He put his hands on the table to steady himself. His head was ringing.

Amberon regarded him warily. "That will not be necessary." He flicked a cautionary glance at the other two wizards.

"Sit down, Vairon," said Korwen. "The Eldest has told you he has already spoken to Silveron, and there is nothing to worry about."

"Yes," added Narwen, "sit, and enjoy your meal."

"And the wine," Amberon said suggestively.

The Master of Beasts stood there, frowning. Why did he feel this way? Corlan wine usually did not have such an effect on him. He shook his head in an attempt to clear it.

"Here we are," said Candreen, reappearing with another bottle. He set it down in front of Vairon. Ari entered carrying a bottle, and put it down in the middle of the table. He went and stood back at his place by the wall.

"No," Vairon said thickly. "I have had enough." He pushed the bottle away.

"Just one more," the Eldest said. "I obtained this wine especially for you, Vairon. I know how much you like it."

The Master of Beasts peered at him. He sat down, and reached for his goblet. "I would not wish to…offend you, Eldest."

Amberon leaned forward, and took up the bottle. "Allow me." He poured Vairon a drink. Vairon bowed his head, and toasted Amberon. With the eyes of the conspirators watching him closely, the Master of Beasts drained the goblet, and leaned forward to put it on the table.

He fell back in his chair. His throat was burning. Vairon coughed, and bright blood flecked his lips. The chair was overturned as he rose shakily and clutched at his chest. The Master of Beasts stared at his companions in shock as the import of the pain struck his muddled mind. They had poisoned him! The other wizards had risen to their feet, and were watching his agonies. Their faces were blank.

Ari came forwards, seeking to help Vairon. Amberon turned his eyes upon the boy, and Ari fell back from his penetrating gaze. He stared at Amberon in horror, realising what they had done. He stood gaping at the dying wizard, wanting to help, but his fear of the Eldest and his powerful magic rooted him to the spot.

Vairon staggered forwards. He tried to speak, but only painful gasps escaped his tortured throat. With an inarticulate cry, he raised his arms above his head, and made an invocation. As the others in the chamber watched, his form shimmered, and became a huge bear. It roared, and rushed towards them, foam flecking its dark lips. Smashing the chairs into splinters as it came, the bear attacked viciously.

The Eldest thrust his hand forwards. The heavy oaken table leapt into the air, and hurtled itself at the oncoming beast. The bowls and plates flew in all directions, and shattered on the stone floor with a crash. Food and knives followed, and the bottles that contained the fatal wine broke into glittering shards as they contacted the floor. The bear bellowed, and brought up its arms, and its claws smashed the table to pieces in a terrible display of power. It came on, and rushed at the wizards.

Korwen was the closest. He was too slow to react. The bear caught him up, and its savage teeth tore his throat open. As his blood fountained into the air, it hurled his body away, and roared. Suddenly flame surrounded it, projected from Amberon's outstretched hand.

But a shield also encompassed the bear, and the Eldest's attack was fruitless. It roared again, and lunged towards them. The wizards scattered, and hurled bolts of lightning and fireballs at it. The shield turned all of their assaults away. The rampaging beast struck at Candreen, but somehow he dodged its attack, and leaped out of the way. The wizards encircled it, and poured fire and devastating bolts of energy at it.

*How could Vairon still be alive?* Amberon thought wildly. There had been enough poison in the wine to kill a horse. The Master of Beast's strength was impossible. He should be dead!

Suddenly, as though Amberon's thought had been turned into action, the bear roared, but this time there was agony in the tones that shook the room. It shuddered, groaned, and fell to the floor with a crash. As they watched warily, it breathed its last, and then its form slowly faded and became Vairon. Cautiously they approached, and Candreen knelt to check to see if life had indeed fled.

He looked up, and nodded. "He is dead."

"I cannot believe that he fought for so long after drinking the poison," said Narwen, amazed.

"He was very strong," Amberon agreed.

Candreen rose to his feet. "It is a great pity that we could not have used such strength."

"He would not have joined us," Narwen said.

"No," Amberon said. He clenched his fist. "Now we have disposed of those who would oppose us. There is no-one to stand in our way." He smiled grimly.

"Where is the boy?" Narwen said.

The Eldest whirled and gaped at the empty wall where the boy had been standing. "After him, you fools! If he gives the alarm, we are done!"

As one, the treacherous wizards raced to the door, and rushed in pursuit of Ari.

Outside, the object of their search ran as fast as he could, gasping, his lungs on fire. His heart hammered in his chest as his mind whirled with the unbelievable thing that he had just witnessed. The Eldest and his companions had murdered the Master of Beasts! His thoughts raced through his head: *Where can I go? Who can I go to?* The remaining Councillors would hunt him down and kill him for what he had seen. As he desperately searched for a solution, he suddenly remembered Telewen. He came to a jarring halt. *Telewen! Yes, I can go to him, and tell him what has happened. He will protect me, and inform the King!* With renewed confidence, he raced towards the Librarian's tower.

Moments later, he had reached it. Ari hid in the bushes, his eyes scanning the area for the traitors. No one was about. Perhaps they thought he had fled into the forest, and had gone there to search for him? Knowing that every second he remained there increased the chances of them discovering him, he took a deep breath, and ran across the open ground to the tower's door, expecting at every step to be struck down by magic.

Ari opened the door, and entered. He closed it behind him, and stood panting with his back against it. He looked up the stairs. Telewen would surely be in his room at the top of the tower, resting. The boy raced up the steps, taking them two at a time. He ran down the corridor, and saw that the Master of Fire Magic's door was open, and light was streaming out of the room. He came to a stop, and glanced in. Telewen was sitting with his back to the door, staring out of the window.

"*Master!*" Ari gasped out, and rushed over to him.

Telewen turned, puzzlement written on his face.

"Ari? What is wrong?"

"Master Vairon, he – he's –"

"Slow down, lad." He rose to his feet. "Here, sit and tell me." Telewen indicated the chair. He guided the boy into it, and placed his hand on his trembling shoulder.

Ari gulped, took a deep breath, and continued: "Master Varion, they *killed* him!"

Telewen frowned. "Killed Vairon?" he echoed. "*Who* killed Vairon?"

The boy shuddered, and then went on in a rush: "The – the Eldest, and Masters Candreen and Narwen. They poisoned him! The wine! He changed into a huge bear, and he killed Master Korwen, but the poison was too much for him..." Ari looked up, and tears ran down his face. "What can we do, Master? They will come for us."

Telewen looked deeply into the boy's eyes. "Are you certain of this? They were not just practicing spells, and you are mistaken?"

"No, Master!" Ari gasped. "I *saw* them kill him! I swear I speak the truth. They murdered him, and now we are in danger."

Telewen looked deep in thought. Ari stared at him, wondering if the Master of Fire Magic's illness had somehow robbed him of his senses. Suddenly, Telewen gripped his shoulder.

"We must go, Ari, and go quickly. This is treason. We must go to the King!" Telewen took up his staff that was leaning against the wall. "Come. You will be safe with me." He walked quickly to the door and peered out. The corridor was empty. The wizard turned and beckoned to the boy. "There is no one there. Let us go."

The boy leapt up. "Yes, Master." He ran over to the door. They looked out into the corridor again to make sure they were alone and safe. It was empty and silent. Telewen nodded to Ari, and they left the room, closing the door quietly.

They came out into the corridor and strode purposefully along it, Telewen taking long strides so that Ari had to almost run to keep up. They descended the stairs rapidly, and came to the door. Telewen halted, and listened. The boy stood behind him, his heart hammering. He hoped that the traitors weren't lying in wait for them.

The wizard whispered; *"Quietly now. Follow me."* He slowly opened the door, and brought his staff up, ready to defend himself. The path in front of the tower was empty. Telewen stepped out onto it. Ari followed, staring all about at the bushes, expecting to see the traitorous wizards. They stealthily made their way towards one of the little used gates in the wall that led out into the forest.

Telewen walked up to it, and spoke the Word of Opening. The door opened, and with one backward glance, he stepped through. Ari followed him, and found himself in a part of the forest that he hadn't seen before. The wizard spoke the Word of Closing, and the door closed. They hurried into the trees.

The pair made their way along a track, and suddenly found themselves in a clearing. They came into the open, and hurried towards the safety of the trees on the other side.

"Hold!"

At the sound of the commanding voice, they stopped and turned.

Narwen was approaching them, his staff ready for combat. He paced towards them, but came to a halt and Ari saw a look of puzzlement cross his face.

"Telewen?" he said. He regarded the Master of Fire Magic uncertainly.

Ari pulled on Telewen's sleeve. "Master! We must go! He will kill us! Master Telewen!" The boy gasped in sudden pain. He looked down, and saw a longknife piercing his chest. He stumbled backwards, and as the blade was pulled free, he clutched at the wound. Blood spurted through his fingers as he stared up into the face of his killer in disbelief. Telewen held the bloody longknife in his hand; his face was blank, and his eyes were cold.

Telewen's face suddenly twisted, reshaping itself. As the mortally wounded Ari watched in amazement, it became Amberon's face. The wizard's robes shimmered and turned into the Eldest's robes.

"I am not Telewen," Amberon sneered.

Ari gaped. He fell to his knees. For a moment longer, he stared, and then he pitched forward and lay on the grass, his lifeblood spreading out in a crimson pool beneath him.

"That was clever."

The Eldest looked across the clearing, and saw Candreen approaching. The wizard came up to Amberon and Narwen, and they all stared down at the dead boy.

"I am glad you approve," Amberon said coldly.

"I did not know what was happening," Narwen said. "For a moment, I thought you actually *were* Telewen, even though I knew he had been slain. I would not have thought to pose as Telewen, and lure the boy into the open."

Amberon gave him a disdainful look. "That is why *I* am Eldest, and you are not." He returned his gaze to the body. The wizard tossed the bloody longknife onto it. He summoned the energy for a fire spell. The other two stepped back.

"Fire," Amberon said. He pointed his staff at the corpse. A tongue of flame leapt from his staff, and instantly the body was wreathed in fire. As it burned with an intense heat, the longknife melted, and both it and the corpse were swiftly consumed. In a matter of moments, only a charred spot on the ground showed where Ari had been.

They became aware of an electric feeling in the atmosphere of the clearing. A vortex formed, and from its whirling centre stepped Darkmor. He came over to them, glanced down at the burnt grass, and then turned his attention to Amberon.

"You could have been exposed," he said icily. His burning eyes swept over them.

"But we were not," Amberon said.

"You were lucky. If this boy had escaped, all of Algol would have been warned, and then they would have informed Anarys. He would no doubt have sent Silveron and Vandaron to investigate. That must not happen. He must remain unaware that you have joined me."

"No-one knows what we have done," said The Eldest. "The death of these three has gone unnoticed. By the time it is known, it will not matter; we will be victorious."

"So you hope," Darkmor replied.

"There is no-one to stand in our way now," Candreen said. "Your forces will crush the Army of Light, and we will help to ensure that your victory is complete. We will deal with –"

Candreen faltered as the sorcerer turned his burning gaze upon him. "I did not give you leave to speak." His eyes flashed, and black flames ran down his staff. A burst of energy leapt from him and engulfed the Elf.

Candreen gasped, dropped his own staff, and clutched at his throat. He was choking. The Master of Void Magic dropped to his knees. The sorcerer raised his staff, and Candreen fell prone. His lungs burned with the need to breathe. Spots danced before his eyes, and his vision began to dim. He gaped like a landed fish, desperate for oxygen. Suddenly the pressure upon his throat vanished. He rolled upon his back and took great gasps of air, staring at his tormenter in fear.

Darkmor loomed over him, his venomous stare piercing the Elf and pinning him to the ground. "You will stay here and do nothing, do you understand?"

Candreen managed to nod shakily, still taking in gulps of air.

"Good. Do not speak to me again." The sorcerer returned his attention to Amberon. "I will inform you when I have crushed the Army of Light. You will then see to it that any who remain are taken care of. I will dispose of Silveron and Vandaron; you and your companions will be the only wizards left. You will have dominion over the Elves. Men will become your slaves."

"And the Dwarves?" asked Amberon. "What of them?"

"They will go back to the Underworld. They only care for their craft."

"There are many of them with the army," Narwen said.

""Then they will die with the army. Once my own forces are revealed, no-one in Erathyn will dare to oppose me. Even now, a vast host descends upon Anarys and his pitiful group." He turned and walked into the vortex, which swallowed him up. It faded, and vanished.

Far away, in the camp of the Army of Light, Silveron came awake with a start. Something was wrong. The Elf sat up on his pallet, and listened to the night. What had woken him? He heard nothing out of the ordinary. He rose to his feet, and walked to the tent's opening. Pulling aside the flap, he looked out. The camp was quiet. Several fires glowed here and there, and sentries paced the perimeter, but most of the army was asleep. Silveron had reported to Anarys what he and Vairon had spoken of in the Sending that he'd made. The Elven-King had been satisfied that all was well in Algol, and had told the wizard that his fear had been groundless.

But Silveron thought otherwise. Something was not right. He couldn't shake off the feeling that there was something strange about how Vairon had acted during the Sending. He knew that The Master of Beasts was not a particularly friendly person, but Vairon had almost seemed dismissive of his concerns, and had been quite abrupt. *That* was not like Vairon.

It was late. Should he try to contact Vairon or Telewen? Both of them were probably asleep. For a few minutes, he considered whether he should interrupt their slumber. Finally, he decided that he would make the attempt in the morning. He returned to his pallet, and lay down. He wondered how Willowen was faring. He had to rescue her, even if it meant his death. Silveron hoped that the Dark One hadn't tortured her in his efforts to unlock the power of the stone from the sky.

With this uncomfortable thought on his mind, the Elf fell into a troubled sleep.

# CHAPTER IV

# COURAGE AND HOPE

Anarys stood in the opening of his tent and looked out at the reddish light that flooded the land. He stared at the blood red clouds that swirled murkily above; they reflected the turmoil of his thoughts. His mind was filled with worry for his daughter. She was headstrong like her mother, it was true, but was that enough to allow her to endure the tortures of the Dark One? The Elven-King knew that Darkmor lusted after the power that was locked within the Starstone, and would stop at nothing to force Willowen to help him unlock such power. Was she strong enough to resist him until the Army of Light arrived to assault him in his stronghold?

"She *is* strong, Sire."

Anarys brought his attention to the speaker who stood before him. "Silveron."

The wizard bowed. "Your Majesty."

"Do you think that Willowen can defy Darkmor until we can arrive to save her?"

"I am certain of it, Sire." A wry smile came to his face. "She defies you; Darkmor has no chance of forcing her to do anything if *you* cannot."

Anarys returned the smile. He reached out and clapped Silveron on the shoulder.

"You are right." He gazed into the wizard's face, a puzzled look upon his own visage.

"What is it, Your Majesty?"

"For a moment, I thought I was speaking to Goldwen. Those were words of comfort that he would have used. Certainly, the humour is much like his own was."

Silveron's smile broadened.

"Perhaps there is more of him within me than you first thought?"

"Perhaps. I sense that your own powers are growing. In time, you may even surpass him."

"I would not even try to, Sire. I am still uncertain of myself."

"My Liege."

The captain of the guard stood there with two of his warriors.

"What is it, Enriss?"

The captain bowed. "Your Majesty, a messenger from the Dark One awaits you outside."

Anarys nodded. "Very well. Bring him before me."

Enriss hesitated.

"Is there something wrong, Captain?" Anarys enquired.

"He is mounted, Sire."

"Upon an O'skaa?"

"Yes, Sire."

"I see." The Elven-King smiled to himself. "Tell him I am coming to hear his message."

Enriss and his warriors bowed. They turned to obey the order.

"Captain."

"Sire?"

"Send Commander Lysanna to me, with four of her bowmays. Tell them to arm themselves."

Enriss smiled. "Yes, My Liege." He bowed.

The group walked away. Silveron and Anarys watched them leave. A few minutes later, Commander Lysanna and her bowmays arrived and bowed. She had been placed in charge of the bowmays while Captain Nilda was away on the scouting mission. She was tall and blonde, with brilliant blue eyes.

"Your Majesty."

"Ah, Commander. Good morning. It appears we have a guest. I wanted you to be here to greet him."

"A guest, Sire?" She looked puzzled.

"Indeed."

The sound of alarmed voices came to them. At first, it was far away, but it slowly came closer. Lysanna and her bowmays formed up in front of the Elven-King, and fitted arrows to their longbows. The susurration of voices grew louder. A crowd appeared, with weapons drawn. They were retreating from something unseen. Lysanna watched in puzzlement. What was it that they were retreating from?

Enriss and a dozen Elven warriors came running up. They drew their swords, and stood between the Elven-King and the approaching group.

Suddenly the host broke apart, and an O'skaa came forward, the cloud of enervating energy that surrounded it preceding its advance. The monsters evil eyes glittered as it approached. Upon its loathsome back was perched the tallest Schaaka that Anarys had ever seen. He was almost as tall as an Elf. He reined in his mount as the bowmays aimed their bows. One of his eyes was scarred over from an ancient wound, and his ugly face was covered with scars from many battles. His gaze roved over the group contemptuously, as he leaned back in his saddle, and raised his goad and let it rest in a pouch that was at his right side.

The Goblin spat upon the ground.

"Is this the way the King of the Bright Ones greets a messenger?" He bared his fangs in a savage grin. He patted his mount's hairy head. "Does my ride frighten you?" he said mockingly.

"Silence, dog!" cried Enriss. "Address His Majesty with respect. Step down and bow to him."

"I am Kherlach. I bow to no one." He stared at them with a disdainful eye.

"You *will* bow to His Majesty, filth," said Lysanna coldly, "or I will send you to join those of your kind who I have slain." She aimed her arrow directly at the O'skaa rider's chest. The bowmays around her drew their arrows back to their cheeks. Enriss and his warriors advanced a pace forwards.

Kerlach regarded Lysanna. He lifted the goad and pointed it at her.

"Do you dare to threaten the messenger of the Dark One?" He said.

"I do. Get off that beast, and bow to His Majesty."

The Schaaka's good eye opened wide, and his nostrils flared. He hissed venomously. The spider echoed his exclamation. It raised its forelegs, and the Elven warriors and bowmays stepped back. Silveron went into a combat stance, his staff came up in a defensive position, and a nimbus of power danced on its tip.

"Hold," Anarys said. He stepped forward, and put his hand on Lysanna's shoulder. "Lower your weapons."

The captain lowered her bow, slowly easing the tension on the bowstring. Her bowmays did the same, and Enriss and his warriors lowered their swords. The glow of Silveron's staff faded, and he stood and held the staff by his side.

Anarys smiled.

"Please forgive them. They only seek to protect me."

Kerlach returned the goad to the pouch. "Protect you? I am only a messenger. I am not here to attack you." His gaze swept over the group standing before him. "Although, if I wished it, my mount could slay you in a moment." He showed his fangs in an evil grin.

"No doubt," The Elven-King replied. "But it is certain that Commander Lysanna and her bowmays would fill you and your mount with arrows immediately after. Or perhaps Silveron would use his magic upon you?"

Silveron's stare bore into the Goblin. Kerlach felt as if the Elven wizard gazed into his very soul. He shuddered, wondering what awful magic the wizard could unleash upon him. He had seen what the Dark Lord could do; surely this Elf was powerful also.

The Schaaka's grin ran away from his face.

Anarys stepped forward, and stood directly before the O'skaa. He fixed his gaze on the monster, and all who stood there could feel the power within him envelope the spider in a battle of wills. Each of them bent their willpower upon the other; Anarys seeking to force the spider to give in to his will, and the creature seeking to reject the Elven-King's command. Finally, the O'skaa shuddered, and in a few moments it lowered its forelegs. Then it lowered its forepart upon the ground in deference. The Elven-King raised his eyes and met Kerlach's amazed stare. None but an experienced O'skaa rider could cow the spiders like Anarys had just done.

"Now," Anarys said, "shall we end this posturing, and hear the message that you have been charged to bring me?"

The Goblin nodded, still amazed at the Elven-King's unexpected display of control over his mount. "As you wish," he said sulkily. He removed a scroll from another pouch that was attached to his saddle. He tossed it to the ground at Anarys's feet.

There was a murmur of outrage at this show of blatant disrespect. Anarys held up his hand to silence it, and then he knelt and picked up the scroll. He rose to his feet and untied the leather thong that bound the scroll. Unrolling it, he looked at its contents in puzzlement. He returned his gaze to the Goblin.

"This is in your tongue. I cannot read it."

Kerlach grinned evilly.

"Then it's lucky I read it myself." He chuckled. "It says: "To the Elf King. I see that you have not taken my advice. I told you that if you or anyone else dared to march against me, I would slay your daughter. Order your rabble to withdraw, or she will die a long lingering death. Darkmor.""

Lysanna cried out, and brought up her bow. Her bowmays followed suit. Enriss and his warriors raised their weapons. Silveron roared angrily, and his staff was raised and pointed at the Schaaka. He began to speak a Word of Power.

"*Stay your hands!*" Anarys cried. He spun about, and regarded them. "Lower your weapons."

The wizard's staff was still pointed at the Goblin. Silveron's eyes burned with fury. Anarys could see that Silveron wanted to destroy the O'skaa rider. He stepped between the furious Elf and his target. Silveron met his gaze. The King shook his head, and Silveron slowly lowered his staff. But his eyes still burned into the Goblin. Kerlach knew he had just faced destruction, and breathed again. The Elven-King turned his attention to the bowmays.

Lysanna's face was burning with hatred. Her eyes glistened with angry tears. Her arrow was aimed at the Schaaka's heart.

"Commander Lysanna," Anarys said, "I order you to lower your weapon."

The Goblins brash demeanour of before had evaporated. He stared at Lysanna and her companions, and sweat beaded his brow. He shifted unconsciously in his saddle.

"Commander," the Elven-King repeated, "lower your weapon." She gave no sign that she heard him. He slowly advanced towards her. *If she should shoot!* He thought. Anarys halted before her.

"Commander," he said, "*that is an order.*"

She blinked.

Anarys reached out his hand tentatively. He could see that her arm was beginning to shake from holding the tension of the bow. *Or is it from anger?* He thought.

"Lysanna,' he said softly. He placed his hand over her right hand gently.

She turned to regard him. She whitened; this time not from anger, but from embarrassment and shame. She had defied her King! She lowered her bow, and as her bowmays followed suit, she knelt abjectly before Anarys. She bowed her head remorsefully.

"Your Majesty, I beg pardon from you, I have disobeyed –"

"Enough," Anarys said.

The commander looked up, and saw that he held out his hand. She gripped it, and he helped her to her feet. He gave her one look that was filled with unspoken command, and then he returned his attention to their visitor.

"A nice display of allegiance." Kerlach laughed. "Is *this* how you rule?" He laughed again, but Anarys could see that he had been shaken to the core.

"These ladies before you are part of the Princess Willowen's bodyguard," he said. "They love her, and will die for her. You would do well to remember that."

"I would die for her also," Silveron added.

The Schaaka sneered, but said nothing.

"We will march until we meet the Dark One's forces, defeat them, and make him give Willowen up," Anarys said. "If he dares to harm her in any way, he will pay dearly."

Kerlach smiled. "Fine words," he said. "Is that what you wish me to tell my master?"

The Elven-King nodded. "No threats against my daughter will stop my army."

"Know this, then," the Goblin said. "My master told me to say to you that his army is coming. He knows the size of your pitiful band, and has sent a much larger force that will overwhelm you. They will come, and they will destroy you. The O'skaa will feed upon you." He raised his arms and spread them wide, indicating their surroundings. "Look about you. This is my master's doing. He has power enough to move the moon out of her place. Can you say that you have any power to match that? He is invincible."

"And yet, he must kidnap my daughter to help him. Is that invincibility? I think not."

The Schaaka's lip curled. "You think so little of her? You would allow her to die?"

"I know she would rather die that let the Dark One triumph," Silveron said.

"Then she will die. She will help my master, and then he will slay her." Kerlach leaned forward in his saddle. "The army of the Underworld will be unleashed. My Queen will destroy you. No force upon Erathyn can stand against us."

"Is that all you have to say?" Anarys said. "I tire of your voice."

"It is."

"Then go back to your master and give him our defiance."

Kerlach snorted. "You are a fool. You will deliver your army into certain death." He stared balefully at Lysanna. "I will find you on the battlefield and give you to my mount." The O'skaa hissed.

"You may try," Lysanna replied coldly.

"I suggest you leave before I allow Commander Lysanna and her bowmays to slay you like the animal you are," Anarys said. "Commander!"

"With pleasure, Sire." Lysanna and her companions raised their bows, and aimed at Kerlach.

"You would shoot me down, although I am only a messenger?" he snarled. "I have offered you no offence."

"You *have* offered offence," Anarys replied. "Your very presence offends me."

"And you insulted the Princess," added Silveron icily. "For that alone, you should die."

"I am sure your mount could find its way home even if you lay dead upon its back." The Elven-King folded his arms. "Get you gone, before I allow them to shoot."

"Let me deal with this foul creature, Your Majesty," Silveron said. He stepped forward.

"No, Silveron. Let him scuttle back to his master."

Kerlach regarded the group in sullen silence for a few moments, and then with a jerk of the reins, he turned the O'skaa about, and they hurried away.

"Your Majesty," Enriss said, "Do you think the Dark One would really kill Princess Willowen? Surely he would not dare?"

Anarys unfolded his arms and regarded him. "I am afraid that he would, Captain. If he can make her do what he wants, he will slay her." He paused, as though he was thinking of something. "We must prepare for an attack. I do not doubt that the foe is on the way. Pass the word to make ready."

"Yes, Your Majesty." Enriss bowed, and then he and his warriors departed. The crowd of onlookers, having heard his command, broke up and went back to their companies to prepare for the defence of the camp.

"Commander."

"Yes, Sire?"

"Send your bowmays to inform your company of my order. Remain here; I would speak with you."

"Yes, Your Majesty." Lysanna nodded to her companions, and they bowed to the Elven-King and departed.

Anarys came to her.

"I do not doubt your loyalty to Princess Willowen, Commander. Nilda chose well when she put you in charge. But..."

Lysanna bit her lip.

"You must govern yourself. To be the leader of the bowmays is to be the perfect example of a disciplined warrior. The display that I witnessed here today must never be repeated. Do you understand me?"

Lysanna nodded. "I do, Sire. The way I reacted is unforgiveable. Captain Nilda would never allow such a lack of control. If it is your wish, I will select another to lead the bowmays, and will step down. I will accept any punishment that you set for me."

A sad smile appeared on the Elven-King's face. He shook his head.

"There is no need for that. You made a mistake. I trust Captain Nilda's judgement. You are a good warrior and leader. But you must realise that that filth will report to his master that my bowmays are an undisciplined rabble. I will not have him laugh at our expense. I have chastised you enough. Go to your company, and make them ready."

"Yes, Your Majesty." Lysanna bowed, and then began to walk away. Then she halted and turned. "I will not fail you, Sire."

"I know you will not."

She bowed low, and then straightened up and continued on her way.

"I disobeyed you too, Sire," Silveron said.

Anarys turned to him.

"Yes, you did," he said. He came over and put his hand on the wizard's shoulder. "But I should not have to repeat the speech I gave to the commander to you. Yours is an important position. I want you to remember that. You must govern your passions."

"I will try, Sire. Control seems to be the hardest thing to master."

The King nodded. "It certainly is." He lowered his voice. "I felt the same way when that dog spoke of killing Willowen. I would have liked nothing more than to feel my blade plunge into his heart." He straightened up. "But I am the Elven-King. Such displays are not allowed to me. I must be seen as resolute; nothing can shake my resolve." He met Silveron's eye. "Go and eat and rest, my young friend. The battle lies before us."

The wizard bowed. "Yes, Your Majesty." He turned to go, and then added: "I will not fail you either, Sire."

Anarys held out his hand, and they shook hands. Then Silveron bowed and took his leave.

Anarys turned his attention to the road upon which the scouting party had left to reconnoitre. There was still no sign of them.

*They are late,* he thought. *They have been gone for a long time. Has something happened? Have they met the enemy?* He stared for a moment longer, and then he turned and made his way to his tent. "Have my armour brought," he said to one of the sentries.

"Yes, Your Majesty."

Anarys realised that he held something in his left hand. He brought it up and gazed at the scroll. The black scrawl upon it meant nothing to him. He already knew of its import. He held it up against one of the torches that stood outside of his tent. He watched the fire ignite and burn the paper. He allowed it to burn down until the flames almost touched his fingers, and then he tossed it on the ground. Anarys watched the fire devour the paper until it was just a blackened remnant. Then he ground it beneath his foot, and approached his tent.

The other guard pulled open the tent flap, and the Elven-King went inside.


Lord Nildoron held up his hand. The scouting party halted behind him. They were following the path that led to Stonebridge. Far below them, the river cut its way through the mountains. He scanned the cliffs that lay on the opposite side of the river. Had he seen something?

Ervin reined in beside him.

"What is it, My Lord?"

"I am not sure. I thought I saw something move."

Nilda rode up and joined them.

"What is it, Father?"

"I think there is something over there." He pointed.

Nilda looked at where he indicated. "Yes," she finally said. "We are being watched."

"Could it be spies of the enemy?" Ervin said.

"Perhaps," Nildoron said. "Or it may just be an animal."

F'Leet came to them and bowed. "I could find out, My Lord," he rumbled.

"Yes," Nildoron said. "Please do. We will hold here."

"Yes, My Lord." The Avianinn leapt into the air.

Across the river, Althar and a party of Schaaka had hidden themselves amongst the rocks. They watched closely as the Avianinn came towards them.

The albino cursed.

"If he sees us..." began one of the Goblins.

"He won't. Keep out of sight."

F'leet came closer and closer. He flew low over them, and circled back.

*"He's seen us!"* A Goblin whispered. He fitted an arrow to his bow.

*"Fool!"* Althar hissed. *"Lower your weapon!"*

The Schaaka ignored him. He was terrified of being discovered. He took aim at the oncoming birdman.

The albino gritted his teeth, and began to crawl towards him. His knife slid from its sheath. He would kill this idiot before he revealed their location.

Too late! F'leet soared above them. The Goblin loosed his arrow. The Avianinn heard the twang of the bowstring, and dodged the fatal shaft.

With an inarticulate cry of anger, Althar rose to his feet, and stepped up to the Goblin. He stabbed him in the back. As the body fell, a cry came from the other side of the river. They had been seen.

"Quickly, you fools!" Althar cried. "Follow me." He ran as the Elven and chokhutai bows sang. Arrows fell about them, and some found their mark. Four Schaaka fell dead as their companions raced after the albino.

"We're going the wrong way," a Goblin said.

"*Imbecile!*" Althar rasped. "We can't go back to the fortress. Ragnak and his Schaaka would be discovered."

"The Bright Ones have horses," another Goblin panted. "They will catch us!"

"This path is too narrow for horses," the albino said. "Run, you dogs!"

"Althar," Ervin said grimly. He turned to Nildoron. His eyes blazed. "I must leave you, My Lord. I have a score to settle."

"I will go with you," Nilda said.

"I forbid it!" Nildoron said.

The Kandaran spurred his horse and sped off in pursuit of the fleeing Goblins. Nilda followed him.

"*Nilda!*" Nildoron cried. "I order you to come back!"

They raced away, ignoring him.

"Ten of you go after them," Nildoron ordered.

Ten of the Elven warriors galloped away after the receding pair. Nildoron watched them for a moment, and then turned his mount to face the way they had been going.

"He has wanted to avenge his people for a long time," Shin said.

"That does not concern me," Nildoron said. "If he puts her in danger..."

"I believe the captain can look after herself," the Goblin said.

"You are correct. However, I am not happy with her attitude. This

Kandaran is the cause of her rebelliousness. I will speak to them both when our mission for the King is successfully completed."

"Forward. We go on to the fortress."

The scouting party continued down the path towards Stonebridge.


Ervin reined in his steed in a cloud of dust. He halted at a small bridge that they had passed not long ago. He leapt down as Nilda came to a stop beside him.

"You'll get in trouble," he said.

She dismounted. "I am always in trouble when I am with you." She grinned.

He laughed.

The Elven warriors came up and halted.

"We are to go with you, My Lady," their leader said.

'You won't need your horses," Ervin said. He gestured at the path across the river. "We're on foot from here." He and Nilda set off at a run.

The Elf nodded. "Two of you stay with the horses." They dismounted and ran after Ervin and Nilda.

Althar looked back over his shoulder. He saw the oncoming group. *Ah, Ervin. Come on, brother. Come and get me.*

"Faster, you slugs!" he called. "The hunters are coming."

Several Goblins cried out in terror. They knew how fleet of foot the Elves were. They sped on, hurtling along the narrow track. Their pursuers rushed after them, slowly closing the gap.

The distance between the two groups lessened rapidly. The Elves and Ervin could run for days, but the Goblins were not used to such a chase. They began to tire as the strain of running at full speed sapped their strength.

Soon they were in bowshot range.

Nilda unslung her bow as she ran. She fitted an arrow and let fly. One of the trailing Schaaka fell.

*"Nice shot!"* Ervin cried. He unslung his own bow, and fitted an arrow. He loosed, but his shaft missed.

Nilda fitted another arrow. She fired, and a second Goblin staggered, and fell off the path, to plunge down towards the river with a shriek.

"And again!" the Kandaran cried. "You'll have to give me lessons."

"Can you afford them?" She winked at him.

Ervin laughed. He looked ahead, to see their quarry disappear around a bend in the path. He slung his bow, and drew his sword and knife.

They raced around the corner, to be met by a hail of arrows. The Goblins had waited for them. Several shafts found their marks. The Schaaka began to reload. The Kandaran hurled his knife. It buried itself in a Goblin's neck. Nilda unslung her bow, and sent arrow after arrow into them. Several of the Elven warriors followed suit, and a storm of arrows tore into the foe. But Ervin charged in recklessly, hewing to his left and right. The Elves slung their bows and drew their swords. The Schaaka scattered. They dropped their bows, and drew their wicked blades.

Nilda shot down a Goblin, and then drew her sword. She waded into the fray. The Elven warriors came behind her.

For a few furious moments, it was hack, slash, and stab. But soon it was all over. The Goblins were scouts, not warriors, and in a short space of time, they lay dead. Winded and exhausted by the chase, they were no match for the Elves. Only Althar remained. He stood upon a ledge that lay at the edge of the path. The river thundered below him.

He backed away, blade outstretched. Ervin slowly advanced towards him.

"What now, *brother*?" the albino taunted. "Will you let your friends here fill me with arrows?" His blood red eyes shifted to Nilda. "Or perhaps your whore wishes to slay me?" he smiled evilly.

Ervin halted. "I'll do that myself."

"Will you now? Have you forgotten that *I* am a better swordsman than you?" The albino reached for the clasp at his throat that fastened his cape to his tunic. He undid it, and let the cape fall to the bloody rocks. "Come then. Let us dance."

The Kandaran advanced, watching Althar's eyes. The albino rushed forwards, and their blades met with a metallic clang. They each dealt savage strokes, but both parried the attacks. They leapt back, and began to circle each other. Nilda and the Elves watched.

"You've improved," Althar said. "I'm impressed."

"I've had plenty of practice killing Schaaka," Ervin replied.

"O'skaa too, I believe. You are like a hero of old. Perhaps they will tell tales of you." The albino saluted him with his blade. "But can you kill *me*? I don't think so."

"Let's see," Ervin said, and rushed at him.

Their swords danced in a medley of strokes. Ervin fell back. A nasty cut on his cheek had opened up, and blood ran down his face. He wiped it with the back of his hand.

Althar smiled. "First blood to me. Come again." He beckoned with his free hand.

This time the Kandaran advanced cautiously. They each stepped carefully, their eyes fixed upon their opponent. A grim ballet of death began. The only sounds were their breathing, and the scrape of their boots upon the rock. They circled each other like predatory beasts that sought an opening to leap upon their prey.

Althar grinned. "Are you tired, brother? Perhaps you should sleep."

"I'll sleep when you're dead," Ervin gritted.

The albino leapt forwards, and swung at the forester's head. Ervin dodged the stroke, and made his own attack, which Althar parried. They both stepped back, and circled again.

"Let us finish this," Althar said. He swung his sword in a figure of eight pattern, and strode towards the Kandaran.

Ervin watched the sword move through the pattern as though mesmerised. Althar smiled and closed in. He reversed the pattern, and struck his opponent on the shoulder. Ervin staggered backwards.

As the Kandaran stumbled, Althar raised his sword with both hands to deliver a killing blow. A wolfish grin was on his pale face.

"*Ervin!*" Nilda screamed.

As the blade descended, Ervin's free hand shot out, and he grabbed the albino's wrists in a vicelike grip. His sword plunged into Althar's chest. The albino gasped. His mouth gaped wide in surprise. Their eyes met. Althar dropped his sword. It fell to the rocks with a clang. His arms fell listlessly by his side.

The Kandaran pulled his blade free. He spun upon his foot, and using the momentum of the spin, swept his sword around and struck at Althar's neck. The albino's head left his body in a spray of pinkish blood. It rolled along the rocks and came to rest face upwards. The eyes held some spark in them for a moment. But only for a moment. The light of intelligence faded from those blood red orbs, to be replaced by the glazed stare of death. The body stood quivering for a moment, and then it took several steps backward and fell off the ledge to plunge towards the river far below. Ervin went to the edge and saw it disappear with a splash.

Ervin walked back, and took up the albino's cape. He wiped the blood from his sword with it, and then went back to the edge. He tossed the cape away and sheathed his sword. He watched the cape flutter downwards like a shot bird. It hit the water, and was whirled away.

"Ervin!" Nilda cried. She ran to him and crushed him to her.

He groaned in pain. She released him and stepped back, and looked at the cut on his face. Nilda reached out and touched it gingerly.

Ervin winced. "It's all right. I've had worse."

Nilda turned to the remaining Elves. "See to the dead."

"Yes, My Lady." They obeyed her order.

She returned her attention to the forester. "Sit," she ordered, pointing at the ground imperiously.

He grinned. "Yes, My Lady." He lowered himself carefully.

Nilda knelt by his side. She tore a strip of cloth from her cape, and wadded it up. Then she took out her canteen, and opened it. She poured some water on the cloth, and started to wipe away the blood from Ervin's cheek.

"You allowed him to strike you," she said disapprovingly. She met his gaze.

He nodded. "Yes. He was right: he was a better swordsman than I. I knew I had to get him to lower his guard."

Nilda looked at the wound on his shoulder. "He could have killed you," she said reproachfully.

"But he didn't. And now my people are avenged." He sighed. "I've waited for this day for so long." A tear formed in his right eye, and then ran down his cheek. Others followed. He sniffed, and wiped his nose with the back of his bloody hand. Nilda reached out and wiped the blood from his face.

She regarded him. "Are you all right? What do you feel? He *was* your brother."

"I feel – relief." He paused, remembering. He took her hand. "When we were young, I had to look after him all the time. Everyone picked on him because he was different. But then..."

Nilda waited for him to go on.

"He was responsible for the death of everyone in the Kandaran villages. He and Granthus came up with the plot that resulted in the death of all those who were at the trading post. Coralyn died there because he thought nothing of them." He clenched his fist.

Nilda packed the wound with the damp cloth, and then she tore another strip from her cape and began to bind it up.

"Ermil's death is on his head too. He was a good boy." He lowered his head.

She finished binding the wound, and placed her hand under his chin. She raised his head. Nilda looked deeply into his eyes, and saw the pain there.

"Now his evil is gone from Erathyn. You have wiped it away. You have avenged your people and your friends. Be of good cheer, Ervin. Come." She helped him to his feet.

"I am the last of the Kandarans," he said mournfully.

"And you are the best of them," she said. "You have done all Erathyn a great service this day. Every race will know of your deed. You have shown great courage."

An Elf warrior came over. He held Ervin's father's knife out to him. "This is yours, I believe."

The Kandaran accepted it with a bow. "Thank you." He placed it in its sheath.

"We are ready to leave, My Lady."

"Good," she said. "How many did we lose?"

"Four. Three were shot and one was slain by the sword."

"Bring them with us. We will honour them."

"Yes, My Lady. We should rejoin Lord Nildoron and the group." He regarded Ervin. "How is your wound?"

The Kandaran made a fist, and then he swung his arm in an arc. "I can still swing a sword. Let's go."

"What of that?" The Elf pointed at Althar's head.

"Let it lie there and rot," Ervin said. He looked at it for a long moment, and then he turned away.

They joined the other Elves and made their way back along the path.

# CHAPTER V

# STONEBRIDGE

Nildoron, Shin, and their warriors lay among the rocks. They had reached Stonebridge and concealed themselves. Now they lay hidden and looked across the bridge to the fortress. All was quiet. Only the wind sighed, and they could hear the distant rush of the river below. But the Elf-Lord was wary. Something didn't feel right. He scanned the walls of the fortress for any sign of life. Nothing met his gaze.

*Nothing,* he thought. *And yet, there could be a hundred Schaaka lying in wait, and we would not know. Where is Nilda? They should have returned by now. If the Kandaran has led her into danger, I will -*

"My Lord?"

Nildoron turned to his left.

"Should we not go and search the fortress?"

"That was the King's order, Alaryn," he replied. "But something here is not right. I can feel it."

"I will take some warriors and go and make sure, My Lord."

"No. We will remain here until Captain Nilda and her party rejoin us."

"But, My Lord, we have already been away from the camp for two days. King Anarys did not expect us to be gone for this long. We need to investigate the fortress, and return."

"I know what we must do, Alaryn. I only wish to make sure that Captain Nilda and her companions are safe."

"But should we not go and check the fortress while we wait? We should not tarry here. I know that you are concerned for your daughter's safety –"

Nildoron rounded on him.

"Are you questioning my orders, Captain?" His mouth set in a hard line.

"No, My Lord. I merely wish to suggest that we carry out our mission."

"That's a good idea. What are you lying there for?"

Ervin and Nilda stood there. They bent low and came over and joined the two Elves.

"Daughter," Nildoron said. "I am glad to see you safe." He met the Kandaran's eyes, and nodded to him. "You were successful?"

"We were. Althar and his band are dead. My people are avenged."

Jhara Shin clapped him on the back. "Well done."

Ervin winced.

Nildoron regarded his wounds.

"But not without cost, I see." He looked behind them, and saw the warriors he had sent off with them. He counted them.

"We lost four warriors, Father," Nilda said. "We brought them with us. They will be honoured."

"Good." Nildoron indicated Ervin's wound. "Can you still fight?"

"I can. I've had worse." He peered across the bridge and scanned the fortress. "Let's go and have a look at Stonebridge. I haven't been there for quite a while."

"The enemy could be laying in wait," the Elf-Lord said. "I do not like it. It could be a trap."

"Of course it's a trap," Ervin said. He grinned. "Althar and his friends tried to lead us off so their comrades wouldn't be discovered."

"You are certain of this?"

"No, My Lord. But it makes no sense for them to go running off into the wilderness when they could have come this way and gained sanctuary in the fortress. Whatever else he was, Althar was no fool. That tells me that some of their friends are inside. So let's go and have a look."

"What if the enemy is there?" Nildoron said. "They will slay you."

The Kandaran shook his head.

"I don't think so. I think they've been ordered to stay out of sight. If they kill us, they'll show themselves and fail their master. And we all know he doesn't like failure."

"Let me go and look the fortress over, My Lord," F'Leet said. "There is less danger to me than to any scout who is on the ground."

"But you couldn't look inside unless you landed, F'Leet," Ervin said reasonably. He turned to Nildoron. "It makes more sense if I go with a small group and investigate."

"I will come with you," Nilda said.

"No," Ervin said. "You're the best shot here. Stay here and cover us. If we do run into the Schaaka, we'll want to beat a hasty retreat."

She was about to reply when Lord Nildoron interrupted her.

"Perhaps you are right, Kandaran. Very well. Captain Alaryn, take five of your warriors and go with him."

"Yes, My Lord."

"But, Father –" Nilda began.

Nildoron held up his hand to silence her.

"What of me?" Lord Shin asked.

"You and your chokhutai are fine shots as well, Shin," the Kandaran said. "You should remain here too."

"Very well. But if you find any Schaaka, leave some for us." He grinned, showing his wicked fangs.

Ervin grinned in return. "I'll do my best."

He and Captain Alaryn rose to their feet. The Elf beckoned to several of his warriors. They came and advanced with the pair until they came to the bridge. The Kandaran's gaze swept the walls of the fortress. He couldn't see anyone. *Doesn't mean no-one's there,* he thought. Ervin drew his sword and stepped onto the bridge. Alaryn and his warriors mirrored his action.

Ervin's gaze swept the fortress walls. It was made of wood, Shaped by the Elves hundreds of years ago. A score of oak trees had been planted here, and grown speedily by the Elves' magic. Then the Shaping had taken place. The walls and buildings had been grown and fashioned artfully. Many people of all the races had come from miles around to see it. It was a wonder to see; an Elf construction out here in the wilderness, where no other such structure existed.

The Forester smiled to himself as he remembered the first time he had come to see it. He and Althar had come with his father. They had marvelled at the beauty and craft that was before them.

"It has been Shaped by Elven magic," Alaryn said, "but this bridge is surely of Dwarf construction."

"Yes," Ervin said. "It was made by both the Elves and the Dwarves, many years ago. All of the races enjoyed coming here. It was a meeting place then, not a fortress." He pointed out modifications that had been added to the walls. "Men did those. After the War of the Races, the Elves and Dwarves wanted nothing to do with the place. Men came and took it over, and fortified it."

"It spoils its beauty," Alaryn said. "My Lord told me it was once called Linador."

The Kandaran nodded. "'High Place.' Yes, my father told me that too. The Dwarves had a name for it, but I've forgotten it. Men called it Stonebridge."

"A plain name for something of great beauty," Alaryn said.

The Forester chuckled. "We were never very good at naming things."

They both fell silent as they advanced across the bridge.

Behind them, Nilda reached around and took her bow from her shoulders. With a swift movement, she fitted an arrow. The Elven warriors who remained followed suit. Jhara Shin gave a curt order to his chokhutai, and the Goblins armed themselves with their short bows. They all knelt there ready to shoot any Schaaka that showed their face. They watched as the Forester and his companions crossed the bridge.

Ervin and Alaryn came to the gates. They were large and wooden, made of a black wood the Kandaran was unfamiliar with. The warriors came up behind them, all eyes sweeping the fortress walls for any sign of the enemy. They listened; only the sound of the wind and the river far below came to their straining ears.

Ervin tried the gates. He pushed against them. They began to open. He gestured to Alaryn, and the Elf came and helped him. With a groan that seemed like the loudest sound Ervin had ever heard, they opened wide.

The courtyard of the fortress was revealed. It was empty. Nothing was there. The group entered cautiously, eyes and ears alert. They spread out, swords ready.

Ervin sniffed. There was something strange in the air. What was it? He'd smelt it before. He waved the warriors on.

"We will check the upper levels," Alaryn said. He pointed to two of his warriors. "Stay here with the Kandaran." He beckoned his warriors forward. They followed him to the main building. They entered and vanished from sight.

Ervin and the remaining Elves advanced and began to search the ground floors of the buildings.

Back across the bridge, Nilda scanned the walls for any sign of the enemy. No-one appeared.

"Perhaps it is empty after all, Father," she said.

"We will soon know," Nildoron replied. "Keep watching."

"It would not be the first time the Schaaka have lain in wait," Jhara Shin said. "I do not like this."

Nildoron didn't reply.

The Kandaran and his companions had searched the ground floors of all the buildings. They had found nothing. They came back to the gates and waited for Alaryn and his warriors.

Moments later, the Captain and his warriors emerged from the main building. They came over to the gates.

"Nothing?" Ervin asked him.

"Nothing at all," Alaryn replied, "although the enemy *has* been here. It seems as though they left in a hurry; we found scraps of food and discarded gear."

The Kandaran nodded.

"We found the same. Let's go and tell Lord Nildoron."

They went through the gates and proceeded to go back across the bridge.

*"What's this?"* A voice bellowed behind them.

Halfway across the bridge, Ervin and Alaryn spun about. A grossly fat Goblin stood in the gateway.

"What are these dogs doing here?" He cried. He stomped towards them. He held a large jug in his hand, and he shook it at them furiously. *"Gorlik! Shoot them down!"* He took a large pull at the jug. He glared at it, and threw it to the ground. It shattered into shards. He drew his sword, and advanced towards the amazed group on the bridge.

Ervin laughed. Was this the only Schaaka left in Stonebridge? A fat drunkard? The laughter died on his lips as two O'skaa and their riders burst from the gates and rushed towards them shrieking. Goblins appeared on the walls, and let fly with their bows. Several Elves fell.

*"Fall back!"* Ervin cried. They turned and ran for the other side.

Nildoron and Shin ordered their warriors to open fire to give them cover.

F'Leet leapt into the air. He took out his small bow, and sent arrows at the Schaaka on the walls. Several fell, but others returned fire, and the Avianinn was forced to dodge their shafts. They kept him moving about so that he had no chance to fire back.

Nilda rose to her feet. She sighted, and loosed an arrow. It sped across the bridge, and punched into Ragnak's chest. The Goblin stopped, and looked down at it in befuddled amazement. He roared, and came on. She fitted another shaft, and fired. This arrow slammed into the Goblin Lord's shoulder. He staggered, but then bellowed and advanced. Nilda nocked another arrow, took more careful aim, and loosed. It pierced Ragnak's left eye. The Schaaka came to a stumbling halt. He swayed there drunkenly for a moment, and then crashed down onto the bridge like a felled tree.

The O'skaa swept past him. Their riders urged them on. The evil energy that surrounded them radiated outwards. They pursued the fleeing Elves. A hail of arrows sped towards them. One of the O'skaa was riddled with shafts. It screamed and fell. Its rider leapt from its back, and rolled along the bridge. As he came to his feet, several arrows pierced him, and he joined his mount in death.

The other spider caught up with the Elves. It grabbed a straggler, and hurled him over the railing. He fell shrieking into space. Its rider reversed his goad, and speared another Elf as he turned and attempted to draw his sword.

*"Turn!"* Ervin cried. "Turn and fight!" He and Alaryn ripped out their swords, and rushed at the monster. The remaining warriors drew their blades and plunged into the fray. Nilda and her comrades held their fire so that they wouldn't shoot their companions down.

A chorus of screams exploded into the air. Nilda looked, and saw more O'skaa coming. Ten of the awful creatures poured out of the fortress gates. Ervin and the Elves on the bridge would be overwhelmed! She dropped her bow, and ran towards them. Her sword leapt from its sheath.

*"Nilda!"* Nildoron cried. He jumped up. *"Endoi!"* He drew his sword, and rushed onto the bridge in pursuit of his daughter.

The Elves around him raced after them, drawing their swords as they came. Shin and his chokhutai dropped their bows, and drew their blades as they followed them.

The single O'skaa on the bridge smashed into the group, hurling them about like dolls. The Forester was thrown down, and looked up to see the rider's spear coming towards him. He rolled, and the spear point scraped across the stone, sending up sparks. He avoided another thrust, and as the Goblin tried to spear him again, his weapon was blocked by an upraised sword.

Nilda parried the weapon, and dodged as the spider attacked her. Ervin leapt to his feet, and desperately looked for his sword. It was nowhere to be seen. All around him, Elves, chokhutai, and spiders were locked in a furious struggle. As he looked, he saw the O'skaa lunge at Nilda. She sidestepped the attack.

The Kandaran drew his father's knife, and hurled it at the Goblin rider. It struck him in the shoulder. Ervin rushed forward, and as the wounded Schaaka brought his spear around and tried to stab him, the Forester grabbed it by the shaft, and wrenched it from his grasp. He jumped back to avoid the O'skaa's rush. A dagger suddenly appeared in the rider's eye. He shrieked, and fell out of the saddle to lie in the blood that covered the bridge.

The monster went mad. It attacked fiercely. Nilda and Ervin dodged its savage assault. The Elf struck out with her sword, and the Kandaran tried to stab the creature with the spear. It lashed out with its forelegs, and swept away their attacks.

Alaryn appeared to one side. He leapt in with his sword. As the O'skaa turned its attention to him, Ervin saw an opening. He thrust the spear into the beast's gaping maw. The shaft plunged deeply into the monster. It screamed in pain and thrashed about. The Kandaran held on grimly.

"*Help me!*" Ervin cried.

Nilda ran up and grabbed the spear shaft. With a flick of his head he indicated to Nilda to help him push the thing over the guard rail. She nodded and added her strength to his own. They heaved, but the monster was too heavy for them to move. Alaryn saw what they wanted to do. He sheathed his sword, and raced up to join them. The three of them gripped the spear, and pushed the monster towards the railing.

"*Push!*" Ervin cried.

They pushed with all their might. The O'skaa's claws scrabbled on the stone, trying to find purchase. It slowly went backwards, screaming. The creature lashed out with its forelegs, but its strength was waning. Ervin took the blows against his shoulders. His wound burned like fire, but he shoved the beast closer to the edge. Another push and the O'skaa came up against the railing. They heaved again, and the creature began to tilt backwards. One final mighty effort, and the arachnid overbalanced, and fell shrieking into the abyss.

Gasping from their efforts, they gave each other a grin, and then they turned and joined their companions. Ervin stopped to retrieve his father's knife, and Nilda's dagger. He tossed it to her, and she caught it expertly. He saw his sword. As she and Alaryn rushed in to help their comrades, he swept it up, and charged in.

Jhara Shin and four of his chokhutai were beset by two of the monsters. They dodged their fangs and claws, and slashed at the O'skaa's legs. Shin tried to pierce an eye, but the spider evaded his thrust. Off balance, the

Goblin-Lord pitched forward to lay sprawled beneath its jaws. Two of his chokhutai raced in, but the O'skaa sunk its fangs into one, and the other was stabbed by its rider. The thing returned its attention to Shin. His comrades saw his peril, but were too busy defending themselves against the other arachnid to help. The awful fangs descended.

Suddenly Nildoron and several of his Elves leapt into the fray. The O'skaa fell back before their flashing swords. Nildoron drew his longknife, and hurled it at the Schaaka. The rider knocked it aside with a sweep of his spear. But this move had left him open to another Elven warrior. He plunged his sword into the Goblin, but then was knocked down by the spider.

Shin had regained his feet, and stood with Nildoron and three of his Elves. The O'skaa rushed forwards. It lashed out, and threw the Elven warriors down. But Nildoron and Shin leapt at it from either side. Their blades sank deep into the loathsome creature's body. It screamed and died.

Jhara Shin pulled out his bloody sword and saluted Nildoron with it. "Thank you, My Lord."

The Elf-Lord bowed to him. Then they both looked about themselves to see if any of the enemy still survived.

The ferocity of the O'skaa's attack had been devastating. Half of the Elves and Shin's chokhutai lay sprawled upon the bridge. But they had given better than they had received. Out of ten spiders, only two remained, and they were beset on all sides. The other monsters and their riders lay dead in their black blood, or had been hurled over the railing to their doom.

The Kandaran rushed towards one of them. It was close to the railing. Ervin leapt up on the rail, and ran along it, perilously close to the edge. He jumped, and came down on the loathsome creature's bloated abdomen. He ran down it, and as the rider realised something was wrong, he turned, and the Forester's sword cleaved him in two. As the Goblin's body fell to either side of the O'skaa, Ervin leapt upon its back. He raised his sword high, and plunged it deep into its brain. The monster shrieked, and expired.

The last O'skaa rider saw that he was outnumbered. He wheeled his beast about, and charged through the survivors, scattering them about. He raced for the safety of the fortress. As they moved away from the Elves, the Goblins in the fortress sent arrow after arrow at the warriors on the bridge. Several fell to the wicked shafts.

*"Back! Back!"* Ervin cried.

As the arrows fell about them, they retreated.

A voice cried out from the fortress.

*"Kerchak! Takhar mo da Cha-den! Kah!"*

The O'skaa rider held up his goad to show that he had heard and understood the command, and then he turned his mount away from the fortress. They hurried along the trail that Althar had taken.

*"Nilda!"* Ervin called, *"your bow! Stop them!"*

She raced to the end of the bridge, and took up her bow. She fitted a shaft, and in a lightning quick move, she fired. The arrow took the Goblin in the side. He slumped forward, but held on. As the Elves and chokhutai gained cover, and began to send their own arrows at the fortress, she nocked another arrow, sighted, and loosed in one fluid motion.

This arrow went through the rider's neck. He fell forward dead. But his mount raced onwards.

*"The spider! Shoot the spider!"* Ervin cried.

She fitted another arrow, and fired. It took the beast in the side. But the vitality of the monsters was well known. It carried on rushing down the trail. Nilda took one more arrow, fitted it to the string, and loosed. It pierced the O'skaa's abdomen, but the beast kept moving. Suddenly, it went around a bend in the trail and was gone.

*"F'Leet!"* Ervin cried. *"Stop it! Don't let it get away!"*

The Winglord raced in pursuit of the fleeing arachnid. A few sweeps of his wings, and he had gone.

The Kandaran came up to Nilda. They crouched down to avoid the Goblin's fire. Nildoron, Shin, and Alaryn joined them. All were splashed with blood. Small cuts on their hands and faces, and tears in their tunics and capes told of the savagery of the fight.

"O'skaa!" Ervin smashed his fist into his open palm, reproaching himself. "That's what I could smell. What a fool!"

"Do not upbraid yourself, Ervin," Nilda said.

"I should have known they were there. Now we've lost good comrades because of me."

"No, Kandaran," Nildoron said. "They would have attacked us regardless."

The Forester turned to him.

"Do you know that for sure? They only showed themselves when that fat Schaaka appeared. They had to do something, because he'd revealed them."

"That is not true, Ervin," Alaryn said. "They were not seen. They could have allowed us to slay him, and remain hidden."

"Yes, Ervin, that is right," Jhara Shin said. "He gave them away. You are not to blame for our warrior's deaths."

"It is too late to argue about how events played out," Nildoron said. "They are dead, our companions are dead, and we know for certain that they occupy Stonebridge. We must go back and tell the King." He turned his attention to the Kandaran.

"What was it that someone called from the fortress?" he asked.

"'Kerchak, Report to the Master. Go.'" Ervin said.

"The Dark One," Alaryn said grimly.

"I'm afraid so," Ervin replied. "They'll know we're here."

"And they will look for the army," Nildoron added. "We must go."

"We can't leave those filth here," The Kandaran said.

"I agree with Ervin, Father," Nilda said. "We cannot leave them here. They must be slain."

"They must already know where our army is, My Lord," Ervin said.

"Why do you say that, Kandaran?"

"It makes sense." He held up his hand and counted off on his fingers. "One; there were the bodies at the edge of the forest. They were killed to prevent them alerting us of the Goblin's presence. Two; Althar and his scouts were roaming the area. You can bet that they have been observing the army this entire time. Three; you have confirmation that the Schaaka have taken Stonebridge. They must know where the army is, and are watching it as it moves. We must stop that."

"Ervin is correct, My Lord," Shin said. "We cannot leave the enemy here. We must slay them all."

Nildoron regarded them.

"The King's orders were very specific: 'Do not engage the enemy.' Are you saying that we should ignore his command?"

"I'd say it's a bit late for that, My Lord," The Forester said.

As Nildoron made to reply, there was a whirl of wings, and F'Leet landed among them.

"Did you get it?" Ervin asked.

The Winglord shook his noble head.

"No," he rumbled. "It disappeared into a large opening in the rocks. I did not follow. I am sorry, My Lord."

Nildoron pondered the Avianinn's words. He knew that it meant that the O'skaa would go back and report to the Dark One. He looked at the bridge, and saw the dead Elven warriors who lay there. His warriors. *They should not have died in vain,* he thought.

"Perhaps you are right," he said. He looked at them each in turn. "We will slay all of the Goblins, and then return to camp and report to the King. Our comrades should not have died in vain. Make ready to attack the fortress."

Ervin grinned. Captain Alaryn moved off to give the order to the remaining warriors. Nilda unslung her bow. Shin signalled to his chokhutai to prepare an attack. Alaryn returned.

"We are ready, My Lord."

"Then let us finish this," Nildoron said. His blade swept from its sheath. He strode to the bridge, and his warriors followed with swords drawn. Ervin and Nilda walked by his side. Shin and his chokhutai followed. The Elf-Lord looked at the fortress. The Schaaka on the walls were holding their fire until they came closer. They must run the gauntlet of arrows and break down the gates to gain entry.

Nildoron held his sword high. *"Endoi!"* he cried, and broke into a run. The others followed. They raced across the bridge. The Goblins still held their fire. Nilda and several of the Elves had their bows in hand, ready to return fire.

As they reached the halfway point on the bridge, the Schaaka began to fire. Four Elves went down, but Nilda and the other Elves armed with bows sent their own arrows sleeting at the walls. Several Goblins were shot down, and fell from view.

They reached the gate. Ervin and Nildoron slammed into it, and pushed. Alaryn and his warriors caught them up, and added their weight against the portal. It shuddered, but held. They attacked it with their swords. Chips of wood flew, but the gates still held. Shin and his chokhutai arrived, and added their own strength to the assault.

Behind them, Nilda and her companions fired upon any Goblin foolish enough to show themselves. The others hammered on the door, and drove their shoulders against it.

A loud crack came to them from inside.

"The bar!" Ervin cried. "It's broken!"

"Push!" Nildoron ordered.

The mass of warriors surged forward, and with a splintering sound, the gates began to give way. With one more push, they burst wide open, and the warriors rushed inside.

Straight into a hail of arrows. Two ranks of Schaaka were there waiting for them. The front rank knelt, and the second rank stood. They loosed as the Elves and Ervin raced through the gates.

The Kandaran felt a heavy blow to his chest. A sharp pain tore at him. He fell, to lie face down in the dirt of the courtyard. The Goblins discarded their bows, drew their curved swords, and rushed in to the attack. Ervin saw a confused view of stamping, struggling feet kicking up the dust as they fought around him. The sounds that came to him; the shouts, the clangour of weapons meeting, and meaty impacts of sword against flesh and bone dissolved into a kaleidoscope of whirling noise.

Someone cried out his name. He stared at his sword. It was still gripped in his fist. He tried to move his hand, but his body was going away. Something heavy fell on him. He gasped as its weight drove the breath from his lungs. His heart was beating more slowly, and with every pump, he felt his lifeblood draining away into the dust. His vision began to fade as the sounds around him became unintelligible. He became numb, and coldness filled him. Its icy touch spread throughout his body like an invading tide of icy water.

Darkness came.

# CHAPTER VI

## SILVERON'S DECISION

Silveron stared into the blood red sky. After the meeting he had returned to his tent. He had lain down to sleep, but had only slept fitfully. After the Elf had tossed and turned for several hours, he had finally admitted defeat, and rose from his pallet. The wizard had crossed the floor to stand in the tent's opening. He had been staring at the ruddy clouds for what seemed like an eternity.

*What power this sorcery displayed!* He thought. His gaze went to where the moon hung in the sky, still blocking the light of the sun. Silveron shook his head in awe.

"And I am to go up against such power," he said to himself. "Can I really defeat Darkmor? If he has such energies to draw upon, how can I hope to win?"

"Winning is not required," a voice answered.

Nomayon stood there.

"What do you mean?" The Elf asked.

"Silveron thinks that he must win in a fight with the Dark One."

"Surely that is so," Silveron replied. "I must defeat him."

The Seer's eyes pierced him through.

"No. Silveron is wrong."

"Wrong?" The wizard echoed.

"Yes. The Council knew that no one in this world could defeat the Dark One. That is why the talisman was made."

Nomayon stepped forward until they were face to face. He regarded the Elf closely.

"Does Silveron understand?"

The wizard considered his words. Nomayon was correct. There was no fight to be won. He nodded.

"Yes. There can be no winning against such a powerful enemy. Only the Spell of Banishment can take his evil away from Erathyn."

The Seer smiled.

"And that is all that is required. No fight, no contest. Silveron must use the talisman on the enemy, and banish him from this world." His eyes went glassy, and the Elf knew that he looked into the future. He remained silent as the Seer regarded what was to come. Finally, Nomayon's gaze returned to normal.

"Silveron will do this. Nomayon has seen it. He will rid us of the Dark One."

"You are certain?"

"Nomayon is certain."

The Elf felt as though a great weight had suddenly been lifted from his shoulders. He breathed deeply.

"But," Nomayon added, "Silveron must not falter."

"What do you mean? What have you seen in your vision?"

"Nomayon must not tell. Everything depends on Silveron. He must use the spell, no matter what happens."

"What are you not telling me? What will happen?"

"Nomayon cannot say. Silveron will know what to do when the time comes."

"What does that mean? Why –"

"Ah! Awake! Good, find you slumbering, I thought I would."

Silveron and Nomayon turned to see Brador. He was ready to march. The Elf saw that he had rested well. He wished he had slept as lightly as the Dwarf.

Brador came forward. He regarded them both in turn.

"Something troubles you, lad. What is it?"

Nomayon shook his head slightly.

"It is nothing. I did not sleep well, my mind was in turmoil." The wizard rubbed his eyes with his knuckles.

"Well," Brador said. "Your friends are here now. Come, have breakfast with us you will."

"I thank you, Brador, but I do not feel like I could eat anything."

"Nonsense! A warrior always eats before the march." He came and took the Elf by the arm. "Come and eat." The Dwarf pulled him along. "Fetch you, Nomayon was supposed to. What were you talking about?"

Silveron smiled. He glanced back at Nomayon, who was following. The Seer put a finger to his lips.

"Nothing of consequence," Silveron said. "We were only talking about which way we should go. Lord Nildoron and his party have not returned, so we cannot have the guidance of Ervin."

"Nomayon's scouts will find the way," the Seer said from behind.

"I hope nothing bad has happened to them," Silveron said.

They arrived at the fire. The rest of the group had already eaten, and were sitting waiting for them.

"Here the wizard is," Brador said. "Feed him heartily."

Egon came forward with a large plate. Upon it were two slices of bacon, two fried eggs, and fried mushrooms. He gave it to the Elf, who regarded it doubtfully.

Egon gave him knife and fork, and bade him to sit and join them. Silveron sat down.

Brador came over with a large mug. Silveron shook his head. He felt queasy.

"No thank you, Brador.  I have had enough wine."

"Ah, water it is only. Eat, lad. You'll soon feel better."

The Elf glanced down at his plate. He looked up and met the Dwarf's stare. He took the fork and speared a piece of bacon. Silveron brought it to his mouth and chewed. It was delicious. He fell to with a will. Soon the plate was clean. He accepted the mug and drained it in one long swallow.

"See," Brador said. "Better, eh?"

"Yes. Thank you, my friends." He rose to his feet. "I see you are all ready to go. I must get my own gear, and bid the King farewell."

"Too long, that will take," Brador said. "Off we must be."

"His Majesty will want to know that we have departed." Silveron made to return to his tent.

"The Elf-King knows Silveron's mission," Nomayon said. "He must depart now. Time grows short." He stared at Silveron enigmatically.

The Elf regarded the Seer. What was it that Nomayon was not telling him? What had he seen in the vision? Silveron knew that King Anarys always trusted the counsel which Nomayon provided. Goldwen had also thought that Nomayon's visions were dependable. His father had told him that Nomayon was the most trustworthy Seer upon Erathyn. But still the thought nagged at him. Why should Nomayon keep something from him? Was it something that spelled danger for him? Or was it something that the entire group should beware of? Perhaps it was something to do with Willowen?

Nomayon's face was blank. Silveron could read nothing in those savage features. He scanned the group around him. Each of them was eager to depart. He knew there was a long march ahead of them. And without Ervin to guide them, it would be longer. They would have to find their own way through the forests and mountains, until they came to

Darkmor's stronghold.

"Do we agree that we should leave at once?" he asked.

A chorus of agreement met this question.

"Very well," he said. "But I still need to fetch my gear."

"Here it is," Nomayon said. He gestured.

M'Shaan and K'Taal stood there with Silveron's staff and pack.

The wizard smiled.

"Such service. I thank you."

The two Plainsmen nodded to him deferentially, and brought his gear over to him.

"Nomayon did not offend Silveron by sending his warriors to fetch his gear?" the Seer asked.

"No. I am not offended. Thank you, Nomayon." The Elf put his pack on, and K'Taal handed him his staff. "Now I am ready. Let us go."

Brador doused the fire as they began to move off. The two Plainsmen led, and after them came Silveron, followed by the rest of the group. He glanced to the side, and saw Egon.

"Your King will understand, My Lord," he said. "You've already spoken of your mission. No need to report to him."

"I hope you are right, Egon. He may have had other things to tell me."

"I don't think so, My Lord." He smiled sadly at the Elf. "King Munare always used to say to me: "Do I have to tell you how to do everything, Egon? What's your brain for?" He trusted me to carry out his will without asking endless pointless questions."

The wizard nodded.

"Goldwen was the same. I would have to work out everything for myself. He sometimes gave me a hint of what the answer was, but he would not give it to me. He always made me work for it." He returned Egon's smile. "I miss him."

"I miss my King, too, My Lord," the Man replied. "I was sent into his service as a young boy. He was like a father to me; he taught me swordsmanship, how to use a bow, and statescraft. I think he wanted me to represent Rewes right from the start."

"Did you like being his agent?"

Egon shrugged. "It took me to places that I had never seen before, My Lord. I met the people of many different races."

The wizard studied his face. He knew Egon was holding something back.

"But you wanted something else."

Egon glanced at him, and then looked away.

"Yes, My Lord," he finally admitted.

"What was that?"

The Man sighed. "I wanted to be an adventurer, My Lord. I dreamed of being a knight; someone who went to foreign lands, and lived by his wits and his sword. I wanted to be someone who rescued fair maidens in distress. You know; a hero."

"And you did not end up living that life?"

"No, My Lord, I didn't. Instead I was sent to ensure the King's orders were carried out, sometimes to make treaties with other races. Other times I had to pore over musty old ledgers to make sure that the merchants weren't trying to swindle my King. That's not the life of a hero."

"Is it not?"

"What do you mean, My Lord?"

"You were charged by your sovereign to carry out certain tasks. Sometimes that took courage."

"Courage, My Lord? I don't see how it would take courage to do that."

Silveron smiled.

"There are those who would shudder to just leave their lands and journey far away, Egon, especially among your people. Goldwen told me of entire communities of Men who had lived and died for generations within the walls of their own villages. Not one of them had ever ventured out to see what the world was like for hundreds of years."

Egon laughed. "That's true, My Lord. You're right."

"And as for living by your wits, I would say you definitely have been doing that, ever since you escaped into the forest with us. I saw how you fought in the fortress too. Your skill with a sword is admirable. King Munare would be proud of you."

"Thank you, My Lord," Egon said softly.

Seeing that he had inadvertently made Egon sad, Silveron changed tack.

"Goldwen once said to me that sometimes we have to do what we do not want to do. Would you agree?"

"Oh yes, My Lord. Absolutely. I've done many things that I didn't want to do."

"Why?"

"Why what, My Lord?"

"Why did you do those things when you clearly did not want to do them?"

"Well, My Lord, sometimes it was because I would be embarrassed, perhaps thought of as a coward. Other times, I did things out of a sense of duty; duty to my King, to my parents, or sometimes to my comrades."

"Is that why you remained King Munare's agent?"

Egon thought for a moment.

"I think that was partly it, My Lord. But the main thing was, I didn't want to let my parents down."

"Why would you let them down?"

"Well, My Lord, they'd given me in service to the King. They wanted me to make something of myself. They didn't want me to lie around daydreaming all the time."

"Daydreaming about being a hero?"

Egon smiled.

"That's right, My Lord." He laughed.

"You don't have to call me 'My Lord,' Egon. We are friends. I am not nobility." He held out his hand.

The Man stared at it, and then grasped it and shook hands with the Elf. He grinned.

"Thank you." He paused, and then said: "Silveron."

"Much better."

They laughed together.

The wizard smiled to himself. When had *he* become the one who gave advice? It wasn't so long ago that it was he who had asked innumerable questions. He liked Egon. The Man could sometimes be closed off, but Silveron knew that was because he was still grieving for his master. As Egon had said, he had been in King Munare's service for a long time. *A long time for a Man, that is,* the Elf thought, *but only the blinking of an eye for an Elf.* Still, he was a good companion, and a staunch ally in a fight. Silveron hoped that Egon would soon get over Munare's death. *If he were an Elf,* he thought, *Egon would still remember his master with fondness, but there would not be this lingering grief.* Elves were taught from the earliest age to control their emotions, and to them, such emotions as sorrow were fleeting, and controlled rigidly.

*Goldwen was one of the exceptions to that rule,* he thought. His father had displayed many of the emotional states that he was discovering in Men. Silveron remembered the sense of humour that Goldwen had. There was also sadness. When he had spoken of things that made him sad, the wizard did not hide that sadness, in the way that an Elf would. Although they were of different races, he had been much like the Men that Silveron had encountered.

King Anarys was like that too. He knew that both the King and Goldwen had spent many years among Men, and during that time, had taken on some of their traits. Men displayed their emotions openly. So too did Anarys and Goldwen. *Willowen too,* he thought. *I hope she is all right.* He sent out a probing thought to see if he could sense her. Nothing came to him. It was as though she had vanished from the world. He ached to see her.

"Silveron?"

The Elf shook himself out of his reverie. He saw Egon smiling at him.

"Now who's daydreaming?" Egon said.

Silveron returned his smile.

The group had been walking through the camp. Now they came to its edge. The two scouts continued on towards the trees. Silveron stopped and looked back. He could see Anarys's tent, and the standard that flew above it. He suddenly had a premonition that he would never see Anarys again. A vision swam before him. He saw the Army of Light standing and waiting. Everything stood out in sharp clarity, but there was no sound.

Anarys sat upon his horse, his gaze was fixed on something that approached. He cried out a command; even though Silveron couldn't hear anything, he knew it was the order to hold. He looked in the direction that Anarys was facing. A vast shadowy mass appeared and rushed towards him. As it neared, he saw that hundreds of the O'skaa and their riders were in the vanguard. A huge arachnid, much larger than the rest, was in the centre of this oncoming force. Seated upon its back was a female Goblin. She shouted a command, again unheard, and the O'skaa riders reversed their goads so they became spears, and the monsters hurtled towards Anarys and the waiting army. With a terrible shock, the two forces crashed together. The vision disappeared. Silveron shuddered. Brador and Nomayon came up to him.

"No second thoughts, lad," the Dwarf said. "On we go."

The Seer looked the Elf deep in the eyes.

"Silveron has seen something."

"Yes," Silveron lied. "I have seen a long hard journey ahead of us."

"No. That is not the truth. Tell Nomayon the truth."

The Elf regarded him. What could he say? Did his vision mean that Anarys and the entire Army of Light would be wiped out by the O'skaa? Their leader must have been the Goblin Queen, Sardia. He had heard that she was immortal. Suddenly he realised that the spell that Darkmor had used to block the sunlight was made for that very purpose. With Erathyn in darkness, the Goblins could come up from the Underworld, and lay waste to everything. With a force of O'skaa that numbered in the hundreds, perhaps thousands, what hope could any army have of stopping them?

"The truth?" he said. "I have seen Anarys and our army overwhelmed by a huge force of O'skaa. There were hundreds of them."

"The giant spiders?" Egon asked. "Hundreds of them?" He went pale.

The wizard nodded.

"Told you that, I did," Brador said. "With the sun gone, come out of the shadows, they will."

"Silveron does not know if that will happen."

The Elf turned to the Seer.

"Visions are possibilities, not certainties," Nomayon said.

Silveron looked into the savage face. As before, Nomayon was unreadable.

"I must warn the King," he said. "Only then can I leave." He made to turn back, but the Seer stepped in front of him.

"Silveron must not go back. Time is running out."

"You will stop me from warning the King?" the Elf said.

"Yes. Silveron's task is before him, not behind. Silveron must take and use the talisman. Everything else is not important."

"The King's *life* is not important? I should let him go to his doom? What of our army? Can I let them go without a word of warning, and be destroyed?"

Nomayon's face was grim.

"Yes. Only Silveron's task matters."

"You would let them all die?"

"If it is their fate, we must let it happen."

"No," Silveron said firmly, "Get out of my way." His eyes blazed. His staff came up, ready for combat.

Something smashed into the back of his head, and he fell into darkness.

"Sorry I am, lad," Brador said. He stood over the Elf, war hammer in hand. "No time for such foolishness," he said to the amazed onlookers.

Egon knelt by the unconscious wizard.

"He's alive."

"Of course he is!" Brador said. "Kill our only hope, I would not."

M/Shaan and K'Taal had come back, wondering what had happened. They stood there silently.

"Give Nomayon your blanket," Nomayon said to M'Shaan.

Wordlessly, M'Shaan came up, and handed it to him. The Seer knelt, and passed the blanket under Silveron's prone form. Egon realised what he had in mind, and came forward. The two Men knelt at Silveron's head and feet, and then they each gathered and took hold of the ends of the blanket. They raised the wizard, and with the improvised stretcher in place, began to walk. The group fell in, and K'Taal went ahead to lead them. They reached an opening in the trees, and he entered. The others followed on, and in moments, they had disappeared into the forest.

# CHAPTER VII

# THE END OF LINADOR

The gates of Linador exploded inwards, and the mass of warriors burst into the courtyard. The Schaaka waiting for them fired their arrows, and then dropped their bows and drew their swords. There was no time for a second volley. They rushed towards the invaders.

Nilda saw Ervin fall. She screamed his name. And then sharp pain tore into her chest. One of the Goblins had seen her distraction, and had stabbed her. She dropped to her knees, and then fell across Ervin. The Schaaka heaved his sword high. Nilda looked up, and waited for the blow to fall.

The next second, the Goblin's own head flew from his shoulders in a spray of black blood. His corpse fell to the dirt.

*"Daughter!"* Lord Nildoron sheathed his sword, and knelt and took her in his arms. He cradled her gently as the chaos of battle echoed around them. Six of his warriors formed a protective circle around them.

Nilda smiled weakly at him.

*"Father,"* she whispered, *"burn us together."* Her trembling hand found his free hand, and she gripped it tightly. She glanced at Ervin, and then returned her gaze to him.

"Daughter –" Tears ran down his face. He shook with emotion. Nildoron stroked her hair tenderly. He brushed some dirt away from her face.

*"Please, Father,"* she begged. She coughed, and blood ran from her mouth. Her eyes began to glaze over. *"I want..to..be with...him..."*

Nildoron nodded to her.

"I will do as you ask," he said, his voice choked. "Rest now, you have fought well." He forced a smile onto his face.

Nilda smiled, and then the light of intelligence went out of her eyes. Her hand was suddenly limp. Nildoron brought it to his lips, and kissed it softly. He laid her down, and closed her eyes with a sweep of his hand. He placed her hands above her breast. He bowed low before her body and wept. Memories flooded into his mind: Nilda as a small child, running, her long black hair streaming in the wind. He recalled the pride that he and his wife had felt when Nilda had been made Captain of the Bowmays. And there was the proud moment when she was chosen to be Princess Willowen's bodyguard.

He looked down upon her. Now, all that was gone, only the memories remained. He threw back his head and howled in anguish. His warriors, shocked by the sudden display of emotion, stepped back. For a moment, he was only an animal, howling for its lost child. Then he regained his senses. He saw Nilda's sword lying in the dirt. Nildoron picked it up, and rose to his feet.

"Captain Alaryn."

"My Lord?"

"Remain here with your warriors. Ensure that no harm comes to my daughter." He made to go off and join the fight.

"My Lord," Alaryn said, "Should not some of us come with you, to help in disposing of the Schaaka?"

Nildoron turned. His eyes blazed with hatred. Alaryn took an involuntary step back. The fury that radiated from Nildoron struck him like a palpable force.

The Elf-Lord drew his sword. He still gripped Nilda's blade in his left hand.

"I will need no help in getting rid of that filth. Do as I say, and remain here."

Alaryn flinched at the rage in Nildoron's eyes. He bowed low.

"As you wish, My Lord."

Nildoron turned. The Schaaka had been forced out of the courtyard. Only bodies surrounded them. But the fighting could still be heard inside the buildings. Nildoron stalked towards them, swords ready to deal death. He strode purposefully across the courtyard, and entered the main hall.

Silveron opened his eyes. His head throbbed. Where was he? He looked up, and saw the reddened sky. The musical sound of running water came to him. Then he was aware of the smell of cooking. The wizard sat up slowly, but then his head began to spin. He gingerly lowered himself to the ground again. He was lying on sweet grass, and as he looked around, he saw there were trees all around him. Silveron propped himself up on his elbows. The sound of water came from a small creek that meandered through the trees.

"Is Silveron feeling better?"

The Elf regarded the speaker groggily. It was Nomayon. The Seer stood in front of him. The wizard looked past him, and saw the rest of the group sitting eating and drinking around a fire in a small clearing. The Seer squatted down upon his haunches, and stared fixedly at the prone wizard. Suddenly, he rose to his feet, and nodded to himself, as though he was satisfied of Silveron's condition.

"Where are we?" Silveron asked.

"In the forest. We have walked for two days, only stopping to rest and eat."

"Two days!" Silveron heaved himself up, but staggered and would have fallen, if Nomayon had not caught him. The Seer helped him over to a large rock, where he sat, his face flushed with his exertions.

"Two days!" he repeated mournfully. 'Now I cannot go back and warn the King!"

"Too late for that, it is."

Brador stood there, a plate in one meaty hand, and a cup in the other.

"Food and drink for you, lad."

Silveron rounded on him fiercely.

"You dared to strike me down! The King –"

"Far from here, he is, and so the army is too." He came and offered the plate to Silveron.

The Elf struck it from his hand. It fell spinning to the forest floor, and the food upon it was scattered. Brador made no remark, but put the cup down on the rock next to Silveron. He bowed and went back to the fire.

"Silveron should not have done that," Nomayon said.

"Why not?" Silveron said. He glared at the Seer.

"Brador is not Silveron's enemy," Nomayon said reasonably.

"I know that," the Elf said irritably. "But he should not have struck me." He winced and rubbed his temples.

"Would Silveron have gone to warn King Anarys if he had not?"

"Yes!"

"So we would have left even later. Time is running out. Silveron must banish the Dark One."

"*I know that!*" the wizard cried. The group at the fire looked over at the pair, alerted by his outburst, but then when they saw that all was well, returned their attention to their food and drink.

"Perhaps Silveron wants to be alone with his thoughts?" Nomayon said. He began to walk off.

"No...I mean, wait, Nomayon."

The Seer stopped and turned.

"Nomayon agrees with Brador. There is no time for foolishness. Silveron is acting like a child. Nomayon would have struck Silveron down, as Brador did."

He turned and walked over to the fire. The Elf sat there alone, his thoughts whirling angrily. His temples pounded.

*A child!* He fumed. *How dare he!*

Silveron glared at the cup that Brador had set down. He slapped it away with the back of his hand. His hand stung from the impact. Suddenly, he was mortified. He had embarrassed himself in front of his friends. The Elf felt ashamed. He knew that Brador and Nomayon were right. King Anarys and the Army of Light would meet their own destiny, with or without his help. The only thing that mattered was the banishment of Darkmor. Everything else, *everyone* else was not important. He looked over at the fire. How could he go to them after he had acted like a fool?

The Elf was suddenly thirsty. He stood up carefully, and walked slowly over to the creek. He knelt down, and cupped the water in his hands. Silveron brought it to his lips, and drank. It was cool and delicious. He repeated this action several times. The throbbing in his head was going away. He splashed the water on his face, and rose to his feet, refreshed.

Silveron went back to the rock, and picked up the plate and the cup. He walked over to the fire, uncertain of the reception he would get after his stupidity. He stood there, wondering what to say.

"Hungry, are you, lad?" Brador said.

"I..." Silveron said, not knowing what to say.

"Bring your plate, then," Brador said, as though the incident of minutes before hadn't even occurred. "Like rabbit stew, do you?"

"Yes, thank you, Brador." He came up to the Dwarf-Lord and held out his plate. "I want to apologise to you."

Brador spooned the stew onto the plate.

"No need for that, lad. Friends we are still, eh?" He grinned.

"Yes, we are friends," Silveron replied. He sat down among them. He put his hand on his head. "But please do not hit me again." He smiled ruefully.

The group laughed.

Silveron ate his food in silence. He knew that Brador had done the right thing. Who knows what would have happened if he had gone back to alert the King of the danger that he had seen in his vision? Would King Anarys have wanted him to stay and help the army against the horde of O'skaa?

"Silveron knows that the Elf-King would not have asked him to do that."

Nomayon squatted down beside the Elf.

"Silveron knows what he has to do."

The wizard finished his stew.

"Some more, lad?" Brador asked.

"No thank you, Brador." He accepted a cup from the dwarf, and drank deeply. He turned his attention to Nomayon.

"Yes, I know what I must do, Nomayon. His Majesty was adamant that my task was the only important thing. His own fate and that of the Army of Light was irrelevant." He was quiet for a moment, thinking. Then he went on: "It does not make my task any easier thinking of such things. I wish I could be there to help them. What if they are destroyed because I am not with them?"

"King Anarys gave you an order," Egon said. "You must obey it."

The wizard nodded.

"I know, Egon. But it is awful to have such a vision, and feel powerless to do something about it."

"Silveron does not know if that vision is true," Nomayon said. "Possibilities, not certainties, such visions are. Silveron must not let them lead him from his path."

"Such questions do not come to Felininn warriors," Yosh-en said. "If we are given an order, we carry it out, even if the cost be our lives. Honour is all."

"Nomayon's warriors would do the same," the Seer said.

The Elf held up his hand.

"Please, my friends. I know that you are trying to help me harden my resolve. Do not worry; I will carry out my task. Do not fear that I will run back to the army."

"We know you won't," Egon said. "We are with you until the end."

"What will that end be?" Silveron said. "Even if I banish Darkmor, the Schaaka will still be here, and will the moon go back to her rightful place when he is gone?"

"Know the end, none of us do," Brador said. "Who does? But as Egon said, stay with you, we will."

There was a chorus of assent to these words.

Silveron smiled.

"Thank you, my friends." He rose to his feet. They prepared to break camp. Silveron glanced over at Nomayon. The Seer met his gaze, and then looked away. The Elf stood there thinking for a moment, and then he looked to see what he could do to help the others.


Darkmor smiled to himself. He had seen all that had occurred to Silveron and his companions. The sorcerer had sent his mind seeking the Elf, and had found them as they had left the encampment of the Army of Light. Darkmor had checked in on them from time to time as they had moved through the forest. He had laughed when the Dwarf felled Silveron with a blow of his war hammer. Now, he had witnessed Silveron's anger, and subsequent apology. He laughed again.

"What fools they are," he said. His voice echoed in the chamber where the pool that provided him his visions lay. He sprawled languidly on the carven chair, and watched as the images of the companions faded.

Darkmor reached out and picked up a goblet that lay upon a small table that was set next to the chair. He drained the wine in it in one long draught. Wiping his lips with the back of his hand, he put the goblet back on the table. He rose to his feet and stretched his back. It was good to have a new and strong young body.

The sorcerer paced over to the door, and with a wave of his hand, the door opened. He strode through, and the door closed behind him. The sound of the bolt sliding home came to him as he walked up the corridor. He was still chuckling to himself as he arrived at another door.

Darkmor stood and listened to see if he could hear anything. No sound came to him. *Was she asleep?* He wondered. He gestured, and the door opened and swung wide. He went in.

Princess Willowen lay upon a rough pallet. As he came into the cell, she became aware of his presence, and sat upright. She turned to face him.

"Have you come to torment me?" she said. Her voice was ragged, as though she had been crying.

He shook his head.

"No. I thought you'd like to know how Silveron is faring."

"You have seen him?" Eagerness filled her voice. "Where is he? Is he well?"

Darkmor came and stood before her. He smiled.

"Well enough. He's coming to save you."

Willowen regarded him with distrust.

"You lie. He would remain with my father's army. He will be at its head when it comes to defeat you."

"You think so?"

"I do."

Darkmor smirked. He watched her closely to see her reaction to his next words.

"What if I said King Anarys himself had told him to come and rescue you?"

He was not disappointed. Her eyes opened wide, and she smiled broadly. Then she remembered where she was, and she quickly subsided.

"Another lie," she said. Willowen assumed an indifferent air, as though she didn't believe anything he had said. He knew the reverse was true.

"You don't fool me," Darkmor said. "I know you love him. It's pitiful."

Her eyes flashed.

"What would you know of love?" she said, her voice unforgiving. "You feel only desire."

"I agree with you. I desire many things. I'm not afraid to admit it."

He came and stood over her. Willowen turned her head to the side and looked away. Darkmor reached out and took her chin in his hand roughly. He forced her to look up at him.

"I'm telling the truth. Silveron *is* coming here. He thinks he can save you." He let go of her, and Willowen backed away from him. She lay back on the pallet, frightened of his sudden display of strength.

Darkmor's gaze roved over her body. *Soon,* he thought.

"It's a pity he lost this," he said. He reached into his robe, and brought out the talisman. He dangled it before her. "Without it, he can't defeat me."

The Princess stared at it. *If only there was some way to take it from him, and get it to Silveron,* she thought desperately.

"Yes," Darkmor said. "You'd like that, wouldn't you?" He put it back inside his robe.

"You should have let me fall to my death," Willowen said.

"Oh, no, I couldn't let you die," Darkmor said. "I need you."

"I will not help you," she said coldly.

"We will see."

The sorcerer's gaze lingered on her for a few moments, and then he turned and walked back to the door. He stopped in the doorway, and delivered a parting shot.

"Oh, by the way, I'm afraid your champion has been slain."

"What?" Willowen sat up.

"Yes. She and her lover were killed in an attack on Stonebridge."

Stony silence met this statement. Darkmor smiled, and then gestured at the wall. A swirl of colour appeared upon it, and resolved itself to an image of the attack he had described. The image moved, and became alive with the struggles of the combatants. Willowen stared in amazement as the fight on the bridge played out before her. She saw the efforts of Ervin and Nildoron and their companions as they pushed at the gates. Then the gates burst open, the warriors rushed inside, and the deadly arrows struck. She gasped as Ervin fell. Then she screamed aloud as Nilda was stabbed by the Goblin.

Willowen leapt to her feet.

"*It is a trick!*" she cried. Tears ran down her face. She stared at the images, shocked to her core.

"It's no trick," he replied. He gestured, and the sequence replayed itself.

The Princess watched as her friend and bodyguard was stabbed over and over. The horrifying scene burned into her brain. An endless montage of Nilda being struck down passed before her unbelieving gaze.

Willowen fell to her knees. She covered her eyes and wept.

"No more," she begged piteously.

"As you wish," the sorcerer said.

Darkmor snapped his fingers, and the awful scene vanished.

Willowen knelt there sobbing.

Darkmor regarded her. *So that iron will can be penetrated,* he thought. *Good.*

"I'll leave you to your thoughts," he said. "When I return I expect you to be more receptive to my proposition regarding the Starstone."

There was no reply. Willowen was lost in her anguish.

Darkmor strode through the door, and it closed behind him. Willowen's sobbing echoed in the cell.

Jhara Shin and Captain Alaryn stood talking in the main hall of Stonebridge. The corpses of the battle had been cleared away. The Schaaka had been taken out of the hall, and cast into the abyss. The Elves and the chokhutai who had fallen lay upon the tables. Each of them had been decently arrayed; their faces had been wiped clean of blood. The bodies of Nilda and Ervin had been laid out upon the main banqueting table. Their faces had been cleaned too, and their raiment had been arranged neatly about them. They lay side by side, one hand grasping the other. The Elf's right hand was clasped in Ervin's left hand. Their other hands had been placed upon their chests. Nilda's left hand grasped her bow, and Ervin's right hand gripped his sword. Khree sat upon Ervin's shoulder and whimpered as she looked down at his peaceful face.

"He was like a son to me," Shin said to the Elf.

"I understand you took him into your clan," Alaryn said.

"Yes," Shin replied. "His people are all gone. He was the last of them."

"They had been betrayed."

"Yes, his own brother did that."

"I was told how Ervin dealt with him."

Shin nodded. "The thought of revenge upon Althar had driven him for years. When Ervin first found out it was he who had betrayed the Kandarans, he could not believe it."

"Were they close as brothers?"

"In a way they were. Ervin used to look after Althar. His brother was teased and tormented because he was different. He was weak, because of his albino blood. Ervin saved him from many beatings when they were young."

Alayrn looked at their peaceful faces. They seemed only to be asleep. But it was a sleep from which they would never awaken.

"Perhaps he would not have protected him if he had known what the future had had in store. Many lives would have been saved."

"Perhaps," Shin agreed. "But such thoughts do not come easily to Men."

"That is true."

They lapsed into silence. It stretched out, until it became uncomfortable.

"You were with Lord Nildoron in the fight?" the Elf asked.

"Yes," Shin said. "He was savage. I have not seen an Elf fight the way he did. And he fought with two swords as well. With every blow, a Schaaka lost his head, an arm, or was cut in two. Never have I seen someone display such consummate skill with two blades before."

"One of your warriors told me that My Lord fought without any thought of defence, only attack."

"That is true. Nildoron was struck several times that I saw, but they were just small cuts, and only seemed to enrage him further. He was furious. He smashed his way through the enemy, cutting them down left and right. They fell back before his ferocity, until there was nowhere to go. Their backs were against the battlements. I saw a dozen of them leap screaming into the abyss rather than face him."

"I should have been by his side, but he ordered me and my warriors to stay with Captain Nilda."

"Maybe he did not want you to see his rage. I know Elves do not like to lose control of their emotions."

"Maybe. But I think he knew that the Schaaka would be no match for him in that state."

"You could be right," Shin said. "They definitely were not."

"Excuse me, Captain. Where is Lord Nildoron?" a voice asked.

An Elf warrior stood there.

"He is outside, with F'leet," replied Alaryn. "He wants the birdman to go to King Anarys and report all that has happened here."

"Thank you, Sir. He wanted to be informed when our fallen had been prepared for the funeral. I will go and tell him they are ready." He turned to go.

"I would not do that if I were you." Shin said.

The warrior stopped and regarded the Goblin.

"Why should I not report to him?"

"It is not necessary, Eridon," Alaryn said.

"But, Captain, he gave me an order."

"Gather our warriors and Lord Shin's together, and bring them here," Alaryn said. "Do not disturb Lord Nildoron. He will join us when he is ready."

"But Sir, he gave me an order. Surely I should carry it out?"

Jhara Shin came forward.

"Were you involved in the fighting in the buildings?"

"No, he was not," Alaryn said. "Eridon here is one of my warriors. He was with me at the gates guarding the bodies of Captain Nilda and Ervin during the fight."

"Ah. So he did not witness Lord Nildoron's fury."

"No, Sir," Eridon said. "I did not."

"I imagine you would like to keep it that way," Shin said. "Interrupting Lord Nildoron would perhaps wake his anger again." He looked at the Elf suggestively.

Eridon looked at them both in turn.

"Perhaps you are right, Sir. I will do as you say, Captain."

"A wise decision," Jhara Shin said.

The Elf bowed and left them.

Outside, on the bridge, Nildoron and F'Leet watched as the dead Schaaka were thrown into space. Nildoron's Elves and Shin's Goblins worked together, an intriguing sight to one who did not know of their alliance. The hulking bodies of two O'skaa lay upon the bridge. Two groups of warriors pushed and shoved them until they too had joined their riders.

An Elf warrior came and bowed before Lord Nildoron.

"All is done, My Lord. The Schaaka and their beasts have been disposed of."

"Very good," Nildoron said. "Have all the warriors clean themselves up and meet in the main building for the funeral. I will join you presently."

"Yes, My Lord." The Elf bowed, and left to carry out the order.

"Do you wish me to stay and observe the funeral?" F'Leet rumbled.

Nildoron shook his head.

"No, it is not necessary. It is more important that you tell King Anarys what happened here. Go and report to him and then return and lead us back to the army. We have been gone too long, and must rejoin them."

"As you wish, My Lord," F'Leet said. "I sorrow for your loss. Captain Nilda was a fine woman."

"Yes," the Elf said softly, "she was. If she had not become involved with Ervin..." he trailed off.

"You should not begrudge your daughter the love that she bore for the Forester, My Lord."

"Why should I not? She may still be alive if not for that – *forbidden* – entanglement."

"You do not know that for certain, My Lord. You should give thanks that she did find love. Ervin was a good Man."

Nildoron stared into F'Leet's golden eyes.

"For many years, her duty to the Princess Willowen was sufficient for her. She loved Nilda as a sister."

"But was that enough?" the Avianinn said. "I will return, My Lord."

With one sweep of his massive wings, he leapt into the sky. Nildoron watched as he sped away, pondering F'Leet's words. Was the birdman right? Was it better for Nilda to have known love, and die, than for her to have never known what it was like at all?

"No," he said to himself, "he is not right."

He walked across the bridge towards the fortress and the funeral that waited.

Lord Nildoron crossed the courtyard. He did not relish the duty that lay before him now. It was one that he had never wished to carry out. The Elf-Lord had always thought that Nilda would live on long after he himself had been slain in battle. It was a stupid thought, he knew that, but in no way had he ever imagined that she would die before he did.

He came to the door of the main building, and halted. He gathered his courage, and entered. The Elven warriors and the Goblin chokhutai were lined up in ranks on either side of the hall. They came to attention as he entered and crossed the floor. Waiting for him were Captain Alaryn and Jhara Shin. They both bowed to him, and then took their place at his side. Alaryn was on his right side, and Jhara Shin was to his left.

Nildoron looked at the array of tables before him. He saw how many casualties that they had suffered. Captain Alaryn had told him the number of their fallen, but to see them was to realise how many warriors they had lost. Destroying the Schaaka had been indeed an expensive undertaking. The cost was high.

*Too high,* he thought, as his gaze came to the main table. He stared at his daughter, and the depth of his emotions almost overmastered him. He held back tears. Nildoron took a deep breath to steady himself, and then he searched his mind for the right words. Ervin's sleakh still whined from her perch.

"We are gathered here to honour our fallen comrades," The Elf-Lord began. He stopped for a moment, and then went on: "They have given the ultimate sacrifice. They gave their lives for Erathyn, so that its folk may live free from the shadow of darkness. Though they are gone from us, we will remember them in our hearts." He bowed low, and the warriors mirrored his action. Nildoron stepped back.

An Elven warrior and a chokhutai came forward. They had been the last in the line of their respective ranks. They held torches, and it seemed to Nildoron that he had only now become aware of the smell of oil that filled the hall. He looked and saw that it had been liberally applied to the tables and the bodies that lay upon them. Beneath the tables were piles of wood. They also had been soaked in oil, and would ensure that the bodies would be burnt quickly. They paused as they saw Khree. Should they try to remove her?

The two warriors looked over at Nildoron. He regarded the whimpering sleakh. Surely she would move once the torches had been applied? He made a decision and made to give them the order to light the pyre.

"One moment," Jhara Shin said. He walked up to stand by Ervin's body. The Goblin regarded Ervin's peaceful face for a moment, and then he took out Ervin's dagger from the sheath that he had put on his belt. Shin held out his left hand over the body, and quickly drew the dagger across its palm. He made a fist with it, and as the blood ran down, he dripped it over Ervin's heart. Then he spread his hand palm down over his own heart.

"Farewell, my son."

He met Khree's gaze and could see the suffering there. Shin reached out and stroked her head. He knew more than anyone else there about the bond that had existed between the Kandaran and his little companion. Now that bond had been broken. What would Khree do? He held out his arm for the sleakh, but she shook her head and returned her attention to Ervin.

Shin took the sheath from his belt, sheathed the dagger, and then placed it by Ervin's side. He bowed low, and then returned to his place by Nildoron's side. The gathering stood silently for a minute to honour the dead.

"Proceed," Nildoron commanded.

The two warriors stepped up, and placed their torches into the pyre. The flames caught quickly, and the fire began to rise. Khree cried out in anguish, and leapt into the air. She flew around the room crying out as the pyre burned. The two ranks passed in front of the burning tables; the Elves saluted the fallen with their swords, and the Goblins placed their hands above their hearts in the same manner Jhara Shin had done. When they had finished, the entire group retreated from the heat, and filed outside.

Shin, Alaryn, and Nildoron watched as the flames rose higher, and set fire to the ceiling. They all bowed to the pyre, and then retreated and joined the warriors outside. As the main building caught fire, they walked across the courtyard, and back across the bridge. They watched the conflagration from the other side of the chasm. Soon the entire fortress was aflame. Within minutes, the main hall had been devoured by the fire, and collapsed in a shower of sparks that went soaring up into the heavens. The blaze rampaged through the other buildings, sending up a tower of black smoke. They could still hear the sleakh's cries. Would she stay in the building with her master and burn?

Suddenly she appeared, hurtling out of the inferno. Now her cries had transformed into a wail that pierced the hearts of all who stood there. She landed in front of Nildoron, and turned a grief-stricken face to him. Tears spilled down her avian face. He was shocked. He had not expected such emotion from an animal. Then he remembered F'leet had told them that they were quite intelligent, and had been used to create the Avianinn themselves.

He knelt down, and Khree flung herself into his arms. He cradled her little form as she sobbed. They remained locked together for a few moments, and then she broke from the embrace, and rose hovering before him. She spun about and took one last despairing look where her master burned, and then she turned to Nildoron again. She bowed to him, and then flew away at great speed. She was never seen again. The Elf-Lord rose to his feet.

Tears blurred Nildoron's vision. He stood immobile watching the inferno. His hands were clenched into fists. The Elf's nails dug into his palms, until blood came forth and ran down to drip upon the stone beneath him. His tears flowed down his face.

Shin glanced sidelong at him, and saw that Nildoron wept. *The loss of his daughter must affect him deeply,* he thought. He knew the Elves did not like to show their feelings, and that they were trained from an early age to control them.

Captain Alaryn deliberately kept his gaze away from Lord Nildoron. He knew that Nildoron suffered greatly due to Captain Nilda's death, but he did not wish to intrude upon that suffering.

"Captain Alaryn," Nildoron said, his voice raw with emotion, "get our warriors ready to march."

"Yes, My Lord." Alaryn bowed and left them to carry out the order, relieved that he could leave the uncomfortable atmosphere.

"A terrible loss of such beauty," Jhara Shin said.

Nildoron did not speak. He stood staring at the blaze, as though Shin wasn't even there. The other buildings had been burnt down, and only the walls still stood. But as they watched, the flames ate away at them too. Soon only ash would remain; ash, and the bridge that gave the fortress its name.

"My Lord?" Shin said.

Nildoron turned. His face was haggard, and the pain that was written there struck Shin to the heart. The Elf-Lord's eyes seemed to look upon something far away. And then they focussed upon the Goblin.

"Did you say something, Shin?" Nildoron asked.

"I said it was a terrible loss of such beauty."

"Yes. Linador was beautiful. I remember coming here many times, usually in King Anarys' retinue. Such a place will never be seen again."

"I was speaking of Nilda, My Lord. She was beautiful, and brave. Her courage and great deeds will be spoken of by my people for many years."

"Thank you, my friend," Nildoron said.

"My Lord?" It was Captain Alaryn. "We are ready to march."

"Good," Nildoron replied. "Let us be off. This smoke will be seen for miles. F'Leet can find us on the way back."

"Yes, My Lord."

The Elf-Lord turned to take one last look at the place where his daughter had died.

"Nephana," he said softly.

Then all three of them went and joined the warriors who stood waiting.

# CHAPTER VIII

# BY THE RIVER

F'Leet flew swiftly over the land. He passed over the great forests, and over the river that lay far below. The Avianinn's far-seeing eyes sought for any sign of the Army of Light. Finally, he saw it, and began his descent. F'Leet came down and landed in front of the vanguard that preceded the army proper. The captain that led the Elven horse held up his hand to stop the advance. The army slowly ground to a halt.

F'Leet watched as the horsemen parted, and allowed King Anarys to ride through. He rode up to the birdman and reigned in his steed. F'Leet bowed to him.

"Your Majesty," he rumbled.

"F'leet. It is good to see you. Where are your companions?"

"Lord Nildoron sent me to report to you, Your Majesty." He paused and gathered his thoughts, and then went on: "We met and slew the traitor Althar and his entire band. They had been hiding in Linador. There were many other Schaaka with them, including some O'skaa riders. These were slain also." He gestured towards the black smoke that still rose in the mountains. "The fortress was burned, so that no other enemy forces could use it."

"That is great news. Althar and his Goblins were a thorn in our side for many years. I imagine Ervin was satisfied that he was finally slain?"

F'leet nodded his noble head.

"It was Ervin himself who slew him in single combat, My Liege."

"Then his people are avenged. What of the O'skaa? Did you slay them all?"

"Alas, no, Your Majesty. One escaped. No doubt it will take word back to the Dark One that we have destroyed Linador."

"That cannot be helped. Surely he knows by now which way we are coming." Anarys said.

"I would agree, Sire."

"What casualties did you suffer?"

The birdman gazed for a moment into the Elf's eyes.

"It was a high cost, Your Majesty."

Anarys was suddenly filled with trepidation. Surely Lord Nildoron had not fallen?

"Lord Nildoron fares well?"

"He does, Sire. He did not fall. But, his daughter..."

Anarys sat back in his saddle. His face went white.

"Captain Nilda was one of the fallen?"

"She was, Your Majesty. Ervin was also slain."

Tears glistened in the King's eyes. He took a deep breath.

"What happened?" he said softly.

"The Schaaka had barricaded themselves in the fortress. Lord Nildoron and his warriors, along with Lord Shin and his chokhutai broke through the gates and attacked. Captain Nilda and Ervin were in this group as they entered the fortress. The Schaaka waited with bows, and they fired upon them. Ervin was struck by an arrow and fell. Captain Nilda was stabbed by one of the Schaaka. During the fighting, we suffered about a dozen casualties."

Tears ran down Anarys' face.

"Lord Nildoron and Lord Shin saw to it that there was a funeral held for them all. They were laid out honourably. And then fire was set to them, as is your custom."

"You saw this?" Anarys asked.

"No, Sire. Lord Nildoron commanded me to reach you speedily."

"You bear both good and bad news, F'Leet."

"I know how much you respected Captain Nilda, Sire. And I believe you came to give the same respect to Ervin."

"That is so," Anarys said.

"Lord Nildoron blames the Forester for his daughter's death. He thinks that if she had never met Ervin, she would still be alive. I know that such a relationship is forbidden in Elven law, but I must tell you that I have never known two people that were so in love with each other."

"Lord Nildoron told me himself that he was displeased with this association," Anarys said. "And in the beginning, I shared that view. But now, I do not know. Perhaps it was their fate to love and die together. My own daughter..." he trailed off.

"You will see her again, Sire."

"That is my hope. Go back and find your companions, and lead them to us. We will advance as far as the Brakoon river, and rest by its banks. Once you have joined us, we will ford the river and make the final push into the Dark One's stronghold."

"I obey, My liege." He tensed, ready to hurl himself aloft.

"Hold a moment," Anarys said. "I forgot to ask if you had seen any enemy scouts on your way to us."

"No, Sire. But I had not been looking for them. Do you believe they are following you?"

"Several have been seen dogging our steps. But none of them will come close. They stay out of bowshot at least. Commander Lysanna's bowmays have taught them that." He smiled. "Now go, and rejoin your companions. Please give Lord Nildoron my profound regrets of the news of his daughter's death."

"I will, Your Majesty."

He leapt up, and with a few sweeps of his wings hurtled back the way he had come.

Meanwhile, in Algol the Bright, the traitorous wizards kept the secret of their murderous acts. No one suspected that anything was amiss. If an enquiry was made of the absence of the wizards Vairon and Telewen, it was an easy matter for Amberon and his cronies to create fictitious excuses. Vairon, it was said, was deep in his magic. He was disappointed in his failure, and did not seek out the company of others. His servant said that he had delivered food to the wizard's door, and when he had knocked and asked to enter, Vairon's voice had boomed from inside; saying that he did not wish to be disturbed. The servant had left the food and retreated. When he had come back, the plate and goblet and cup were empty. He replenished them several times a day, but had not seen Vairon. Everyone in Algol knew how ill-tempered Vairon was, so it was no surprise to them that he had taken to avoiding company.

Telewen's absence, on the other hand, was explained away in a different manner. Amberon let it be known that Telewen's illness had taken a turn for the worse, and that he had been confined to his tower. Melandor the healer was puzzled at this, but Amberon had assured him it was for Telewen's benefit. When Melandor had asked if he could send one of his healers to tend to the Master of Fire Magic, Amberon had told him that he had assigned his own servant to look after him. Thus Ari's absence was explained too. The Eldest was praised for his generosity.

When asked of the whereabouts of Korwen, Amberon told the questioners that he had sent the wizard on a mission, and that it was of vital importance that none of the details were made known to all and sundry. The Dark One had spies everywhere....

So it was that the three remaining wizards came together to discuss the future, safe in the knowledge that their evil deeds had not been discovered. They sat in Amberon's tower, drinking and congratulating themselves on their subterfuge.

"It was an easy thing to make Vairon's servant believe that he was still in his room," Narwen was saying. "I only had to throw my voice, and make sure all the food and drink was gone." He took a long pull of his own drink.

"No-one questions Telewen's state either," Amberon said. "Even Melandor believes that he is ill, and must rest."

"That was a fine touch to tell him that Ari was serving him," Candreen offered.

Amberon glanced at him. His lips were pursed.

"Eldest," Candreen added.

Amberon regarded him a moment longer. Then he sat back languidly.

"Yes," he finally said. "I thought it would make the boy's disappearance logical. Of course, Melandor did not gainsay me."

"So now no-one knows what we have done," Narwen said. "They are completely ignorant of these deaths. What do you propose to do now, Eldest?"

Amberon rose to his feet and walked over to the window. He looked out, gathering his thoughts. His companions waited for him to speak.

The wizard turned away from the window.

"Darkmor has told me he wants to restore the Black Circle, and to that end, he wishes us to join him."

"The Black Circle?" Candreen echoed.

"Yes. He is now the sole surviving member of that sorcerous group, and is possessed with all of its dark knowledge. We should join him.

Think of the secrets we would be shown!" His voice had risen to a feverish pitch.

"But what of Silveron?" Narwen said. "He has the Talisman of Banishment. If he should use it..." He placed his empty goblet on the table with a clink.

"That boy? Pah! He is nothing. He cannot even control his powers."

"He could banish Darkmor, Eldest," Candreen said.

Amberon rounded on him.

"Imbecile! He does not even know how to use it! Goldwen had no time to tell him the spell that activates it."

There was a sudden chill in the room. They all stopped speaking, knowing that Darkmor's presence was there among them.

A black spot appeared on the wall. It grew, spinning into a vortex of power. Darkmor stepped from it.

He regarded them as one would look upon worms. He reached into his robe, and brought the talisman forth. He dangled it before their unbelieving eyes.

"Is this what you refer to?" He laughed.

"How –" began Amberon.

"I took it from Silveron. We had a – *disagreement* – in the Goblin King's banqueting hall." He smiled. "That was not all I took from him." The sorcerer turned and gestured.

Willowen stepped out of the vortex. She glared at them angrily.

"So," she said acidly, "you are traitors to the realm, and to your King."

"We do not serve him anymore," Amberon said. "Magic is the only thing that matters; only magic and power."

The Princess laughed.

"Are you such fools to believe that Darkmor will allow you to join him? He will destroy all who stands against him, and then he will crush you like the insects you are. He does not share power willingly."

Narwen and Candreen looked doubtfully at Darkmor, and then returned their gaze to Willowen.

"Is that the best you can do?" sneered Amberon. "Try and set us against each other?"

"You would not last a moment against him," Willowen replied. "You are an old dotard, and your cronies have not the merest speck of power that Goldwen had."

"Having such power did not save him," Narwen said.

"Yes," added Candreen, "if he and the others had not poured most of their strength into the talisman, they may have triumphed."

The Eldest spread his hands.

"But here we are. Darkmor is now the most powerful sorcerer in Erathyn. There are none that can stand against him. Goldwen is dead. He can no longer help Anarys and his Army of Light."

"And you would help to destroy that army," Willowen retorted, her voice harsh. 'You, who have sworn to protect Erathyn and all of its folk. You would join Darkmor, and see darkness and evil reign supreme."

"You are correct," Amberon said reasonably. "The time of the Elves upon this world is coming to a close. You know yourself that your father wanted us to return to Glindarion. I prefer to remain here."

"And be Darkmor's slave?" she said witheringly.

"Say rather his servant. I would rather be a servant here than your father's lackey in Glindarion."

The sound of clapping hands resounded in the chamber. They all regarded Darkmor, who was applauding. All through this exchange, he had watched them argue, a smile upon his face.

"Oh, this is such wonderful entertainment," he said. 'Do go on."

Willowen subsided into silence. She still seethed with anger, but held her tongue.

"Don't let me stop you," Darkmor said, grinning.

The Princess made no response. She clenched her fists, and maintained her stubborn silence. Then she wondered where Telewen and Vairon were. Hadn't Goldwen told them to remain in Algol to keep an eye on Amberon and his confederates? She suddenly feared the worst.

"Yes," The Eldest said, catching her thoughts. "We had to dispose of Goldwen's friends."

"They would have exposed us," Narwen said.

"I do not believe you," Willowen said.

Amberon raised his eyebrows. He gestured at the opposite wall. Images suddenly swam upon it, and to her horror, Willowen saw Telewen stabbed, and the fight with Vairon when the treacherous wizards had poisoned the Master of Beasts, and killed him. She watched with tears in her eyes as Amberon deceived Ari, and killed him also. The awful scenes faded, and vanished.

"You do not think I try to trick you?" Amberon said.

"No. I know you show me the truth. Darkmor has shown me Nilda and Ervin's death. I know you have done these things." She lowered her head in sorrow.

"Then you know that there are no wizards to help your father," The Eldest said.

Willowen made no reply.

"Vandaron is with the army," Candreen said.

"Vandaron!" Amberon scoffed. "We will make short work of him."

"What of Silveron?" Narwen asked.

"He's nothing without the talisman," Darkmor said. "I'll let him stumble through the woods, and allow him to enter my tower. Then I'll kill him." He reached out, took Willowen's chin in his hand, and raised her head. He stared into her eyes. "Maybe I'll kill him in front of you." He smiled wickedly.

The Princess wrenched herself from his grasp.

"Silveron will defeat you," she said fiercely.

"Do you think so? Remember I outmatched him before, I'll do it again. He stands no chance against me without his little trinket." He reached out and pushed her into the vortex. She disappeared.

"She *is* entertaining," he said, and laughed. Then his gaze swept over the wizards, and they shuddered in spite of their allegiance.

"Make yourselves ready," he said. "Anarys has almost reached the Brakoon. I'll send some nuisance raids against him, and then order my Schaaka to retreat. They'll pull back without engaging the enemy. He'll advance cautiously, until he reaches me." He smiled. "I'll have a surprise waiting for him in the valley. I'll send word when I want you to come to me."

"Yes, Master," Amberon said. "We will be ready."

"Good," the sorcerer said. He turned and stepped back into the vortex. As he vanished from sight, it shrank and collapsed upon itself, and then it too disappeared.

Silveron and Nomayon lay upon a ridge that overlooked Darkmor's tower. They had been looking down into the valley, and making a count of the sorcerer's forces. They could see thousands of Cobrans, as well as Schaaka. O'skaa riders were in evidence too, although Silveron had expected Darkmor's army to be almost uncountable. Were these all the warriors he had at his disposal? Surely there were many more. Perhaps they were in hiding? But why would that be? Darkmor had no idea that they had penetrated into his mountain fastness.

*Or does he?* The Elf wondered.

The others sat a short distance away. From time to time, Silveron would tell them what they could see.

"Here is the birdman," The Seer said.

Silveron looked, and saw K'Reel winging towards them. He landed behind them, and they rose and went to met him.

"What have you seen?" Silveron asked.

"Much the same as you have. I could not get close, as I would have been discovered. I think you can see better from here."

"Did you find a way into the tower?" the Elf said.

"I believe so," K'Reel rumbled. "Look." He went over to the edge and lay prone.

They followed and lay beside him. The Avianinn pointed.

"The tower is at the end of the valley. It almost backs up against the cliffs that rise there. There is a small door at the rear of the tower, which cannot be seen from here or from anywhere else in the valley. One would have to know it was there, for it is hidden among bushes."

"Is it guarded?" Silveron said.

K'Reel's noble head nodded.

"Yes. There are eight guards. Four are Cobrans, the others are Schaaka. One of them is an O'skaa rider. There is an O'skaa with him as well."

"Eight only, and a spider too," Brador said. "Good odds they are."

The others had come and joined them. The three of them came away from the edge, and sat with the group.

"Are there any patrols?" Egon said.

"I did not see any."

"Why do we wait, then?" Brador said. "Let us go and get this over with."

"It could be a trap," Egon said.

"How could that be?" the Dwarf said. "The Dark One does not know Silveron lives, or that on his doorstep we are."

"Nomayon doubts that," the Seer said.

"Why do you say that?" Brador said.

Nomayon didn't reply. He merely looked at Silveron.

The Elf sighed.

"Brador, I am sure Darkmor knows I am alive."

"How do you know this?" Toran-en said.

"I have felt his presence. He knows I live, and what my task is."

"Then waits for us he does, like a spider," the Dwarf said.

"Yes."

"Does he expect us to walk into his web, like fools?" Egon said.

"I think it more the case that he does not consider us a threat," Silveron said. His gaze swept the group. "He knows I am no match for him. Not without the talisman."

"Do you know where it is?" Egon said.

The wizard shook his head.

"I have tried to sense it. Something blocks me. I think he keeps it on him at all times."

"Then we have come all this way for nothing," Yosh-en said.

"No," Silveron said. "I am going to enter the tower, and find the talisman."

"Enter the spider's web you will?" Brador said.

"I will. It is my task. I must have faith that I will find the talisman, and use it." He regarded them in turn. "I do not ask any of you to come with me."

There was a chorus of disagreement at this.

"Friends we are, lad," Brador said. "With you, we are."

"Yes," Egon added, "We won't desert you now."

"Nomayon is pleased to serve, and his warriors too."

"My son and I are with you," Yosh-en said.

"My Winglord would not want me to leave you now," K'Reel said.

"I thank you for your faith in me, my friends," Silveron said. "I hope I can justify that faith. K'Reel, I do not expect you to come. Your wings would be useless underground."

"Then I will stay here and watch and wait, and hope for your success."

"Let us rest for a while, and then go down," Silveron said.

They all lay down and took what rest they could.


Lord Nildoron and the surviving warriors from the battle at Stonebridge rode into the camp of the Army of Light. They rode past the tents and towards the place where the horses were corralled. They gave their mounts to the care of the ostlers, and then Nildoron and Shin told their warriors to rest and eat while they reported to King Anarys. They walked over to his tent that was set upon a hill that overlooked the river. F'Leet had been sent on ahead. King Anarys had told him to search the other side of the river for any sign of the enemy.

The sentries at the tent came to attention as Shin and Nildoron arrived. One of them opened the flap and announced them.

Anarys came to the opening and greeted them himself.

"My friends," Anarys said. "Come, eat and drink while you give me your report."

They followed him inside, and sat in chairs that were set about a wooden camp table. He sat and waited until they had filled their plates with food. A servant boy came and filled two goblets of wine. They drank them down with relish, for the ride had been dry and thirsty work. Then the pair set to with a will on their plates. In moments, they were clean and empty. They sat back, their hunger sated.

"So," began Anarys, "Linador is no more."

"Yes, Your Majesty," Nildoron replied. "It is only ash in the wind." His face was sad.

"We did not wish to leave such a place to the enemy," Jhara Shin added hastily, noting Nildoron's visage.

"I understand," the King said. "I would have done the same thing myself."

An uncomfortable silence fell. Anarys broke it.

"Lord Nildoron. My heart is broken for the loss of your daughter. She was a fine warrior, and a great friend as well as bodyguard to my own daughter. I will not forget her."

"Thank you, Sire."

"She was a fine shot too, Your Majesty," Shin said. "No wonder she was the leader of your bowmays."

The King nodded.

"She was indeed. They were desolated by her loss. I have promoted Commander Lysanna to be their captain. She will be a good leader, but Lysanna is nowhere near as fine a captain as Nilda was."

"Thank you, Sire," Nildoron said.

"F'Leet told me one of the O'skaa escaped."

"Yes, Sire," Shin said. "It was shot several times, but you know how hard the things are to kill. F'Leet said he pursued it until it went underground."

"No doubt it will go and report to the Dark One," Anarys said.

"Have any other spies been seen, Your Majesty?" Nildoron asked. "Two O'skaa riders followed us, but they pulled back when we reached the camp."

"Yes, Nildoron, they have been spotted shadowing us. They keep their distance, though. Several have been shot and slain, but they will not engage any force that I send out."

He rose and began to pace.

"It is unusual. We have met no resistance at all. If any O'skaa riders are seen, they retreat immediately. It is as if the enemy wants us to come on before he will commit any of his forces to battle."

"I would agree with that, Sire," Shin said. "It is a strategy of the Schaaka. They will never attack first. They probe an enemy's defences, and test his steadfastness. They will try to draw you to a place that is of their choosing. The Schaaka will never fight unless they have numerical superiority, and the advantage of the better position."

The tent flap opened.

"Your Majesty," the sentry said, "Lord F'Leet has arrived."

"Good. Send him in."

"Yes, Sire."

The Avianinn Winglord entered, and came over to Anarys. He bowed low.

"Your Majesty, My Lords."

"Did you fly over the river? Have you seen anything?"

"I did as you ordered, Your Majesty. There is no sign of the enemy. They must have retreated."

"I would not be so sure of that, F'Leet," Nildoron said. "They could be in hiding. Is there any cover across the river?"

F'Leet nodded his noble head.

"There is a dense wood that comes almost to the water's edge. It was not possible for me to enter and search it."

"I can take some of my chokhutai and search it," Shin offered.

Anarys was about to reply, when there came the sound of Elven horns blowing.

*"An attack!"* Anarys cried.

They leapt to their feet and rushed out of the tent. Anarys grabbed up his sword belt that was near the opening. He buckled it on as they ran towards the sounds of battle. Horses screamed in terror, and the clash of arms echoed all around. The screams of O'skaa pierced the air. The Elven horns continued to blow. All around them were warriors racing to come to grips with the enemy.

They came upon a chaotic scene. The O'skaa were running amuck. Horses lay dead, or galloped about, rearing and screaming. The Schaaka were stabbing anyone who came within reach of their goads, and some of them were armed with short bows. These riders were causing havoc among the handlers and warriors who were attempting to stop them.

"*The horses!*" Nildoron cried. He drew his sword and rushed towards the fight.

The others followed suit. They ran into the whirling melee.

Nildoron ran towards one of the monsters. He swung his sword, and the Schaaka upon its back was cloven in two. The spider spun about, attempting to knock the Elf-lord down, but Nildoron leapt out of its way. He jumped in again, and this time his blade plunged into the evil creature's brain. It died with a squeal.

Jhara Shin's chokhutai had caught up with him. They surrounded one the beasts, dodged its attacks, and leaped in to deliver their own thrusts. The rider upon its back skewered one of them on his goad, but his cry of triumph ended in a gurgle as Shin tossed a dagger that pierced his throat. As he fell, the chokhutai all rushed in and stabbed his ride in a flurry of strokes.

King Anarys and five of his warriors were beset by two of the O'skaa. They cut and thrust at the monsters, but had to dodge the attacks of both of them at the same time. For two of the Elves, it was too much, as they fell to the fangs and claws of the arachnids. Another of the Elves was stabbed by a rider, and the two warriors and Anarys were hard put to fend off their enemy's assault. One more Elf fell, leaving Anarys and a single warrior. Now they were over matched and desperately fighting for their lives.

Suddenly, a voice cried: "*Your Majesty! Get down!*"

Anarys dropped to the ground. His companion however, was too slow. One of the riders speared him. An instant later, a shower of arrows riddled both riders and O'skaa. Anarys turned his head and saw Captain Lysanna with a company of her bowmays. As he watched they fitted arrows and released another barrage.

Eight more of the monsters were shot through. Their riders died upon their backs, or were thrown sprawling. The bowmays restrung their bows and fired again, and the Schaaka fell.

The harsh braying of a Goblin horn shattered the air. The remaining riders turned their mounts and raced away. Lysanna's bowmays sent arrows sleeting after them, and the two at the rear of the pack fell. The others disappeared into the woods on either side of the camp. A dozen Elven warriors began to go in pursuit.

"*Stay!*" Nildoron cried. "They will be waiting for you in the woods. See to the wounded." He spotted Captain Enriss. "Captain, set a watch on the woods."

"Yes, My Lord."

Anarys came to his feet. He was wiping the blood from his sword upon an O'skaa's back when Lysanna rushed up to him.

"Your Majesty! Are you hurt?"

"No. Excellent work, Captain." He sheathed his blade, and came and put his hand on her shoulder. "That was fine work, Lysanna. Please tell your bowmays I am most impressed with their skill." He smiled. "And your impeccable sense of timing."

Lysanna blushed.

"Ah, thank you, Sire. I am glad you are unhurt."

"There are many who are, though. Please help with the wounded."

"Yes, Your Majesty." She smiled like a girl and ran off to obey his order.

Mocking laughter echoed from the other bank. Anarys looked, and saw the rider who had given him the Dark One's message. It seemed like a lifetime ago. It was he who had blown the horn. There were several O'skaa riders sitting upon their mounts on either side of him.

"It seems that you have lost some of your horses," Kerlach shouted. "Would you like to borrow some of our O'skaa?"

Uproarious laughter met his words. The Schaaka howled derisively.

"I would rather walk," The King replied.

"Then you'd better start walking," Kerlach said disdainfully. "It's a long way to my masters' stronghold."

At this, the Schaaka roared with laughter, and made obscene gestures.

"Your Majesty. Shall I teach them a lesson?"

Anarys realised that Lysanna stood by his side. Her bow was already nocked with an arrow.

"Please do," Anarys said.

Lysanna stepped forward.

"You will pay your respects to His Majesty." She didn't raise her voice, but it carried across to the other side.

The Schaaka ignored her, hooting and howling.

Lysanna drew back the shaft, and let loose. The arrow sailed over the river, to impact on the bank far short of Kerlach and his companions. The Goblin's eye opened wide, and he laughed again.

"*This* is your finest shot? I am disappointed."

His comrades howled with mirth.

Lysanna fitted another arrow.

"Please, try again!" Kerlach said gleefully. He opened his arms wide. "Hit me, if you can."

Lysanna released the arrow, and it crossed the river, only to fall into the water. It had not gone as far as the first shot.

The Schaaka were beside themselves.

The Captain fitted another shaft.

One of the Schaaka jumped down from his mount, and edged closer to the rivers bank. He turned and displayed his backside to her, slapping it and laughing.

Anarys watched Lysanna. A smile crept onto his face.

Lysanna pulled the shaft back and took precise aim.

The bowmay loosed her shaft. It sped across the water, and slammed into the Goblin's back between his shoulders. As he fell, his companions cried out in shock. Lysanna fitted another shaft and sent it speeding across the water. It smashed into the horn in Kerlach's hand, sending it spinning away. He snarled, and turned his mount and fled. The Schaaka scattered, milling in confusion. Lysanna nocked an arrow and fired again, and the last rider fell from his mount. In moments, they had disappeared into the woods on the far bank.

A cheer went up.

Lysanna turned to see Elf and Goblin roaring out her name and cheering her marksmanship. She bowed graciously.

"That was excellent shooting, Captain," Anarys said. "Even Captain Nilda herself could have done no better."

"Thank you, Your Majesty. That is high praise."

"And that was clever thinking, too. To make them think that you could not hit them, make them lower their guard, and only then show your skill. It was well done."

"Thank you, Sire."

"Your Majesty?" It was Captain Enriss.

"Yes, Captain. How did we fare?"

"It is not good, Sire. Fully half the horses were lost. Some were slain outright, and some we had to put out of their misery."

The King's face was grim.

"That is indeed not good. It was the strength of our horse that had smashed through the enemy in times past. He had no mounted forces then. There are no foot soldiers on Erathyn who can withstand a charge of mounted warriors."

"But now he has the O'skaa, Sire," Lysanna said.

"Yes. They are a powerful force. Hard to kill, and ferocious in combat." He looked up into the blood red sky, where the moon still occluded the sun. "If it were not for this sorcery that allows the creatures to come up from the Underworld, we would make short work of his army." He returned his attention to Enriss. "What are our casualties, Captain?"

"There are forty five dead, Your Majesty. Both Elf and Goblin fell. There are others who are badly wounded who will not last the night."

The King sighed wearily.

"They are but the first. Set a watch, Captain. Be vigilant, for the Schaaka always seek to take advantage of any laxity."

"Yes, Your Majesty."

He bowed and left them as Jhara Shin and five of his chokhutai came up.

"What news, Lord Shin?"

The Goblins bowed to Anarys.

"The O'skaa had dug tunnels under the river. That was how they caught us by surprise. The tunnels came out behind the woods on either side of the camp. We entered them, and made sure none of them were still there. Then we followed the tunnels over to the other side. We could not find any of the enemy."

"The O'skaa riders have gone?" Anarys said.

"It seems so, Your Majesty."

"Do you think this is part of the strategy to lead us on that we spoke of earlier?"

"I am sure of it, Sire. It is the way of the Schaaka. They always try to lure their enemy into a place of ambush."

"Then we must be careful as we advance. Go and get some rest, all of you. We will ford the river tomorrow."

"Yes, Sire," Shin said. He and his chokhutai bowed, and departed.

"I hope we meet that Kerlach again, Sire."

"Why is that, Captain?"

"I have an arrow that I would like to put through his good eye."

The King smiled.

"Good night, Captain."

"Good night, Your Majesty." She bowed.

Anarys walked back to his tent.

# CHAPTER IX

# THE VALLEY OF DEATH

The O'skaa that had escaped from Linador finally arrived at Darkmor's stronghold. It had hastened there, driven by the need to report to him. The arachnid made its way past the frozen warriors, and into the camp at the end of the valley. There it was stopped by two riders.

"Where have you come from?" One of them asked. "Where is your rider?"

*I come from Sstonebridge. He wass ssslain.*

"What happened to the company there?" The other asked.

*Sslain. All sslain. By the Bright Oness and their alliesss.*

"We must report this to the Master."

*Yess, yess, the Masster. The Masster musst be told.*

"What must I be told?"

The two Schaaka turned. Darkmor stood there with staff in hand. They dropped to one knee, and the O'skaa lowered its forepart to the ground.

"Master, this O'skaa comes from Stonebridge. It says the company there was destroyed by the Bright Ones."

*Sslain. All sslain. By the Bright Oness and their alliesss,* The O'skaa sent.

"Allies?" Darkmor queried. "Which allies do you speak of?"

*A Man. And Goblinss were with them too.*

"The Man would be Ervin the Kandaran," The sorcerer said. "The Goblins would be those under Jhara Shin's command."

He stood lost in thought. The two riders and the O'skaa did not interrupt his meditation. They knew that even though he wore the Elf's young body, his mercurial temperament and fierce temper were still a part of him.

"It is of no matter," he finally said. "Stonebridge and Gorlik's company there served their purpose." He started to leave, but then recalled a thought. He pointed his staff at the O'skaa. "What happened to Althar? I haven't had any message from him, and I can't sense him."

*He was sslain, Masster.*

"How? What happened?"

*The Man sslew him in combat, Masster.*

*So, Kandaran. You finally avenged your people,* Darkmor thought. He smiled.

"Althar served his purpose too," he said. "Put this O'skaa in with your mounts. Send riders to every company. They must leave the valley, and go into the mountains. I'm going to cast a spell. Ensure that no-one is left behind, or they'll die. I'll begin in one hour."

"Yes, Master," chorused the riders.

Darkmor turned and raised his staff. He lifted off the ground, and flew to the top of the tower. He saw the O'skaa riders taking his message to the different companies that were camped in the valley. His gaze left them and swept over the stilled warriors. For over a thousand years that spell had held, but now it was time to undo it.

Darkmor put his hand into his robes and withdrew Willowen's pendant.

"Soon,' he said to himself. He put the pendant back in his robes.

He walked over to the door and let himself in with a wave of his hand. The door closed behind him with a thud.

On the ledge above the tower Silveron and Nomayon lay side by side. The Seer's eyes were vacant, and the Elf knew that Nomayon had seen and heard what Darkmor had said to the Schaaka. He had seen some of it himself in his mind, but he didn't dare to intrude in case Darkmor sensed his presence.

Why were Darkmor's forces breaking camp? Why were they leaving the valley? He watched and saw them marching away into the mountains. Why had they done this?

"Nomayon knows."

Silveron saw that Nomayon's eyes were clear.

They both backed away from the edge, and rejoined their companions, who had been waiting for them.

"Nomayon saw and heard the Dark One," The Seer said.

"What were his orders, Nomayon?" Silveron asked.

"The spider told him of a battle," Nomayon replied. "A group of his Schaaka were all slain by a force that had both Elves and Goblins in it."

"Ah," Brador said, "Lord Shin's chokhutai."

"Yes Brador, I agree," The wizard said. "That makes sense. Go on, Nomayon."

"Ervin was with them. He slew the traitor Althar in single combat."

"So he has finally avenged his people," Egon said. "That is good news."

"Where was this battle, Nomayon?" Yosh-en enquired.

"At Stonebridge in the mountains."

"Stonebridge?" Silveron echoed.

"That is what Men called Linador," K'Reel said. "It was once a meeting place for all of the races. The Schaaka must have used it to spy on our army."

"Mmm. Yes, remember Stonebridge, I do," the Dwarf said. Fine work was done there, by both Elf and Dwarf."

"Why did Darkmor's forces leave the valley?" Silveron asked.

"The Dark One is going to cast a spell," Nomayon said.

"What kind of spell?" Egon said.

"Nomayon does not know. But he goes now to the stone from the sky. He has Princess Willowen's pendant."

"Trying to unlock the Starstone's power, he must be," Brador said.

"Yes, but why?" Silveron said. "What can the spell be?"

"It must have something to do with his forces leaving the valley," Egon said.

"It makes no sense," Yosh-en said. "Why would they have to leave? There is nothing in the valley..." he trailed off.

"The warriors from a thousand years ago, there are," Brador said.

"Could he be going to release them from that spell?" K'Reel said.

"I do not know," the Elf said.

"Even if he did, can they be alive after all this time?" Egon said.

"We must assume that they could be," Silveron replied.

"If that's true," Egon said, "then the forces that faced him all those years ago would still be against him."

"Would they?" Silveron said. "Surely he would not free them from the spell, only to have them as his enemy again. I fear he would also be able to turn them into his allies."

"Makes sense, that does," Brador said. "Go and stop him before he casts this spell, we should."

"We do not know where in the tower he is," The wizard said. "We should wait here and make sure that he is going to lift the spell."

"But waste time that does," Brador argued. "Go now, we should."

"Silveron is right," Egon said, "we don't know how to find the Dark One. It's better that we stay here and watch and wait."

"I agree," Yosh-en said. "If it turns out that he does lift the spell, we will have to warn King Anarys."

"That is where I come in," K'Reel said.

"Good, K'Reel," Silveron said. "We will wait here and see what happens." He exchanged a glance with Brador. "But once we see what the result of his spell is, we will go down and enter the tower by the hidden door."

The Dwarf grinned.

"Acceptable that is." He lay down and closed his eyes.

The Elf smiled. He knew that Brador, as a seasoned campaigner, was taking his rest while he could.

"That is a good idea," he said. "All of you rest. Nomayon and I will keep watch, and wake you if necessary."

The group made themselves comfortable, and Silveron and Nomayon crept back to the edge.


Far below them Darkmor came to the door that led to the Starstone. The two Schaaka there bowed to him. He waved his hand, and the huge metal bolt pulled back with a screech. The door opened slowly, and a wave of heat gusted out. He entered, and the door closed behind him. He traversed the narrow bridge that led to the platform on the far side. The lake of fire grumbled and hissed in the depths below. He was half way across and his face was already shining with sweat.

The sorcerer stepped onto the platform. He strode purposefully up to the raised area where the Starstone sat. It shrieked at him, a metallic howl that echoed in the chamber. Hate and fury were in that cry. Darkmor knew that if the intelligence within the stone were released from the sorcerous bonds that he had bound it with, it would seek to destroy him.

He stood before it, his gaze sweeping the sigils that he had put in place. They were all as they should be. Even so, he knew that the thing had been straining against its prison.

"So, you still don't accept me as your master."

A metallic wail answered his statement. It went on, changing pitch and timbre. The thing was trying to communicate with him. But there was only fury and detestation in the sounds. The sorcerer knew that it was venting its hatred for him in a tirade that he couldn't understand, but he felt its rage nonetheless.

He stepped closer, and the intensity of the sounds increased.

"You'd like to escape, wouldn't you?" He smiled. "You'd like to break out of your prison, and destroy me."

A harsh metal grinding was his only answer. It sounded like the frustrated sound a beast would make that couldn't reach its prey. It rose to a deafening pitch.

He pulled Willowen's amulet from his robe and dangled it in front of the Starstone. The howling shut off as though it had been cut with a knife.

"Ah. Good. I'm glad to see that I have your attention."

A whine came from the Starstone. It sounded like a whipped puppy.

"Now," Darkmor said. "I want you to give me your power."

He raised his staff and began to chant...


Two hours later Darkmor appeared upon the tower's top. He hadn't bothered with the hundreds of stairs that led to the chamber below. With the help of Willowen's amulet, he had unlocked the Starstone's power. It filled him. He felt like he was filled to the utmost part of himself with blazing energy. He walked to the edge and looked out over the valley.

The sorcerer raised his staff with both hands and closed his eyes. He formed in his mind the sigils that corresponded with the words of the incantation. The eyes of the serpent bracelet kindled, and a ball of black fire appeared at the staff's tip. Black flames ran down the staff.

"Chah!" Darkmor cried. A sigil formed before him made of black flame, as though an unseen hand was writing in the air.

"Mok!" Another sigil joined the first. The air around him began to shimmer, as if Darkmor were wreathed in a heat haze.

"Dahk!" A third sigil appeared and blazed alongside the others.

"Chekh!" A fourth sigil burned upon the air.

"Toh!" The fifth sigil was added.

"Ley!" The sixth sigil appeared.

"Dun!" The seventh sigil was added.

Darkmor opened his eyes and stared fixedly at the blazing sigils. Only one more remained, and the spell would be complete. He took a deep breath.

"Mahk!" He cried. The eighth and final sigil appeared.

Darkmor brought the staff down with both hands and slammed its base against the tower. The sigils vanished with a thunderclap. A shock wave radiated outwards.

Under the blood red light of the occluded sun, the wave of energy pulsed outwards from the tower. It flowed over the stilled warriors. A low humming accompanied it, making the walls of the valley vibrate. It went on for a few moments, and then the wave dissipated, and the sound stopped. There was stillness.

A vast groan went up. It came from the throats of the thousands of warriors who had been held in the Spell of Stasis. Here and there were small movements as they began to move. Slowly, these movements intensified, until it could be seen that all of the warriors had turned to face the tower.

"Come to me," Darkmor said.

Slowly, the host began to advance towards him. Like sleepwalkers, they came on, the sound of their tramping feet and the hooves of their mounts rumbled like thunder. Elf, Man, Cobran, Dwarf, Avianinn, Felininn, and all the nameless things that had made up the Army of Darkness came closer. They advanced right up to the tower's base and stopped.

"I am your master," Darkmor said. "Go into the mountains until I call for you. Do not interfere with my forces there. Go!"

As one, the immense horde began to move away. Darkmor watched them for a time, and then he lifted his staff and vanished.

Silveron and Nomayon had watched everything unfold. They hadn't had to wake their comrades; the sound of the shockwave and movement of the warriors crossing the valley had woken them. They lay upon the ledge, staring at the thousands moving below them. Thousands, that for centuries had remained locked in the sorcerer's spell.

"They are all under his spell," Egon said.

"Bad, this is," Brador said. "Even the Elves obey him."

"We must send word to King Anarys," Silveron said.

"I am ready," K'Reel said.

"Tell His Majesty what has happened," the wizard said. "We will wait here until you return."

"I obey." K'Reel leapt into the air, and with a sweep of his wings, hurtled away.

"Look, Silveron," Egon said, pointing.

Silveron saw a majestic figure upon an Elven horse. Her golden armour looked dull under the blood red light. Her cape was a dirty brown. Even her hair looked red, although Silveron knew it was a golden mane. She led a large group of Elves that were mounted, and behind them came Elven foot soldiers.

"Queen Nerolynn," He said.

"Loath King Anarys will be to face her in battle," Brador said.

"We must ensure that that never happens," Silveron said.

"How can we do that?" Yosh-en asked.

"I do not know. Perhaps if I can find and use the talisman to banish Darkmor, this spell will be broken."

"Will they not die if that happens?" Brador said.

"I do not know," Silveron replied.

"Better to die than be a slave of the Dark One," Egon said.

There was a murmur of assent at this statement. They all returned their attention to the host marching below.

"Why are the birdmen walking?" Egon said. "They should be flying."

The Avianinn walked along with the rest of the host. Their wings hung slackly.

"Lucky for us they do not," The Dwarf said. "Find us, they could."

"There are some Felininn amongst them too," Silveron said.

The feline warriors sat upon their giant birds. Hundreds of them rode along with the horde that was marching into the mountains.

"Yes," said Yosh-en. "Lord Tong-en was sent to answer the call of the Elf-King. But I do not see him. Perhaps he has fallen in battle."

"That would be an honourable death," Toran-en said. "But this, this is unnatural. I would rather die."

"No argument here," Brador said.

"Well, we must await word from King Anarys," Silveron said. "We should stay out of sight, even though we have seen no patrols."

They backed away from the edge. The tramp of marching feet and the sound of shod hooves upon stone continued on for a long time.

K'Reel saw the Army of Light advancing below him. He went lower, and landed in front of them. Captain Enriss called the army to a halt. King Anarys rode forward, accompanied by F'Leet and Vandaron. The wizard was riding a horse, but F'Leet was on foot. He had just returned from scouting ahead.

"Your Majesty, My Lords," K'Reel said, and bowed with his wings opened behind him.

"K'Reel. Why have you come to us? Is something wrong?" Anarys regarded the Avianinn with trepidation. *Has Silveron failed?* He thought.

"There is, Sire. Silveron sent me to report to you."

"Have you met with resistance?" F'Leet said. "Do you have casualties?"

"No, My Lord," K'Reel replied. "But something – strange – has happened. Silveron thought it was imperative that I report it."

Captain Enriss rode up.

"What is your order, My Liege?"

"Captain. K'Reel has an important message from Silveron. Go and tell the section leaders the army may rest here for a while. Tell them to be ready to march again at a moment's notice."

"Yes, Your Majesty." He turned his horse and rode off to obey the order.

King Anarys dismounted. Vandaron followed suit.

"Well, K'Rell, please give me your report."

"Yes, Sire. We had found a hidden door at the back of the tower. Silveron had decided to see where it led. He wanted us to go inside to try and find both Princess Willowen and the talisman. But before we could do so, Darkmor appeared on top of the tower and cast a spell."

"I see," Anarys said. "And this spell, did it release the frozen warriors that were in the valley?"

"It did, Your Majesty. How did you know?"

"I thought Darkmor would do this if he could manage it. Go on."

"Many of the host were released. They all came to the tower at his bidding. He ordered them to go into the mountains." He stopped, unsure how to go on.

"These warriors, were they all from the Army of Darkness?" Vandaron asked.

"No, My Lord," the Avianinn answered. "Some were Elves, some Dwarves, and Men and Avianinn and Felininn too. All obeyed Darkmor."

"I know what you are hesitant to say, K'Reel," King Anarys said. "Queen Nerolynn was among them, was she not?"

"She was, Sire. She was on horseback, and led a vast group of Elves, both mounted and foot soldiers."

"What a cunning mind Darkmor has," Anarys said. "He will make us fight our own people. He knows that will take the fighting spirit out of our warriors."

"It would be a terrible thing for you to fight your Queen, Sire," Vandaron said.

"Indeed, Vandaron. That is just what Darkmor wishes us to think. K'Reel, where are Silveron and his companions now?"

"They await my return, My Liege."

"F'Leet, go and fetch Lord Nildoron and a dozen of your best wingmen."

"Yes, Sire." F'Leet leapt into the air.

"What do you have in mind, Your Majesty?" Vandaron asked.

"F'Leet and his wingmen will follow K'Reel back to Silveron and his friends and wait while they enter the tower. Nildoron will go with them. When Silveron has rescued Willowen and banished Darkmor, they will fly them back to join us."

"Do you still think Silveron will achieve this goal, Sire?" Vandaron said. "Remember how Darkmor struck him down, and took both Princess Willowen and the talisman."

"I have not forgotten, Vandaron. But I have faith that Silveron will be successful."

"Let us hope that your faith is justified, Sire. Perhaps I should go, and assist Silveron in this task."

"Do you expect him to fail, Vandaron?"

"No, Your Majesty. I hope he succeeds, but if he does not –"

"All will fall. I know you think he is not capable of achieving victory. I have watched you belittle him before us."

"Sire, I –"

King Anarys held up his hand. Vandaron's mouth shut like a trap.

"I will hear no more of this, do you understand? It is Silveron's task, and no other. Goldwen had faith in him, so do I. That is the end of the matter. Do I make myself clear?"

The wizard nodded.

"Yes, Your Majesty."

"Good. Ah, here comes Nildoron."

The Elf-lord reigned in his mount, and dismounted and bowed before Anarys.

"You sent for me, Sire?"

"Yes. I want you to go with F'Leet and his wingmen and wait for Silveron and his companions. When they have rescued Willowen and Silveron has banished Darkmor, you will fly them back to us."

"I understand, Sire."

As this exchange was taking place, F'Leet and his wingmen arrived. They landed and bowed before Anarys.

"What is your order, Your Majesty?" F'Leet asked.

"Take Lord Nildoron and follow K'Reel to where Silveron and his companions are. Lord Nildoron will enter the tower with them. Once they have rescued Princess Willowen and the sorcerer has been banished, you will fly them all back to join us."

"We obey, Sire." He walked over to Lord Nildoron. "My Lord, I will carry you myself." He went behind Nildoron, reached under the Elf's armpits, and wrapped his arms around Nildoron's chest. "Are you ready?"

"Yes," Nildoron said. He grabbed the Avianinn's arms, and held on for dear life.

F'Leet spread his wings. His wingmen followed suit. He nodded to Anarys.

"We go, Sire." All of the Avianinn hurled themselves into the air.

With K'Reel in the lead, they sped away.

Anarys and Vandaron watched until they had disappeared from view.

"Vandaron," the King said, "do not tell anyone about what Darkmor has done."

"But should we not tell them, Sire?"

"No. Many of us will have to face old friends in combat. That is bad enough."

"But would not the shock be lessened if they were forewarned?"

"Perhaps it would. But I believe our warriors would worry if the truth were known. They would wonder who of their old comrades were now under Darkmor's spell, and worse than that, they would wonder if they could slay them in battle."

Vandaron knew that Anarys was thinking of Queen Nerolynn. Surely it was torture for him to know that his own wife was under Darkmor's spell, and that he might have to fight and kill her on the battlefield? *If they could be killed,* Vandaron thought.

"As you wish, Your Majesty. I will not speak of this to anyone."

"Good. Here comes Enriss."

Captain Enriss reigned in his steed. He bowed to Anarys.

"What is your command, Your Majesty?"

"Captain. I believe we should be moving again. Please send a groom to take Lord Nildoron's horse."

"Yes, Sire." He turned his mount, and rode off to give the order to march.

King Anarys and Vandaron mounted their horses. A groom rode up and bowed to Anarys.

"I will lead Lord Nildoron's mount back to his troop, Your Majesty." He led the horse away.

Captain Enriss returned and bowed to the King.

"We are ready to march, Sire."

"Proceed," Anarys said.

Enriss held up his hand, and then waved it forward. The army started to move again.


Willowen awoke to the sound of the bolt of her prison cell drawing back. She rose from her sleeping pallet and stood. Who was it? Had Darkmor come to torment her again? He had the amulet. No doubt he had worked out how to use it. Perhaps he had used it on the Starstone?

The door opened wide, and Kalindra appeared in the doorway. She was carrying a tray that had a plate of food, eating utensils, and a bottle and two goblets.

She entered the room. One of the Schaaka who stood guard closed it behind her. The girl came over to Willowen and bowed.

"Your Highness."

Willowen smiled.

"I am glad it is you, and not Darkmor."

Kalindra returned her smile.

"Will you eat, Your Highness?"

She walked over to the table and placed the tray on it. Willowen came and joined her. The girl put a plate of food in front of Willowen and filled a goblet and placed it before her. Willowen sat down. The food smelt good. She picked up the goblet and tasted the drink.

"This is honey wine," she said, surprised.

Kalindra sat down.

"Darkmor said that you could have it now. Are you pleased? He said it would please you."

"It does indeed. As does your company." She raised her goblet and toasted the girl.

"Thank you, Your Highness."

"Has something happened? There was a sound like thunder, and I thought I heard many warriors on the march." Willowen took up the small knife and fork and used them to cut the meat. She popped some in her mouth and chewed. It was mouth-watering.

The girl nodded.

"Darkmor used a spell to free the warriors that were frozen in the valley. It was amazing. P'Kaani and I watched it from the window. They came to the tower. Darkmor ordered them into the mountains. We could hear his voice commanding them."

The Elf paused in the act of taking another mouthful.

"Were they all freed?"

"All except those who had been slain in battle."

"What happened to them?"

The girl went pale. Her freckles stood out. She licked her lips nervously.

"Oh, Your Highness," she said, her voice filled with horror, "it was awful."

"Tell me."

Kalindra took a deep breath, and then went on in a rush.

"They turned to dust! It was as if the centuries had finally caught up with them. They had been frozen in time for so long, and it seemed as if all of those years were laid upon them all at once. I turned away, but P'Kaani is a Plainswoman, and is made of sterner stuff. She watched it all. She described it in great detail. I wanted to stop up my ears, but she kept on."

"Is that what happened to the Army of Light and its allies?"

"Oh no, Your Highness. The ones who were – *summoned* – by Darkmor, came and marched with his own forces that he had freed. I saw a beautiful Elven Queen, mounted upon an Elven steed. She led many of your warriors."

Willowen put her knife and fork down. She gazed at the girl in shock.

"Your Highness? What is it?"

"The Queen you saw is my mother. She has been lost to us for a thousand years."

"Oh, Your Highness, how terrible for you." The girl reached across and put her hand over Willowen's.

"Thank you. I remember when my father came here to try and free them. He had with him Goldwen, who was the mightiest wizard of the time. But whatever they tried, they could not free them. They had to admit defeat, and leave them as they were. My mother was lost to us." She frowned. "Why would they not resume their fight with Darkmor once they were awakened? My mother hated the Black Circle. The enemy then was the Man Malkaar, and he was the last of that sorcerous group, but now his soul possesses Darkmor the Elf. Surely they would have continued the fight against him?"

"They seemed to be under a spell, Your Highness. They obeyed him as his own warriors did."

"What happened then?" Willowen asked.

"P'Kaani and I watched as the others marched away. It seemed to take a long time. There were thousands of warriors."

"I see." Willowen was lost in thought. Her mother lived! There must be some way to save her.

"Your Highness, I think I know what Darkmor wants to do."

"And what is that?"

"He came to us and used us as before. But afterwards, he was boasting. He said something about King Anarys and his warriors not being able to

166

face their own people in battle. He thought it would take the fight out of them. And he said there was another force that no-one knew about."

Willowen took the girl's hands in her own.

"Kalindra, I must escape. I have to warn my father. Can you get the talisman for me?"

"I will try, Your Highness. Darkmor is tiring of me. I know he will get rid of me soon. Can I come with you?"

"Of course you can."

Willowen picked up the bottle and filled their goblets. She raised hers in a toast. Kalindra followed suit.

"To freedom," Willowen said.

"To freedom," Kalindra echoed.

The goblets clinked together, and they drank.


Meanwhile, F'Leet, Nildoron and the Avianinn came to the valley. Nildoron had had a brief moment of terror when they had first taken to the air, but now he found it exhilarating. He had spoken to F'Leet while they were flying, pointing out features of the landscape that they passed below.

"The valley, F'Leet, and Darkmor's tower," he said. He had needed to raise his voice to be heard above the wind that rushed by.

"I see them, My Lord."

"There is something different," Nildoron said, his voice puzzled.

"The warriors are gone," the Avianinn rumbled.

"You are right. It is completely empty. Are they now all under Darkmor's spell?"

"I do not know, My Lord."

As they entered the valley, Nildoron swept his gaze over the land below. Not one warrior remained. But there was a grey ash or dust that covered the valley floor. He wondered what it was.

Ahead of them K'Reel began to lose height. F'Leet and the others followed him. They came down and landed where Silveron and his companions were waiting.

F'Leet released Nildoron and stepped back.

"Thank you, F'Leet," Nildron said. "That was breathtaking. I now understand the love you have for flying."

"It is my honour to serve you, My Lord." He bowed.

"Greetings, My Lord," Silveron said. "I did not expect you to bring so many Avianinn with you."

"It was the King's idea. I am to join you in the search for Princess Willowen and the talisman. F'Leet and his wingmen will wait here for us. When we have rescued her and the talisman has been found and used, they will fly us back to the army."

"I must thank His Majesty for his confidence in my success."

"Tell me about this spell," Nildoron said.

"Darkmor came to the top of his tower. He spoke several Words of Power, and sigils appeared before him. There was a thunderclap, and then moments after, the warriors who had been frozen came to life and made their way to the tower. He spoke to them, and commanded them to go into the mountains."

"He sent them into the mountains? Why would he do that? Would he not have them form up in battle formation and prepare to meet our army?"

"Mayhap an ambush he prepares," Brador said. "Empty the valley is now. An inviting emptiness, it is."

The Elf-Lord nodded.

"You may be right, Brador. But King Anarys would not march across it without considering it a trap. Silveron, did all of the warriors leave the valley? Surely there had been some who had been cloven in two, or had lost limbs or head in the conflict. Would Darkmor's spell revive them and make them whole again?"

"No, My Lord, that did not happen. Did you see the dust on the ground in the valley?"

"I did. I wondered what it was."

"That is all that remains of the warriors you speak of."

"They turned to dust?" Nildoron said.

"Aye," the Dwarf said. "Freed from the spell they were, and all the years that they had stood there were finally laid upon them heavily."

"You saw this happen?"

"We did," Egon said. "Thousands of them crumbled to dust before our very eyes."

"What an awful thing to have been frozen for a thousand years and then just turn to dust." Nildoron shook his head.

"There is something else, My Lord."

"What is that, Silveron?"

"Queen Nerolynn was among the warriors that Darkmor released."

"The Queen?" Nildoron said.

"She went into the mountains with thousands of your people," Egon said.

"The Queen is under Darkmor's spell," the wizard said.

"I told His Majesty of this," K'Reel said.

"What was his reaction to this news?" Nildoron asked.

"He said that he would not inform the army that the Queen and so many of your own people were now under the Dark One's spell."

"He did not even inform me," Nildoron said. "Darkmor has done this so that she and all the others who were once our allies may now be turned against us."

"That is what I thought too," Silveron said.

"I cannot imagine how the King would react if he were to meet her on the field in battle," Nildoron said.

"Stay his hand, it would," Brador said. "Cunning, Darkmor is to make friends into foes."

"He is indeed cunning," Nildoron said. "We must not let that fight happen. Silveron, where is this door you found?"

"Come, I will show you."

Silveron walked over to the ledge and lay prone. The Elf-Lord came and joined him. The wizard pointed to the back of the tower.

"See there? The door is hidden among trees."

"Is it guarded?"

"Yes. There are eight guards. Four Schaaka, four Cobrans, and one of the Schaaka is an O'skaa rider. His spider is with him."

"That is all?"

"Yes."

"Then we should go. The army is getting closer every moment. If you can carry out your task before they arrive and are forced to fight Queen Nerolynn and her warriors, banishing Darkmor should negate his spell."

"What if negating the spell destroys them as the warriors in the valley were destroyed?" the wizard said.

"We must take that chance. If we wait until the army arrives, they will fight. It will be too late then."

"I agree."

The pair backed away from the ledge and rejoined the others.

"We are going now," Nildoron said. "F'Leet, you and your wingmen remain here until we return."

"What if you do not return?" the Avianinn rumbled.

"Then you are to join His Majesty and fight to the end."

"Yes, My Lord." He bowed.

"Come, Brador," Silveron said. "It is time to put your war hammer to work."

The Dwarf grinned.

They walked over to a path that they had found and began the descent to the door.

# CHAPTER X

# THE DEATH IN THE VALLEY

The Army of Light advanced under the blood red light. They were getting closer to Darkmor's stronghold with every mile that they travelled. Several of his O'skaa riders had been seen following them, but when any of King Anarys' forces were sent to capture them, they fell back rapidly, and disappeared. This game of cat and mouse had been going on ever since the army had crossed the Brakoon. Some hit and run raids had been carried out when the army had stopped to sleep. The O'skaa riders had suffered casualties in these raids, but that did not stop them returning and shadowing their enemy.

Hidden among some trees watching the army pass by was Kerlach. He was still fuming over how foolish Lysanna had made him appear before his warriors. With him were ten of his riders. Another ten were on the far side of the column, peering through the trees.

"Will they rest tonight?" one of his riders asked.

"Yes," he answered. "They are slow. Half of their force is on foot."

"Pity we didn't kill all their horses," another said. "They are good eating."

*Horsesss,* Kerlach's mount sent. *Give them to usss.* It moved restlessly beneath him.

Kerlach patted the creature's head.

"Patience, my pretty," he said. "You'll have horseflesh soon enough."

"And other sweeter meats besides, eh, Leader?" a Schaaka said, and laughed.

An Elven outrider turned their way. He drew his sword and pointed it in their direction. He cried out something that they couldn't hear.

A dozen mounted bowmays gathered and headed towards them, fitting arrows as they came.

"*Scatter!*" Kerlach bellowed, and his riders went in all directions.

The bowmays reached the trees and went in hurried pursuit of the scuttling arachnids. One was lagging behind the others. It was riddled with shafts, and as it fell, its rider rolled along the ground. He sprang to his feet, only to have an arrow punch through his back.

Kerlach and one of his riders were rushing towards the dense forest. Once there, they knew that the bowmays would not venture inside, and they would be safe. Kerlach turned and looked over his shoulder. The closest Elf was too far away for a clear shot. He laughed, but then his blood ran cold as he realised that it was Captain Lysanna herself that was bearing down on them. He urged his mount to a faster speed.

His companion fell behind. Lysanna took aim, and fired. Her arrow took the Schaaka in the back. He dropped to the ground. His O'skaa turned with a scream, and hurtled towards the Elf.

Lysanna reigned in her steed, and nocked two arrows. She sighted, and held her ground. The spider raced towards her, shrieking.

Kerlach had reached the safety of the forest. He stopped his mount, turned and watched.

The O'skaa was almost upon Lysanna. It reared, baring its fangs. The Elf loosed her arrows, and they sped and pierced both of the monster's main eyes. The O'skaa screamed, and died. Kerlach cursed.

"Come out!" Lysanna cried.

"You won't fool me again!" Kerlach responded.

"You are content to hide in the shadows?" Lysanna cried. "You are a coward."

An inarticulate explosion of hate came from the trees.

"I'm no coward!" Kerlach shouted. "I'm no fool, either. You have a longbow. My bow doesn't have the range yours has."

Lysanna's comrades rode up. One of them reported to her.

"Captain, the O'skaa riders are either dead, or have run."

"What are our losses?"

"We lost three riders, and two mounts, Captain."

"Thank you, Melandra. Go and tell the King. Four of you remain here with me."

"Yes, Captain." She wheeled her mount and headed back towards the army. Half of the bowmays followed. Lysanna returned her attention to the forest.

"Goblin! Are you still there?"

Silence was the answer.

"Goblin!"

A shadowy shape appeared among the trees. The O'skaa crawled out onto the grass. Its rider held aloft his goad.

"I am Kerlach!" the Schaaka bellowed. "Fight me on foot, if you dare!"

Lysanna returned her bow to the harness that lay next to her saddle. She dismounted.

"Captain –" one of the bowmays began.

Lysanna held up her hand to silence her.

"If this Schaaka kills me, you will let him leave here without harm."

The bowmays looked at each other.

"Did you hear me?" Lysanna said.

There was a chorus of reluctant agreement from the bowmays.

"Good." Lysanna gave her mount's reins to one of them, and began to walk towards the waiting Kerlach. Her companions watched in trepidation. Could they trust the Schaaka? He could just order his mount to kill Lysanna.

Kerlach grinned. He plunged the spear end of his goad into the ground, and used it to vault down from the O'skaa's back onto the grass. He reached behind his head with his right hand, and drew his own blade from the sheath that was strapped to his back. He swung it back and forth with both hands as he advanced towards the Elf. His O'skaa made to move, but he spoke a single word, and it stopped and stood like a statue.

The two closed the gap until they were only ten paces apart. Lysanna looked her enemy over. She had wanted to meet him in battle ever since he had refused to show respect to King Anarys. How she wished he were here to see her deal out justice to this filth.

Kerlach had stopped swinging his sword. He planted its tip on the ground in front of him, and leaned on the pommel.

"Well, I didn't think you'd accept my invitation," he said, and grinned. "You're taking a chance."

The Elf watched his eyes for any indication of intent.

"I can still order my bowmays to fill you full of arrows. You are in range now."

Kerlach leered. "You wouldn't do that. Your King wouldn't like it."

"No, I would not. He –"

She stepped back and dodged as Kerlach sprang forward, whipped up his sword and made a cut at her. He swung again, and their blades met with a metallic clang. They exchanged several furious strokes, and then backed away from each other.

"Good, Elfling, good," Kerlach said, smiling. "I've caught more than one enemy with that trick."

"It is an old trick," she replied curtly.

They began to circle each other.

"But a good one," Kerlach said, grinning.

They continued to circle; each of them watching the other closely, and waiting for the opportunity to strike. Lysanna's companions looked on with bated breath. She was well known for being an excellent shot with the bow, but how would her swordcraft stand against such a brute? Even though he was a Goblin, he was the tallest one any of them had ever seen, and he was much bulkier than the Elf. And his sword made hers look like a paring knife in comparison.

He made a feint with his blade, and Lysanna stepped back. He laughed.

"You're pretty good with a bow," he sneered, "but not much with a sword. How many have you killed with yours?"

"Enough," she said.

Kerlach leapt forward, but instead of making a stab at her, he spun on the ball of his right foot and turned. Lysanna's thrust met empty air. The Schaaka whipped his massive blade around, and sliced open her chin. He dodged as she struck at him, and stepped back.

"Ah," he said with satisfaction. "Now it's your turn. Hit me if you can."

Lysanna wiped the back of her hand across the cut. She looked at the blood there. Her eyes narrowed. Blood began to run down her neck. She felt it trickle between her breasts. She watched Kerlach. His eyes strayed from hers, and he gazed at her breasts for an instant.

It was enough. The Elf lunged forward, and slashed at him. She stepped back and took a guard position.

A long cut had opened up along his left forearm. Black blood seeped out, and began to run down his arm. He had been swinging his sword with both hands. Now, he gripped it with his right hand, and clenched and unclenched his left. He winced with pain.

"Very good, Elfling," he said. "Come again." He hefted his blade.

They returned to circling. Both were now wounded. Which of them would succumb to the loss of blood first? Drops of their blood fell upon the grass, and as they moved, became intermingled. The footing beneath them became slippery.

Lysanna's bowmays cried out as she slipped. But even as Kerlach began to move in, the Elf managed to retain her balance. She brought up her sword to block any of his attacks.

Melandra and her bowmays rode up. With them were King Anarys, Lord Merys, and eight Elf guards. They reined in, and watched the combatants stalk each other.

"We have an audience," Kerlach said. "Your King has come to watch me kill you." He chuckled.

Lysanna made no reply.

"Your Majesty," Melandra said, "should we not intervene? The Captain is wounded."

Anarys addressed the bowmays who had stayed behind: "What was the Captain's order, ladies?"

"Sire, we were ordered not to interfere, and if the Schaaka killed her, we were to allow him to leave unharmed."

"Then let that order stand. Captain Lysanna knows what she is doing."

"Very well, Sire," Melandra said.

Watching from the depths of the forest were a dozen O'skaa riders. One of them smiled to himself. He was Mordakh, the Schaaka who had laughed and given their position away. Now he leaned forward in the saddle, and watched as Kerlach and Lysanna battled. He had no love for Kerlach. In fact, if the truth were to be told, he hated the big Goblin. He imagined that it should be he, and not Kerlach who should be in charge of the riders.

"Mordakh, shouldn't we go and help?" one of the riders asked.

He shook his head.

"No. Kerlach got himself into this; it's up to him to get himself out of it." He grinned.

"But there's only a handful of them. Our O'skaa would make short work of them."

"Be quiet, you'll give us away," Mordakh snarled.

"You already did that," another rider said.

Mordakh turned with a hiss.

"Who said that?"

None of them owned up. He fixed his gaze upon them, but they all had blank faces. He spat on the ground, and returned his attention to the two combatants. When this was all over, he would get rid of this group. They owed their allegiance to Kerlach. He would gather another group of riders that would call *him* Leader.

"That's the Elf King," one of them said, breaking his reverie.

"What?" he said angrily. "Where?"

"That one," the Schaaka said, and pointed at Anarys with his goad.

"Are you sure?"

"Yes. Kerlach and I followed him for a day. He usually has a bigger bodyguard, but I guess he thinks we ran off."

Mordakh's evil little mind began to consider how he would be treated if he brought the Elf King to the Master as a prisoner. He stroked his chin, thinking. Yes, that would be good. He would take the Elf King prisoner, and bring him before Darkmor. *And Kerlach?* He thought. *Perhaps he would be killed in the attempt. How unfortunate.* He snickered.

"Good. Tarakh, you take six riders around to the left. Makaar, take your lads around to the right. I'll give you a few minutes to get into place. Then I'll blow my horn. That's the signal to attack. Take the Elf King alive. Kill all the others. Go."

A murmur of agreement met this statement. The group broke up, and moved away as his order had entailed. He watched, smiling. Soon he would be a group leader; no, a *Captain* of four groups, or even more! He would cut Kerlach down himself, if no one else did. At long last he would be rid of the big Goblin and his heavy handed leadership.

He watched the stealthy movement of the riders as they moved into position. They finally reached their assigned spots. He lifted his horn and wet his lips. *Goodbye, Kerlach,* he thought vengefully.

The horn blared.

The O'skaa riders exploded from the forest and rushed towards the King and his companions. The spiders screamed as they attacked.

"*O'skaa!*" Melandra cried. "*Swords!*" She and her bowmays drew their blades.

"Protect the King!" Lord Merys commanded. The Elven guards drew their swords, and surrounded Anarys.

Kerlach laughed, and bowed mockingly to Lysanna.

"Until we meet again." He turned and ran back to his O'skaa.

Lysanna stood her ground. The O'skaa rushed towards her. She was too exhausted to run as Kerlach had. *I will make an end worthy of the Captain of Bowmays,* she thought.

"*Captain!*"

Lysanna spun about. Melandra was there, holding out her hand. Lysanna sheathed her sword, and grabbed hold. Melandra swept her up onto the horse, and they raced away. They hurtled across the grass with the O'skaa in hot pursuit.

They reached the others in moments. Lysanna jumped down from Melandra's mount. She saw with dismay that the bowmays were armed with swords.

"*Bows!*" she ordered, and the bowmays sheathed their swords and grabbed up bows and fitted arrows. They loosed hastily at the oncoming riders. Two of the arachnids went down, and three of the Schaaka were slain.

Then the O'skaa were upon them.

An O'skaa leapt upon a bowmay who was trying to draw her sword.

She fell to its fangs. Her horse shied, and knocked two of the other bowmays down. As one got to her feet, the O'skaa rider speared her with the sharp end of his goad. The other bowmay dodged away, and ripped out her sword. She and the Goblin traded blows, and with a savage thrust, she plunged her blade into the spider. It shrieked and died. The Schaaka leapt from its back, and engaged her with his wicked curved sword.

Lysanna hurled her longknife at one of the riders. It pierced his throat. He fell off his mount, to be trampled beneath its many feet. The Captain drew her sword, and leapt in. She fended off the spider's attacks, and sent her blade home in its brain.

Half of the King's guard had fallen. Anarys and the four remaining guards fought desperately against the O'skaa. Lord Merys was engaged with one of the riders. They exchanged blows from atop their mounts. The Elf-lord saw an opening, and stabbed the Schaaka in the eye. As he fell, Merys backed his horse, and pulled on the reins. The horse reared, and plunged its hooves into the monster's brain. The Elf-lord looked about himself quickly, and then took out his horn. Taking a deep breath, he blew, and its bright tones echoed in the clearing. He continued to sound it.

Kerlach had slain three of the bowmays himself, and had just seen Lysanna, when the horn began to sound. He cursed. He wanted to finish the Elf off.

A large group of mounted bowmays appeared, and rushed towards them.

"*Metekh!*" he bawled. *Retreat.*

The surviving O'skaa riders saw the incoming Elves, disengaged from the fight, and spurred their mounts towards the forest.

"After them!" Melandra cried, and she and the remaining bowmays joined in the pursuit.

"No, wait!" Lysanna called out. "*Melandra! Leave them!*" She was unheard due to the pounding hooves thundering by. She stood there and watched them race after the retreating O'skaa riders.

Kerlach cast a look over his shoulder. He grinned.

"This way!" he cried, and turned his mount to the right where a trail led deep into the forest. His riders followed him, and they in turn were followed by the bowmays. They were only ten hours ride from Darkmor's tower. *The Elfling's may have fresh mounts,* he thought, *but they aren't as hardy as our O'skaa.* He would lead them into the valley. *There's always a watch there, and then we'll have them.* It was too bad Lysanna hadn't taken the bait, but at least they would deal with these Elflings. He laughed.

Both groups disappeared into the forest.

Captain Lysanna watched them go in disbelief. She sheathed her sword.

"That is a nasty cut, Captain. You had best let Shelarindel see to it."

She looked up to see King Anarys.

She bowed. "Yes, Your Majesty. I must apologise for Commander Melandra's conduct."

"There is no need, Captain," Anarys said. "She is not as seasoned a warrior as you."

"She knows better than to call for swords when bows are needed."

Anarys nodded.

"She made a mistake. It is understandable, considering the circumstances. We were under attack. The Commander panicked."

"A Commander of Bowmays does *not* panic."

"This one did."

A silence fell between them.

"They are already dead," Lysanna said flatly.

"Yes, they are." The King's face was grim. "I am sorry, Lysanna."

She looked him in the eye.

"Sire, with your permission, I will have this trifle seen to, and then I shall choose a Commander from among my bowmays."

Anarys regarded her for a moment.

"You may go, Captain."

She bowed to him and went to look for her horse.

Melandra urged her bowmays to close the gap between them and their quarry. She had thought they would have caught up to the O'skaa riders by now. The miles had flown by; first they had followed the enemy through the forest trail, and then they had come out into the open. The closeness of the trees had restricted their mount's speed, but once they were free of that restriction, they had gone into a full gallop. Melandra had thought the O'skaa riders would have left them behind in the forest, but the tail end of their group was always in view. It was as though they were teasing the Elves; as though they were remaining just beyond their reach. It was as if they were daring them to come and take them...

A terrible thought formed in Melandra's mind.

*What if they are just leading us on? Luring us...*

*"Commander!"* One of the bowmays cried.

The O'skaa riders had halted and turned. They were arming themselves with bows. Melandra laughed. Their short bows did not have the range that their Elven bows had. They could halt and fill their quarry with arrows, and none of the Goblin's shafts would even reach them.

"Bows!" She ordered, and her bowmays took them up and nocked arrows. They would go a little closer. The O'skaa riders were gathered in the opening of a valley. Perhaps their mounts were spent, and their leader had ordered them to stand and fight. It would be his last order. She gauged the distance between them. They were close enough. She held up her hand.

"Halt!"

The bowmays came to a stop.

"Form combat line!"

The group of bowmays spread out in a line, facing the enemy.

The harsh sound of a Goblin horn rent the air. Kerlach was sounding it. It was answered. A chorus of horns brayed. Three groups of O'skaa riders appeared. Two came from either side of the bowmays, and another group closed off their retreat. In moments, Commander Melandra and her companions were surrounded. They formed a protective circle with their bows aimed outward at the encircling Goblins.

Melandra automatically counted the enemy. There were sixty of them; thrice the number of bowmays under her command. They looked as if they were veterans of many battles. She looked at the group that had cut off their retreat. Could they smash through them, and run? *No,* she thought, *even if we did break free, our mounts would be run down quickly.* The O'skaa that had joined them were fresh, and as she now realised, they were a hardier mount than their horses were.

Kerlach rode his mount up. He was grinning. A dirty cloth was wrapped around his wound. It was stained with his blood, but it had obviously stopped the bleeding. He bowed mockingly from his saddle.

"Welcome, ladies. We were wondering how far you'd chase us." He turned and gestured with his goad into the valley that lay behind him.

Melandra looked past him. The valley opened up, and at its end was a tall shape. She gasped as she realised what it was. Darkmor's tower seemed to touch the reddened sky. They had come all the way to the enemy's stronghold! Her blood went cold. She had led her bowmays into a trap.

"Lower your weapons," Kerlach said.

Melandra stared at him. She had underestimated the Goblin. This had been his goal; perhaps to begin with his plan had been to kidnap the King, but he had failed to accomplish that. He would be satisfied with their capture. She looked again at the Schaaka that surrounded them. There was no way that they could fight their way out of the situation.

"Do as he says," she said.

"Commander?" One of the bowmays queried.

"We are outnumbered, Salmaris. Drop all weapons."

"We could fight and die," Salmaris said.

Melandra nodded.

"Yes, we could. But I choose to surrender. Drop all weapons."

Salmaris met her gaze. For a moment, it seemed she would ignore the order, and fight. But then she slowly lowered her bow, and tossed it onto the ground. Her sword and longknife followed. The other bowmays disarmed themselves.

There was a clattering as bows, quivers, swords and longknives were dropped onto the grass. Several Schaaka dismounted and came and collected them.

"What now?" Melandra asked.

"Now you are our guests," Kerlach said.

Her gaze met his one good eye.

"I would ask that you let my bowmays go."

He laughed.

"Now why would I do that?"

"If you do, I will give myself over to you as a prisoner. They only obeyed my command; it is my fault that they have come to this."

Kerlach regarded her. She had not disarmed. He thought for a moment, and then smiled to himself.

"I have a better idea," he said. *"Mordakh!"*

Mordakh rode his mount up and halted it next to Kerlach. It did not surprise Kerlach that the wily Schaaka was still alive. He had a talent for dodging combat. *Until now, that is,* he thought wryly.

"Yes, Leader?"

"This Bright One here has asked that we let her companions go. What do you think of that?"

"I wouldn't agree. Take them all prisoner."

"But they fought well. Shouldn't we take that into account?"

"No. It doesn't matter. She made the mistake of chasing us here."

"That's right. But should her warriors suffer for a mistake that she made?"

Mordakh turned and looked at him quizzically.

"They should all suffer for that blunder."

Kerlach smiled.

"No. I'm feeling generous today."

"What do you mean?"

"I mean we will give her the chance to redeem herself."

"Redeem? I don't –"

Kerlach turned abruptly away, ignoring him.

"Commander," he said. "I will accept your request under one condition."

"What condition would that be?"

"That you meet Mordakh here in single combat. If you win, your friends can leave. If you lose..."

Mordakh gasped and went pale.

"I understand," Melandra said. She looked Mordakh up and down. Her practiced eye showed that he was no expert in combat. In fact, she thought that he looked like someone who went out of his way to avoid any kind of fight. "I accept."

"But, Leader –" Mordakh began.

Kerlach rounded on him.

"*You are an O'skaa rider,*" he said fiercely. "Act like one." His one eyed stare burned into Mordakh like fire.

Mordakh flinched.

"Yes, Leader," he said contritely. Inside, his thoughts raced. How was he to survive this? Whenever there was any fighting, he had always managed to hang back. His mouth was suddenly dry.

"You will both dismount," Kerlach said. "You may not use your bows."

Melandra dismounted. She drew her sword and walked forward. The ring of O'skaa parted and let her through, and then closed up again. Melandra came and stood thirty paces from Kerlach.

"I am ready. I am Melandra. Come and face me."

"The lady is waiting, Mordakh," Kerlach said with a grin.

The Schaaka slowly dismounted, and walked over to stand before the Elf. She brought up her sword. He raised his goad. It was reversed, so that the spear tip faced her. Kerlach smiled as he saw that Mordakh's hands were shaking. Melandra saw this also. She also saw the sweat that was beading the Goblin's face. She smiled. He licked his lips nervously.

"Begin," Kerlach said.

Melandra lunged forward. Her blade was deflected by Mordakh's spear, but only barely. She cut and slashed, and the Goblin fell back, desperately blocking her attacks. Kerlach laughed, and the O'skaa riders did too.

"That's not how it's done, Mordakh! Stand your ground!" Kerlach was enjoying himself.

The Schaaka's face burned with shame. He was being humiliated in front of his companions. They were smiling and laughing at his predicament. They knew what he was.

Suddenly, he was filled with rage. How *dare* Kerlach treat him like this! How *dare* they laugh at him! He would show them all. With an angry cry, he leapt forwards, brandishing his spear in a frenzy of stabs. His impetuous rush took Melandra by surprise. His spear penetrated her defence, and she cried out as it tore through her shoulder. Mordakh backed away as she struck back at him, amazed that he had scored a hit.

"Well done, Mordakh!" Kerlach cried gleefully. "Do it again!"

The O'skaa riders cheered and laughed.

Now the combatants began to circle each other. The crowd went silent, as they could see that the combat had now begun in deadly earnest. Before, it was comical how the Elf had made Mordakh look the fool. But now that he had wounded her, all there knew only death could now finish the contest. But whose death would it be?

Melandra shifted the grip on her sword. The blood that flowed from her wound made it slippery. She kept her eyes fixed on her enemy. His unpredictability made him a dangerous opponent. Such furious attacks were hard to foresee and defending oneself against them was difficult.

Mordakh was still amazed that he had actually hit the Elf. He knew that she was a more seasoned warrior than he was, but even so, his strike had hit home. He looked for another opening, but now saw that his opponent was watching him closely. Maybe he should try to wait her out? Maybe her wound would make her weak, and he could strike. *Yes,* he thought, *I'll wait until she's weakened by her wound.*

Melandra saw the concentration on his face. She made a guess at what he was thinking. He had not attacked since his lucky blow. Perhaps he was waiting for her to succumb to blood loss? She would see. She stumbled, and he leapt forwards.

There was a brief exchange of strokes, and then the combatants backed away from each other.

She was right. He *was* waiting for her wound to weaken her. Melandra watched his eyes. She would only get the one chance. She deliberately made her movements slow. She staggered. Mordakh would have attacked, but was now wary of her. She would have to make a blatant fall. It was taking a chance, but she thought and hoped that the Goblin would fall for her ruse.

*Good,* she thought.

Kerlach smiled. He could see what Melandra planned. It was all to the good. He would be rid of Mordakh. *Good riddance,* he thought.

Melandra cried out and fell. Mordakh rushed forward, intending to stab her as she lay prone. She swept up her sword, and buried it in his chest. The Elf rose to her feet, with the impaled Mordakh staring and gasping at her from her sword's point. She withdrew it slowly. He choked, dropped his goad, and fell onto the grass and lay still. The Elf wiped her blade on him, and stood facing Kerlach.

"I have defeated your warrior," she said. "Let my bowmays go."

Kerlach smiled.

"I'm afraid I've changed my mind. Tarakh!"

Tarakh raised his bow and loosed.

The arrow sped and punched into Melandra's chest with a meaty thwack. She looked down at it, and then looked up and met Kerlach's gaze. A look of shocked surprise was frozen on her face. She staggered, dropped her sword, and fell.

"Kill them all," Kerlach commanded.

The Schaaka's bows twanged, and the bowmays joined Melandra in death.

*Horsess,* Kerlach's mount sent. *Give them to usss....*

At least half of the bowmays mounts had been shot down with them. The others milled about aimlessly, their eyes rolling in terror.

"Patience," Kerlach said. He patted his mount on its furry head.

"Tarakh, bring me their heads. I have an idea."

"Yes, Leader." Tarakh motioned to several of his companions. They walked over to the corpses, and took the bowmays heads with one swing of their swords. They came back and stood before Kerlach with their grisly trophies.

"Good. Pile them here. Now fetch me some spears."

Tarakh grinned. He knew what Kerlach had in mind.

"Yes, Leader. Come on, lads."

They tossed the heads onto the ground and went to get the spears. Kerlach addressed his riders: "Dismount and let our O'skaa feed."

The riders dismounted. Kerlach leapt down from his O'skaa.

"Feed, my pretty. Horses and Elves for you."

The spiders screamed and closed in on the horses in a rush. In seconds, the spent Elven mounts had disappeared under a confusion of white fur. The screams and whinnies of the horses were cut off abruptly. The riders came and joined Kerlach. It was not good to be near the giant arachnids at such a time. In their feeding frenzy, they would strike out and eat anything. The gruesome feast continued on.

Standing watching on the ledge overlooking the valley were K'Reel and F'Leet. They had seen everything from the time that the bowmays had chased Kerlach and his companions into the valley and the trap had been sprung.

"We should have done something," K'Reel said.

"No," F'Leet replied. "We cannot reveal ourselves."

"But we let them die. We should have intervened."

"No," F'Leet said. "We are here for Princess Willowen and Silveron. We were right not to get involved."

K'Reel turned away from the awful sight below.

"Why did they come here?" he said. He was puzzled. "Surely they must have known that they could not enter the Dark One's lair unchallenged?"

"I believe they were tricked into following those O'skaa riders."

"Tricked? How can that be?"

"Sometimes in the heat of battle such things can occur."

"But they were bowmays, F'Leet. They are among the best warriors the Bright Ones have. Would they lose their composure and pursue an enemy into a trap like that?"

"I am not sure. But it is the only explanation. Our army must be close by now. Perhaps these O'skaa had made a raid upon it. The bowmays were fighting them. The O'skaa fled, and the bowmays gave chase. It was a mistake; a grave mistake that cost those bowmays dearly."

"Should we report this to King Anarys?" K'Reel asked.

F'Leet turned to him.

"No. Our task is clear. It is unfortunate that they were killed; however, we must remain here and wait for Silveron and his companions. Our army will be here soon enough. The King will see for himself what has happened."

He returned his attention to the valley below. The spiders had finished their gruesome repast. Kerlach and his riders were mounting up. In a moment they were moving off. Tarakh and ten riders had remained, and were planting spears in the ground. F'Leet guessed at the import of that.

The Schaaka took the heads of the slaughtered Elves and began to impale them upon the spears. F'Leet had guessed correctly. He and K'Reel watched the Goblins as they went about their task. They finally finished, and began to walk across the valley towards Darkmor's tower. The bowmay's heads stood forlornly atop the spears. A mess of strewn bones, both Elf and horse, lay upon the grass beyond in the valley's opening.

"Let us rest," F'Leet said. "We can do nothing for them."

They moved away from the ledge and joined their comrades.

# CHAPTER XI

## MALOR AND SHELARINDEL

The Army of Light had made camp. King Anarys had called a halt so that they and their remaining mounts could be refreshed. The loss of the horses from the raid was a heavy blow. The once mounted warriors were now afoot, and their pace slowed the army's progress. The camp was settling down. The ruddy light that covered all made it hard to judge what was day and what was night, but hunger and thirst were good indications of how time had passed.

Anarys stood talking with Captain Lysanna in front of his tent.

"We went as far as we dared to go, Sire," she was saying.

"And you did not see Commander Melandra and her bowmays?"

"No, Your Majesty. There were plenty of signs that they had pursued the O'skaa riders through the forest path." She stopped.

"And then?' Anarys asked.

"The trail came into the open, and went across grassland towards the Dark One's lands. We did not go any further. I ordered a return to camp, so I could report to you."

"You did the right thing, Captain."

Anarys could see the sadness on her face.

"Lysanna, it was not your fault. Commander Melandra took charge of those bowmays and gave pursuit. That Goblin must have known they would give chase, so he led them on into the Dark One's lands.

"That Kerlach," she said. "I will make him pay dearly for what he has done. I would like to meet him on the battlefield."

"Maybe you will meet."

A silence fell between them.

"Your Majesty?"

Captain Enriss was there. He bowed to Anarys.

"What is it, Captain?"

"Sire, Lord Malor is here. He has brought two hundred mounted warriors with him from Oakendean."

Anarys smiled.

"Ah. That is good news. Please ask him to join me."

Enriss bowed again.

"Yes, Sire." He made to leave.

"Enriss."

"Yes, Sire?"

"Please send someone to bring the Lady Shelarindel to me."

"Yes, Your Majesty." He left them to carry out the order.

"Well," Anarys said, "That is a pleasant surprise."

"I thought Lord Malor had decided to remain in Oakendean, Sire?"

Anarys smiled wryly.

"There was more to it than that. He thought Silveron had failed when he and Darkmor faced each other in Sirlyk's banqueting hall. When Darmor took the talisman, Malor felt that we could not succeed against him. So he decided to return to Oakendean."

"Captain Nilda also told me that Lord Malor was grieving for his brother. Perhaps that was something that helped him to make that decision?"

Anarys nodded.

"Yes, I believe that is true. They had been close as children, but when Malin left to join the Council of Light, their friendship suffered." He thought for a moment, and then continued on. "When Malin became Goldwen, and ascended to become the Eldest; the Leader of the Council, that friendship was broken. They did not speak to each other for years."

"You sent for me, Your Majesty?"

Shelarindel stood there. She bowed.

"Shelarindel. Welcome. Come and join me." He gestured to the tent opening.

"Thank you, Sire."

"You may leave, Captain," Anarys said. "Thank you for your report."

Lysanna bowed.

"Your Majesty." She left them.

"Come, Shelarindel. I have some honey-wine." He opened the tent flap.

"Thank you, Your Majesty."

They entered the tent. Anarys crossed the floor to a small table. Upon it was a bottle of wine, and several goblets. He filled two of them, and carried them across the floor and gave one to Shelarindel.

"Thank you, Sire."

They both drank. Anary gestured to two camp chairs, and they both sat down.

"How are your patients doing?"

"We have not lost any more wounded," she replied.

"That is good."

"But I fear that the battle ahead will be fierce," she said. "Casualties will be appalling."

"Not if Silveron is successful. There may not even be a battle at all if he can banish the Dark One before our two forces meet."

"Do you think he can succeed?"

"It is my hope. I believe he can. We must have faith that he can."

"Your Majesty."

One of the sentries stood in the tent opening.

"Lord Malor is here, Sire."

Shelarindel gasped.

"Send him in."

The sentry bowed.

"Yes, Sire."

Malor entered. He saw Shelarindel, and stopped. Then he mastered himself, crossed the floor, and knelt before the King. He bowed his head.

"Your Majesty," he said, "I have come to offer you the service of myself and my warriors."

"And you are most welcome. Rise. Come have some wine."

Malor rose to his feet. He did not look at Shelarindel.

"Thank you, Sire."

The King stood, and went to pour Malor some wine.

"You know the Lady Shelarindel, I believe."

Malor bowed to her.

"My Lady."

Shelarindel stared at him coolly.

"My Lord," she said. Her voice was cold.

The King crossed the floor and held out the goblet to Malor. When Malor went to take it, Anarys gripped it tightly. He looked into Malor's eyes.

"That is enough. Stop treating each other like strangers. Sit, and be civil."

"Your Majesty –" they both protested.

"*Sit!*" he commanded.

They both lapsed into silence. Malor took the goblet from Anarys, and they went and sat down.

"Now," Anarys said, "this foolishness will cease. I know that you love each other." He turned to Malor. "You are the Lord of Oakendean. I know you think that the responsibility of that position is more important than anything or anyone. I know you feel that our cause was lost when Silveron failed. You thought that we had no chance against the Dark One without the talisman, so you returned to Oakendean. I could have commanded you to remain with the army, but I did not. Why have you decided to come to me now?"

Malor glanced once at Shelarindel, and then turned his attention to Anarys.

"Sire, it was the right thing to do. I must ask your forgiveness. I made the wrong decision. I should never have returned to Oakdean."

"Is that all that you are sorry for?" Shelarindel asked.

Malor looked over at her. His face was troubled. He seemed to be full of words that he wanted to say, but was unsure how to proceed. She saw the confusion in his eyes. Malor was obviously struggling with some inner conflict. Then she saw determination come to his visage. She knew he had made a decision. He was about to speak, when the King addressed him again.

"It was the right thing to do?" Anarys said. He took a drink, and then continued: "Malor, the right thing to do would have been to stay with the army. No matter how you thought Silveron had failed, your duty is to me and to our people."

"I know, Your Majesty. But it was difficult for me to do that. I felt I had to leave."

"Why?" the King said. "What was difficult? You only had to follow me."

Malor did not answer. Anarys could see that he was holding something back. What was he loath to say? He looked sideways at the healer. Her look was imploring. She was looking at Malor as though she were begging him to say something.

The King rose and walked over to the table. He poured another drink. He crossed the floor and sat down. Shelarindel and Malor had regarded each other without speaking. An uncomfortable silence had descended between them.

"How long will this go on?" Anarys asked.

"Sire?" Malor said.

"Your Majesty?" Shelarindel said.

"May I venture a guess as to why you left us, Malor?" Anarys said.

Malor glanced quickly at Shelarindel.

"There is no need, Sire. I will tell you." Malor took a deep breath, and carried on. He avoided looking at the healer. "Before Goldwen died, he gave Shelarindel and I his blessing to be together. For a time, we were happy. But then I thought that I was unworthy of her. I had loved her from afar for many years. But she had loved him, so I had not interfered. When we had finally become involved, I somehow thought I was betraying him. Being with the army day after day, I saw her all the time and this feeling became overpowering."

He looked at her. Tears were forming in his eyes.

"I felt I had to leave. I am sorry."

"Why did you not tell me of this?" Shelarindel said. "I did not understand why you left so abruptly. We could have talked about it."

"We are at war with the Dark One. Our personal problems pale into insignificance when they are measured against Erathyn's fate."

Shelarindel rose to her feet.

"So you thought you would just go back to Oakdean, and those problems would just go away?" Her lip trembled.

"It was easier. You had your work. I had Oakdean to manage."

"So you did not care about how you would hurt me by leaving without any explanation?" Tears came to her eyes.

Malor got to his feet. He made to go to her, but then stood still. Uncertainty was written all over his face.

"You did not care," she said. She wept.

"No, that is not true. It is because I cared that I left."

"I loved Goldwen that is true. But now he is gone. I have accepted your love. Why did you not stay with me?" Her tears ran down her face unheeded.

Malor stared at her. What was he to do? He had thought that he could report to the King, and keep away from Shelarindel. But now that he saw her, he realised that his love for her still burned in his heart.

"Shelarindel –" He faltered. All of the words that he had meant to say had vanished from his mind. He looked over at Anarys. The King motioned with his eyes that he should go to her. Malor knew that that was what he should do, but somehow he stood rooted to the spot.

"Shelarindel –" Malor said. It made his heart ache to see her filled with sorrow. He walked slowly over to her. She looked up at him. Her eyes were red from weeping. She suddenly threw herself into his arms. He clumsily put his arms around her. Malor stroked her hair as she cried. But this time, her tears were of happiness.

"That is better," Anarys said. He lifted his goblet to Malor in a toast as if to congratulate him on making the correct move.

Malor gave him an apologetic smile. He looked uncomfortable; he had not wanted the King to see this emotional scene. He realised that it had been foolish of him to think that he could avoid Shelarindel once he had returned to the army.

"Your Majesty," he said, "I must apologize for my conduct in this matter. If I had known how much sadness I would cause Shelarindel, I would not have left."

"No," Anarys said, "you would not have. But now that we know the reason for your leaving, it is easy to understand." The King put his goblet on the ground and stood up. He came over to them.

"I had no idea. I thought Goldwen's death, and Silveron's failure to defeat Darkmor were the cause of your departure. I thought you had lost faith, and just wanted to return to Oakendean and wait for the end."

Malor shook his head.

"No, Sire. I was troubled about Goldwen's passing for a long time. But I have accepted it. Silveron's failure was something that disturbed me also. But now I have been told that he and a small group have infiltrated the enemy's stronghold. I had thought he was dead. I am overjoyed to learn he still lives."

"If you had stayed with us, you would have known that," Shelarindel said. She was gazing at him in adoration. A smile came to her lips.

Malor grinned.

Anarys came closer. He put his arms around both of them.

"You are my friends. It pleases me greatly to see that you are reunited."

Malor coughed in embarrassment.

"Thank you, Sire. Once again, I am sorry for any trouble I have caused."

The King stepped away from the embrace.

"You are forgiven. What does the Lady Shelarindel say?"

"I forgive him as long as he does not do it again." She reached up and pulled Malor's head down, and they kissed. When they broke from the kiss, Malor glanced at the King. The Lord of Oakdean's face was red.

"Do not be embarrassed, Malor," Anarys said. He was smiling. "Shelarindel is beautiful. She deserves to be kissed."

"*Sire!*" Shelarindel said. She gaped at him in shock.

The King laughed. After a moment, Malor and Shelarindel did too.

"Well, I am glad that ridiculous situation has been resolved. I was worried that you had fought. It is good that you have rectified the situation, Malor." Anarys went and picked up his goblet. He went over to the camp table, took up the bottle, and filled it. "More wine, my friends?"

Malor picked up his and Shelarindel's goblets. He came over to the King.

"Thank you, Your Majesty."

Anarys filled them up. Malor took them over to the healer, and gave her one of them.

"Please sit," Anarys said.

They resumed their seats. They each took a drink of honey-wine.

"Sire, please tell me of this mission Silveron has undertaken." Malor drained his goblet and sat back.

"It has always been in his mind to venture into the Dark One's tower," Anarys began. "We spoke of it in depth. Goldwen came up with the original plan. He and some of the Council members created the Talisman of Banishment. But you know that. Silveron took it upon himself to finish what Goldwen had set in motion. But it seemed that it was all doomed to fail when Darkmor defeated him and took the talisman from him in Sirlyk's banqueting hall." He looked thoughtful. "He took Willowen too, as you recall."

"Princess Willowen," Malor said. "Has there been any word of her? I am sorry, Sire. I should have asked you about her right away."

"You had a lot on your mind," Shelarindel said.

"That is no excuse, Your Majesty."

"Do not upbraid yourself, Malor. Silveron told me she lives. He was convinced of it. Now he has slipped into Darkmor's lair to rescue her, and to find the talisman and use it."

"That is dangerous. How will he accomplish that?"

The King shrugged.

"I do not know. But if he succeeds, Erathyn will be rid of Darkmor for good. The great battle we are preparing for may never happen."

"I would welcome that," Shelarindel said. "The casualties from a battle of that size would be overwhelming."

"That is the truth," Malor said. "It could even mean the end of our army."

"Indeed," Anarys said. "An O'skaa rider came to me as the messenger of the Dark One. He bragged to me that the enemy has forces that far outnumber us. Darkmor has kept them in reserve for this battle."

"I saw when I arrived that you have suffered casualties along the way. I was told that the O'skaa riders performed raids that slew many of our horses."

"Yes. We lost a company of bowmays too."

"Was there a pitched battle, Sire? I thought there had only been the raids?"

"No. There was no battle. That Goblin messenger I just mentioned; he and his companions were the ones who raided us. We managed to slay some of them, but most of the time they evaded combat." He and Shelarindel exchanged a glance.

"What happened, Your Majesty?"

"Captain Lysanna had run him down and challenged him to single combat. I was sent for, and when I arrived, an ambush was sprung from the trees. His riders had been hiding in the forest, and thought to capture me. Lysanna's bowmays and my guard protected me. When the company of mounted bowmays appeared, the Schaaka saw that they would be overwhelmed, and so they fled. Commander Melandra gave chase, and the company followed her."

"How far did they follow, Sire?"

"We do not know. Lysanna went to look for them. She found signs that they had pursued the enemy into the Dark One's lands."

Malor looked shocked.

"Why would she do that? It should have been obvious to her that the Schaaka were leading them into a trap."

"As I said to Lysanna, Melandra made a mistake. In the heat of battle, a decision can sometimes be made that is a mistake. It is unfortunate."

"Do you think they could still be alive, Sire?" Shelarindel said.

"I do not think so, Shelarindel. I think that the Schaaka have slain them all."

Anarys drank from his goblet. "We do not know if they are dead, but I fear that could be the case. The truth is we are not certain of their fate."

"What happened to the Goblin that led them?" Malor asked. "Did Lysanna slay him?"

"Unfortunately, no. She is filled with the desire for revenge. Lysanna hopes to meet him on the battlefield and finish him."

"I hope she does," Shelarindel said. "That Goblin is responsible for many deaths."

"Anything is possible," the King said. He rose to his feet.

Malor and Shelarindel stood in respect.

"My friends, I grow tired. Malor, I would think you are weary also. It is time to sleep."

"Yes, Your Majesty. When will we be moving out?"

"I have called a halt here to wait for Lord Kitar-en and his warriors. There are two thousand of them, all mounted on warbirds. They will reach us in three days."

"That should make up for the loss of horses that you suffered, Sire."

"Yes. But the bowmays are a great loss." He rubbed his face. "Forgive me, I must sleep."

"Of course, Your Majesty."

Malor and Shelarindel bowed to him.

"Enjoy the rest while you can, my friends. Even though I still hold hope that Silveron will be successful, we must prepare for battle."

"My warriors are ready, Sire. As am I."

"I do not doubt it. Good night."

"Good night, Your Majesty." Malor bowed.

"Good night, Sire," Shelarindel said. She bowed. "Thank you," she said, smiling.

He nodded to her and raised his goblet to them both.

"Be good to each other."

They bowed to him and took their leave. Anarys drank the last of the wine, and put the goblet on the table. He yawned, and went over to his pallet.

Malor and Shelarindel walked through the camp. The discomfort that had been between them was gone. They talked easily, as they had done before he had left.

"Did you bring all of your warriors with you?" The healer asked.

"No," Malor said. "I left one hundred of them to guard Oakdean."

"I see. I remember a time when you could have brought a thousand warriors to battle."

"Yes. That was before the war. We suffered many casualties, as you know. Our numbers dwindle. You know that the King wants us to return to Glindarion. This world is harsh and unforgiving."

"Many agree with him. They feel that we should leave this world to Men."

Malor nodded.

"Goldwen and I spoke of it. He agreed with the King. To begin with, Men were like children, as you recall. Then we showed them many things. It is time for them to live without our assistance. But first, we must ensure that this world is free of the Dark One and his minions."

She turned a concerned face to him.

"Do you think we can beat him? If what Kerlach said is true, Darkmor has forces that will devastate our army. Can we defeat them?"

"I do not know. We can hope that we can. But if Silveron is successful, as we hope he is, we may not even have to face such overwhelming odds."

They walked in silence for a few minutes, each of them filled with thoughts of the future and what it may hold. They came upon a group of Elven bowmays, who were sitting around a fire. Captain Lysanna was with them. She rose to her feet as they approached.

"Lysanna," Malor said. "It is good to see you."

"And I you. I was surprised to hear that you had joined us."

Malor looked embarrassed.

"Malor decided that he would come and serve the King," Shelarindel said.

"I see. That was a good decision, My Lord."

"Where is Captain Nilda? Is she with Ervin?" Malor asked.

A look of pain wrote itself across Lysanna's face.

"She was slain in battle."

"I am sorry to hear that," Malor said, mortified that he had caused Lysanna sorrow. "I have been with the King. I had no idea. What happened? Was it one of the raids that the O'skaa riders carried out?"

Lysanna shook her head.

"No. She and Ervin and Jhara Shin, along with Lord Nildoron and a number of warriors, were sent to scout ahead of the army. F'Leet had reported seeing something strange, so they investigated. They found many dead at a crossing, and signs that the enemy had retreated. When they went further, they encountered Althar and his companions near Linador. The Forester gave chase, and Nilda followed him, although Lord Nildoron had ordered her not to. Ervin slew his traitorous brother, and the Goblins were all slain. They returned, and Lord Nildoron decided to investigate Linador." She stopped speaking. In her mind, Lysanna could see all that she was describing. Even though she had not been present, she knew all that had occurred.

"What happened then?" Malor asked.

Lysanna looked at him as though she were just waking from a dream. Then, clarity came into her eyes.

"They sent some scouts ahead. They went into the fortress and searched. The scouts found nothing. But as they returned, a drunken Schaaka came onto the bridge, bellowing and roaring. Nilda shot him down, but as she did, O'skaa riders appeared and attacked them. The fortress was suddenly filled with Goblins. They fought their way across the bridge, and broke into the fortress. A group of Schaaka stood waiting for them with bows at the ready. They shot down Ervin and several of our warriors. Nilda was distracted by his fall, and one of the Schaaka took advantage of her distraction and stabbed her. Lord Nildoron ordered some of his warriors to stand guard over her, and they took the fight to the Goblins. They slew all of them. After the fight, our dead were honoured. They put them in the main banqueting hall, and set the flames to them. The fortress burned. Then they returned to the army." Tears glistened in her eyes.

"Lysanna," Malor said, "I grieve for your loss. Nilda was a beautiful and courageous woman. I respected her deeply." He bowed deferentially.

"Thank you," she said. "Will you join us?"

Shelarindel took Malor's arm. He could sense that she wanted to leave.

"I thank you for your offer. I must decline. I am weary from the ride. Please excuse us."

"Good night, then. Good night, My Lady."

"Good night, Captain."

Lysanna watched them leave. *At least they seem to have resolved their differences,* she thought. *May they be happy together.* She rejoined her bowmays by the fire.

"That was embarrassing," Malor said.

"Do not feel badly about it," Shelarindel said. "As you said to her, you have been with the King. You did not have time to learn what else has been happening."

"She was devastated," Malor said. "I could see that Nilda's loss still weighs heavily upon her."

"Yes. She misses her deeply. She was the light of her life. Lysanna was so proud when she became Princess Willowen's bodyguard, and also when she was promoted to be the Captain of Bowmays. Nilda and Lysanna had been friends since they were young. Lysanna always looked up to her."

"It seems she almost worshipped her."

"I believe that to be true. It must be hard for her."

"Lord Malor! Lady Shelarindel!"

Jhara Shin and several of his chokhutai stood there before them. They were drinking from tankards.

"Welcome!" Shin said. "Come have some fine ale."

"I have had enough to drink, my friends. Shelarindel and I shared some wine with the King. But I thank you for the offer."

"We drink to honour Ervin and Nilda and all of our companions who fell at Linador," Shin said. "Will you not have just one mug?"

Malor and Shelarindel exchanged a look.

"Well," Malor said, "perhaps just one to honour our friends."

"I will fetch them, My Lord." One of the Goblins walked over to a tent, and went inside.

"I was sorry to hear of your losses," Malor said. "I was shocked to hear that Ervin and Captain Nilda were among the fallen. I am sorry; I know that the Kandaran was like a son to you."

"Indeed he was. Thank you, My Lord."

The chokhutai returned with a tray that held three tankards. He picked up one of them and gave it to Malor.

"Thank you."

The Goblin picked up another tankard and offered it to Shelarindel.

"I am sorry," she said. "I do not like ale."

He grinned.

"It is not ale. Good honey-wine for My Lady Shelarindel. Come, take it."

The healer regarded the tankard dubiously. Hadn't she already had enough wine for one evening? She glanced at Malor. He nodded.

She accepted the tankard. The chokhutai took up the last one and raised it high.

"To our friends that have fallen. They will always be in our hearts."

"To our friends," the others chorused. They took a drink.

"Come sit by the fire with us," Shin said.

They all went and sat down on some camp chairs that ringed the fire. For a few moments they all drank in silence, their thoughts on their fallen comrades.

"So, Malor," Shin said, "you spoke to the King. Did he tell you of Silveron's mission?"

"Yes, he did. I was surprised to hear that he was alive. The King hopes that he will be successful; both in rescuing Princess Willowen, and in finding and using the Talisman of Banishment."

"What do you think, My Lord?" one of the chokhutai asked. "Is it that powerful? Can it rid us of the Dark One forever?"

Malor shrugged.

"I do not know. I only know that Goldwen and his companions from the Council of Light thought it was the only weapon that we could use against him."

"Then we must put our faith in it," Shin said. "And in Silveron and his friends who ventured into the enemy's land." He took a deep pull at his tankard.

"I wonder how they are faring," Shelarindel said.

"We must hope that they are successful," Malor said. "What they do is far more important than what we will do in three days. But no matter if they succeed or not, we must meet Darkmor's forces in battle."

"Lord Kitar-en is coming with two thousand Felininn warriors," Jhara Shin said. "They will be most welcome."

"His Majesty told me of them." Malor shook his head. "During the war, they could have fielded ten times as many warriors."

"Their numbers dwindle and fade," Shin said. "Vast, the Goblin army was once as well. Now, it is only a shadow of its former glory."

"Even so we are glad to have you with us," Shelarindel said.

Jhara Shin smiled, and saluted her with his tankard.

"It is the same with the Elven forces," Malor added. "Like you, we suffered much during the war. I remember a time when we had a hundred times the force we have now."

"The only race that seems to be increasing in number is the race of Man," another chokhutai said.

"True," Malor said. "But it is their world. When all this is over, King Anarys wishes the Elven people to return to Glindarion."

"Will you go, Malor?" Shin asked.

"Yes. Goldwen is gone. I have seen much sorrow upon Erathyn. I long to return to our homeland."

Shelarindel put her head on Malor's shoulder. He knew she was letting him know she wanted to leave. He put his arm around her and helped her to her feet.

"Please excuse us, my friends. Lady Shelarindel is tired, and I grow weary myself."

"Of course," Jhara Shin said. "Thank you for joining us."

"Good night, Lord Shin," Malor said.

"Good night."

The two Elves left the fire, and continued through the camp. Shelarindel was unsteady on her feet. Malor could feel the heat of her body against him. He pushed it out of his mind. Surely the healer would not welcome any advance from him in the state she was in?

"I think I have had too much wine," Shelarindel slurred. She burped, and then giggled like a little girl.

Malor smiled.

"Which way is your tent? I will make sure you get there safely."

"That is nice of you. I like it when you are nice." She smiled broadly at him.

"Thank you. Where is your tent?"

They stopped for a moment. The healer looked about, her face confused.

"This way," she said, and pointed.

They walked in that direction. Suddenly, she stopped, nearly knocking Malor over.

"No. Wait," she said. That is not right." She peered into the night, trying to remember the location of her tent.

"I do not know where it is," Shelarindel said. She shook her head groggily.

As they stood there, two Elven sentries came towards them. They saw them and bowed.

"Where is the healer's camp?" Malor asked.

One of the Elves gestured to their right.

"It is down that way, My Lord."

"Thank you." Malor made to move off.

"Do you need any help, My Lord?" the other Elf said. "The lady seems poorly."

"No. I will take care of her. Thank you."

"Good night, My Lord, My Lady."

"Good night."

Malor and Shelarindel walked down the indicated direction. The camp was quiet. *Surely everyone but the patrolling sentries was asleep?* Malor thought. *How much further do we have to walk?*

They finally came to a group of tents. It was the encampment of the healers. Shelarindel stepped out of his arms and walked unsteadily over to one of the tents. She opened the flap.

"Here we are. This is my tent."

"Then I will say good night," Malor said. He made to leave.

The healer dropped the flap and went over to him. She took his arm.

"Do you not want to be with me?" Her voice was husky.

Malor looked into her eyes, and saw the love she bore him within their depths. He stroked her hair.

"More than anything," he said. His voice shook with passion. "But my warriors will wonder where I am. I must go and join them."

Shelarindel put her arms around his neck. She pulled his head down, and they kissed for what seemed like an eternity. He grabbed her hips and crushed her to him. Malor could feel her breasts against his chest. They broke from the kiss. Each of them was breathing fast. Their hearts pounded together, and their ears rang with the blood that rushed around their bodies.

"Let them wonder," she said, and took him by the hand. She led him to the tent, and opened the flap. They entered, and the flap closed behind them.

# CHAPTER XII

# INTO THE LABYRINTH

Silveron peeked through the bushes. The door that led into Darkmor's lair lay before him. But there were also the guards. He looked them over. They did not seem to be very alert. They were sitting and talking, and not paying attention to their surroundings. Still, they would have to be dealt with before he and his companions could enter the tower. He felt movement at his side.

*"Slay these sentries, we will,"* Brador whispered. *"Let us be about it."*

The wizard grabbed his arm.

*"We must be cautious. Look there."* He motioned with a nod of his head.

Brador looked in the direction he had indicated. Hanging from a wooden frame was an alarm bell.

*"If that sounds..."* Silveron whispered.

*"Lost we will be."*

The Elf closed the gap in the bushes, and they both turned stealthily away. They padded quietly through the trees until they reached their companions.

"Well," Egon said. "Do we go?"

"There is an alarm bell," Silveron said. "We must ensure that it never sounds."

"Swift, we must be," the Dwarf said.

"I have an idea," Nildoron said. "Nomayon, how far can your warriors cast their spears?"

"At least four hundred paces. They are both great warriors.'"

"Good. And both Egon and I have bows." His gaze swept the group. "We should strike from a distance with these weapons, and then rush the survivors. If the four of us can slay one guard each at the outset that will make our task easier."

"Forget not that the O'skaa rider has a horn," Brador said. "As dangerous to us as the alarm bell, that is. And the spider itself, if it screams...."

"You are right, Brador," Nildoron said. "We must choose our targets wisely. M'shaan, you and K'taal, you slay the O'skaa and its rider. Egon, you and I will shoot down any guard who is close to the alarm bell. Silveron, how did the sentries appear to you? Are they vigilant?"

The Elf shook his head.

"I would say that they are bored. They are just waiting until they are relieved."

"Good. What are their positions?"

"The O'skaa rider stands by his mount by the door. The other three Schaaka are sitting on chairs nearby. The four Cobrans are off to one side sitting under a canopy. None of them is keeping a proper watch."

"That stands to reason," Egon said. "The door is so well hidden. They don't expect anyone to surprise them. I bet it's the most boring duty in the Dark One's army. All they do is sit around and wait for it to finish."

Silveron smiled.

"What is it?" Nildoron said.

"Let us give them a surprise."

"What do you mean?" Yosh-en asked.

"How do you think they would react if Darkmor himself appeared unannounced?"

"There'd be a mad scramble," Egon said. "They would –" He grinned. "Can you do that?"

"Darkmor is my twin. I think I could fool them for a moment. At least long enough for you to strike anyway."

"Look like him you do not," Brador said. "See through your ruse, they would."

Silveron regarded him.

"Give me a moment." He closed his eyes.

The wizard stood there, breathing slowly. He did this for a few minutes. Then he raised his staff, and murmured a spell in a low tone. Blackness appeared in his hair at the top of his head. It swept down and turned his mane dark. His robe shimmered, and turned black. Dark Magic symbols appeared upon it. His staff turned to ebony. Black flames suddenly wreathed it, and ran down its length to the ground. He was the very image of Darkmor. He opened his eyes, and they burned with multi-coloured fire.

Brador gasped and stepped back. The others did also, shocked at this transformation.

"Well, Master Dwarf?" He said. His voice was sibilant and evil. The wizard's eyes penetrated Brador's soul.

Egon drew his sword in a rush. The others armed themselves.

The fire went away in the wizard's eyes.

"It is all right, my friends," Silveron said. "I am not Darkmor." The flames on his staff died and went out.

"Made my blood run cold, you did." Brador said, amazed. "Powerful your magic is."

"I thought the Dark One had somehow taken you over," Egon said. He sheathed his sword. "It's incredible."

"Now, here is what I propose. I will show myself to the guards. Nildoron, Egon, M'shaan and K'taal, you slay your targets. They will be confused, and we will have the element of surprise. We will rush the others before they can sound a warning."

"Make sure you kill the O'skaa too," Egon said. "Don't let the thing scream."

M'shaan nodded.

"Are we all agreed?" Nildoron asked.

There was a chorus of assent.

"Good. Let us go."

"After you, Darkmor," Egon said with a grin.

The wizard grinned wickedly, and started towards the door.

Moments later, they were hidden in the bushes where Silveron and Brador had spied on the guards. They peered out. Nothing had changed. The sentries were still sitting about. Silveron regarded each of his companions in turn.

*Ready?* He mouthed soundlessly.

They all nodded. He concentrated, and the fire came into his eyes. He stepped out onto a path that ran down to the door.

*"What is this!"* he roared. He strode purposefully towards the startled guards. They had leapt up at the sound of his voice.

"Master!" The O'skaa rider cried. The others milled about, confused. They finally formed into a line and dropped to their knees. The rider hurried over to stand before Silveron and bowed low.

"What happens here?" Silveron said imperiously. "You are supposed to be on guard. Instead I find you lolling about! I should feed you to the males!"

"Master!" The rider cried out in fear. "Forgive us!"

His Goblin companions whimpered in terror. The Cobrans made no sound, but obviously understood the threat he had made.

"W-we did not expect –" The leader began.

*"Silence!"* Silveron bellowed.

The Schaaka's mouth snapped shut like a trap.

"I have never seen such laxity. Leader, when does your relief arrive?"

"In four hours, Master."

"When they replace you here, you will go and report to your commander. He will punish you all for your laziness." He fixed the Goblin with a freezing gaze. He lowered his voice menacingly. "You are lucky that you will all be needed in the battle ahead. Otherwise..." He trailed off suggestively.

The Schaaka gulped in horror. He bowed several times.

"Thank you, Master. Thank you, thank you."

"Enough of that," Silveron said brusquely. "Open the door for me."

"Y-yes, Master. I have the key. P-please follow me."

The Goblin turned and almost ran over to the door. He fumbled with a ring of keys that he wore on a belt about his waist. He inserted several keys, but none of them were the right one. He glanced over his shoulder and saw Silveron staring at him impatiently. He hurriedly turned back to his task, and finally found the right key. He inserted it and turned it in the lock. He pulled the door open wide and stood holding it for the wizard. He bowed to Silveron.

With a meaty thwack, M'shaan's spear tore into the O'skaa's brain. It died without a sound. K'taal's spear punched into one of the Schaaka, and he fell dead. The others, galvanised into action, leapt to their feet. There came the sound of Nildoron and Egon's bows, and two of the Cobrans dropped to the ground.

Silveron whipped out a dagger and stabbed the rider. The Schaaka gaped at him in shock, and then he fell back against the wall of the tower. He gurgled and slid down the wall, leaving a streak of black blood on the stone.

Silveron's companions burst out of the bushes and rushed at the other guards. One Goblin turned and ran for the alarm bell. He never got to it.

K'taal hefted his war axe and sent it spinning through the air. It crunched into the Schaaka's back, and he fell lifeless.

Brador smashed the skull of one of the Cobrans, and turned to block the thrust of a sword wielded by his comrade. He drove his war hammer into the snake man's chest, and knocked him down. He lifted his war hammer high, and then brought it crashing down on the Cobran's chest, which caved in under the heavy impact.

The last Schaaka threw down his sword and started to run. Nildoron's bow sang, and the arrow took the Goblin in the throat. He joined his comrades in death.

Silveron was wiping his blade clean on the rider when Nildoron, Egon, and the two Plainsmen came out from hiding. They came over, checking the bodies as the others were doing. M'shaan and K'taal retrieved their spears, and K'taal went and pulled his war axe from his victim's back.

"Went well, that did," Brador said. "All are dead."

"I'm glad you're on our side," Egon said to Silveron.

The wizard smiled, and his image shimmered. Standing before them was Silveron.

"That was well done," Nildoron said.

"Thank you, My Lord," Silveron replied. "I had not tried that spell before."

"We are glad that it worked," Yosh-en said. "Now our way is open."

"What of the bodies?" Nomayon asked.

"Lay them out as if they are sleeping," Nildoron said. "That will fool their reliefs for a moment."

"But only for a moment," Silveron said. "We must go."

As the others laid the corpses out under the canopy, Nildoron and Silveron spoke together.

"How will you find Princess Willowen?"

"I can sense her, My Lord. I might be able to send a message to her using mind-speech."

"Very good. What of the talisman? If we cannot find it, our mission is of no use."

Silveron stood there concentrating. Nildoron waited for him to speak. At last, the wizard turned to him.

"I can sense it too. There is something different. Darkmor does not have it in his possession."

"Are you certain?"

"Yes. Someone else carries it on their person." He probed with his thought. "A young woman has it. I can see her hurrying through the corridors below."

"What does this mean?" Nildoron was puzzled.

The wizard shook his head.

"I do not know, My Lord. But it should be easier to get it from her than it would be to take it from Darkmor."

"Perhaps she stole it from him?"

"Perhaps."

"Ready to go, we are," Brador said.

The others had finished their task and were waiting.

"Let us go, then," Silveron said.

He stepped through the door, and his companions followed. The last one in was Nomayon, and he closed the door behind them.

Kalindra ran through the corridor. Her heart pounded in her chest. She had done it! She had stolen the talisman! She could not believe how easy it had been. Images swam into her brain. Kalindra saw again what had happened. She and P'kaani had been with Darkmor in his chamber. They had all been sleeping on the huge bed. The girl had woken up, and stealthily opened one eye. Her companions had been sleeping soundly. She had waited for a few minutes to make sure that they were both really asleep, and then she had slipped naked out of the bed and padded over to the window.

She had looked out for a moment, and then had turned back to see if either of them had awakened. Both of them had still been asleep. Kalindra had tiptoed back to the bed, and looked down upon Darkmor. She had stared at the talisman where it lay upon his chest. He wore it all the time. She had never seen him take it off.

The girl had wondered how she could remove it without waking him. The sorcerer had then moved in his sleep, and she had started in alarm. But he had not woken. Looking closely, she had seen a small clasp at the back of the chain that the talisman was attached to. It had slipped around from the back of his neck when he moved. Taking a deep breath, she had leaned in and tried to open it. It had defied all of her attempts. She had moved back and sat on the edge of the bed. Kalindra had looked at the clasp and wished that she had something to help her open it.

Her gaze had gone to the side table. They had eaten and drank before Darkmor had taken them both. An empty plate and goblets along with a bottle had sat on the table, as had a small dagger that had been used to cut the meat. She had eased herself off the bed, and picked it up. She had gone back to the bed and stood over P'Kaani and Darkmor again.

Kalindra had raised the dagger. She could have killed him while he slept unawares. For a long moment, she had stood there, dagger poised above the sorcerer's heart. It would have been easy to plunge the dagger into him. Erathyn would be rid of him.

But instead, she had slowly reached out, and used the tip of the dagger to pry open the clasp. She had then removed the talisman, hoping that she would not wake him. When she had it safely in her hands, she had backed away from the bed. She had found her clothes on the floor, and picked them up, one eye on the sleeping forms. She had dressed hurriedly, and crossed the floor to the door.

Kalindra had opened the door quietly, and quickly stepped out into the corridor. She had closed the door softly. Then she had quickly ran to the kitchen. She had told the Goblin there that she was to take a meal to Princess Willowen. He had given her a tray with a plate of meat along with a bottle of wine and two goblets.

Now she was almost at the cell where the Princess was kept. She slowed to a walk, and then stopped to catch her breath and compose herself. After a moment, she went on, and coming around a corner in the corridor, she came to the cell. Two Schaaka stood guard there, which was usual. She went up to them.

The Goblins looked her over.

"Is it feeding time, pretty?" One of them said.

The other snickered.

"Yes. I am to take this to the Princess."

The Goblin who had spoken stepped closer to her. He reached out and stroked her red hair. Kalindra shuddered. His gazed roved over her body. He took her by the arm and leaned in closely. The girl tried to back away, but his grip was like a vice.

"Maybe we could come in with you?" He said suggestively. "Perhaps the Princess is lonely?"

Kalindra's green eyes flashed.

"The Master would not like that," she said coldly. "Shall I tell him his guards have mistreated us?"

"He wouldn't care. Give us a kiss." He leaned in towards her.

Kalindra pulled away, disgusted.

"Wait, Korpek," his companion said, "you'd better not. She's one of the Master's favourites."

"What? Are you sure?"

The Schaaka nodded.

"I've seen her with him."

Korpek looked at Kalindra. He knew what would happen to him if he were to mistreat one of Darkmor's women.

He released her. His lip curled in a snarl.

"Open it up," he said curtly.

The other Schaaka took out a ring of keys, and opened the door. Kalindra walked past both of them haughtily. The door slammed behind her. Her heart was pounding again after the confrontation with the Goblins.

Willowen was sitting on her pallet. She smiled as the girl crossed the floor.

"Kalindra, it is good to see you. I am famished."

They went and sat down at the table.

"I have more than food and wine, Your Highness."

She reached into her robe and brought out the talisman. She offered it to Willowen.

The Princess took it and held it in her hands. She stared at it in amazement, and then regarded the girl.

"You did it! Well done, Kalindra."

"Thank you, Your Highness. Now all we have to do is get out of this cell, and escape the tower."

"Is that all? Well, after succeeding in stealing this from the Dark One, I think that that should be easy by comparison."

The girl smiled.

Willowen took up the bottle and poured them both a drink. She gave a goblet to Kalindra.

"To success," Willowen said.

"Success," Kalindra replied.

They both drank.

Meanwhile Silveron and the others were trudging along the corridor. The wizard led, his staff emitting a soft light to show their way. They had been walking for hours, but it seemed like days. Suddenly they came upon an open space. Silveron entered the chamber and walked to its centre and paused, looking about himself. There were three huge open doorways set into the walls; one to his right, one straight in front of him, and another to his left. His companions stopped, glad for a rest.

"We came this way before," Toran-en said.

"Are you sure?" Egon said.

"Yes. We took the doorway on the right before."

"A maze this is," Brador grumbled. "Lost we are."

"I never thought I would hear a Dwarf say that," Egon said.

"Know these tunnels I do not," Brador replied. "Around and around we go. If in my own home we were, lost we would not be."

"How long have we been walking?" Yosh-en asked.

"It has been eight hours," Nomayon said.

"Eight hours!" Egon said. "Are you sure?"

"Nomayon is hungry. His belly tells him how long we have walked."

Silveron came over to them.

"We may as well call a halt and eat and drink. I am not sure which way to go. All of these chambers look the same."

"Toran-en says we have been this way before," Nildoron said.

"Is that right, Toran-en? Are you sure?"

The Felininn nodded.

"Yes." He pointed to the doorway on the right. "We went down that way."

"Then go down another one we should, eh, Silveron?" The Dwarf said.

"Perhaps. If we could mark the doorways somehow..."

"Nomayon knows how."

The group regarded him.

The Seer took a pouch from his pack. He opened it, removed something, and held it up for them to see.

"Here is chalk. Nomayon uses it for some spells. We could mark the doorway, and if we come back this way, we will know which doorway we have already tried."

"Excellent idea, Nomayon," Nildoron said. "Let us have some rest first."

"And food!" Brador said. "Nomayon is not the only one who hungers."

A murmur of assent greeted his words. They all went and sat along the wall. For a while they were all busy eating and drinking. When they had finished, they sat quietly for a few minutes.

Silveron rose to his feet.

"We should be going. Nomayon, bring your chalk."

The Elf walked over to the right hand doorway. Nomayon joined him as the others got to their feet and prepared to move. The Seer handed the chalk to Silveron, who drew a rune upon the rock wall. He handed the chalk back to Nomayon.

"There. Now we know we have been that way. Which way should we go now?"

Nomayon gestured to the middle doorway with his staff.

"Nomayon thinks we should try this way."

"Very well. Come, my friends." Nildoron handed him his pack. "Thank you, My Lord. Let us go."

They crossed the floor and entered the doorway.

Hours later they came into another chamber that was just like the one they had left. They walked into the space wearily; fatigue was weighing on them heavily. Brador crossed the floor to the right hand door. He cursed bitterly.

"What is it?" Egon said.

"Look!" Brador grated. "The same doorway it is. In circles we are going still!"

The companions walked over and joined him. He was right. On the wall was the rune that Silveron had drawn. They had gone in a large circle.

"This cannot be," Silveron said. "We went a different way. How could we end up in the same chamber, and arrive from the same direction as we did the first time?"

"Work of the Dark One, this is," the Dwarf said angrily.

"Nomayon agrees. A dark spell hides the way from us."

"How could he know we are here?" Egon said.

"The dead sentries would have been discovered by now," Nildoron said.

"Would he not send some Schaaka after us? Or maybe even O'skaa?" Yosh-en said. "He would not let us wander his stronghold unopposed."

"Perhaps that is exactly what he is doing," Silveron said.

"What do you mean?" Egon asked.

Silveron regarded them.

"If Darkmor knows we are here, and it seems that he does, it would suit his humour to have us stumble around these corridors until we died. If he has placed a spell on us, that would explain our wanderings. And the lack of pursuit tells me that this is so. Otherwise, it would be as Yosh-en said, we would either be prisoners or being hunted down."

"Tried the left hand door we have not," Brador said.

"Do you still want to try it?" Silveron said.

"Aye! Lie down and die, I will not. Nomayon, your chalk."

The Seer came and gave him the chalk. Brador walked back to the doorway from which they had entered, and scrawled a mark against the wall. He came back to them, and handed the chalk to Nomayon.

"As pretty as yours it is not, lad. But serve as a marker, it will." He walked over to the left hand doorway, and glanced at them over his shoulder. "Coming, are you?"

"I think we should sleep for a while," Nildoron said.

"I agree," Silveron said. "We are all exhausted."

"You've already marked the doorway," Egon said reasonably. "We know which way to go."

Brador returned to them.

"Mayhap you are right. Tired, I am."

"Then let us sleep then," Nildoron said. "We will all need our strength."

"Who will stand guard?" Egon said.

"I do not think we will need to," the wizard said.

"Yes," Toran-en agreed. "If the Dark One had sent anyone or anything after us, we would know by now. I think Yosh-en and Silveron are right; he is content to have us roam these tunnels until we die."

"Let us sleep, then," Silveron said.

"We should sleep in the middle of the chamber, just in case," Egon said.

"Good idea, Egon," the wizard said. He allowed the light of the staff to dim.

They went to the centre of the room and took off their packs. They lay down using them as pillows. It was neither hot nor cold, so they did not need their blankets. Silveron spoke a word, and the light from the staff went out. In a few moments, they were all sleeping like babes.


Several hours later, Silveron awoke. He sat up. Had he heard something? His companions were still asleep. He listened intently, but heard nothing. Was he mistaken? Had he heard a noise that had woke him up? He picked up his staff and rose to his feet, looking about himself. The four doorways yawned blackly. He spoke a Word of Power, and the light at the top of his staff kindled. The chamber was lit up by the soft light. Nothing was in there with them. But he could not shake the sensation that he had heard a sound. He walked towards the closest doorway.

Silveron shone the light down the corridor. It only went a short way, so he spoke again. The light brightened, and sent a beam down the corridor. It was empty. He stared down it for a few moments, and then turned and made his way to another of the doorways.

He repeated his actions, shining the light down the corridor. It too was empty. He frowned. Was he imagining things? *No,* he thought, *something definitely woke me up.*

He crossed the floor to the right hand doorway. He raised his staff, and let the light shine down the tunnel. Once again, it was empty. That only left the doorway that Brador had marked. It was the only one that they had not traversed. Or had they? Perhaps the spell made them lose all sense of direction. Maybe there was only the one chamber, and all the tunnels led to it.

A clicking sound came to him. He cautiously went over to the last doorway. The clicking stopped. He lifted his staff, preparing to send a bolt of force down the passage. But nothing met his gaze.

Suddenly, he heard whispering. It was made up of many voices. He listened closely, but he couldn't make out what the voices were saying. They just went on and on, echoing in the large space.

A sense of being watched stole upon him. It felt as if he were under the scrutiny of many eyes. He spun about, and sent the light beaming around the chamber. Could it be some device of Darkmor's? But it didn't seem like the sensation he had felt from the sorcerer.

It *did* feel like...

A feeling of dread came upon him. He had felt such a feeling before. It was the debilitating energy that surrounded the O'skaa. He turned about, casting the light everywhere. But none of the monstrous arachnids came into view.

The sensation grew and became stronger. How could this be? They would have to be close for him to sense, but none were there in the chamber. Was it his imagination? Perhaps he was still asleep, and only dreaming? *No,* he thought, *I am awake. This is real.*

The clicking sound came again. Something fell pattering to the floor behind him. He whirled, and saw some dust and small particles raining down from the ceiling. An awful foreboding suddenly filled him. He slowly looked up, and raised his staff.

A dozen O'skaa were on the ceiling. Their eyes glittered in the staff's light. Several of them bared their fangs at him.

He gaped at them for a few seconds, shocked to his very core.

The spiders dropped towards him.

Coming out of his shock, Silveron cried out a warning.

*"Wake up! O'skaa!"*

The arachnids screamed as they fell.

Silveron's companions scrambled to their feet and armed themselves. The spiders dropped to the floor, and rushed to attack.

The wizard sent a bolt of energy that consumed two of the monsters. Then he had to dodge the assault of another.

Nildoron took up his bow, and sent a shaft into one of the creature's brains. It shrieked and died. But its sisters came on. He dropped his bow and drew his sword.

M'shaan hurled his spear. It impaled one of them. It squealed and expired.

K'taal cast his spear, but the O'skaa he had targeted knocked it away with one of its forelegs. It rushed towards him. He drew his knife and raised his war axe. As it lunged at him, he spun and used his knife to slash off one of its legs. As the monster screamed in pain, he brought his war axe down between its eye cluster.

Egon was trying to draw his sword, but he was groggy and still half asleep. An O'skaa grabbed him, and sunk its fangs into him. It turned and ran, dragging the unfortunate Man towards one of the doorways.

"Egon!" Brador cried. He went to go to his aid, but was blocked by one of the O'skaa. He roared in frustration and brandished his war hammer.

The spider scuttled towards the doorway with its prey as the others fought. Egon hung limply in its jaws.

Suddenly, its way was blocked by Nomayon. He stood in the doorway with raised staff. The O'skaa reared up, and lashed out at him. The Seer dodged its attack, and began to chant. The monster struck at him again, but he leapt out of the way. He was still chanting as he evaded the murderous assaults. He struck the O'skaa with his staff, and it dropped Egon. The Man rolled across the floor, out of harm's way.

Nomayon cried out a single word, and the monster shrieked. It burst into flame, and danced about, screaming in agony. It became a living torch. Nomayon watched dispassionately as it burned and squealed in its death throes. Finally, it was dead. Smoke rose from the corpse and filled the chamber.

The Seer went to Egon's side and knelt down. He rummaged in his pack.

The others had managed to kill all the other spiders. They came over and stared at the incinerated O'skaa in amazement.

"By my Longfathers!" Brador exclaimed.

Nomayon had taken a stone from his pack. It was adorned with swirling symbols. He placed it on Egon's forehead, and began to chant.

"Check the doorways for more O'skaa," Nildoron said.

The others turned and headed towards them. Nildoron and Silveron stood over Nomayon as he chanted. They did not interrupt him.

Their companions returned.

"There is no sign or sound of any more spiders," Toran-en said.

"That does not mean that they are not there," Nildoron said.

"Right you are," Brador said. "Go we must. Dangerous to linger here, it is."

"We should have set a watch," Yosh-en said mournfully. "Now, Egon is dying."

The Seer rose to his feet.

"No. He lives, but is stricken with the spider's poison. Nomayon will do what he can for him."

"Will he survive?" Silveron asked.

"Nomayon does not know."

"We cannot stay here," Nildoron said. "More O'skaa are sure to come. Can he be moved?"

"Nomayon would not like to move him. But we must leave this place. Nomayon will move him."

He gestured to his silent warriors. They came to him and M'shaan took off his pack. He removed his blanket, and unrolled it and laid it out flat beside the prostrate Man. Then he and K'taal gently lifted Egon onto it. They took hold of either end of the blanket, and raised him up.

"Now we go," Nomayon said. "Does Silveron still want to try the last doorway?"

The wizard shook his head.

"No. I do not think any of the doorways lead out. I think the spell always leads us here because there is only this one chamber. I think we must search the corridor for a hidden exit."

"Easier to defend than this chamber," the Dwarf said.

"Good," Nildoron said. "Let us go. Lead on, Silveron."

The wizard regarded the doorways. He strode towards the one they had first traversed. The others followed him, weapons at the ready. M'shaan and K'taal walked in the middle of the group, carrying Egon in the improvised stretcher. The Seer walked beside him, looking down from time to time. The light from Silveron's staff lit their way. They entered the tunnel, and were gone.

An hour later, the wizard called a halt.

"This seems to be about the centre of the tunnels. I can sense the chamber ahead. If we went into it, we would just be repeating our meanderings. I think we should stay here. I feel that the hidden doorway is here somewhere."

The two Plainsmen lowered the unconscious Man to the floor. Nomayon knelt by his side. Egon's face was sweaty and pale. The Seer lifted one of his eyelids, and checked his eye. It was bloodshot. He lowered the eyelid, and felt Egon's neck for a pulse. It was there, but it was weak and thready. Nomayon took a small cloth bag from his pack and opened it. Inside it was a thick grey paste. He dipped his finger in it, and using the finger traced a design on Egon's forehead. It blazed out whitely for a moment, and then faded. He replaced the bag in his pack.

The others had moved to watch both ends of the tunnel. Silveron walked to and fro, searching with his thought. Could he sense where the doorway was? He was not sure. But to continue to roam the corridor and end up in the chamber was certain death. He *must* find the doorway, or they were finished. He placed his hand on the wall, and sent out feelers of thought. An image began to form in his mind. Was it an opening? Then, just as quickly as it had come to him, it was fading away.

"Can you sense anything?" Nildoron asked.

"No, My Lord. Darkmor's spell keeps breaking my concentration. I begin to see something, but then it is wiped away by his sorcery."

"Find the doorway you must, or we are done," Brador said.

Silveron stopped pacing.

"Have you sensed something?" Toran-en asked.

"No. But I have an idea. It is dangerous, but it could be the only way to find our way out."

"Tell us, Silveron," Nildoron said.

"I could release my Self, and explore the tunnels in spirit."

"Are you sure you could find the doorway that way?" Nildoron asked.

"I believe so. But I will be vulnerable. If the O'skaa come again..."

"Protect you, we will, lad." Brador hefted his war hammer. "No spider will touch you."

Silveron smiled.

"Then I will try."

He sat against the wall, and closed his eyes. He began to breathe deeply.

# CHAPTER XIII

# WILLOWEN AND SILVERON

Silveron sat back against the wall, and closed his eyes. He began to breathe deeply. The wizard focussed his attention within. He could sense his Self deep inside himself. Silveron relaxed all of his muscles, and let all of the tension in his body go. He could feel his body relaxing.

Good. That is what I want.

His Self gathered together like smoke. It rose from the top of his head, and looked out at his friends. They were gathered around him, and watched him intently. The Self rose, and looked about the tunnel. It could see a dim red light at the tunnel's end. It floated over to it.

The light was made up of thin lines. They formed the frame of a doorway.

*Good, that is the way out.*

The Self made to go back to its body. Suddenly, a voice it knew well came to it.

*Silveron...*

*Willowen! Where are you!*

*Come to me.*

The Self sent out feelers of thought. It could sense where Willowen was. It flew along the tunnel, and passed through a wall. It made its way through the solid rock, passing through it easily. The Self found itself in the main part of the tower. It kept going along the corridor, homing in on Willowen's presence. It came to the cell where she was imprisoned. With barely a glance at the two Schaaka on guard, the Self passed through the cell door.

Willowen stood in the middle of the cell, her eyes closed. The young woman that Silveron had sensed before sat on a chair to one side.

The Self manifested itself into the image of the wizard.

The girl let out a gasp and leapt to her feet. Her chair fell to the floor.

*"Your Highness!"*

The Princess's eyes snapped open. She stared at the apparition that was before her.

"Silveron!"

The Self bowed.

"Here to serve you. Have you been treated well?"

Willowen stepped forward, and made to embrace the image.

"You cannot touch me," it said, raising a hand. "I am merely a projection."

The Princess halted, confused.

"Silveron's body is in the tunnels above you," it said.

"I see," Willowen said. She smiled. "How powerful you have become."

The image smiled in return.

"We have learned a few things."

"Your Highness, is this a trick of the Dark One?" Kalindra asked. She had stood gaping at the figure in shock.

Willowen turned to her.

"It is all right, Kalindra. This is Silveron. He is on our side."

"I do not know," the girl said doubtfully. "I have seen how Darkmor tricks people. Are you sure?"

"I am certain."

"Perhaps I can convince you that I am not the Dark One?" The figure said.

"How can you do that?" Kalindra asked.

"I will tell the Princess something that only she and Silveron know. She can confirm that what I say is the truth. Will that convince you?"

The girl regarded the image dubiously.

"Maybe."

"Forgive me, Your Highness," it said. "When was the first time that you and Silveron became intimate? Was it not at Jhara Shin's home in the Underworld?"

Willowen blushed.

"Yes. That is correct. That is the truth, Kalindra. I am satisfied that this is not a work of Darkmor."

"Then I accept it also," the girl said.

"Silveron," Willowen said, "this is Kalindra. She has brought me the talisman." She reached inside her dress and brought it forth.

"Good work Kalindra," the image said. "Silveron sensed you going through the corridors with it. Is Darkmor aware that it has been taken?"

"I do not know," Kalindra said. "He and P'Kaani were sleeping when I took it. But that was some time ago."

"Silveron and his companions are above," the figure said. "They were trapped in a spell that created a maze that they could not escape from. But now the exit has been found. I came to see what your condition was. I am overjoyed to see you. Now we can escape the maze and come to you. Silveron can use the talisman, and banish Darkmor."

"Do you know how to do that?" Willowen asked.

The image shook its head.

"No. But Goldwen told Silveron that the spell would come to him when he needed it. The first thing to be done is for me to return and help my comrades escape the maze. Then we can make our way to you."

"What about the guards outside?" Kalindra asked.

"Silveron has fought and slain O'skaa in the tunnels above. Two Schaaka will not pose a threat to him. I will leave you now, but he will return with his friends shortly."

The image shimmered and began to turn transparent.

"Wait!" Willowen cried.

The figure became solid again.

"What is it?" it asked.

"My mother, Queen Nerolynn, is one of those who have been released from the spell that was on the two armies fighting in the valley centuries ago."

"I know this. Silveron and his companions watched the breaking of the spell. She and many others who were once allied with the forces of Light are now under Darkmor's command."

"Can they be freed?" The Princess asked.

"I do not know. Malkaar's sorcery was powerful. Now that he has taken an Elf's body, that power seems to have grown in strength. You have seen that he commands even the moon herself."

"I have heard Darkmor bragging of his powers," Kalindra said. "It is the Starstone that allowed him to do that. It has strange powers of its own, and is somehow alive, even though it has come down from the skies above."

"He would not have succeeded in unlocking those powers without my amulet," Willowen said. "Forgive me, Silveron. He took my knowledge and used it for his evil ends." She looked humiliated.

"It is not your fault, Willowen," the figure said.

"I should have died rather than give up that knowledge," she said sorrowfully. "How many have died because I gave him that which allowed his Goblins to come up from the Underworld?"

"There have been many who have died," the image replied. "But you must remember that because of your actions, Jhara Shin and his Goblins have also been able to come to the Overworld and assist us. Not all the consequences of your actions are evil."

"Thank you. You are very kind. How I long to see you in the flesh again."

"That will be soon. Silveron longs to be reunited with you also."

The sound of a key being inserted in the door came to them.

"Do not go," Willowen begged, as the image began to fade.

"I will remain, but you will not see me," it said.

It shimmered and vanished.

The door opened. Darkmor strode in, and behind him was P'Kaani. Three Cobrans were with her. One of them was carrying a staff and was dressed in the robes of a wizard. His ophidian eyes regarded the two women coldly. Kalindra shrank from his scrutiny. She had seen the Cobran wizard before, and he terrified her. She lowered her head and stared at the floor.

Darkmor bowed to Willowen. The door shut.

"Your Highness." He gazed around the cell. "Who were you speaking to?"

Willowen and Kalindra exchanged a glance.

"Why, Kalindra, of course."

He came over and stood in front of her with his hands on his hips.

"Don't take me for a fool. Who was it?"

"I tell you it was only Kalindra and I."

He reached out and grabbed her by the hair. He pulled her roughly towards himself, and dragged her backwards, until she tottered on unsteady feet staring up at him. Her back was arched painfully. She gripped his arms, which felt like iron under her fingers.

"Don't play games with me, Willowen," he said harshly.

"*It was Silveron!*" Kalindra blurted out. "Please don't hurt her!"

The sorcerer smiled, and threw Willowen sprawling on the pallet.

"There, you see, that's better. Your servant knows not to defy me." He turned and regarded the trembling girl.

Kalindra was beside herself with terror. She goggled at Darkmor, and sweat began to bead her face. She licked her lips nervously.

Darkmor crossed the cell floor to stand before her. He looked her up and down. He seemed to peer into her very soul. He put out his hand in the gesture of one who expected to receive something.

Kalindra swallowed.

"Give it to me," Darkmor said.

The frightened girl glanced swiftly over at Willowen. The Princess shook her head the tiniest amount.

"Give what to you, Master?" Kalindra asked.

"You know what I mean," the sorcerer said. "Give it to me."

"I –" Kalindra began. Her terror overwhelmed her, and she could not go on. She merely stared at Darkmor.

The sorcerer's eyes suddenly blazed with many coloured fire. The girl started in shock, but could not turn her gaze away. She stared fixedly at Darkmor.

*Where is it?* The sorcerer's Voice demanded. It seemed to penetrate her flesh like knives. The girl gasped as if she had been stabbed, but made no reply.

Darkmor reached out, and placed his hands on either side of her head. He stared into her eyes. The girl screamed.

*Where is it?* Came the Voice again.

Kalindra tried to shake her head in negation, but his grip was too tight. She screamed again, a piercing sound that filled the cell.

Willowen sat bolt upright.

"She knows nothing. Stop it!"

She ran over to stand at Darkmor's side.

"Stop it, I beg you!"

Darkmor slowly turned to regard her. She flinched as those fiery orbs stared into her eyes, but she held her ground. He smiled wickedly.

"As you wish," he said.

With a quick movement, he turned the girl's head to the right. A sharp snap like the sound of a branch breaking echoed in the cell. Kalindra dropped lifelessly to the stone floor.

"*No!*" Willowen cried. She dropped to her knees and cradled the girl's corpse.

"Pitiful," Darkmor said scornfully.

The Princess turned a tearstained face to him.

"Why did you do that?" She sobbed.

"She stole from me." He said reasonably. "I had to teach her a lesson."

He held out his hand, and Willowen stared at it for a moment. Then she realised that he meant to bring her to her feet. She took his hand, and he helped her rise.

"I'm afraid we still have a little puzzle to solve," Darkmor said.

"Puzzle?" Willowen echoed.

"I know Kalindra took the talisman from me," he said. "Surely she would bring it to you."

"I do not know what you are talking about," she said. "Kalindra had only brought my meal –"

"I grow tired of this, Willowen," interrupted Darkmor. "Give me the talisman."

"I swear to you that I do not have it."

Darkmor's eyes thinned into slits.

"Very well." He turned to the Cobran warriors. "Strip and search her."

"*You would not dare!*" Willowen cried. "I am the Princess Royal –"

The sorcerer spun and faced her. His gaze froze and silenced her on the spot.

The Cobrans came forward.

"Wait!" Willowen said. She undid the clasp at her neck that closed her robe. She stared at the others in the cell for a long moment, and then she let the robe fall. Under the robe she wore a light shift. She slipped the shoulder straps over her shoulders and let it fall to the floor. Now the only article of clothing she wore was a small loincloth.

Darkmor gestured, and she slipped it off. She stood there naked but for her light shoes. The sorcerer indicated that she turn, so she turned about slowly. She felt degraded by the scrutiny of those in the cell. She could feel their gaze upon her flesh. Willowen burned with shame. She faced them again.

Darkmor picked up her clothing. He inspected it minutely, searching for hidden places in the folds of cloth. Finally, he was satisfied with his inspection. He held the clothes out for her to take.

Wordlessly, the Princess dressed.

"It's not here," Darkmor said. "Kalindra must have hidden it somewhere."

"I told you I did not have it," Willowen said frostily.

"So you did."

Darkmor walked over to Kalindra's body. He addressed the Cobran warriors: "Search this one."

They crossed the floor and began to undress the corpse.

"She won't have any objection, will she?" Darkmor said. He smiled.

Willowen was disgusted. She looked away.

"Sshe doess not have it, Masster," one of the Cobrans said.

Willowen came over and took Kalindra's dress from his companion. She knelt, and covered the girl's body decently. She rose to her feet and regarded the sorcerer.

"What now?" she asked.

"The talisman must be found. Perhaps it's in this cell?"

Willowen paled.

"Ah. So it *is* here somewhere. Search the cell."

The two Cobrans began to search. Willowen stood like a statue. The sorcerer did not take his eyes off her for a moment.

One of the Cobrans searched through the blanket and then tossed the mattress off the pallet. Something fell to the floor with a metallic clink. The Cobran knelt and picked it up.

Beads of sweat stood out on the Princess's brow. Darkmor smiled to himself.

"Masster," the Cobran said. He came over and offered the talisman to Darkmor.

"Good work. I wonder how it came to be there?" He placed it inside his robe.

Willowen made no reply.

"Masster," The Cobran wizard said. "It iss almosst time."

"Ah. Forgive me. Your Highness, this is Essissnarr. He has come with his forces to meet Anarys."

Essissnarr bowed to her. He stood and his tongue flicked in and out as if he were tasting her scent. A look of revulsion wrote itself upon Willowen's face.

"A pleassure, Your Highnesss."

Bile rose in Willowen's throat. The Cobran sickened her.

"Well," Darkmor said. "I have what I came for. Come, Willowen."

"Where do you want me to go?"

"I have something to show you." He made to walk to the door. He stopped and turned. "But perhaps you wish to remain here with your servant? I'm afraid the conversation would be one-sided."

Willowen looked down at Kalindra's body. The poor girl had not deserved the death that Darkmor had dealt her. *She died for me*, Willowen thought. *I must not let it be for nothing. I must get the talisman from him.*

"Very well," she said. "I will come with you."

The sorcerer regarded her. He raised his hand and waved an admonishing finger.

"I know what you are thinking, my dear. Put it out of your mind. You won't take the talisman from me. Your hero will never possess it again."

He looked around the cell.

"Where is he? I know it was Silveron that you were speaking to."

The Princess made no reply.

Darkmor walked about the cell.

"Where are you, *brother*? Are you too afraid to show yourself? Have you finally realised that you've lost? The talisman is mine; nothing else that you possess can defeat me."

There was no answer. Willowen searched the cell despairingly. Silveron said that he would remain. Had he left her to Darkmor's mercy? *No,* she thought, *he would not do that. He would* never *do that.*

"You disappoint me, brother. I have Willowen too. Think of the many nights I'll enjoy her –"

The image of Silveron appeared in the middle of the cell.

"Ah. There you are, hero." Darkmor bowed mockingly.

"Release the Princess," the image said.

The sorcerer folded his arms.

"Or what?" He sneered. "You'll take her? Come and try."

The figure did not respond.

Darkmor unfolded his arms.

"You see, my dear? He's impotent. He can't help you."

Willowen stepped forward.

"Help me, Silveron," she begged. "Take me with you."

"I don't think you'd like to go where he is," Darkmor said.

"And why is that?" The figure said. "You do not even know where I am."

"Ah, but I do," the sorcerer replied. "I've watched your little band as it travelled through my lands. I saw you kill the guards and enter by the secret door. I watched as you entered the maze. I've enjoyed seeing you wander there aimlessly."

A look of surprise came to the image's face.

"Yes," Darkmor said with relish, "your little plan has failed. You'll never escape the maze."

"We will see," the image said.

"You'd better return to your comrades," Darkmor said. "I've sent wave after wave of O'skaa against them. They can't stop them all. It's only a matter of time before they're all killed and eaten."

He stepped up to stand beside Willowen.

"Aren't they supposed to be guarding your body while your Self is travelling?" Darkmor asked.

"You lie," the image said.

The sorcerer raised his hand and gestured at the wall. The serpent's eyes in the bracelet upon his wrist glowed. A point of light formed upon the wall. It expanded, to show Silveron's companions in a desperate struggle against the monstrous arachnids. They could see Silveron's body sitting against the wall. It was being shaken by Brador. The Dwarf was yelling and pounding the listless form with his meaty fists in a frantic attempt to wake the Elf.

"Off you go," Darkmor said. "Hurry, or you and your friends will be O'skaa meat."

He put his arm around Willowen. She flinched, but made no move to escape. Her attention was fixed upon the awful vision on the wall.

"Do not despair, Willowen," the image said. "Silveron will come back for you."

The figure vanished. It fled back the way it had come. It entered the tunnel through the doorway, and came upon a nightmare scene. The tunnel was filled with O'skaa. His friends held the monsters back at both ends of the corridor. They fought with desperation, knowing that if his Self did not return, they would all perish horribly at the jaws of the giant spiders. The creature's size meant that only one of them at a time could fit into the corridor to attack. This was the only reason that the companions had not been overwhelmed by the arachnid's numbers. Even so, they were tiring from the constant fierce assaults. The O'skaa could sense this, and attacked relentlessly.

The Self sped over to Silveron's body, and lowered itself into it.

Silveron woke with a gasp.

"Lad! Save us!" Brador cried. "Too many of them, there are."

The wizard rose to his feet, picking up his staff. He turned to his left, where Egon, M'shaan, K'taal and Nildoron were holding the spiders at bay.

*"Get down!"* He cried.

He raised his staff and sent a bolt of energy down the corridor, and the arachnids there disintegrated in its blazing light. He turned to his right, where Yosh-en, Toran-en, and Nomayon fought the beasts. They saw his intent, and dropped to the stone floor. He repeated his action. The spiders were incinerated by a tongue of flame that poured from his staff.

His friends rose to their feet. The tunnel was filled with superheated air, and smoke rolled along the roof. Not one O'skaa remained. His companions came over.

Brador slapped him on the back.

"Timely, that was, lad. Glad to have you back." He grinned.

A chorus of approval met his words.

There came the sound of clapping. They spun about, and standing there was Darkmor, applauding. Nildoron brought up his bow in a lightning swift movement, and loosed at the same time that M'shaan and K'taal cast their spears at the sorcerer. The shaft and spears passed through Darkmor, hit the stone wall, and clattered to the floor.

"That's a poor greeting," Darkmor said admonishingly.

"Stay your hands," Silveron said. "This is only a projection."

"Just so," Darkmor said. The image looked around the corridor. "I'm impressed. I didn't think your friends would survive so long without your protection."

"More surprises we would show you, if appeared in person you did," Brador growled. He hefted his war hammer.

"I don't think so, Master Dwarf. I've more important things to do."

"And what would they be?" Silveron asked.

"I have to oversee the destruction of the Army of Light. My forces now outnumber them greatly."

"This lie you have told before, sorcerer," said Brador. "Believe you we do not."

"Must you doubt everything?" The image said. "You were all eager to join Silveron in this foolish escapade. He gave you no certainty of its success. Why didn't you doubt him?"

"That is different," Nildoron said. "It is a matter of faith."

"Faith?" The image echoed.

"Yes, faith," Egon said. "We have faith in his powers, and we believe he will succeed."

"Then you are all fools," The figure said.

"Better to be fools than slaves," Yosh-en said.

"You followed Silveron here to meet your doom just based on your faith in him?"

"If that is what our fate is to be," Nildoron said.

"Where is Willowen?" Silveron asked.

An image appeared beside the sorcerer.

"She's here. At my side. Forever. You've lost, Silveron. How does it feel to be the one who allowed me to rule Erathyn? Tell me how it feels to realise that you're the one who failed in his task?"

"There is still time yet for me to accomplish that task."

The image shook its head.

"I'm afraid not. There are more O'skaa on the way. Many more than you can handle. Soon you'll be dead, and I'll destroy Anarys and his forces. With them gone, no-one can stand against me. My army will march all over Erathyn, and crush anyone foolish enough to try and stop us. A greater force has never been seen before in this world.

"So you keep telling us," the wizard said. "Where are these overwhelming numbers? I believe they only exist in your feverish brain."

The sorcerer gestured to the wall on his right. An image began to form there. It was the valley. It lay empty, but the vision moved. As they watched, they seemed to be soaring above the valley like a bird. They came to the top of the valley. The scene now before them was unbelievable. Thousands of O'skaa riders filled their view. In their centre was a huge O'skaa. It was many times the size of the others. Upon its back was seated a female Goblin. The view suddenly spun around, and they were shown the other side of the valley wall. Many more O'skaa riders waited there too.

Then it was if they swooped down to the valley floor. The vision moved swiftly until it reached the tower. It loomed above them for a moment, but then they passed it and saw what lay beyond it.

Queen Nerolynn sat her horse there with hundreds of her kin. With them were many Men; afoot or on horseback. Avianinn and Felininn were there also, standing and waiting. All of these were once on the side of Good, but now Darkmor was their master. It was true. His forces outnumbered those of King Anarys by a great margin.

The vision faded.

"Well?" The figure said.

"A trick it is," Brador said.

The image regarded them.

"Fools. Don't you believe your own eyes?"

"Nomayon knows that the Dark One is full of tricks. He does not believe your vision." The Seer's savage face was set like stone.

"Don't believe it then. Come, my dear. I'll show you my army myself. The O'skaa are coming. Can you hear them?"

A single shriek echoed in the corridor. It was followed by a chorus of screams. It was a fair distance away, but was rapidly coming closer.

"Goodbye, brother. I wish I could stay and watch, but as I said, I have things to do. I have enemies to destroy, and I have a world to conquer. Die well."

The O'skaa's screams became louder. Their skittering claws could now be heard on the stone as they hurried nearer. Suddenly, they were upon them. The companions turned to defend themselves.

"*No!*" Willowen's image screamed. "*Silveron!*"

It reached out, and tried to go to the wizard. Darkmor's image clutched it in its arms.

"Goodbye, brother." The figure laughed, and then they were gone.

The O'skaa rushed to the attack.

# CHAPTER XIV

# THE MASSACRE

Warlord Kitar-en rode his warbird at the head of his warriors. It had taken them many days to travel from their island home. He was looking forward to seeing the Army of Light. An experienced warrior himself, he lived for combat, and nothing pleased him more than to see a mass of warriors in action. He had fought in many battles, and had served his Empress with distinction. There was only one other Felininn warrior who was more esteemed in her empire than he was, and that was Warlord Yosh-en.

*Ah, Yosh-en,* he thought, *it will be good to see you again.*

He cast his mind back to several battles where he and Yosh-en had fought together. Their comradeship was closer than brotherhood. They had saved each other's lives many times over.

"My Lord?"

Kitar-en came out of his reverie. One of the advance scouts was before him. Kitar-en raised his hand, and the column came to a halt. He reined in his warbird.

"What is it?" he inquired.

"My Lord, the trail ahead passes through a thick forest. Captain Jodar-en does not like the look of it. He sent me back to report to you."

"Has he seen any sign of the enemy?"

"No, My Lord, but he feels that it is a perfect spot for an ambush."

Kitar-en looked ahead. He could see the trees in the distance. The woods there were indeed thick. Conceivably, thousands of the enemy could be hiding and waiting for them to advance. Five small figures were Captain Jodar-en and the rest of his scouts. They were waiting in the open for Kitar-en and his column. Just beyond them the trail continued on through the trees.

"I see," Kitar-en said. "What is your name?"

"Vosh-en, My Lord."

"Vosh-en, go and fetch Captain Jodar-en for me."

Vosh-en bowed in his saddle.

"At once, My Lord."

He turned his warbird and they raced off.

Kitar-en became aware of a presence at his side.

"Is there trouble, My Lord?"

The Warlord turned to the newcomer. It was Captain Tando-en, his Second.

"I do not know."

Tando-en looked at the forest ahead. He could see that the trail entered part of the forest.

"Hmmmm. Yes, that could be a dangerous spot. It was wise of Jodar-en to call a halt." He looked back along the column. "Do you want me to break up the column and form defences?"

Kitar-en shook his head.

"No. Let us speak to Jodar-en. See, here he comes now."

Vosh-en and Jodar-en were racing towards them. They came to a halt before the Warlord. They both bowed to him.

Jodar-en was a veteran of many battles. He had seen much more combat that even Kitar-en had seen. His pelt was starting to fade, and here and there were gray hairs. Several lines in his pelt told the tale of wounds that he had suffered and recovered from. In contrast Vosh-en was a completely different warrior; young, and probably inexperienced. His youth was evident in the rich colours that his pelt displayed.

"My Lord," Jodar-en said, "I report as ordered."

"So you are not happy about our route through the trees?" Kitar-en asked.

"No, My Lord."

"Have you seen any sign of the enemy?"

"No, My Lord. But that does not mean that he is not there."

"I agree, My Lord," Tando-en said. "This trail could be a trap. Can we not go around this forest?"

"No," Kitar-en replied. "We must meet King Anarys in one more day. We cannot afford to change our route. He plans to attack the Dark One's stronghold in two days. We must meet his army at the time that was agreed upon."

"Very well, My Lord," Tando-en said.

"Jodar-en, have you scouted any of the trail where it enters the forest?"

"No, My Lord. I felt I should report my misgivings to you first."

"You were right to do so. But now we must go that way. Any deviation would add more time to our journey than we can afford. We must take this trail."

Jodar-en regarded the Warlord. He made to speak, thought better of it, and then bowed.

"Then, My Lord, with your permission, Vosh-en and I will rejoin my scouts, and we will see what the trail ahead is like."

"Very good," Kitar-en replied.

The two scouts bowed to him, turned their mounts, and raced away to rejoin their companions.

Tando-en raised his hand. He waved it forwards, and the column began to move. Kitar-en and he urged their mounts on. They advanced towards the trees. In a few moments, they had reached the opening in the forest. The scouts had vanished ahead of them. They entered and followed the trail.

Two hours later they were still traversing the forest. The trees about them were densely packed together. If they were ambushed, it would be impossible for the warbirds to penetrate such thick woods.

There was silence all around them. Not a bird or insect was seen or heard. They continued on. The only sound was the musical accompaniment of their gear as they rode along. It was very warm. They and their mounts began to tire in the heat.

In the depths of the forest, unfriendly eyes watched them as they passed by. Thousands of Cobrans shadowed the column on either side of the trail, weapons in hand. They moved stealthily through the trees, soundless.

Tando-en and Kitar-en saw a scout heading back to the column. Tando-en raised his hand and the column came to a halt. As the scout came nearer, they could see that it was Vosh-en. The scout reined his mount in before them and bowed.

"What is it, Vosh-en?" Kitar-en said.

"My Lord, the trail ahead is blocked. Many large trees have been felled across it."

Kitar-en and his Second exchanged a glance.

"How far does this obstruction go?" Kitar-en asked. "Can it be cleared away?"

Vosh-en shook his head.

"No, My Lord, it cannot. Two of us went to see how far the trail had been blocked. It extends for a long way. It would take many days to clear it."

"I see."

"My Lord," Vosh-en said, "we have found another trail beside the blocked one. It seems to lead in the same direction."

"But," Kitar-en said, "I sense that there is something about this trail you do not like."

"Yes, My Lord. It is narrow, with only enough room to ride our warbirds in single file."

Tando-en looked back at the column. As per the usual Felininn riding order, it was arranged in ranks of four. He turned back and addressed Kitar-en.

"I would not advise breaking our ranks, My Lord."

"Captain Jodar-en was of the same mind, My Lord."

Kitar-en looked thoughtful.

"It would mean that the column would be stretched out over a great distance, My Lord," Tando-en said.

"Yes, I know. But what choice do we have? We must reach Anarys in one day. If we turn and retrace our steps, it will take us far too long to get to him. Vosh-en, is this other trail clear?"

"It appears to be, My Lord."

The Warlord thought for a moment. What could he do? There was no other way that they could reach Anarys in time. They must go this new way. But what if it led them in another direction? He stifled that thought.

"Tando-en."

"Yes, My Lord?"

"Go back and break the column into single file."

Tando-en regarded him for a moment. He looked as if he would say something, but then he just bowed.

"As you wish, My Lord."

He turned his warbird and went to relay the order that Kitar-en had given him.

*An order that he does not like or agree with,* Kitar-en thought. He knew his Second well. They had served together for many years.

In a few moments Tando-en rejoined them.

"It is done, My Lord," he said.

"Very good. Vosh-en, lead us to Captain Jodar-en."

"Yes, My Lord. Please follow me."

The three of them continued on. The warriors, now in single file, streamed after them. Shortly they came to where Captain Jodar-en and his scouts waited. Tando-en halted the column. Jodar-en rode up and bowed.

"My Lord, you can see how the trail ahead is blocked." He gestured at the felled trees.

Kitar-en and Tando-en looked at the mass of intertwined wood. It would be impossible to clear in the time that they had left to them.

"However," Jodar-en continued, "if you look here, there is another trail. It is narrower, but appears to be clear of obstructions."

They looked in the direction he indicated. There was another trail, but it looked as if it had not been used in a long time. The trees met at the top, giving the impression that it was a tunnel.

"Do you recommend we go this way?" Kitar-en asked.

"No, My Lord, I do not. But I know that we are in haste. It would seem that we have no other choice but to take this trail."

Kitar-en rode a bit closer to the trail. He could not see far into it, but there were no blockages. The way ahead seemed to be clear. He turned his mount.

"What does my Second say?"

"I am doubtful of this new way, My Lord."

"How so?" Kitar-en said.

"The main trail is blocked, and just by luck, we have found another way to go. Does that not strike you as strange?"

"What do you mean?'

"Could this not be a trap? Someone has barred our way, but has also given us another option. Could they not be driving us in the direction that they want us to go?"

"It is a possibility," Kitar-en replied. "But time is against us. What do you say, Captain?"

"I would advise caution, My Lord. Lord Tando-en could be right. This could be a trap. If it is, the narrowness of the trail would restrict our movements. There would be no room to manoeuvre and fight."

"We have seen no sign of the enemy," The Warlord said. "Perhaps they blocked the trail, and left the area. Maybe they did not know of the other trail."

"I think that is doubtful, My Lord. We found it easily enough."

The Warlord turned his mount to face the new trail. Was he doing the right thing? Were his Second and the Captain right? Was it indeed a trap? He knew they were waiting for his decision. He made up his mind.

"We will go along this new trail. Tando-en, give the order to move."

There was a moment of silence.

"Yes, My Lord," Tando-en finally said. He rode back to relay the order to the waiting warriors.

"Lead on, Captain," Kitar-en said.

Jodar-en made no reply, but he and Vosh-en bowed, and rode their mounts over to where the other scouts waited. They all entered the trail, and in a few moments, Kitar-en and Tando-en went after, followed by the long line of warriors. Soon they had disappeared from view.

An hour later the column was still traversing the trail. The trees above them shut out the reddish light from the occluded sun, but the heat had remained. It was not long before it became stifling. Both mount and rider suffered in the heat, tiring and sweating freely. Still they pressed on, not knowing how far the exit from the tunnel like passage would be.

The Cobrans had shadowed them unseen and unheard. Thousands of them moved silently through the trees on either side of the trail. The snake-men were used to the heat. It was just like the jungle that they came from, so they were not uncomfortable like the Felininn were.

The end of the column had entered the tunnel not long ago. It wound back to the head, spread over a large distance. Two Cobrans watched as it passed by. They had been given orders to sound a horn when the end of the Felininn force was deep in the forest. A large force of Cobran warriors had advanced to the tunnel mouth. When the horn was sounded, they were to attack the tail end of the column, and force them deeper into the forest.

Kitar-en rode on. He undid the strap on a water bag that hung on his saddle, and took up the bag. With one hand, he removed the stopper, and brought it to his parched lips. The liquid was cool and felt pleasant as he took a drink. He replaced the stopper, and hung it back on his saddle.

"Are you all right, My Lord?" Tando-en asked from behind him.

"Yes. It is just the heat. It would be good to stop and rest for a while."

"I would advise against doing that, My Lord," his Second said. "We must press on until we get out of these trees."

"I know. You may have been right."

"Right, My Lord? What do you mean?"

"We should not have entered this trail. We do not know how far it goes. What if it leads us astray?"

"We must hope that it does not, My Lord."

The Warlord made to reply.

The harsh sound of a Cobran horn rent the air. It was answered by a chorus of other horns. The warriors looked about themselves. It seemed like the forest was filled with the strident sound. Their mounts began to shy nervously. The column slowed and halted.

The Cobrans who watched from the shadows stopped too. They were led by a huge Cobran. He regarded the Felininn for a moment, and then he raised his curved sword and hissed. As he did so, all of the snake-men on his side of the forest followed his action. Then the Cobrans on the other side of the trail echoed them. The hissing drowned out the sound of the horns.

The warbirds were uneasy. They had not liked the close confines of the forest trail, and now the sound that the Cobrans were making was making them jittery. A finer mount could not be found upon Erathyn when it came to fighting on open ground, but the lack of room on the trail was upsetting them greatly.

The Cobrans at the end of the trail entered the tunnel, and ran towards the end of the column. They drew their swords and hissed. It seemed as if every Cobran in the world was there. They smashed into the rear of the column. The Felininn there had no chance. They could not move, because the trees hemmed them in. They died without having any opportunity to defend themselves. The snake-men advanced, slaughtering warriors and mounts alike. Desperation seized upon the Felininn. If they could not fight, they must retreat. They rushed to escape, trampling their companions in a desperate effort to get to the head of the column. The retreat became a rout.

At the same time, the snake-men on the sides of the trail loosed their bows. A hail of arrows sleeted into the halted column. Felininn warriors and warbirds went down, filled with the deadly shafts. Screams of pain and panicked cries echoed in the forest.

*"Fire back!"* Tando-en cried. *"Bows!"*

Some of the Felininn obeyed the order. They armed themselves with bows, and fitted arrows. They fired, but the Cobrans ducked behind the trees. All of the shafts missed their mark. None of the snake-men were slain, and the arrows passed harmlessly into the forest, or embedded themselves in trees.

As the Felininn were fitting new arrows, the Cobrans emerged from cover and rushed towards them. The Felininn dropped their bows and hurriedly ripped out their swords. Savage hand to hand fighting ensued.

The advantage that the cat-men would have enjoyed in open ground was lost to them. The Cobrans took a heavy toll on them as they struggled. Without the room to manoeuvre, the Felininn were being slaughtered.

The terrified warriors at the end of the column continued to trample their comrades. The only thing that mattered to them was to escape the carnage. They ran, and were shot down or cut down as the Cobrans caught up with them.

Kitar-en struck down one of the enemy, but another leapt upon his mount's back. The Cobran wrapped his scaly arm about the Warlord's neck. His fangs dripped with venom, and he leaned in to bite Kitar-en. The Warlord desperately tried to avoid his fangs.

The Cobran suddenly stiffened, and fell from the warbird. Kitar-en looked, and saw Tando-en. He had flung his dagger with deadly accuracy and slain the Cobran. Kitar-en raised his hand in thanks.

Another Cobran rushed at him. He made his mount sidestep, and as the snake-man stumbled, Kitar-en slashed his head off with one stroke. The Cobran's blood sprayed like a fountain into the air.

*"My Lord!"*

Kitar-en turned towards the shout. He saw Vosh-en waving frantically.

*"My Lord, the way ahead is open! Quickly!"*

The Warlord looked past the scout, and saw that Vosh-en was right. The trail ahead was empty of the enemy. He looked back at the struggling mass of Felininn and Cobrans. They must escape this deadly trap. He saw Tando-en.

*"Tando-en!"* he cried.

His Second heard him, and raced over to his side.

"Look, Tando-en. The trail is clear ahead. Sound the retreat."

Tando-en nodded, and took up the horn that was hung about his neck. He took a deep breath, and blew it. The horn's note echoed in the forest. Kitar-en's warrior's heard the horn and immediately attempted to fight their way free and retreat down the trail. As soon as they saw this, Kitar-en and Tando-en turned their mounts and plunged towards Vosh-en. Some of the Felininn broke free of the conflict, and followed in a rush.

The Warlord and his Second reached Vosh-en. The scout whipped his mount up, and all three of them raced through the gloom.

"There is a clearing ahead, My Lord," the scout said. "It is not far."

"Good," Kitar-en said. "We will see how the Cobrans fare when we have plenty of room to fight." He cast a glance over his shoulder, and saw his warriors coming on.

"My Lord, look," Tando-en said.

Kitar-en returned his attention forward. He could see the opening in the tunnel of trees. Captain Jodar-en and his scouts sat their mounts there. They urged their warbirds to a faster pace. In moments they had reached the opening. Jodar-en and his scouts moved aside, and they rushed out into the open. The scouts fell in with them.

"My Lord," Jodar-en said, "we must make a stand."

"You are right. Halt here. Our warriors are coming to join us." He reined in his mount, and the others did the same. They sat waiting, eyes on the opening.

In seconds the surviving Felininn reached the opening and poured out into the clearing.

"Tando-en, sound battle formation," Kitar-en said.

The Second raised his horn and blew the call for formation. The oncoming warriors fell into ranks, and formed up facing the opening.

"*First rank, bows!*" Tando-en cried.

The front rank of warriors armed themselves with bows. They nocked arrows and waited.

"*Second rank, spears!*" The Second cried.

Those warriors in the second rank who still had spears levelled them. The others just had their swords at the ready. Kitar-en rode behind the formation, counting them. There were only one hundred and fifty warriors left out of the force of two thousand that he had led. He returned to the centre of the formation.

"*Here we hold them!*" he cried.

"*Cho-dah!*" his warriors shouted. *We obey.*

The Cobrans exploded from the tunnel of trees, and hurtled towards them. There were thousands of them. They hissed as they came on, and displayed their fangs.

*Here we die,* Kitar-en thought.

The boiling mass of snake-men rushed across the grass, eager to come to grips with the remaining Felininn. With every second they closed on them. Tando-en measured the distance that still remained between them.

"Hold. Hold. Let them get closer."

The Cobrans raced towards them. Now their ophidian eyes could be seen.

"*Loose!*" Tando-en cried.

The bows sang, and their deadly shafts tore into the oncoming enemy. Many of them fell, but their comrades pressed on.

"*Second rank, charge!*" Tando-en bellowed.

The first rank sidestepped their warbirds, and the second rank spurred their mounts through the gap and charged the Cobrans. They met with a bone-jarring shock. Felininn spears found their mark, skewering snake-men all along the line. But not all were successful. Here and there a spear was struck aside and splintered. The Cobrans leapt in, and pulled down the warbirds to get to their riders. A wild melee ensued as the enemy's superior numbers overwhelmed the fallen cat-men. In moments all those Felininn who had charged had been slain. The Cobrans resumed their attack.

*"Bows! Fire at will!"* The Second cried.

Another volley of arrows ripped into the Cobrans doing their lethal work. But then the enemy was upon them, and bows were useless. Swords rose and fell, spraying blood and brains as the Felininn fought desperately for their lives.

Kitar-en found himself pressed by four of the snake-men. He hewed about himself feverishly in an attempt to block their sword strokes. A blade passed under his guard, and tore into his side. One of the Cobrans stabbed his mount. It shrieked and fell. The Warlord managed to roll free of its carcass. Now he faced his foes on foot, wounded and bleeding. He blocked another thrust, turned his opponent's blade, and sank his own sword into the Cobran's chest. As he fell, another of the snake-men slashed Kitar-en's arm. The Felininn cried out in pain, and only managed to duck a swing that would have taken his head off.

Suddenly there was a stunning blow to his head, and he dropped to the blood stained grass. He looked up, and saw a Cobran heaving his blade high.

The snake-man suddenly lost his head. His headless corpse tumbled down next to Kitar-en. Four mounted Felininn struck down the other Cobrans.

*"My Lord!"*

Jodar-en was there. He leapt down, and helped the Warlord to his feet. Kitar-en was groggy from the blow on the head. The scout helped him to mount.

"Go, My Lord! We are lost!"

Kitar-en shook his muddled head.

"No. I will not leave my warriors. Get word to King Anarys."

"I will not leave you, My Lord."

"I gave you an order. Obey me."

Jodar-en beckoned to one of the riders. He came to them. It was Vosh-en.

"Vosh-en," Jodar-en said, "we are done for. Go and find King Anarys and tell him how we died."

"Captain, I –"

"*Go!*"

The young scout looked at them for what seemed a long time. Then he bowed to them both, turned his mount and raced away from the battle. The sounds of conflict receded in his ears as he hastened away.

Kitar-en and Jodar-en watched him go.

"Good, Jodar-en," the Warlord said. "I like him. He does not deserve to die here." He stared at the pitiful remnants of his command as they continued to resist. "In time to come, they will speak of how my mistake cost all these warriors their lives. I will be regarded as a fool."

"No, My Lord," Jodar-en replied. "They will speak of how the enemy tricked you, and of how your loyal warriors fought bravely with you to the bitter end."

Kitar-en regarded him.

"Thank you, my friend."

Then there was no more time for words as a wave of Cobrans swept towards them.

Vosh-en rushed towards the trees, tears streaming down his matted and blood soaked fur. None of the blood was his. He had fought well, and had been lucky enough to not be injured in the fight. He wept for his comrades, and for his Warlord. He felt like a coward, running away from those who depended on him. He pulled on his warbird's reins, and brought it to a halt. He turned, and saw that the battle was nearly over. Only small groups of Felininn still fought in a futile effort to survive. He was suddenly filled with the desire to rejoin them.

He made to spur his mount, but then remembered Jodar-en's order.

He could not disobey him. His brain whirled. How could he leave them behind? Surely King Anarys would find out how they had perished?

He ripped his sword from its sheath. He would go and die with his comrades.

"Scout."

He whirled, and saw four Goblins standing there.

"We are friends," one of them said.

"We go to join King Anarys," another added.

He stared at them. Where had they come from? The meaning of their words penetrated his befuddled wits.

"Go and tell him that Lord Kitar-en and all of his warriors were ambushed and slain by the enemy. I go to join them. Farewell."

Vosh-en made to spur his mount. Two of the Goblins rushed in. One grabbed the reins, and the other grabbed the Felininn's boot and toppled him from his warbird. Vosh-en leapt up, sword at the ready. The warbird shied, but the Goblin holding its reins brought it under control.

'I will kill you all," the scout said fiercely.

"I think not," one of the Goblins said. They had not drawn their swords.

"Come with us," another said.

"No. Give me back my mount, and let me go to my comrades."

"They are all slain. Look for yourself."

Vosh-en looked back at the battlefield. The fighting had ended. The Cobrans were leaving the field, satisfied that they had annihilated their enemy.

Vosh-en was filled with remorse. He dropped his sword, and stared through tear-filled eyes. He fell to his knees and sobbed. Everything went away. The only thing that existed was the deep sorrow for his comrades. His heart ached for the loss.

An arm was laid about his shoulders. He started in shock. One of the

Goblins had come to console him. He turned a tear-stained face to him.

"It is all right. Come with us. We will look after you."

"But my comrades, they –"

"You cannot do anything for them. Come with us."

The Goblin helped him rise to his feet. Another of them picked up his sword, and offered it to him. Vosh-en accepted it, and re-sheathed it.

"My chokhutai will take care of you," said the Goblin who had comforted him. "What is your name?"

"I am called Vosh-en."

"I am Ando Chun. Two of you, take him to King Sirlyk."

Two of the Goblins came forward, and bowed.

"As you command, Lord Chun," they chorused.

"Lord Chun?" Vosh-en said. He bowed to the Goblin, embarrassed. "I apologise, My Lord. I thought you were only a scout, like me."

Chun grinned.

"But I am a scout. I am not offended. Go with them. My companion and I will quickly inspect the battlefield."

"Let me come with you."

"No. I think you have had enough heartache today."

"But some of my friends could still be alive. Maybe Lord Kitar-en still lives too."

Chun shook his head.

"I do not think so. The Cobrans are without mercy. They slay all they meet in combat."

"Then why do you go and look?'

"I go because the King ordered me to."

He put his hand on Vosh-en's shoulder.

"Was this your first battle?"

"Yes, My Lord. I should have stayed and died with my comrades."

"Why did you leave the field? Were you frightened and ran?"

"No, My Lord, I wanted to stay and fight, but Captain Jodar-en ordered me to go and find King Anarys."

"Then you obeyed his order. You should not be ashamed. Go with my chokhutai. I will follow shortly."

Vosh-en bowed to him.

"Very well, My Lord."

He went over to his warbird. The Goblin holding the reins gave them to him. He mounted up.

"This way," one of the Goblins said.

They led off, going towards the tree line. The scout urged his mount forward and followed them. Vosh-en looked back and saw Chun and his companion set off towards the battlefield. He returned his attention to the Goblins ahead of him.

In a few moments they had reached the trees. They entered by a small path. It was well worn, and had obviously been there for many years. They continued on, until they came into a large open area. Before them was a camp. The two scouts led Vosh-en through a line of sentries who guarded the perimeter. They led him on until they came to a Goblin who was sitting on a camp chair. He was armoured much like all the other warriors were, but Vosh-en knew that he must be the Goblin King.

The Goblin scouts bowed to him. Vosh-en dismounted and did the same.

"Your Majesty," one of the Goblins said, "this is Vosh-en, of the Felininn people."

"I greet you," Sirlyk said. "I wish we had met under better circumstances."

"Thank you, Your Majesty. Your scouts have been very kind to me."

"You are welcome. Where is Lord Chun?"

"He went to inspect the battlefield, as you ordered, Sire," one of the Goblins answered.

"When he returns, we will set off immediately."

"As you command, Sire," the Goblins chorused.

"Are you hungry or thirsty?" Sirlyk said.

Vosh-en was suddenly aware that he was famished and his throat felt as dry as dust.

"Yes, Your Majesty."

"Go and fetch him food and drink," the King said. "Water his mount."

"As you command, Sire," the Goblins answered. They bowed to him.

One of them took the reins from Vosh-en. He led the warbird away as his companion left to find food and drink.

Sirlyk indicated another chair that was set up by his side.

"Now, Vosh-en, come and tell me of the battle."

The scout came and sat down. He gathered his thoughts. *What should I tell him?* He wondered. *Should I tell him that My Lord made a mistake?* He measured his feelings for a moment. *No,* he decided, *I will not sully My Lord's memory.*

"It was not much of a battle, Sire," he said. "The Cobrans ambushed us on the forest trail where our warbirds were disadvantaged. There was no room for us to manoeuvre. They attacked us from the forest, and forced the end of our column along the trail. Men and mounts were trampled in the rout. When we finally emerged into the clearing, many warriors had been slain."

"A sad tale, Vosh-en," Sirlyk said. "If only we had met up with you before the battle, we could have escorted you through the Underworld tunnels that we have been using. We have not met the enemy."

The Goblin who had gone to get food returned with a plate and mug. He gave them to Vosh-en. It was good meat and bread, and the mug was filled with cool water.

"Eat and drink," The King said. "I do not stand on ceremony."

The scout fell to with a will. Until Sirlyk had asked him, he hadn't realised how hungry he was. He finished the food in a short time, and took a drink. The water was soothing and cool and satisfied his thirst. He gave the plate and mug back to the Goblin, who had been standing by waiting for him to finish his repast. He bowed to the Goblin King, and departed.

"Thank you, Your Majesty. That was excellent."

Sirlyk smiled.

"Even the simplest of food and drink seems so to one who is hungry and thirsty. Ah, here comes Lord Chun."

Chun and his companion came up to them and bowed.

"What do you have to report, Chun?"

"Sire, we went to the battlefield as you ordered. All of the Felininn have been slain. We entered the trail, and went along it for a fair distance. It was littered with many bodies; Felininn, warbird, and Cobran alike."

"Did you follow it to the end?"

"No, Your Majesty. There was a group of Cobrans about half-way along the trail. We did not let them detect us. We returned to the camp."

"Captain Jodar-en estimated the trail to be about ten miles," Vosh-en said.

"I would say that the entire trail was filled with corpses," Chun said.

"Did you find Lord Kitar-en?" Vosh-en asked.

"Yes. His body was amongst the slain. There were many dead Cobrans around him. It appears he fought courageously. I am sorry, Vosh-en."

"He was a great leader and commander of warriors," Vosh-en said.

"We will honour him and his warriors when we reach King

Anarys," Sirlyk said. "Lord Chun, take Vosh-en with you. He can join your group. Help him to clean himself up."

"Yes, Sire."

Vosh-en rose to his feet.

"I am honoured to accept your hospitality, Your Majesty." Vosh-en bowed.

"Tell Lord Shen we are breaking camp immediately."

"Yes, Sire," Chun replied.

He and Vosh-en bowed and departed.

"We will wipe that blood from your fur," Chun said.

"Thank you, My Lord."

They went in search of Chun's group.

# CHAPTER XV

# THE TOWER

The O'skaa closed in, shrieking. Their screams echoed in the enclosed tunnel. The companions stood fast, ready for the onslaught. But in each of their minds the uppermost thought was of the end. It was impossible to defeat so many of the giant arachnids.

*Defeat?* Silveron thought. *No, we do not have to* defeat *them.* Suddenly, he knew what he had to do.

"My friends, gather closely around me. Take hold of my belt. Quickly!"

His comrades obeyed, coming in close. They each took hold of the wizard's belt. He raised his staff high.

The O'skaa closed in, fangs a-drip with venom. Their prey disappeared beneath them as the spiders rushed in to rip and tear them to shreds. For a moment, nothing was to be seen but the pallid whiteness of the arachnids. Those at the back were screaming and scrabbling to get close enough to taste the flesh of their quarry.

A deep boom that was more felt than heard reverberated in the corridor. The O'skaa who covered the wizard and his companions were flung away as a bright sphere suddenly appeared and pushed outwards rapidly. As it contacted the spiders, they squealed and were incinerated on the spot. The sphere of death expanded rapidly in the tunnel. The

O'skaa turned to flee, but it caught them and turned them to ash. The sphere grew larger, expanding and forcing the spiders to retreat. It grew until it blocked off both ends of the corridor.

Standing in the centre of the sphere were Silveron and his companions. They looked about, amazed at the sudden destruction and retreat of the arachnids. The monsters were amassed at either end of the tunnel where the sphere kept them at bay. They did not dare advance into its destructive area, but they hissed at the companions.

"You can release my belt now," Silveron said.

They all let go of his belt and stepped back.

"A good trick, lad," Brador said.

"I thought we were done for," Egon said.

"I thought you were dead," Silveron replied.

"No. Nomayon healed me. I feel a bit sick, but I can fight."

"Nomayon thought the herbs that combat snake bite would help," The Seer said.

"And so they did,' Nildoron said. "What now, Silveron? Do you know how to escape this maze?"

The wizard nodded.

"I do. Look at the wall to your right. Can you see some thin lines in the rock?"

The Elf-Lord peered at the wall.

"Yes. I can see them."

"Good. That is a hidden door. It is easy to operate. You just push it inwards. The mechanism will do the rest."

"What are we waiting for then?" Yosh-en said. "Let us get out of here."

"Wait a moment," Silveron said. "I can only keep this shield up for a short time. We must open the door, and then you all should go through it. I will keep the shield active to keep the O'skaa away. Then you must cover me as I drop the shield and join you. The door must be closed quickly to keep the spiders out."

"Then let us be about it," Toran-en said.

Nildoron went over to the hidden door. He pushed on the middle of it, and it swung inwards and upwards. The corridor outside came into view. He cautiously went and looked out, and then ducked back into the tunnel.

"The corridor is empty. Let us go."

He stepped through the doorway. The others came over and followed him. When they had all gone through, he and Egon appeared in the doorway, armed with bows.

"Come, Silveron," Nildoron said.

The wizard started towards the door. The shield began to shrink. The O'skaa screamed and advanced as the shield diminished in size. Suddenly it vanished completely, and the spiders shrieked and rushed to attack. Silveron leapt through the doorway, as Egon and Nildoron loosed their arrows at the oncoming arachnids. They jumped back just in time as Brador pushed the door back into place. A high pitched shriek was cut off as the door closed. One of the O'skaa had had one of its forelegs pinched off, and it lay on the floor twitching. The muted sound of the spiders scratching and clawing against the rock came through the wall. Their screams were dulled, but could still be heard.

"Can they push the door in?" Egon said. He was backing away from it nervously.

"No," Brador replied. "Found a lock, I did."

The Man looked relieved.

"Good. I think I've had enough of those things."

The Dwarf slapped him on the back.

"Agree with you, I do, lad. Nasty creatures they are."

"Which way do we go now, Silveron?" Nildoron asked.

The wizard was standing there listening. He looked up and down the corridor.

"I am not sure. Willowen was down that way, but Darkmor has taken her."

"What of the talisman?" Nildoron asked. "Do you know where it is?"

"Yes. Darkmor has it."

"What happened to the girl that you saw in your vision?" Nildoron said. "Didn't she steal it from him?"

"Yes, she did," Silveron said. "But Darkmor found her with Willowen, and slew her. Willowen had hidden it, but he found it and took it back."

"Then we have failed," Egon said glumly.

"Not yet," Silveron said. "I see his thoughts. He is showing Willowen his forces in an attempt to impress her. He will unleash them upon our army. But I sense that he grows weak. The sorcery that he used to hold the moon in place greatly sapped his strength. He intends to go down to the cavern where the Starstone is, and obtain more power from it."

"Can he do that?" Nildoron asked. "I thought he needed Princess Willowen's help in achieving that goal."

"He did. But now he has her amulet, and knows how to use it. He now has the knowledge of a Shaper of Stone."

"Then go down to the cavern we must, and take them both from him."

"You are right, Brador. I can sense the Starstone. It is somehow alive, and its thoughts are strong. We can follow them and ambush Darkmor, take the talisman, and save Princess Willowen."

He began to walk down the corridor. The others followed. They had their weapons ready, and moved as quietly as they could.

An hour passed without them meeting a single soul. The corridor was dim, but every now and then cressets were set burning upon the walls. Silveron did not dare to use the light of his staff, but luckily the light from the torches was enough for them to find their way.

The wizard came to a door at the end of the corridor. He raised his hand, and the group came to a stop. Nildoron came up to him.

"What is it? Is that the way to the cavern?"

"I am not sure. But I do know it leads to the lower levels. I know the Starstone is far beneath us."

"Then go that way, we must," Brador said.

"Is it locked?" Egon asked.

Silveron tried the door. It opened easily. He cautiously opened it up wide, and looked through. The corridor on the other side was empty. He motioned for the others to follow him, and then stepped through the doorway. The companions followed. Nomayon, who was the last in line, closed it softly behind them.

The corridor had a damp smell about it. It was darker than the other corridor that they had just traversed. The cressets were fewer, so the light was a bit dimmer. They continued on cautiously, watching their footing. After a while, their eyes adjusted to the dark, and they walked with more confidence.

"No guards," the Dwarf said. "Strange, eh?"

"Perhaps Darkmor thinks his stronghold is impregnable, and doesn't bother with them," Egon said.

"I doubt that very much," Nildoron said. "I think the truth is he has emptied his tower of guards so that they may join the forces that are ranged against our army."

"I would agree," Silveron said. "He wants to crush any opposition."

"Make sure he fails in that ambition, we must," Brador said.

"Indeed," Nildoron said. "If he succeeds, all of Erathyn is lost."

"*Quiet!*" Silveron suddenly whispered. "*I hear something ahead.*"

They advanced silently. Soon they could all hear talking. They listened intently. It seemed to be two people; Goblins, by the harsh sound of their voices. They were coming in their direction.

The companions stopped. They had to hide. But where could they go to? The corridor was empty of doors.

The voices became louder, and now they could hear the sound of footsteps upon the rocky floor.

"*Slay them, we must,*" Brador said softly. He raised his war hammer.

"*No,*" Silveron whispered. "*It is too risky.*"

"*If they raise the alarm...*" Nildoron said quietly.

"*All of you, get back against the wall, and make no sound!*" The wizard husked.

They all did as he asked. Silveron was whispering a spell. The companions looked down the corridor. The sounds were getting louder. Suddenly two Schaaka appeared. They were arguing. They came closer, until they were almost on top of them.

"I tell you, Karaak, it's the big one, this time."

"No, it's not, Grelk. The Bright One's army is nowhere near us."

"Ha! That's what you think. Tercha told me –"

"Tercha! *That* fool! What does he know?"

"More than you do. He's a Leader –"

"*A Leader?* Haha! He couldn't lead his finger up his..."

They both stopped.

"What is it, Grelk?" Karaak asked.

"I don't know. Something smells funny." He drew his curved sword. His comrade did the same. Both of them sniffed the air.

They were standing right next to Silveron.

"Smells Elfish, don't it?" Grelk said.

"Yeah. You're right. Could a prisoner have escaped?"

"Impossible."

They advanced, sniffing. The companions were standing to either side of them. The Goblins looked about themselves, but appeared not to see them. They came closer, until they were almost standing on the invisible group who were spread against the wall.

They were so close that Egon could reach out and touch them. He thought that they would be discovered at any moment. Could the Goblins hear him breathing? He held his breath.

"I thought I could hear something," Grelk said.

His comrade cocked his head to one side, listening.

"What? I can't hear anything," Karaak retorted.

"It sounded like breathing."

"Breathing? Ha! You've been down here too long, Grelk."

Grelk snarled, but made no reply. He stepped closer to the wall.

Egon was about to stab him, but Brador closed his meaty fist about his sword arm. As the Man regarded him, the Dwarf shook his head. Egon lowered his blade.

Suddenly, Grelk snapped his fingers.

"Ha! I've got it. It must be that fancy Elf bitch the Master took upstairs." He snuffed in a lungful of air.

"Smells nice, don't she?" Karaak said. He grinned.

"Ha ha! I wonder how she *tastes*?" Grelk replied.

They both laughed uproariously.

They sheathed their swords, and continued on.

"I'd like to show her some things," Karaak said.

"Get in line," Grelk replied.

Their laughter continued, and faded as they went down the corridor.

Silveron listened until their voices disappeared into the distance. When he could no longer hear them, he stepped away from the wall, and spoke a Word of Power. The others gathered around.

"Another fine trick, lad," Brador said.

"Thank you," Silveron said. "But the Spell of Invisibility is taxing. I cannot do it for very long."

"Then we must find somewhere to hide while we wait for Darkmor," Nildoron said.

"Let us go on down to the lower levels," Silveron said. "We should be able to find a storeroom or something down there that will suffice."

"Can you sense the Starstone?" Nildoron asked.

The wizard stood and listened for a moment. The Starstone's metallic thoughts came to him. They were stronger than before.

"Yes. They are increasing in strength. This way."

He went down the corridor, and the companions followed on.

Not long after they came to another door. Silveron tried it. It was unlocked, like the other had been. He opened it cautiously, looked in, and then waved his friends on. He stepped through, and they all followed. Nomayon closed it behind them as before.

In front of them were some stairs that led downwards. Silveron looked up, and saw them spiralling up away into the distance far above. He went over to them, and looked down. The stairs led down into the darkness.

"This is the way," he said.

"Are you certain?" Nildoron said.

"Yes. The Starstone's thoughts are stronger. They come from below. This is the way to go."

He went over to the stairs and began to descend. The others came and followed suit. They went down and down, as silently as they had crossed the corridors. After what seemed a long time, they came to the end of the stairs. It was hot, and the air was close and humid. Condensation dripped from the walls. A corridor led away from the stairs.

Silveron advanced along the corridor. There were several doors set into the walls. He passed them by. They walked along the corridor, eyes and ears open.

The wizard suddenly held up his hand. The companions halted. Nildoron came to his side.

"What is it?" he asked.

"There are two guards ahead and below us. I can sense them. They guard a large door. It must lead to the chamber where the Starstone is kept."

He sent his thought probing ahead. The door was locked and bound by a spell. He sent his thought further, and saw an image of the Starstone in his mind.

"I was right. The Starstone is in a chamber in a level that lies below us. It is locked and bound with a spell." He looked back the way they had come. "We must hide in one of these rooms."

He and Nildoron turned and came back to the companions.

"Here is where we wait and hide," he said. "Let me find an empty room for us."

He went back along the corridor, sending his thought into the rooms. One of them was a storeroom filled with barrels. He stopped at the door. It was locked, but no spell was on it.

"This is good. I will try to open it."

"Let me," Egon said.

He came forward, and took a pouch from his belt. It had a set of lock picks in it. He inserted two of them into the lock, and began to manipulate it. He listened closely as the mechanism was engaged. A final turn and the door opened.

"Good work, lad," Brador said.

"I used to steal cheese from the King's larder." He grinned. He put the lock pick back into the pouch, and hung it at his belt.

The Dwarf slapped him on the back.

"Full of surprises you are."

"Let us go in and make ourselves comfortable while we wait for Darkmor," Silveron said.

He went into the room, and the others filed in after him. The door closed, and the corridor was empty and silent again.

Meanwhile, far above them, Darkmor stood on the top of the tower, looking out at the valley. Willowen stood at his side, and P'kaani, Essissnaar, Essaarkun, and the two Cobran guards stood behind her.

"See here, Willowen, the place where Anarys and his army will be destroyed."

The sorcerer spread his arms wide to indicate the valley below them.

"I cannot see these overwhelming forces that you speak of," she said.

He turned.

"They are there," he said, smiling.

She folded her arms.

"I do not believe you."

"No?"

"No."

"Must I show you?"

"Thiss wench iss tessting you, Masster," Essaarkun said.

"She wants to see proof of my words," Darkmor said reasonably. "Very well, then."

He made a gesture, and an image swam before them in the air. It showed the top of the valley to their right. Thousands of O'skaa and their riders were gathered there, and in their midst was a huge O'skaa, much larger than the others. Upon its back sat a Goblin woman. She was armoured and crowned.

"That is Sardia, the Queen of the Schaaka," Darkmor said.

He moved his hand, and the image changed to display the valley to their left. There were many O'skaa and riders there also. They were led by a huge Goblin with one eye.

"He is Kerlach," Darkmor said. "Both of them have thousands of O'skaa riders with them."

Willowen looked unimpressed.

"There is also a large force of Essaarkun's Cobrans behind Anarys and his army. They dealt with some reinforcements the other day. And behind the tower –"

The Princess yawned, feigning disinterest.

Darkmor regarded her.

"This doesn't impress you?" he asked.

"No. You are like a little child showing off his toys."

"There are many more warriors than Anarys and his pitiful little force can handle," he retorted.

Knowing that she had hit a nerve, Willowen smiled to herself.

"Are you so afraid, then?" she asked.

"Afraid?" he echoed. "What do you mean?"

"You must be afraid if you need such overwhelming numbers to support you."

The sorcerer's lip curled.

"I fear nothing. I only wish to make sure that Anarys and his army are totally destroyed."

"But you can move the moon to block the sunlight. Can you not deal with a mere army without assistance?"

"Sstay your tongue, female," Essissnaar hissed.

Darkmor had made no reply. All there upon the tower's top could sense the anger that burned within him. He made to step closer to Willowen, but then stopped.

"I forget to show you something," he said. Looking her in the eye, he raised his right hand, and snapped his fingers.

A vortex appeared in their midst. A dim figure could be seen within its swirling energies. The sorcerer beckoned, and the figure stepped from the vortex onto the tower top.

It was Nerolynn. Willowen gasped and rushed over to her. She stared into eyes that were dull and white. The Queen stood like a statue.

Willowen spun on her heel.

"Release her!" she cried.

"Aren't you happy to see your mother alive?" Darkmor said.

The Princess stormed up to him.

"She is *not* alive. You have brought her back from the dead, and put her under a spell."

"You're both right, and wrong. She *is* alive. She has been alive ever since I cast the Spell of Stasis centuries ago. But she *is* under my control."

"You lie," Willowen said coldly.

Darkmor waved his hand. The colour returned to Nerolynn's eyes, and she looked around herself dazedly.

"What? Where –" She was plainly confused.

"*Mother!*" Willowen cried. She ran and wrapped her arms around her.

"Willowen? What is this?"

She held Willowen out at arm's length, and stared at her dumbstruck.

"How can you be here? I do not understand. I was leading the charge –" She stopped speaking as she realised where she was.

"This is Malkaar's tower. What has happened?" Nerolynn saw Darkmor. "Who are you?"

The sorcerer bowed.

"Allow me to introduce myself. I *was* Malkaar, but now I have an immortal Elf body. I am Darkmor."

Nerolynn pushed Willowen away from her, and drew her sword. The two Cobrans drew their blades, and Essissnaar raised his staff. Darkmor held up his hand, and they lowered their weapons.

"Then you are the enemy," Nerolynn said. "I will kill you."

"There's no need for that," Darkmor said reasonably. "You can join me."

"I would rather die."

"Is that any way to show gratitude to one who has kept you alive for a thousand years?"

"What do you mean?"

"Look out upon the valley. Centuries ago, when my army was about to be defeated, I cast a spell that froze everyone in time. You were among them."

"How can you be here now then?" Nerolynn asked. "You were only a mortal Man. You should have died many years ago."

He smiled.

"I was mortal then. Shaarla cast the Ice of Foreverness, and I was imprisoned in my own tower. I was trapped in the ice for centuries."

"How did you escape then?"

He spread his hands.

"I don't know. But here we are."

"And here you die," Nerolynn stepped forward, and raised her sword high.

Darkmor raised his hand, and she stopped abruptly, as though she had walked into a solid wall. Nerolynn tried to force her way forward, but try as she might, she could not move. The sorcerer made another gesture, and the Queen lowered and returned her sword to its sheath. She stopped struggling, and stood still. But her eyes were filled with hatred.

"That's enough of that," Darkmor said. "You see, Willowen? Your mother *is* alive. But now she is my servant."

Nerolynn fixed him with a freezing gaze.

"You don't like that, do you, Your Majesty?" He laughed.

He walked over to stand before her. The Queen glared at him in impotent fury.

"You'd love to chop me up with that sword of yours, wouldn't you? But

I'm afraid you won't have that opportunity. What you are going to do is command your warriors to charge and engage Anarys's forces."

Nerolynn gritted her teeth and tried to move. She shuddered with the effort, but was still rooted to the spot. She gaped like a fish out of water, as if she was trying to speak.

"You *are* strong," Darkmor said. "But not strong enough. You can't break free."

The Queen's gaze went to Willowen. The Princess came a step closer, but halted. The sorcerer regarded them both. Nerolynn still struggled to speak, but no matter how hard she tried, she couldn't make a sound. Darkmor raised his hand and Nerolynn gasped.

Realising that he had allowed her to talk, Nerolynn turned to him.

"Let my daughter go. She has no part in this."

"Oh, but she has. She helped me with the Starstone."

"I do not understand. What is the Starstone?"

"You don't have to understand. Besides, I recently lost one of my companions, and only have P'Kaani there to attend me. She and Willowen will serve me."

"She is not a slave," Nerolynn said icily.

"She is now." He turned and walked over to look out upon the valley. "I'm disappointed in you, Nerolynn. I thought you would see the logic in joining me. There are none who can oppose me."

"Silveron can," Willowen said.

Darkmor slowly turned and regarded her.

"The O'skaa feasted upon him and his friends. You saw that yourself."

"I saw them surrounded by the spiders. I did not see them slain and eaten. He still lives. I can sense it."

The sorcerer came and stood before her.

"Are you sure?"

"I am certain of it. Can you not feel it?"

"No."

"Then your senses are dulled. I know he lives, and as long as he lives, he will never cease in his attempts to destroy you."

"Enough of this. Say farewell to your mother. She goes now to command the warriors who will slay your father. I wonder, Nerolynn, if the sight of you will stay his hand? Will he stand there stunned to see you, and be struck down? Even perhaps by your own blade?"

The Queen cried out in rage, and tried to move. But as before, her struggles were pointless. There was no way that she could break the hold that Darkmor's spell had over her.

"I wish I could let you go into battle with all of your faculties," Darkmor said, "but it wouldn't serve my purpose. But I want you to go with the knowledge that you face the one who you once loved, and you won't stop the fight until he and all of his army are slain."

Nerolynn groaned like an animal. Tears filled her eyes, and spilled down her cheeks. Darkmor gestured, and her eyes went blank again. She turned and stepped into the vortex. It shrank and disappeared.

"You are heartless," Willowen said. Her own tears ran down her face.

"Only to those who oppose me. I made her a fair offer. She can still join me once Anarys and his army are gone. If she still lives after the combat, that is."

"She told you she would rather die."

"It doesn't matter. I have you. I would have liked to have had you both by my side, but if she still refuses, I can simply use a spell on her to make her mine."

"But you would not like to do that, would you? You want those that you desire to join you freely, and not be under your magical control. Why is that? Is it because you cannot bear to be rejected by anyone?"

"Be careful, Willowen. Remember who you are speaking to."

"What will you do? You will not harm me. You want me to be your slave."

"I have P'Kaani. Your mother can join her. I'll dispose of you if you continue to mock me."

"But my mother may be slain in the battle ahead. Will you take that chance?"

"It's a possibility. She may die, it's true. But I believe the Elves won't fight their own."

"Are you certain? Those who were lost in the battle centuries ago have already been mourned by their kin. My own father did his grieving for my mother, as did I. But we accepted the fact that she was gone."

"But what if they see old comrades and friends in the army that faces them? What then? Will they take up arms against them?"

"I believe they will. My father and his warriors will know that they are ensorcelled, and are under your power. They would consider it a release from your spell if they slew them in battle."

"You think Anarys would slay Nerolynn himself if they met on the battlefield?"

"I think he would. He would rather her die at his own hands than let her be your slave."

"*Pah!* Ridiculous! I know that his love for her was strong."

"That is why he would not hesitate to slay her and release her from your sorcery."

"You're a fool, Willowen. You think that love can conquer anything. Your mind is filled with the romantic foolishness of a young girl."

She smiled.

"Perhaps it is. But your own mind is only focussed on thoughts of power and desire. You will never know the true meaning of love."

"Love? Love is for those who are weak."

"No. You are wrong. Love is strong; perhaps it is the strongest force of all. Those who are in love will die for the one they love."

"Like you would have died for Silveron?"

"Yes, and he would have done the same for me. This simple emotion is beyond your understanding or grasp."

"It's too bad he's dead," Darkmor said coldly.

"Is he?" Willowen replied. "Can you not sense him? I can."

The sorcerer stared at her for a moment, and then cast his thought outward. He sent it probing, searching for any sign of the Elven wizard. Surely Silveron was dead, eaten by the rampaging O'skaa? He sought for any sign that Silveron was alive, but nothing came to his roving mind. Satisfied, he pulled his thought back.

"I couldn't sense anything. He's dead." A contented smirk spread across his face.

Willowen laughed. Darkmor scowled at her.

"Silveron," she said. "Come to me."

Nothing happened.

The sorcerer folded his arms and regarded her with amusement.

"Silveron," Willowen repeated.

No image of the Elf appeared; no sound of his voice was heard.

Darkmor laughed and clapped his hands.

"What entertainment," he said, grinning. "Do go on."

Willowen glared at him.

"Silveron," she said for the third time.

Darkmor was about to laugh, when a point of light appeared in the air. It grew, and they could see a figure within it. It formed itself into an image of the wizard. Darkmor gaped in astonishment.

"I am here," the image said.

The sorcerer was beside himself with rage. His initial shock had given way to anger. How could Silveron have survived the assault of the O'skaa? He clenched his fists in fury.

As if the image had read his thought, it turned and addressed him.

"Darkmor. Silveron created a shield that kept the spiders off. He found the hidden door, and used it to help himself and his companions escape."

"This is a trick!" Darkmor cried. "You couldn't have escaped!"

"It is no trick. Silveron and his friends are alive. They are going to stop you."

Darkmor bared his teeth. He rummaged in his robe, and brought out the talisman. He flourished it triumphantly.

"Not without this you won't!"

"Silveron does not need the talisman. He has found another way to destroy you."

"Where are you? I'll find you!"

"He is waiting for you."

The sorcerer moved quickly, and grabbed Willowen by the throat.

"I'll kill her," he hissed venomously.

The image regarded Willowen.

"Willowen is prepared to die to ensure that you are destroyed," it said.

"You won't let me hurt her. You love her."

"Yes, Silveron loves her. And she loves him. But both of them will die rather than let you become the master of Erathyn."

"That is the truth," Willowen said.

With a wordless exclamation of ferocity, Darkmor cast Willowen down upon the rooftop. He stepped closer to the image.

"I'll find you," he said fiercely. "I'll kill you." His eyes blazed with many-coloured fires. The eyes of the serpent bracelet kindled and burned with red flame upon his wrist.

"You are welcome to try," Silveron said. "Come, let us end your reign of terror."

The figure gestured, and an image formed in front of Darkmor. It was the door that led to the Starstone. It was wide open, and the two Goblins who guarded it lay dead upon the stone floor. The vision of the image appeared to move; inside the chamber it went, and over the bridge that spanned the lake of fire. It came to the platform where the Starstone lay. Silveron and his companions were there. The wizard's form lay prone on the floor, and his friends surrounded it. As Darkmor looked upon the Elf, Silveron smiled.

"*Impossible!*" Darkmor cried. "Only *I* know the spell to unlock the door."

Silveron's image gestured again, and the vision disappeared.

"Can you be certain that we have not broken into the chamber?" it said. "We have found the source of your power. We can destroy you."

The image turned to Willowen.

"Have courage, Willowen. Soon you and Silveron will be together."

It bowed and vanished.

Darkmor clenched his fist and shook it.

"Yes, you'll be together; together in death! Bring her!"

As the Cobrans dragged the Princess to her feet, Darkmor stormed towards the door that led downwards. The others followed.

Far below, Silveron sat up.

"Prepare yourselves. He is coming."

# CHAPTER XVI

# WHEN FRIENDS MEET

Anarys washed his face with water from a silver bowl. He picked up a towel from the small camp table and dried his face and hands. He put the towel back on the table and walked over to the map table that lay in the middle of his tent. He was poring over it when he heard one of the sentries opening the tent flap.

"Sire."

"What is it?"

"One of our scouts has reported a large Goblin force advancing towards us."

"*What!* Sound the alarm! Muster all of our forces to defend –"

"There's no need for that."

King Sirlyk stepped into the tent. He grinned.

Anarys shook his head, and then laughed. He crossed the tent, and they gripped hands in the way of Men.

"Sirlyk! It is good to see you!"

The Goblin-King pounded him on the back.

"How did you like my joke?"

Anarys smiled.

"You completely fooled me. I was about to throw on my armour."

Anarys regarded the sentry. The Elf looked down, embarrassed. He then went down on one knee.

"Your Majesty, if I have offended you, I will accept any punishment you see fit to give me."

"What is your name?"

"Landor, Sire."

"Rise, Landor. Look at me."

The sentry came to his feet and looked Anarys in the eye.

"I am not offended. I know that this was King Sirlyk's idea. What did you threaten him with, Sirlyk?"

"Oh, I suggested that if he did not do what I wanted, I would make sure he would be sent to look after the horses." He grinned.

"Not a very good trade off for one of the King's Guard." His eyes twinkled with merriment. "You may go, Landor."

"Thank you, Sire." He bowed and made to leave.

"What of the King's other guest?" Sirlyk said.

Landor's face reddened.

"I had forgotten. Your Majesty –"

The Elf-King held up his hand.

"Just send them in. Thank you, Landor."

"Yes, Sire." He bowed and backed out of the tent. Relief was written all over his face.

Vosh-en entered and bowed.

"Your Majesty. I am Vosh-en."

"You are one of Lord Kitar-en's scouts?"

"Yes, Sire."

"Where is he? He is late."

Vosh-en and Sirlyk exchanged a glance.

"What has happened?" Anarys asked.

"They were ambushed by Cobrans in the forest," Sirlyk said. "All but

Vosh-en here were slain."

"All of them?" Anarys said, aghast.

"I'm afraid so, Sire," the scout replied.

"How did this happen?"

"We were following the trail, and we came upon some felled trees that blocked it. Another way through the forest was found, and we took it. But when we had gone forward for about an hour, a Cobran force attacked our column from the rear. Our warriors there were driven along the trail. At the same time another attack came from both sides of the forest. Lord Kitar-en ordered the retreat. There was only one way we could go. Forward. We came out into a clearing, and held our ground, but we were vastly outnumbered. As the fight went on, Captain Jodar-en ordered me to leave the battlefield and find you and report what had happened. The Cobrans showed no mercy, and slew all on the battlefield."

Vosh-en's eyes brimmed with tears.

"I am sorry," Anarys said.

Sirlyk crossed the floor to the table where a bottle of wine and several goblets stood. He filled one of them, and came back and offered it to Vosh-en. The Felininn took the goblet and drained it. He handed it back to Sirlyk and bowed.

"Thank you, Your Majesty."

"What a terrible thing to happen," Anarys said.

"They were good warriors, Sire," Vosh-en said. "Lord Kitar-en was a great leader, and stayed with them until the last. His warriors thought highly of him."

"I am sure they did. We will honour them before we depart in the morning."

"Thank you, Sire. What do you wish me to do now?"

"Perhaps you should join Lord Shin's group. He has some scouts that you could work with."

"I would like that, Your Majesty."

"Good. Landor!"

The tent flap opened, and the sentry appeared. He bowed.

"Yes, Your Majesty?"

"Take Vosh-en here to Lord Shin. Tell him that I have attached Vosh-en to his scouts for the time being."

"Yes, Sire."

Vosh-en bowed to the two kings.

"Thank you for your kindness, Your Majesties."

He and Landor left.

"Well, Sirlyk. Come and have a drink with me and tell me your thoughts on this matter."

They walked over to the camp chairs. The Goblin-King sat down, while Anarys poured them both some honey-wine. He brought the goblets over, gave one to Sirlyk and sat down.

"So, my friend," Anarys said, "what is your opinion? Please tell me what you saw."

Sirlyk took a drink. He sat back in his chair.

"I'm afraid I didn't see anything. Lord Chun was the one who was at the edge of the battlefield when they encountered Vosh-en. Perhaps you should ask him."

The Elf-King regarded Sirlyk curiously.

"But surely you have an opinion of what happened?"

Sirlyk took another drink. He nodded.

"Yes, I do. But as I said, I didn't witness any of it. I was in camp, and Chun came to me and reported."

"I see. What are you not saying?"

"What do you mean?"

"I know you are not telling me what you think. Why?"

The Goblin-King rose and went and refilled his goblet. He came and sat down. His face was troubled.

"Do you think they were betrayed?" Anarys asked. "Do you think there was a spy among them?"

Sirlyk shook his head.

"No. I don't think so."

"Then why are you so reluctant to give me your thoughts?"

Sirlyk rose from his chair and began to pace.

"What is it that disturbs you so?" Anarys asked.

The Goblin-King stopped pacing. He faced Anarys.

"I don't want to dishonour Lord Kitar-en's memory."

"I do not understand. What do you mean?"

Silryk came and sat down.

"Kitar-en was one of the most decorated warriors of the Felininn peoples."

"I know that."

"I believe he made a grave error. It cost him dearly."

"You mean that he should not have taken the other trail."

"Yes. From what Vosh-en told me, it was an obvious trap, but Kitar-en still made his force march into it."

"I think he felt he had no other choice. He knew we were going to march on Darkmor's stronghold, and he had to meet us before that. The Felininn are extremely loyal, and will follow orders sometimes even to their own detriment. We made them that way. It was a mistake."

"It was a terrible mistake. Chun said he saw thousands of corpses. He and some scouts went a fair way down the trail, and he said not a foot of ground was free of them."

"The Cobrans fight and slay without mercy," Anarys said. "They take no prisoners."

"Do you still intend on marching tomorrow?" Sirlyk asked.

"I must. We have delayed far too long. Now we must do without Kitaren and his warriors."

"You have my own sword, and my chokhutai," Sirlyk said.

"I thank you for coming. You are most welcome. This will be the last battle between the Elves and the Dark One. We either destroy him, or are destroyed ourselves."

"What if we are victorious? I heard you wished to return to Glindarion."

"Yes, I do wish that. This world has brought us much sorrow. My people have suffered much. We have lost many friends. We will leave Erathyn to Men."

Sirlyk raised an eyebrow.

"Men?" he echoed. "They are like children."

"Children must grow up," Anarys replied.

Sirlyk smiled wryly.

"Has there been any word of Silveron and his party? I was told that they went secretly into the Dark One's lair."

"That is right. Silveron sent an Avianinn back to report. They had managed to get past all of the sentries, and had found a rear entrance to the tower. He and his group intended to enter there and find both Willowen and the talisman. I sent F'Leet and a group of his wingmen to aid them in escaping when they achieved their goals."

"I see. Do you think that Silveron can succeed?"

"I do not know. But we must hope that he can. In any case, we must march on the morrow. Even if we are only a diversion, we must play our part."

"What is known of the enemy's strength?"

"Not much. His numbers are unknown. Apart from small raids by O'skaa riders, his forces always fall back, and do not engage us."

Sirlyk looked thoughtful.

"Hmmm. The Schaaka do the same thing. But in their case, it is always a ploy to lure you on, and to lull you into a false sense of security. Then they attack with full force."

"That has been my thought also. We must march regardless."

"Have the O'skaa stopped their raids?"

"Yes. None have been seen for two days."

"Then we must be careful, Anarys. That is also a part of their strategy. They leave the area, but keep you under watch. They want your warriors to feel relief at their absence, and become lax in their awareness."

"I have issued orders that everyone must be vigilant, especially when we are so close to Darkmor's stronghold."

"There could be thousands upon thousands in his army," Sirlyk said. "What of the Schaaka? Perhaps Queen Sardia has allied herself with Darkmor. She has many O'skaa riders at her disposal. They are fanatical, and worship her as though she is a goddess. They are savage fighters, and the O'skaa are terrible foes, as no doubt you remember."

"I do. I recall the battle where Captain Nilda slew the Queen of the O'skaa with a single arrow. It was a magnificent shot." His face grew pensive.

"I understand the Captain was lost to us," Sirlyk said.

"Yes. Both she and Ervin the Forester fell at Linador, along with many fine Elven and Goblin warriors." He drained his goblet.

"I heard the tale. They will be sorely missed." Sirlyk finished his drink, and stared into the empty goblet. "Ervin was a great friend to me and my people. He lived among us for a while. He was a fine swordsman, and good with a bow." He looked up. "And he was well loved. I will miss him."

The Elf-King rose to his feet, and walked over to the table. He stood in thought for a moment, and then picked up the bottle. He came back to the chairs. Sirlyk held out his goblet, and Anarys filled it, and then filled his own. He set the bottle down, and took up his goblet.

"Let us drink to them," he said.

They both drank.


Meanwhile Landor had escorted Vosh-en through the camp until they had reached Jhara Shin's tents. The Goblins were sitting around a fire. The pair advanced and bowed.

"Lord Shin. This is Vosh-en. The King has attached him to your scouts."

"Thank you, Landor," Shin replied. "You may leave us."

"My Lord." The Elf bowed and departed.

"Come and join us, Vosh-en. Have you eaten?"

"I was not hungry, My Lord."

"Well, you must have something now. Would you like some wine?"

Vosh-en came and sat in a chair that one of the chokhutai gave up.

"No thank you, My Lord. King Sirlyk gave me some honey-wine earlier. Water is fine."

"Ah, so you drank some of King Anarys's honey-wine? How did you like it?"

"I found it too sweet, My Lord. I prefer water. My own comrades..." He trailed off.

An uncomfortable silence fell. Shin and his warriors had all heard of the massacre. The chokhutai who had given up his seat returned with a plate that had meat and bread on it. He offered it to the Felininn. Vosh-en looked up at him and accepted it.

"Thank you," he said softly.

"Bring him some water, too," Shin said.

"Yes, My Lord." The warrior left.

Vosh-en was staring down at the plate.

"Eat up, my friend," Shin said.

The Felininn began to pick at the food, and then found that he was famished. He fell to with a will. The chokhutai returned with a metal cup. Vosh-en took it and drained it. The water was cool and refreshing.

"Much better, eh?" Shin asked.

"Yes. Thank you, My Lord."

The chokhutai held out his hands. Vosh-en gave him the plate and cup, and the warrior took them away to be washed.

"You have our sympathy, Vosh-en," Shin said. "Everyone in the camp knows the sorrow that you bear. I am certain that King Anarys will honour Lord Kitar-en and his brave warriors before we march in the morning."

"He told me that he would do that, My Lord."

"How long have you been a scout, Vosh-en?"

"Two years, My Lord."

"Did you see any combat during those years?'

The Felininn shook his head.

"No, My Lord. The Empire has been at peace for many years. I went on several scouting missions, but at no time did I come into contact with the enemy. I was also involved in training exercises, but that is not the same."

"No," Shin said. "It is not."

"When the message came from King Anarys and I was chosen to be one of Lord Kitar-en's scouts, I was..." He searched for a word.

"Excited?"

"Yes. That was it, My Lord. I was excited. I was finally going to see some action."

"But you found the reality completely different? The chaos and madness of combat is something that must be experienced. No-one can understand its nature until they are in the thick of it."

"That is true, My Lord. Everything happened so fast."

"Did you slay any of the enemy?"

Vosh-en looked uncertain.

"Three, perhaps four fell to my sword. I am not sure. I was not injured in any way. Then I was ordered to leave the battlefield to find King Anarys and report what happened."

Shin put his hand on Vosh-en's shoulder.

"Then you served your lord well. To slay the enemy is one thing, but to depart the field and leave knowing that your comrades are doomed is another. You wanted to stay and fight?"

"Yes, My Lord. I felt like I was running away. I wanted to die with my comrades."

"To follow an order like that is commendable, Vosh-en. I will be happy to have you as one of my scouts. Captain Shen."

One of the chokhutai rose to his feet and came over and bowed.

"My Lord."

"Vosh-en can join your group."

"Yes, My Lord."

"Please take him to meet your warriors. Supply him with any gear that he may need, and find him somewhere to sleep."

"Yes, My Lord."

Vosh-en rose to his feet.

"Thank you for your hospitality, My Lord. I will serve you well." He bowed.

"Of that I have no doubt. Good night. I will see you in the morning. Good night, Captain."

Captain Chen bowed.

"Good night, My Lord. Come, Vosh-en."

They departed. Shin came to his feet. He stretched, and yawned cavernously.

"I think it is time we all retired. Good night, my friends."

His chokhutai wished him a good night, and then they all went to their tents.

At the same time, in Algol the Bright, the traitorous wizards had met in Amberon's tower. They had enjoyed a fine meal, and had drunk several bottles of honey-wine. Now they sat and listened as Amberon spoke of his plans for their future.

"Darkmor is certain to defeat the Army of Light. Anarys and his rabble have no chance to win against the force that Darkmor has mustered."

"Can we be sure of that?" Candreen asked.

Amberon turned and regarded him coldly.

"Eldest," Candreen added.

Amberon continued to stare at the younger wizard until Candreen cast his eyes downwards. Satisfied that he had cowed the young upstart, Amberon went on.

"Only *I* have seen and know the vastness of Darkmor's army. He has brought Queen Sardia up from the Underworld. Her O'skaa are numbered in the thousands."

"And his own warriors are numerous as well," Narwen added. "Such a force must be successful."

"What do we know of Silveron?"Candreen asked. "If he obtains the talisman, he could still succeed in banishing Darkmor."

"Yes, that is true," Narwen said. "Have you had any word of him, Eldest?"

Amberon shook his head.

"No. But Darkmor would surely know where the boy is, and that he poses no threat to him. Do not concern yourselves." He drank deeply from his goblet.

"When did he tell you this?" Candreen asked. "He has not appeared to us since we disposed of Telewen and Vairon."

"He must be busy organising the coming battle," Narwen said.

"It does not matter," Amberon said. "He will triumph, and then we will have our chance."

"Our chance?" Candreen echoed.

"What do you mean?"' Narwen said.

Amberon looked at them both in turn.

"I mean that Darkmor will destroy Anarys and the Army of Light. But it will cost him dearly. He is already weakened from the sorcery that he uses to keep the moon where it is. The battle will surely drain most of his remaining strength." He smiled suggestively.

"And then what?" Narwen said.

"And then, we take control. We slay him, and take the power of the Starstone for ourselves. And do not forget the mastery of Dark Magic that he possesses. Surely there are many tomes of such forbidden knowledge in his library that we can take." Amberon's eyes shone with fervour.

Candreen gasped.

"That is dangerous. Surely he will sense what we are up to, and destroy us."

"No," Amberon said with relish, "as I told you, he is too busy with the arrangements for the battle to come to sense anything we plan."

"I do not know, Eldest," Candreen said. "I am concerned with this plan. It is reckless. The risk of discovery –"

"Is nonexistent," Amberon interrupted. "Think! Darkmor has not contacted us; he has no idea what we plan."

"Can you be sure, Eldest?' Candreen said. "He could be spying on us at this very moment." He stared around the room nervously.

"So because of your misgivings, you are not willing to risk all so that we can become the masters of this world?" Amberon sneered.

"I only advise caution, Eldest."

"What do you say, Narwen?"

"I am willing to take the chance, Eldest. The secrets of Dark Magic would be ours. No-one else on Erathyn would have them."

"Good. That is the correct attitude."

"However," Narwen continued, "I think it would be wise to have one of us present at the battle, to see its outcome."

Amberon stroked his chin in thought.

"Yes, I agree. We must know how it turns out. Which of you will go?"

"I will go," Narwen said. "I will disguise myself as Vairon."

Candreen looked relieved. Amberon and Narwen both knew that he would never have volunteered for such a dangerous mission. They exchanged a glance.

"Very good, Narwen," Amberon said. "That is how it shall be. You will go, and report back to us. Then we will decide when to make our move. Candreen, the honey-wine is nearly gone. Go and find Neldriin and tell her to bring more."

Candreen bowed.

"Yes, Eldest."

Candreen left the room. He could feel the other wizards staring at him as he departed.

"I am disappointed in our young friend," Amberon said. "It seems he does not share our desire to rule."

"He does appear to be unwilling to take any chance against Darkmor, Eldest."

"What should we do about it?"

"Perhaps we should dispose of him? Two can share power more easily than three."

A slow smile spread upon Amberon's face.

"Good, Narwen. I see that we are both of the same mind. Yes, let us get rid of Candreen. When he returns, I will distract him." He took up one of the knives that they had used to eat their meal, and handed it to Narwen. "Do it quickly."

Narwen smiled and nodded. He hid the knife in his sleeve.

Outside the door, Candreen paled as he heard their plan. He had eavesdropped on their conversation. Sweat stood out upon his brow. He whirled and hurried away.

He raced down the corridor, his mind spinning. Now he realised that Amberon had no loyalty but to himself. Everyone who he perceived as a threat was disposed of. *What can I do?* He thought desperately. If he exposed Amberon's treachery, he was done for. His own involvement would see to that. But there must be some way to lay bare Amberon's plots, and save his skin.

He skidded to a stop as he heard someone approaching him. He stood, panting, his heart hammered in his chest as though it would break through his ribs and fly away. Then with relief, he realised that they were coming from the opposite direction of The Eldest's chamber. He took several deep breaths to steady his nerves, and composed himself.

Neldriin appeared, carrying a tray. Upon it sat a fresh bottle of honey-wine, and a plate of sweetmeats. She knew well of Amberon's love of the finer things, and had anticipated that he would call for more wine.

She stopped as she saw Candreen. She bowed to him.

"Master, I was just bringing these to The Eldest. Can I help you with something?"

*You certainly can,* Candreen thought. He thought quickly. He came and took the girl's arm, and hustled her back the way she had come. Neldriin gazed at him in shock.

"Master? What is wrong?"

He pulled her into one of the side rooms, and closed the door.

"*You must be quiet,*" he hissed.

"Why? I do not understand." She stared at him, puzzled by his strange behaviour.

"I have just heard Amberon and Narwen plotting to slay the King."

"What? Are you certain?"

"Yes. I was sent to get some more wine. I had forgotten to tell The Eldest something, and went back. When I stood at the door, I heard them talking. Something made me stand and listen. When I had heard their conversation, I knew I had to get away."

"Are you sure of what you heard?"

"I am. I knew if I had opened that door, I would have been slain."

The girl went white.

"What can we do?"

"We must go. We must leave Algol, and report to King Anarys."

"But Master, how can we do that? The army is many miles away."

Candreen drew himself up proudly.

"I am the Master of Void Magic. I can create a portal for us. We can go to the King now, and inform him of their treachery."

"But the wine, I must take it to them."

Candreen fixed his eye upon her.

"If you go into that chamber, you will not leave it alive. Come with me now. Leave that."

Neldriin nodded. She put the tray down on the floor. She licked her lips nervously.

"Will it hurt?" she asked apprehensively.

The wizard smiled.

"No. You will only feel a tingling sensation. Stand next to me."

She did as she was told.

Candreen closed his eyes. He sent his thought outwards, searching for the King. Over the many miles his thought travelled, until he perceived the Army of Light in its camp. The King's tent appeared. He fixed its position in his mind, and spoke the Words of Power for a portal softly to himself. The portal shimmered about them. The girl gasped and drew closer to him in fright, but he ignored her and activated the spell. The portal spun with electrical fire, and they both stepped into it. Their forms were swallowed up by it, and the portal contracted and slowly vanished. The room was empty.

Anarys was tired. He and Sirlyk had drunk wine and spoken together for hours. It had been good to see him, but now Anarys was weary, and wanted nothing more than to sleep. Sirlyk had departed to join his own warriors.

The King sat down on his pallet. He rubbed his sleepy eyes.

A small spot of colour appeared in the middle of the tent. He stared at it as it grew, and formed a portal.

He shook his head groggily Surely he had not drunk *that* much wine?

Anarys could see two figures within the portal. As he watched, they stepped forward into the tent. Anarys rose to his feet as the portal collapsed in on itself.

"Master Candreen. Why have you come to me at this hour?" He regarded the girl at the wizard's side. He had seen her somewhere before.

Candreen and the girl bowed.

"Your Majesty. I must report to you a plot on your life."

Anarys frowned.

"Continue."

"Sire. I heard Amberon and Narwen plotting to slay you."

"Amberon? The Eldest?"

"Yes, Sire."

"What did you hear?"

"They spoke of the end of Darkmor. Amberon said that once the sorcerer had been defeated, they would find a way to slay you as well. Then they would rule Erathyn."

"Hmmm. Did you hear this conversation, girl?"

Neldriin knelt.

"No, Your Majesty. But I believe what Master Candreen says."

"Rise," Anarys commanded. "What is your name?"

"I am called Neldriin, Sire."

"The Eldest's servant?"

"That is correct, Sire. I served Master Goldwen, and now I serve Master Amberon."

"Not for much longer if what Master Candreen has to say is the truth. Come, wizard, tell me more of what you heard."

"Yes, Your Majesty."


Amberon and Narwen watched an image of the King and Candreen upon the wall. They had waited for Candreen to return, but when the wizard had not come back, they had wondered what had happened. A simple spell had shown them Candreen and Neldriin meeting in the corridor. Then they had both watched and listened as Candreen had lied to the girl and created the portal. They saw the pair disappear into it. Another spell had located them, and then they had seen and heard the conversation Candreen had had with Anarys.

With a snarl, Amberon waved his hand, and the image vanished. He began to pace the floor restlessly.

"He has betrayed us," Narwen said.

"*The fool!*" Amberon hissed. "Now Anarys is aware of our plan." He clenched his fist angrily.

"What can we do?" Narwen asked.

The Eldest stopped pacing. His face became thoughtful. Narwen did not interrupt him, as he knew of Amberon's temper, and did not wish to face his wrath.

"We will do nothing," Amberon finally said.

"But he has exposed us. Anarys knows what we plan, if Darkmor also finds out –"

Amberon rounded on him angrily.

"Darkmor will *not* find out. As I told you, he is too busy with preparations for the coming battle."

"What if he contacts us?"

"Then we will present ourselves as the same obedient servants as before."

"What if he suspects something?"

"He will not. We must behave as if nothing is out of the ordinary." Amberon regarded him. "Can you do that? Or must I dispose of you as well?"

The threat made Narwen's blood run cold. He knew that Amberon would snuff him out without thinking. He had seen how merciless he was when someone was in his way.

"I will do as you say, Eldest. You may count on me."

"Are you certain you can maintain a calm demeanour? If Darkmor does come to us, and you give him any reason to doubt us, we are lost."

Narwen placed his hand over his heart.

"I will not fail you, Eldest. I give you my word that Darkmor will not suspect anything on my account."

Amberon stared at him fixedly. Narwen wondered what he was thinking. Was Amberon considering disposing of him, as he had threatened? He let the knife slip down into his hand, and watched the other closely. The tension in the room became palpable.

Amberon turned and walked over to the table, deliberately turning his back on Narwen, and giving him an opportunity to strike without warning. He picked up the bottle, and filled a goblet with the last of the wine. He drank it down, and then put the goblet down with a clink.

Narwen wondered if he could close the distance between them, and plunge the knife into Amberon's back. What should he do? Should he risk an attack on Amberon? Would he be fast enough to carry out the assault without facing any response from Amberon? He stood there sweating, lost in indecision.

"We can do nothing about this," Amberon said, still with his back to Narwen. "Worrying about it can accomplish nothing either." He turned to face Narwen. "Do you agree?"

Narwen watched him carefully. Was Amberon ready to strike him down? He looked at the other's eyes, and sought in them the small signs that indicated that Amberon was about to attack him. He looked at Amberon's form, to see if his body held any tension, which would be also indicative of an assault. Amberon seemed calm.

"I do agree, Eldest. Please excuse my doubts of before." He bowed.

Amberon sat down in his place at the table.

"Very good. Now, since Neldriin has taken our wine, go and find another bottle and bring it here. We will enjoy it while we make our plans."

"As you wish, Eldest." Narwen bowed, and walked towards the door.

"Narwen."

He stopped and turned.

"Eldest?"

"You may leave the knife."

Narwen smiled. Of course Amberon had known he had thought about stabbing him. He walked back to the table, and laid the knife down. His eyes met Amberon's. The Eldest's gaze seemed to say: I know what you were thinking. Do not try anything against me. I will crush you.

Narwen bowed, and then went in search of the wine. Amberon sat back in his chair, pleased with himself.

# CHAPTER XVII

# INTO THE DARK LANDS

Anarys and Sirlyk stood together, resplendent in their armour. Before them was the Army of Light. Formed up in their respective groups, the army had gathered to honour the memory of Lord Kitar-en's fallen warriors.

Anarys looked over at Jhara Shin's contingent. He searched the rank of scouts until he saw Vosh-en. Their eyes met, and Vosh-en nodded deferentially to the Elven-King. Anarys acknowledged this with a nod of his own.

He stepped forward.

"We are gathered here today to honour the memory of Lord Kitar-en and his warriors. You have all heard how they were ambushed. They fought valiantly against a force that outnumbered them, but were overpowered and fell in battle. We will not forget them."

He drew his sword. The many warriors before him followed suit. He raised his blade, and they did the same. Thousands of swords shone red in the light.

"We salute them, and give thanks for their service."

"We salute them," the army chorused.

He looked to his right, where a group of Elven trumpeters stood.

Their leader gave an order, and they lifted their instruments to their lips. The Fanfare for the Fallen rang out. As the echoes of it died away, they sounded another tune. This time it was the Anthem of the Empress, the Felininn national anthem. They lowered their trumpets. Anarys sheathed his sword, and the army before him mirrored his action.

"Now we go into Darkmor's lands," Anarys continued. "We may all fall in combat, but we will meet the Dark One's forces, and do what we may. Silveron and his companions have made their way into the enemy's tower, and are seeking both Princess Willowen and the Talisman of Banishment. We must have faith, and hope that they achieve both of these goals, and rid Erathyn of the Dark One for all time."

He turned to his left.

"Lord Merys, make the army ready to march."

Merys bowed.

"Yes, Your Majesty." He addressed Captain Enriss: "Captain, form marching order.

"Yes, My Lord."

Enriss stepped forward and took a deep breath.

"Form marching order!" he cried.

The army began to fall in.

Sirlyk came to Anarys's side.

"Now we come to it at last," he said.

"Yes," the Elf said, watching the warriors form up. "I wonder how many of us will be alive on the morrow?"

Sirlyk took him by the arm. Anarys turned to him, his face distracted.

"It's not like you to be so pessimistic before a battle," Sirlyk said.

Anarys shook his head, as though he was waking from a dream.

"Forgive me, my friend. I am only tired."

"Perhaps you should have some more wine?"

The Elf laughed.

"I believe we already had too much last night."

"Indeed we did." Sirlyk grinned.

"Your Majesty?"

Candreen stood there. He bowed to them.

"What do you wish me to do, Sire?"

Anarys regarded him.

"I want you to assist Master Vandaron, Candreen. You are to make the shield to protect us. Vandaron will carry out any attack against the enemy."

"As you wish, Sire." He bowed and left them.

"What did Vandaron think of Amberon's betrayal?" Sirlyk asked.

"He did not believe it at first. *I* did not believe it. But Candreen and Neldriin convinced us of their treachery. It seems that Amberon has been in league with the Dark One for a long time. He has fooled everyone."

"What does he think to gain from this involvement? Surely he knows that the Dark One will not share power with him?"

"I do not know, Sirlyk. He is a fool. Darkmor will destroy him, or I will have to."

"That may prove difficult."

"I know, but such treachery must not go unanswered."

"Can Candreen be trusted? I get the impression that he is only concerned about himself."

"As do I. He may even have been involved in some way. I sense that he is not telling us the whole story." He frowned. "Or at least, he is twisting it somehow to favour himself."

"I agree, my friend. There is cunning in that one, to be sure."

"Your Majesty?"

Lord Merys stood there. He bowed.

"The army is on the march, Your Majesty." He turned and waved a groom forward who was holding the reins of the Elven-King's horse.

The groom bowed. "Your mount, Sire."

"Thank you." Anarys put his foot in the stirrup, and climbed into the saddle.

"I'll go and join my lads," Sirlyk said. He went to leave, and then stopped and turned.

"What of the girl who was with Candreen?"

"Neldriin? I sent her to assist Shelarindel. She seems quite capable. She was once Goldwen's servant and then became Amberon's."

"Ah. Very good. I like her."

"I thought Shelarindel would appreciate her help."

"I'm sure she would. I'll go and see how my lads are doing."

"I will see you when we reach the valley."

Sirlyk nodded, and then left them.

"Lord Merys, let us be off."

"Yes, Sire."

They joined the long line of the army as it marched out. The scouts were in the lead, riding ahead of the main body. Captain Shen led his group, which also included Vosh-en across the desolate landscape. Any trees that they saw were dead and blackened, and the grass had died. Ash blew in the wind, and wisps of smoke drifted forlornly in the distance over the dead lands. The blood red light covered all in a ruddy twilight.

The scouts looked about themselves, wary and alert for any sign of the enemy. No sound came to them. No beast or bird was seen. Even the hum of insects was absent. It was as though they had come to a dead world, where everything that had once lived and thrived had perished and vanished into oblivion.

On they rode, with no change in the bare landscape. The same desolation met their eyes. They came to a small creek. It was choked and full of stagnant slimy water. The reek of it stung their noses. They passed it by with relief.

"Captain, look ahead," one of the scouts said.

Shen looked, and saw the opening of Darkmor's valley. He held up his hand, and the group came to a halt. They stared into the distance. Darkmor's tower reared up into the sky, a massive edifice, even this far away. Shen brought his hand forward, and they rode on. He kept his eye on the tower, and scanned the valley walls for any sign of the enemy. All was bleak and empty. The wind moaned in the valley; a mournful noise. The clop of their mount's hooves was muffled by a fine dust that covered everything on the valley floor.

"Captain," a scout said. He pointed.

Shen looked in the direction indicated. Spread along the valley's opening were some spears, as though Darkmor's minions had put them there as a warning. He frowned. There was something on the end of the spears. They came closer, and with horror, he realised that they were heads.

The group rode up and halted in front of the awful sight. They looked closely, and could see that the heads were those of Elven bowmays. Their long hair blew in the wind, matted and soaked with blood. Almond shaped eyes stared blankly into nothingness. Mouths gaped, and dried blood covered the spears and had pooled on the ground.

Shen's mount shied, and something crunched under its hooves. He looked down, and for the first time noticed the bones underfoot. He had not seen them before due to his attention being fixed on the grim sight before them. There were Elven bones as well as horse's remains there. Some of the bones were marked with deep punctures. *O'skaa,* he thought with dread.

"What an awful death," Vosh-en said, appalled. "Their captors let the spiders eat them."

"Take them down," Shen said, his voice raw with emotion.

His scouts dismounted, and went to carry out his order.

"Vosh-en."

The Felininn rode up to him.

"Yes, Captain?"

"Return to the army, and report to King Anarys. Tell him that we have found Commander Melandra and her bowmays. We will bring them back to be honoured."

"Yes, Captain, at once." Relieved to get away from the awful sight of the bowmay's grisly demise, he turned his warbird and sped back the way that they had come.

Watching them from above was Sardia. She was mounted upon Oolikhorr. Her O'skaa riders surrounded her. She smiled as she imagined the reaction the Elven heads had had upon the scouts.

"That will give them pause," she said.

*They will sstill come,* the giant arachnid sent.

"Of course they will. They cannot allow Darkmor to conquer all Erathyn."

*They will fall. Our numberss far outnumber them.*

"And then you will feast on their flesh."

*Yess. Flessh. It will be ourss.*

*Flessh, flessh,* the spiders around them chorused.

They watched the Elves go about their gruesome task.

The Army of Light advanced. Lord Merys held up his hand, and that advance ground to a halt. He pointed.

"A rider, Your Majesty."

The figure of a solitary rider was coming into view. Anarys looked beyond. The tower of the enemy was getting closer.

"It is Vosh-en, Sire."

The scout reigned in his mount before the Elven-King and bowed.

"Your Majesty, Captain Shen sent me to report that we have found

Commander Melandra and her bowmays."

"Dead?" Anarys enquired.

Vosh-en looked upset.

"Yes, Sire."

Anarys regarded the scout. It was plain to see that something had unnerved him.

"What is it, Vosh-en?" Anarys asked.

The Felininn lowered his head. He could not meet the Elven-King's gaze. They sat their mounts in an uncomfortable silence.

"It is awful, Your Majesty," he finally said. He raised his head, and looked Anarys in the eye. "They were all – *eaten* – by the O'skaa..."

"Go on," Anarys said. His face was grim.

"The Schaaka, they..."

The Elves waited for him to continue. They could see that he had been shaken to the core of his being.

Mastering himself, Vosh-en continued.

"The Schaaka, they had captured the bowmays. It appears that they gave them and their horses to the O'skaa. And then, they put their heads upon spears that they had driven into the ground. They formed a line across the entry to the valley."

"*Monstrous*," Merys choked out. His face was livid. He turned to Anarys. "Let us go and avenge their deaths, Sire. Such an offence must not go unpunished."

"Calm yourself, Merys," Anarys replied. "That is what the enemy wants us to do. He wants us to charge in there filled with anger so he can cut us down. I would wager that both sides of the valley are swarming with O'skaa riders ready to come down upon us."

"Forgive me, Sire," Merys said, abashed. "You are right. I allowed myself to become angered."

"It is all right, Merys," Anarys replied. "I *am* angry. To think that those filth would try to provoke us with such a disgusting act." He regarded the other, and Merys could see the hatred that burned in the Elven-King's eyes.

"Captain Shen bade me tell you that he is bringing them to be honoured, Sire," Vosh-en said.

"Good, good, Vosh-en. Go and rejoin him and lead them back to us."

"As you wish, Your Majesty." The scout bowed, wheeled his warbird, and raced away.

"Go and give the order to prepare to receive the honoured dead," Anarys said.

"Should we not prepare for battle, Sire?"

"No," Anarys replied. "The enemy has used Commander Melandra and her bowmays to incite our anger. We will show them that we Elves have command of our emotions, and will not allow this to goad us into rash action. We will honour the memory of these brave women."

The Elven-King leaned across, and put his hand on Lord Merys's shoulder.

"Make no mistake, Merys. Those scum will pay dearly for what they have done. We will first show them how we honour our fallen. Then we can make preparations for battle."

He lowered his arm, and looked ahead. Malkaar's tower lay before them. Anarys knew that the Dark One was watching them even now.

"Go and give the order," Anarys said.

"Yes, Your Majesty." Lord Merys bowed, turned his horse, and rode towards the army.

*Every moment we delay we give Silveron more time to be successful,* Anarys thought. He stared at Darkmor's tower, as if by the force of his will he could make the enemy know that he had not succeeded in breaking the army's morale. *I must hope that that is so,* he thought. He wheeled his mount, and rode towards the gathering warriors.

An hour later, and the warriors had assembled. Shen and his party of scouts had returned with the defiled heads of Commander Melandra and her bowmays. They had been laid out in rows, with the Commander's head in the front. They were decently covered with silks, so that their tortured features could not be seen. The Elves had washed the blood from their faces, and had doused them with pure water to purify them. Now they sat upon a wooden bier, which had been liberally soaked with oil.

Standing before them were King Anarys, Vandaron, and Candreen. The Army of Light was arrayed behind them. Two ranks of Elven trumpeters stood waiting, their instruments by their sides. The sun was slowly going down. Shadows were lengthening, and a hush had fallen over the valley. Two Elves stood with flaring torches, ready to touch off the oil.

King Anarys stepped forward. His raised voiced echoed from the valley walls.

"We are gathered here to honour our fallen dead. These our sisters have fought the enemy, and in doing so have upheld the honour of all Elvenkind." He paused for a moment, thinking. Then he went on: "The enemy has defiled them, thinking that this will give us pause. It has not. It has instead filled us with the resolve to destroy him utterly. You all know of Silveron's mission. Our battle is not as important as his task. But we will face Darkmor's forces nonetheless. Let us remember Commander Melandra and her bowmays, and strike the enemy hard on the morrow."

He drew his sword. Thousands of blades were drawn in response. He held his sword high, and the army echoed his action. The trumpeters raised their silver trumpets, and the Fanfare for the Fallen rang out.

"We hereby swear to destroy the enemy. We swear by the blood of our fallen sisters here, and by the blood of all those who have been slain by the actions of the enemy."

*"We so swear!"* The warriors chorused. Their voices echoed in the silence.

He turned and faced the bier, and the two torch men advanced, and set their torches to the oil. The flames caught quickly, and the aromatic oil sent up sweet smelling clouds that rose into the air. They also blocked the smell of the burning heads.

Anarys stood for a moment longer, and then he sheathed his sword. The army followed suit in a shirring of steel. He turned and faced the warriors.

"Now go and take what rest you may, for tomorrow we take the fight to the enemy."

He nodded to Lord Merys, who began to shout orders. The gathering dispersed. The funeral pyre burned on as each warrior sought his blanket. In minutes the army had vanished. Only the sentries remained.

Merys came and bowed to Anarys.

"What now, Sire?" he asked.

"We will not attack at night," Anarys replied. "Let our warriors sleep. The day will bring the last battle."

"Will not the enemy send some raids against us?"

"Perhaps he will. But we must not respond. Inform all the sentries that they are not to be drawn away from the camp. They may repel any attack that comes, but must hold fast, and not pursue."

"I understand, My Liege."

"It is my hope that this pause will give Silveron more time to be successful in his mission. You do realise, Merys, our battle is only a distraction in the scheme of things."

"So you have told me, Sire. I understand how important his task is." He shook his head. "I wish we had the full strength of arms that we possessed hundreds of years ago. You remember, Sire. Our army was many times the size of this pitiful remnant you now command. It was all made up of Elven warriors too. There was no need to have assistance from any of the younger races. It was a glory to behold."

The King clapped him on the shoulder.

"I do remember, Merys. Many battles we fought with that army. It was indeed glorious. But I also remember that we did not come to Erathyn for battle. It was supposed to be a home for us. Instead we have found much sadness and death."

He removed his hand and grasped his sword.

"My Queen was lost on this world. Many of our friends have fallen also. Perhaps it was a mistake to lead us here. I am the one who has brought such misery and suffering to my people."

His knuckles turned white as he gripped his sword harder. Merys noticed this, and replied.

"No, Your Majesty. It is not your fault that these things have befallen us. You must not upbraid yourself. We will follow you anywhere. You are our King."

Anarys regarded him. He gave the Elf-lord a wan smile.

"Do you really believe that, Merys?"

Merys nodded.

"I do, Sire." He bowed. "I will give the section leaders your orders." He bowed and departed.

"'*We will follow you anywhere,*'" Anarys repeated to himself as he watched him walk away.

He turned and looked at the funeral bier.

"You may all follow me into death, Merys," Anarys said to himself softly.

The Elven-King regarded the pyre until it burned down to ashes, and then he bowed to it and retired to his tent.

Sardia looked down upon the encampment that lay far below in the valley. She smiled to herself. The enemy had not taken the bait that had been offered. It was to be expected. She knew the Elves were masters of their emotions. It was no surprise that they had made camp and not charged into the valley, filled with rage. *Ah, if only the army had been made up of Men,* she thought, they *would have come running to the slaughter.* She laughed.

*What iss it, Sisster Queen?* Oolikhorr sent.

"I was only thinking that the Elves had held fast, where Men would have raced headlong into our trap."

*Yess,* the arachnid sent, *Men are foolss. The Bright Oness are ssmarter. But the Bright Oness are tastier My Queen,* an O'skaa at their side sent.

*True, sisster,* Oolikhorr replied. *Their meat is ssweeter.*

"And you shall have your fill of them." Sardia said.

*Sshould we not ssend a raid againsst them?* Oolikhorr sent.

"It would be a waste of time," Sardia replied. "Anarys would not allow his warriors be led away, as those bowmays were. Such a pity."

*But look at Kerlach over there,* Oolikhorr sent. *He iss bored, and his Sschaaka are too. I can also ssense the hunger in their O'sskaa. They long to attack.*

Sardia looked across the valley, and saw Kerlach sitting upon his mount. He was restless, that was certain. She smiled, and raised her goad. He acknowledged her signal by raising his own goad. She swept her goad around and pointed down at the camp. He nodded, grinned, and began to give orders to the warriors around him. Twenty of them made to move off. He raised his goad again, bowed to the Goblin Queen, and then turned his O'skaa to lead the raiding party.

Darkmor and his companions hastened down the stairs. The sorcerer's mind was filled with the image that had been shown to them. *Silveron must not reach the Starstone!* He thought wildly. If the Elf could negate the sorcerer's spell and the sun be released, then Darkmor's allies from the Underworld would scatter before its harsh light. Such a thing must not happen. Without the overwhelming numbers that the Schaaka and the O'skaa provided, the Army of Light could well prevail. *No!* He fumed to himself. *They must be destroyed!*

They came down to the ground level of the tower, and happened upon a dozen Schaaka who were making ready to go out into the valley.

"You!" the sorcerer barked, "Follow me."

Their leader saw who had addressed him.

"Yes, Master." He bowed as Darkmor swept past him, and then he and his warriors fell in behind the group as they took the stairs down to the lower levels.

Hustled along in their midst, Willowen smiled to herself. If Darkmor was this agitated, then he must be afraid that Silveron posed a very real threat to him. She glanced about as they hurried down the stairs. *I must be ready to escape,* she thought. She smiled once again as she thought that soon she and Silveron would be together again.

Silveron and his friends were making themselves ready. They were listening for any sound of the approaching Darkmor. Swords were drawn, and Brador hefted his war hammer in his meaty fist.

"Do they come, lad?" he asked eagerly.

"Yes. They are coming to us." The wizard listened. "A dozen Schaaka have joined them."

He regarded his companions.

"We must not allow him to get to the Starstone. It is the source of his power."

"He won't live to use it," Egon said. He raised his sword suggestively.

"You cannot harm him with your weapons," Silveron said. "I alone must deal with him. His friends, however..."

"Strike them down, we will," the Dwarf said. He clapped his hand on Silveron's shoulder. "Worry not, lad. Interfere they will not." He bared his teeth in a grin.

"I know I can rely on you, my friends." A thoughtful look came to the wizard's face, and he added a word of warning.

"Willowen is with them," He said. "Take care you do not harm her."

"The Princess will not be harmed," Nildoron said. "All of you take care of where your blows fall."

There was a murmur of assent at this.

They stood waiting, weapons clenched in fists. Silveron prepared his mind for the battle to come. *Now it has come,* he thought. *I must not fail. The fate of Erathyn hangs in the balance. Father, help me.* No presence came to him. Surely Goldwen would not abandon him now?

Kerlach and his raiders halted at the edge of the camp. He swept his gaze over the massed force that lay before them. It was only a nuisance raid, he knew, but it would do two things. One, it would make the enemy unsettled, and an uncertain foe is a good thing. Two, it would ensure that his own warriors were satisfied that they had struck a blow against the enemy. The O'skaa and their riders were champing at the bit to engage the Army of Light.

He saw the horses were they were penned. Only four Elves guarded them.

He grinned. *Staked down like prey for my O'skaa,* he thought. He motioned with his goad, and indicated the horses. His warriors made ready to charge. Kerlach brought up his horn and sounded a charge. The harsh note echoed in the air. His Schaaka cried out at the top of their lungs and goaded their mounts forwards. They hurtled towards the horses.

The Elven sentries drew their swords as the O'skaa rushed towards them.

*"Alarm!"* One of them cried. "Raid!" His voice was stilled as a black Schaaka arrow tore into his chest. He fell face first into the ash.

Then the O'skaa were among the others. They struck down the sentries, and exploded into the pen. The horses screamed with terror and milled about as the monsters attacked them savagely.

Kerlach laughed to see such carnage. Then, as the sound of silver horns came to him, he snarled in fury, and brought his own horn to his lips. He sounded the retreat, wheeled his mount, and rushed back into the valley. He flung a disgusted look over his shoulder, and cursed as he saw that his riders had been cut off. He urged his mount into a faster gait, and disappeared into the shadows.

Lord Malor led a contingent of mounted Elves against the O'skaa riders. He sat upon a white horse with his sword drawn. Sirlyk and his Goblins were with him, and a company of the bowmays stood with bows aimed. They were between the enemy and safety.

The O'skaa riders paused, seeking a way out. There was none. Their escape to the valley was blocked. They were outnumbered. They had thought to make a lightning raid, and retreat without loss, but they now faced destruction. They regarded each other, and then glared at their foes. With harsh cries, they leapt forwards as one.

A hail of arrows tore into them as the bowmays loosed their shafts. Fully half of the invaders and their mounts crashed to the ground as they were pierced through. The others came on, shrieking war cries and brandishing their weapons on high.

Lord Malor goaded his mount forwards, and his Elves came behind him. Sirlyk and his chokhutai rushed after them, wicked curved blades ready to deal death. The bowmays had reloaded, but held fast with bows ready to take down any enemy that tried to escape.

The two groups met with a bone shattering shock. Malor hewed about himself in a frenzy. Several riders went down under his flashing blade. His Elven warriors charged in, and slashed and hacked. Sirlyk spitted a Schaaka rider with his sword, and as the rider fell, the Goblin-King dodged his mount's attack, and plunged his sword into its brain. His chokhutai fell upon the foe, attacking fiercely.

In moments, it was all over. All of the raiders and their mounts lay dead, but not one of the defenders had been slain. They had only sustained cuts and bruises.

Sirlyk leapt up onto the back of one of the O'skaa. Malor reined his horse in beside him.

"Ha!" The Goblin-King exulted. "We slew all of the dogs with no loss to ourselves!" He grinned wickedly. He raised his sword, and his warriors cried out in delight.

"You are wrong, Your Majesty," Malor said. "There were losses."

"What?" Sirlyk said, perplexed. "What do you mean?"

"Do not forget the horses that were slain. The raid achieved its purpose."

An Elven warrior came up to Malor.

"How many horses did we lose?" The Elf-lord asked.

"Twenty were slain, and six others were severely wounded, My Lord. They may die before dawn."

"What of the sentries?" Malor asked.

"All of them were slain, My Lord."

"You see, Your Majesty, there *were* losses on our side."

Sirlyk's face was grim. He sheathed his sword in disgust.

"They are more lives that the Dark One must pay for," he growled.

Watching from the darkness, Kerlach clenched his fist furiously.

What would the Master do to him for such a stupid mistake? *They were waiting for us,* he thought grimly. For a moment, he considered making his way stealthily out of the valley, and hiding away before he could be blamed for losing his riders.

He shook his head. "There is nowhere to hide. The Master would find me no matter where I went." He turned his mount and slowly returned to report his failure to Queen Sardia. *She won't be pleased either,* he thought. "Either she kills me, or The Master will."

But Darkmor had much more important things on his mind at that very moment. He wasn't even aware that the raid had been sent out, or that Kerlach had lost his group. His brain seethed with the knowledge that Silveron was now close to the Starstone, and if the wizard destroyed it, much of his own power would be gone. Without it, The Army of Light would defeat his army, because once the spell that held the sun at bay was negated, the light would scatter his forces like bugs before a flaring torch. He increased his pace, hurrying down the corridor. His underlings hastened to keep up with him.

In their midst, Willowen smiled to see how exasperated the sorcerer was. She looked about at her guards. They were more interested in not lagging behind than in her at the moment. She watched and waited for her opportunity to escape. *Silveron,* she thought, *I know that you are here somewhere. I hope we will be together soon.*

One of the Goblins pushed her from behind. She stumbled and fell, and a rough hand dragged her to her feet. The Schaaka pulled her close.

"Don't even think about getting away, girl," he hissed. His breath stank.

Willowen flinched, and the Goblin flung her after the others. He laughed.

"I've got my eye on you," he chuckled. They came to a set of stairs, and hurried downwards.

Below them, Silveron and his companions waited with bated breath. This was the moment; the moment that would decide the fate of all Erathyn. They knew they must prevent Darkmor from reaching the Starstone. Nothing else mattered. If they should all be slain in the attempt, it would be of no account as long as the sorcerer's plan was foiled.

*And if he succeeds?* Silveron thought. *No, he* cannot *succeed. I* must *be the one to achieve victory. And rescue Willowen.* He grasped his staff tightly.

"Worry not, lad," Brador said. "Fail you will not."

The Elf met the Dwarf-Lord's gaze. He looked at his other friends. They had come a long way, and endured many trials.

"Thank you for being here with me, my friends," he said.

Brador gripped his arm.

"Ready, we are."

*"Hush!"* Nildoron whispered. *"They are close. Get the door, Egon."*

Egon grabbed the handle of the door and waited. The tension in the room was palpable. Their ears strained for the sound of the enemy, but nothing came to them. Only Nildoron and Silveron could hear the foe's approach. A few moments more went by, with the Elves listening intently.

*"Now!"* Silveron cried.

Egon flung the door open, and they rushed into the corridor.

Darkmor cursed as they appeared, and raised his staff. A blast of energy hurled Silveron and his companions to the floor. The sorcerer raced forwards, and as he and his entourage passed the stunned wizard, he cried out to the Schaaka who followed.

"Slay them all! Let none escape!"

Then he and the others fled down the corridor as the Goblins drew their swords and attacked.

Hardier than his companions, Brador leapt to his feet, and blocked a Schaaka's swing. He smashed the Goblin's helmet and skull with one blow of his war hammer. He waded into them, dealing crushing blows to left and right.

Egon stepped in and engaged one of them. Their blades met with a clang.

Nildoron drew his longknife and hurled it. It sank into one of the Schaaka's throats, and he slumped to the ground with a gurgle. The Elf-lord drew his sword and rushed into the fray.

K'taal and M'Shaan threw their spears. Both found a target, and as the bodies fell, the savage warriors drew their axes and knives and joined the fight with piercing war cries.

Toran-en and Yosh-en roared, and drew their own blades. In moments, they were in the thick of the combat.

Darkmor and his followers ran down a flight of stairs, descending towards the door that led to the chamber in which the Starstone lay. The sounds of combat receded behind them.

"Masster," Essissnarr hissed, "That will not hold them for long."

As they came to the end of the stairs and set foot on the floor, the sorcerer stopped and turned.

"Then we must ensure that they are delayed further," he said. He looked the Cobran in the eye, and made sure that he had his attention. He indicated the Plainsgirl with a flick of his eyes, and then nodded.

The Cobran understood his intent, and returned a nod of his own.

"Good," Darkmor said, and turned and hurried on.

Essissnar grabbed P'kaani by the arm, and waved the others on. They hastened after Darkmor. As Willowen and her Goblin guard passed them by, she saw the look of fear in the girl's eyes, and then they were gone.

The Cobran released the girl's arm.

"Go to the sstair and ssee where the enemy iss," he said.

P'kaani bowed, and went to obey the order.

Essissnarr lashed out with his staff. The snake-head smacked against the girl's neck with a ringing slap. She fell to the floor and thrashed about.

The Cobran watched for a moment as she writhed on the floor, his tongue flickering in and out. He looked around the corridor for a door. One lay to his right. The Snake-man went over to it, and raised his staff. He hissed a command, and the door was flung wide.

Essissnaar returned to the girl. Her thrashings had ceased, but now her back was bowed, and she breathed stertorously. The Cobran knelt down, and grabbed her by her long black hair. He dragged her across to the open door, and lay her down on the floor of the room inside.

He regarded her for a moment longer; an evil smile came to his lips. Then, he hurried away down the corridor in the direction Darkmor and his followers had gone.

# CHAPTER XVIII

# THREE QUEENS AND TWO KINGS

Anarys sat upon his horse and looked into the valley. Darkmor's tower loomed in the distance. Was he watching them even now? Perhaps he considered the Army of Light not worthy of his attention? Not one enemy scout had been seen since the previous night's attack.

But the Elven-King knew that thousands of Darkmor's followers lurked in the shadows, waiting for him to give the order to advance. *O'skaa, too,* he thought. *Thousands of them led by Sardia and Oolikhorr themselves.*

He smiled. The last time he had seen the monstrous arachnid was when Nilda had shot her in one of her great eyes. It had been a fine shot. *One of many that Nilda had made,* he thought sadly. He had thought that that had been the end of the creature, but now he knew that she still lived.

*And still she hungers for Elven flesh,* he thought.

*Sardia wants to destroy us, too. The Schaaka have hated us for centuries. Well, perhaps today they will get their wish.*

He peered into the distance, seeking a sign of any foe. None met his piercing gaze. It was as if the valley was empty of all life, good or otherwise.

"Don't be fooled by the emptiness."

Sirlyk sat his mount to his left. It was a huge warbeetle. It was much bigger than the Elven-King's horse. Its dark green carapace shone with a red glow under the occluded sunlight. He grinned.

"I'll wager that there are thousands of them, just waiting for us to come into their trap."

"I would not take that wager," Anarys replied, "for I know you are right."

"What do you wish to do, then? Shall we keep them waiting a bit longer?"

Anarys nodded.

"Yes," he said. "The longer we delay, the more time Silveron has. Let the enemy think that we are hesitant to enter his valley."

"Hmmm. We won't be able to do that for very long. Eventually, they'll get bored and attack." Sirlyk smiled knowingly. "I know Sardia. She's impatient. If we sit here, she won't be able to contain herself, and will come charging in."

The Elven-King smiled.

"Good. Then that is what we will do. Lord Merys."

"Your Majesty?"

"Go and pass the word that we will wait here until there is sign of the enemy."

Lord Merys bowed in his saddle.

"As you wish, Sire."

He rode off to pass the order.

"Now comes the last battle, Sirlyk. We are outnumbered. That is a certainty. The enemy has three queens and all of their forces at his command. Sardia, Oolikhorr, and my own lost queen are all his servants. I hope that I do not face her on the field."

"But we have two kings, Anarys." Sirlyk reached over and clapped him on the shoulder. "Two kings can beat three queens."

The Elven-King took his hand. They shook hands in the way of Men.

"Are you always so optimistic, my friend?" Anarys said.

"Always," Sirlyk said, grinning. "If we are to die, let us die well. I've had a good life." He gazed into the valley. "I'd like to face Sardia, though. I would die happily if I could cut her down." He patted his warbeetle on its head. "Chukdah here would like that too." The warbeetle mewed.

"What about Oolikhorr? I imagine she would not make such a task easy for you."

"You're right there. That monster is a fearsome enemy. She's much more dangerous than her many sisters. I hear that she is at least ten times the size of them."

The Elven-King thought for a moment.

"She is huge, but not as large as that. I would say she is about four times their size."

"Still too big for a Goblin," Sirlyk said, smiling.

"Even the King of the Goblins?"

"Ha, Ha! Even him. But I hear he is a great fighter."

"And a great drinker."

Sirlyk slapped Anarys on the back.

"That's true!" Sirlyk laughed. "Sometimes both at the same time."

They both smiled.

Anarys smile faded.

"I am glad that you are here by my side, my friend. We have seen many battles. Perhaps this will be our last one."

"Perhaps, but anything is possible. What will happen if Silveron is successful?"

"I do not know. Darkmor will be thrown out of this world. More than that, I cannot be certain of."

"What of his army? Will we still have to face them, or will they scatter when his spells are gone?"

Anarys shook his head.

"I do not know," he repeated.

"What of those of your kin who are under his command? Your Queen, and all of her folk. Will they know who you are?"

"Perhaps. Or maybe they will just turn to dust, as all of the others did." He indicated the thick dust on the valley floor.

Sirlyk made a face.

"How awful. We must hope that that does not happen."

"It may be preferable to facing Nerolynn and all of her warriors in combat."

"How can you say that, Anarys? She was your greatest love, and your staunchest supporter."

"I know. But I have already lost her. Goldwen and I came here a thousand years ago, after the final conflict with Malkaar. We went through the High Pass, but were delayed by Malkaar himself. With his sorcery, he threw the mountainside down upon us. We were lucky to survive. By the time we managed to get here, it was all over. Shaarla had cast the Ice of Foreverness, but before she did so, Malkaar had put everyone in the valley under a Spell of Stasis. Then he was frozen in ice himself."

"I remember," Sirlyk said. "Your day of triumph was accompanied by tragedy."

"Goldwen tried every spell he knew, but nothing he did could break Malkaar's sorcery. He was the most powerful wizard on Erathyn, but even he had no success in freeing Nerolynn and the others. Finally, he admitted defeat. It was a heavy blow to him. He admired Nerolynn greatly, and for him to not be able to release her was torture to him. He felt he had let me down, and it almost broke him. Goldwen then left us and wandered in the wilderness for ten years, struggling with the fact that he had failed."

"I wish he were with us," Sirlyk said.

The Elven-King nodded.

"As do I. His powers are most needed now. With him beside us, I could almost believe that we could win. All of our hopes are with Silveron, but this test could be too much for him. If he fails..."

"He won't fail. You told me that Goldwen had given him much of his power."

"True. But power without control or experience can amount to nothing. An untrained warrior who flails about with a sword has a slim chance of winning a fight."

"But sometimes he may get in a lucky stroke, and take down his enemy."

Anarys regarded him.

"I have missed your unfailing positive attitude, my friend. I wish we had more time. I would like to sit and talk as we did of old."

"I'd like that too. Perhaps we will, after the battle."

"Perhaps. If we are still here."

"Your Majesty?"

"Yes, Lord Merys?"

"The army is standing by as you ordered, My Liege."

"Good. Go and rest. Make sure that a watch is kept on the valley for any sign of the enemy."

Lord Merys bowed in his saddle.

"Yes, Sire. Your Majesties."

He rode off.

Lord Malor rode up to them and bowed in the saddle.

"Your Majesties. We are not going to advance?"

Anarys shook his head.

"No. I have decided to make Sardia and her friends wait for us."

"I see. I wonder how long she will be able to do that."

"Not long," Sirlyk said with a grin. "We were just talking about that.

She is impatient. I'll wager she will get tired of waiting for us to come, and rush to the attack."

"You speak the truth," Malor said. "I have seen her act that way before. It is a weakness, her short temper."

"A weakness that we should make use of," Anarys said. "Now we wait."

"This is the part that I hate," Sirlyk replied.

"As do I," Malor added. "I would rather be in battle than just waiting for it to happen."

The Elven-King dismounted, and his companions followed suit. Three Elven grooms hurried forwards to take the reins from them. Two of them led the horses a short distance away. The third groom looked at Sirlyk's warbeetle doubtfully.

"It's all right," Sirlyk said, "She won't hurt you." He held the reins out.

The groom took them from him gingerly.

Sirlyk patted Chukdah's flank.

"Go with him."

The warbeetle chittered and allowed herself to be led away by the groom.

Anarys and Malor smiled. Then the two kings and the Elf-lord sat down on the ground.

Sirlyk stretched and yawned.

"I wish we had some of your honey-wine," he said. He looked up at the top of the valley. "Look there, Sardia and Oolikhorr are watching us." He waved merrily.

The Queen of the Schaaka scowled. She could see the tiny figure of Sirlyk waving.

"I'll lop that hand off," she hissed angrily.

*Pay him no mind, Ssisster Queen,* Oolikhorr sent. *They are all doomed.*

*We will crussh them, and rule thiss world.*

"You are right," Sardia said. "They cannot hope to succeed against us. Even without Nerolynn and her warriors, we are more than a match for their pitiful force." She smiled wickedly. "When they are gone, I will take Sirlyk's kingdom for my own."

*Perhapss the Masster will keep the moon where it iss? Then we would never have to return to the Underworld. We could make a new kingdom here.*

"Perhaps. I never considered that. I thought that he would negate the spell once our enemies were destroyed, and we would return home." She thought for a moment. "I would like to remain here. The open spaces are pleasant. I even like the light the way it is. We were forced away from Sirlyk's lands, and we retreated into the darkness. Even the dimness of the upper caverns was denied us. We lingered for centuries in the shadows, sending forth raids from time to time. You remember this."

*I do. I alsso remember the hate that you bear Ssirlyk, and hiss friendss, the Bright Oness.*

"That is a hate that is matched by your own, Great One."

The arachnid hissed, and venom dripped from her fangs to sizzle on the rocks beneath them. She moved agitatedly beneath the Goblin.

*Yess,* she sent, *I wissh to meet the one that did thiss to me.* She scratched irritably at the arrow lodged in her eye. *It burnss me. The pain never sstopss. I will make her ssuffer for a long time before I sslay her..."*

"I am sure you will, Sister Queen. How fine it will be to wipe the Elves from the face of Erathyn. Sirlyk and his Goblins will be slain too. Men, Dwarves, all of them will fall. They will all be destroyed."

*Not all of them,* Oolikhorr sent. *We musst leave ssome of them alive. My children and I musst have something to eat.* A wheezing sound came from the monster. The Queen of the Spiders was laughing.

Sardia laughed.

"You will have your fill of their flesh. I am sure the Master will supply you with a plentiful stock of them." She peered down at the small figures of Anarys and Sirlyk. "Enjoy the last moments of your existence. You will not laugh at us for much longer, Sirlyk."

*Perhapss you would like to laugh at him and the King of the Bright Oness?*

"What do you mean?" Sardia said.

*Why do you not sshow them what Queen Nerolynn hass become? They would not laugh then.*

Sardia smiled.

"That would indeed give them pause. I would love to see Anarys's face when he sees that she still lives and how she has been put under Darkmor's control." She stroked the arachnid's head. "But I will keep that secret for a while longer. I want it to be a great shock for the King of the Bright Ones. I want him to hesitate when I reveal his pretty Queen and her warriors to them. I want the revelation of her existence to stay his hand, perhaps fatally. Will he take up arms against his love? Or will he not be able to force himself to fight against her on the field?"

*I would not think sso,* Oolikhorr sent. *They are weak, thesse creaturess. If one of my ssisterss were to attempt to fight me, I would sslay her in an insstant. I would have no qualmss about doing sso. The ssentiment that they feel for each other iss one of their great weaknesssess.*

"You are right," Sardia replied. "Anarys and his ilk do not have the strength of conviction that you and I have. It *is* one of their greatest failings. I have seen it many times when we have fought them. Where we would slay any who stood against us, regardless of who they were, or even what they meant to us, they would pause and let their weak emotional attitudes rule their actions. Sometimes that would mean that they would be slain themselves. I have never understood that flaw in their character."

*Nor have I. But it iss a weaknesss that we can take advantage of, Ssisster*

Queen. *That iss all that matterss.*

"I agree, Great One."

There was a commotion behind them. Oolikhorr turned around. Coming towards them was Kerlach. He rode his mount right up to them, and then he and his O'skaa bowed.

Sardia regarded him with distaste. The Goblin's face was sweaty, and he did not meet her eye. He knew how she and Oolikhorr rewarded failure. He glanced once at the huge form of the Queen of the Spiders, and then lowered his head.

Sardia did not speak. *Let him tremble in fear for a moment,* she thought with relish. Beneath her Oolikhorr hissed. Kerlach flinched at the sound.

"What have we here?" Sardia finally said.

*Iss thiss not Kerlach?* Oolikhorr sent. *He losst all of hiss riderss. He failed uss, Ssister Queen."*

The Goblin's head came up. His good eye was wide with terror.

"N-no, Great One...."

*"We did not give you leave to speak!"* Sardia screamed. She fixed him with a terrible gaze.

Kerlach lowered his head, dismayed. His huge frame began to tremble.

The Queen of the Schaaka leaned forward in her saddle.

"Perhaps you are not capable of following our commands?" She asked icily. "Was your raid successful?" She paused, and then screamed: *"Or did you lose your entire squad?!"*

Kerlach could not reply. He was shivering with fear.

*Sspeak!* Oolikhorr commanded.

The rider looked up. He stared at them, his mouth open. He attempted to say something, but his terror overmastered him. Gone was the swaggering demeanour that he had previously shown. Now he was paralysed with horror.

"How do we reward failure, Sister Queen?" Sardia asked knowingly.

*With death,* Oolikhorr sent. *Thosse who fail uss desserve nothing lesss...*

The other O'skaa around them began to stir. They were anticipating a feast. Kerlach and his mount would serve as a fine meal. The rider looked around at the encircling arachnids and swallowed nervously. One command from Sardia or Oolikhorr and he and his spider would be torn to shreds and eaten alive.

"I –I –" he stammered.

"You are pathetic, Kerlach," Sardia said, her lip curled in a sneer.

*We give you command of a hosst of O'sskaa riderss, and thiss iss how you sshow your gratitude?* Venom dripped from the monster's fangs and fell to smoke upon the rocks.

Kerlach found his voice. He took a deep breath to steady his nerves, and went on in a rush.

"W – we slew many horses...and the sentries too."

The two Queens stared at him impassively.

"I beg Your Majesties to let me make amends for my failure."

"Why should we do so?" Sardia asked.

The rider stared at them, searching his mind for a reason that would be acceptable for them to allow his mistake to be forgiven. He found none. His error had cost the lives of his entire squad, Goblin and O'skaa both. There was no excuse that he could use to justify that loss.

*Well,* Oolikhorr sent. *Why sshould we forgive your failure?*

Kerlach licked his lips.

"I know there is no excuse for my mistake," he said. "But I have served you both well in the past. Surely that is something that counts in my favour?"

"Do you ask us for mercy, Kerlach?" The Queen of the Schaaka said. "Do you wish us to ignore your error of judgement that cost the lives of your squad?" Her eyes narrowed. "And I believe you also missed the opportunity to capture King Anarys himself. With him as our prisoner, his army would have been forced to submit to our demands. They would not have dared to oppose us. The battle would have been won without a fight."

The rider searched Sardia's face. It was set like stone. Mercy was not to be found there. He looked at Oolikhorr. The monstrous arachnid's main eyes were expressionless. One of them only held great hunger, and the other was dull and dead; he stared at Nilda's arrow that still protruded from it.

"I do ask for mercy, My Queen." He bowed in the saddle.

Sardia allowed silence to descend. The O'skaa around them still shifted restlessly, but no other sound was heard. She regarded Kerlach. The Goblin still trembled. Sardia knew that her next words would decide his fate. She relished the power that that gave her.

"What do you say, Great One? Does Kerlach's long service to us make up for his error? Do we show mercy?"

The Queen of the Spiders regarded the trembling Goblin. Kerlach wondered what was going on in her mind. The O'skaa were unpredictable, and with her horrid wound she was probably going insane. He waited with bated breath for Oolikhorr to comment.

*No,* Oolikhorr sent. *We musst make an example of him.*

Kerlach gasped. His life was done.

"I agree." Sardia addressed the leader of the closest group of O'skaa riders. "Garduk, tell your riders to dismount and move to a safe distance, so that they may not suffer Kerlach's fate."

"Yes, My Queen. Dismount!"

Twenty riders jumped down from their mounts, and backed away hastily. They had all seen how the male O'skaa devoured victims. None of them had ever seen how the females fed. The arachnid's claws tapped on the rocks impatiently. They began to hiss in anticipation of the feast to come.

Only Garduk remained seated on his mount. He regarded Kerlach with a grim smile.

*"No,"* Kerlach whispered. His good eye brimmed with tears. He tossed away his goad, leapt down from his O'skaa, and prostrated himself before the two queens.

"I beg you, Your Majesties." He looked up, and saw Sardia's stony visage. "Mercy," he pleaded. His tears spilled over and ran down his terrified face. He clasped his hands together in supplication. His eye searched Sardia's face for any sign of mercy.

The Queen of the Goblins stared down at him with disgust.

"Take them," she ordered coldly.

With a chorus of shrill screams, the O'skaa rushed in. Kerlach screamed once, and then he was covered by the mass of ravenous spiders. He screamed several more times, and then his agonised shrieks were cut off abruptly. The monsters scrabbled and fought over Kerlach, and his severed arm was thrown clear of the feasting creatures. It had hardly landed on the rocks before one of the O'skaa snatched it up and devoured it. As they tore him and his mount apart and ate them alive, Sardia and Oolikhorr looked on dispassionately. The other riders stared at the feast aghast. Even they were appalled at Kerlach's awful death. Only Garduk remained impassive. His mount made to join the other O'skaa, but at a curt word from him, and a sharp tug on her reins, the O'skaa subsided and merely watched.

Down in the valley, Anarys had been describing to Sirlyk what had happened to the unfortunate Kerlach. His far-seeing Elven eyes had shown him the Goblin's horrific demise.

"You could call that justice," Sirlyk said.

"Yes, you could," Anarys said. "Kerlach suffered the same terrible death that he meted out to Melandra and her bowmays. It was what he deserved."

"It's too bad," Sirlyk said.

"What do you mean? Surely you do not think that that evil creature did not deserve his end?"

"Not at all," Sirlyk said. "I merely thought that Captain Lysanna will be disappointed that she can't slay the dog herself." He grinned.

Anarys shook his head and smiled wryly.

On the cliff top above the valley, the O'skaa had ended their horrific repast, and had backed away from the spot where Kerlach and his mount had met their dooms. Blood lay upon the rocks, and only mere tatters of clothing and a pair of boots showed where the unfortunate Goblin had been eaten. His sword lay upon the rocks, and Garduk dismounted, walked slowly forwards, knelt, and picked it up. He faced the two queens.

"Well, Garduk, you are now given Kerlach's position. It is only right that you take his sword."

The Schaaka bowed.

"Thank you, My Queen. I will not fail you."

"See that you do not." Sardia's gaze swept the feasting area, and then she met his eye. Garduk did not need her to say any more. He knew that any failure on his part would ensure that he met the same grim end that had befallen Kerlach. He walked back to his O'skaa, and leapt into the saddle. He held Kerlach's sword in his hand.

*You know what will happen if you fail uss..* Oolikhorr sent.

"I do, Great One." He slung the huge sword at his back.

"Good," Sardia said. "Take charge of your riders. You are to command Kerlach's force on the other side of the valley."

"Yes, My Queen." He turned and beckoned his riders forwards. *"Mount up!"*

The Schaaka came forwards, and mounted their O'skaa. They looked at the blood and remnants on the rocks, and then turned their attention to their new leader.

"*Bow!*" he cried.

The Schaaka bowed in their saddles, and their mounts lowered their foreparts onto the rocks in obeisance.

"Now go and wait for the order to attack," Sardia said.

"We obey, My Queen. *Turn about! Ride!*"

The greater mass of O'skaa opened up a way for them, and Garduk and his riders went through the gap and disappeared from view. The O'skaa closed up.

"Now, Sister Queen," Sardia said, "I have an idea."

*And what would that be?* Oolikhorr sent.

"I think that you are right; we will show Anarys and Sirlyk what Queen Nerolynn has become. That should take some of the fight out of them. Imagine how the Elven warriors will react when they see that their queen and many of their former friends are arrayed against them."

*Yess,* Oolikhorr sent; *let uss go down to them.*

"Arakh, bring twenty of your best O'skaa riders to escort us."

"Yes, My Queen."

Oolikhorr moved off, and the O'skaa fell in behind her.

Minutes later, Anarys rose to his feet. He frowned.

"What is it?" Sirlyk asked. He stood and looked in the direction where the Elven-King's attention was focussed.

"A large group of O'skaa comes. Oolikhorr and Sardia are at their head. There is also a contingent of mounted warriors on horses behind them. I cannot make them out yet."

"Horses? I thought the Goblins disdained such mounts. That's strange."

"Indeed." Anarys continued to watch the oncoming group.

"Sire?"

Lord Merys sat his horse beside the two kings. He bowed in the saddle.

"What do you wish me to do?"

"Bring up some bowmays, and some mounted warriors. Have the bowmays arm themselves, but do not fire unless I give the order. It seems that Sardia and her monster wish only to talk."

"Maybe they want to surrender to us?" Sirlyk said. He grinned.

"I doubt that, my friend. Go, Lord Merys."

"Yes, Sire."

He rode off.

Anarys could finally make out the group of mounted warriors. He gasped.

"What is it?" Sirlyk said.

"See for yourself."

The Goblin looked, and saw a figure resplendent in golden armour leading the mounted warriors. Her hair was golden too. She rode a fine white horse.

"Nerolynn..." Sirlyk said, amazement in his voice.

Oolikhorr came right up to the two kings. Sardia regarded them both with a smile. The bowmays came and formed up in front of Anarys and Sirlyk, and fitted arrows to string. The mounted Elves arranged themselves in battle order behind them. The entire Army of Light made itself ready for battle.

Lord Merys rode up. He stared at the mounted Elves, and looked at their leader with shock on his face.

"The Queen?" He said, confused. "Sire, how can this be? Is it a trick?"

"It is no trick," Sardia said. "Here is your Queen Nerolynn, Anarys." She beckoned, and Nerolynn rode forwards. She halted in front of them. She showed no sign of recognition. Her face was blank, and her eyes were white and empty of emotion.

Several shocked voices were heard from the forces gathered there.

"*The Queen!*"

"She lives!"

"How can this be?"

Anarys regarded her beautiful face. How many times had he wished that she had not been lost to him? *Thousands of times,* he thought. Now she was here before him. His heart ached with longing for her. He wanted to rush to her and take her in his arms. *But that is just what the enemy wants me to do,* he thought.

*Well, Bright One, do you not wissh to greet your love?* Oolikhorr wheezed with mirth.

"Yes," Sardia said mischievously, "why do you not greet her warmly?"

The Elven-King tore his gaze away from Nerolynn. He met Sardia's eye, and the fury in his own gaze made her flinch.

"Because she is *not* my Nerolynn," he said coldly. "My Queen died many years ago."

"Not so," Sardia said, recovering her poise. "This *is* Nerolynn. I myself saw how the Master resurrected her."

*Sshe sspeakss truly, Bright One. Hiss magick iss sstrong.*

"Why has he done this?" Anarys knew why; he just wanted to see what Sardia had to say.

"Why, to bring you both together, of course," The Goblin Queen said. "Do you not want to be with her?"

Anarys nodded to himself. Of course.

"What would the price for that be?" he asked.

Sardia smiled, and leaned back in her saddle.

"You would accept the Master as your rightful overlord. You would pledge your allegiance to him, and serve him forever."

"Is that all? That seems to be an easy thing to do."

"It is, isn't it?" Sardia said. "Be reasonable, Anarys. Accept this offer, and Nerolynn will be yours again." She smiled. "Think of your warriors, too. Would they not hate to fight those who they have loved? Surely there are Elves in Nerolynn's company who are well known to your own warriors. To have them face each other on the field of battle would be a terrible thing."

"That is just what the Dark One wants," Sirlyk said gruffly. "That is why he cast his spell upon them."

Sardia glanced at him once, and then returned her attention to Anarys.

"Such bloodshed could be averted, Anarys. It is up to you. What is your decision? Do you accept the Master's offer?"

The Elven-King regarded her, and then looked at Nerolynn. Her face had not changed at all, save for the blank expression. A thousand years had not left its mark on her. Her hair was still rich and golden, just as he remembered it.

"You cannot do this, Anarys," Sirlyk said.

The Goblin Queen's lip curled in a snarl.

"It is not your decision, Sirlyk," she said acidly. "Anarys commands the Army of Light. Only he can make this choice."

*Yess,* Oolikhorr sent. *Keep your wordss to yoursself.*

"Suppose I do accept this offer," Anarys said, "what will happen to Sirlyk and his chokhutai?"

Sardia smiled wickedly.

"We will slaughter them."

"That doesn't seem reasonable," Anarys said. "What of the Dwarves, the Avianinn, and the Felininn? Will you slay them all too?"

"They will all die, yes," The Goblin Queen answered. "They are not part of this bargain."

"It appears to be no bargain to me," Sirlyk said.

Sardia rounded on him.

"Silence, fool! I'm not interested in you."

Sirlyk laughed.

"I'm glad of that. Do you really think that Anarys would surrender his entire army, and allow the rest of us to be slain? You are as insane as that creature you ride if you believe that."

Oolikhorr hissed, and made to leap upon the Goblin. The bowmays brought up their bows, and aimed at the arachnid. Sardia's face was suddenly white with fear. At her back, the O'skaa prepared to rush to the attack. The mounted Elves brought up their spears, and levelled them in preparation of a charge. Nerolynn drew her sword, but made no other move. A tense silence descended.

Which was broken by the Elven-King's chuckle.

"You are as outspoken as always, my friend." He clapped Sirlyk on the back, and took a step forwards.

"Sirlyk is impetuous, but his words echo my thoughts."

Sardia's eyes were slits. She hated that her fear had been witnessed by everyone there.

"So you decline this proposition?" she asked coldly.

"I do," Anarys replied. "I cannot surrender my army just for the opportunity of having Nerolynn by my side again."

*But sshe wass your great love. How can you refusse thiss?*

The Elven-King looked at the monster.

"I can refuse it by remembering that she was lost to me a thousand years ago. I have grieved for her, but I have continued on with my life. How can she be the same? The Dark One has control of her now. She and her warriors are neither alive nor dead, but in some strange undead state."

Sardia had been listening to all that Anarys said. Her face flushed with fury.

"You are as foolish as Sirlyk," she spat angrily. "Now, the next time you see Nerolynn will be on the battlefield. I hope that you will relish fighting her."

Anarys looked at Nerolynn. She stared blankly, with no sign of intelligence in her eyes. *But I imagine she would be able to fight,* he thought. A vision of them both locked in mortal combat came to him. Could he face her on the field? Would he be able to strike her down, or would his hand be stayed? He didn't know. Would the fate of Erathyn be decided by his hesitation? *No,* he thought, *this battle is nothing compared to the task that Silveron has been set. If I fall to Nerolynn's sword, it is my fate.*

"If that is what is to be, then I cannot deny it," he said.

The Goblin Queen laughed harshly.

"Perhaps you are not concerned about your life because you still hold onto the hope that your wizard will be successful." She smiled. "That is a forlorn hope. He and his companions are dead."

The Elven-King regarded her.

"You lie."

Sardia shook her head.

"I do not lie. Silveron and his friends were lost in the Master's labyrinth, and the O'skaa dined on them."

*Thiss iss true. I ssaw it in my mind,* Oolikhorr sent.

"Your mind has been twisted since that arrow pierced your eye," Sirlyk said roughly. He glanced at Anarys, worry filling his heart.

The huge arachnid hissed.

"No," Anarys said. "He cannot be dead."

"Why do you say this?" Sardia said. "Can you sense him? Do you have a connection to him? Can you feel that he is alive?"

"No, but I have faith that he still lives, and will succeed in his task."

"Faith, ha!" Sardia cried. Your warriors on The Great Plain had faith that they would win. Many of them perished. Your warriors at Lindemar had faith that their cause would succeed. They were slaughtered. Those stupid Felininn who died in the forest had faith in you. They all fell. Faith is nothing but a foolish dream. *Power* is the only thing that matters, and you are powerless before the Master."

"You may be right," The Elven-King replied.

"Of course I am right. Without Silveron's magic, you have no others to stand up to him. You know by now that even Amberon and his companions have turned against you. Your fate is to die a needless death."

"Yes, I am aware of Amberon's treachery. The Council of Light is broken."

She leaned forwards in her saddle.

"Anarys, there is no way that you can win. Think of your warriors. Will you let them give their lives for a hopeless cause? If you will only pledge allegiance to the Master, they will all live. I ask you again, be reasonable. Accept this offer, and save them all. If you don't, they will all die."

"Death would be preferable to serving him as slaves," Sirlyk said.

Sardia glared at him, but said nothing.

"Should I give you some time to consider? I'm afraid I can't give you long." She smiled.

"I do not need time," Anarys replied. "You know what my answer must be."

Sardia's smile faded. She shook her head.

"You are a fool, Anarys. You should have agreed. Now all of you will die."

"If that is our destiny, then we cannot escape it."

The Queen of the Goblins regarded them both for a moment.

"So be it," she said. She regarded the bowmays. "Will you allow us to leave, or shoot us down?"

"Let them go," Anarys said.

The bowmays lowered their bows, and the mounted Elves lowered their spears.

Sardia turned Oolikhorr with a pull on the reins. The O'skaa riders turned and followed, and Nerolynn's mounted warriors formed up and rode after them.

"You did the right thing," Sirlyk said.

"I know. Lord Merys."

"Sire?"

"Prepare for battle."

"Yes, Your Majesty."


Above them, watching in amazement at Nerolynn's appearance, F'leet and K'reel turned to each other.

"The Queen lives?" K'reel said, in disbelief.

"Surely it is a trick of the Dark One," one of the Avianinn said.

"No," F'leet rumbled. "It is truly Queen Nerolynn."

"How can this be?" K'reel asked. "She was lost to us over a thousand years ago."

"I do not know," F'leet answered. "The enemy's sorcery is powerful. Somehow he has made her live again."

"What should we do, Lord?" K'reel asked. "Should we go down to the King?"

F'leet stood staring down at Sardia's group as they made their way back to their own lines. What was going through Anarys's mind? What would Nerolynn's sudden appearance have upon his resolve? Could he actually face her in combat? Then it came to the Winglord. He understood Darkmor's plan. *Ah*, he thought. *That is just what the enemy wants. He wants Anarys to be shaken by this. Darkmor wants Anarys to lose his fighting spirit. How cunning.*

"No," he said aloud. "We have been given a task. We must carry it out."

K'reel regarded him for a moment, and then looked down at the battlefield. His gaze lingered on the departing queens. He watched them for a moment longer, and then returned his attention to F'leet.

"As you wish, My Lord," he said, and bowed.

# CHAPTER IX

# THE VALLEY OF DEATH

The O'skaa that had escaped from Linador finally arrived at Darkmor's stronghold. It had hastened there, driven by the need to report to him. The arachnid made its way past the frozen warriors, and into the camp at the end of the valley. There it was stopped by two riders.

"Where have you come from?" One of them asked. "Where is your rider?"

*I come from Sstonebridge. He wass ssslain.*

"What happened to the company there?" The other asked.

*Sslain. All sslain. By the Bright Oness and their alliesss.*

"We must report this to the Master."

*Yess, yess, the Masster. The Masster musst be told.*

"What must I be told?"

The two Schaaka turned. Darkmor stood there with staff in hand. They dropped to one knee, and the O'skaa lowered its forepart to the ground.

"Master, this O'skaa comes from Stonebridge. It says the company there was destroyed by the Bright Ones."

*Sslain. All sslain. By the Bright Oness and their alliesss,* The O'skaa sent.

"Allies?" Darkmor queried. "Which allies do you speak of?"

*A Man. And Goblinss were with them too.*

"The Man would be Ervin the Kandaran," The sorcerer said. "The Goblins would be those under Jhara Shin's command."

He stood lost in thought. The two riders and the O'skaa did not interrupt his meditation. They knew that even though he wore the Elf's young body, his mercurial temperament and fierce temper were still a part of him.

"It is of no matter," he finally said. "Stonebridge and Gorlik's company there served their purpose." He started to leave, but then recalled a thought. He pointed his staff at the O'skaa. "What happened to Althar? I haven't had any message from him, and I can't sense him."

*He was sslain, Masster.*

"How? What happened?"

*The Man sslew him in combat, Masster.*

*So, Kandaran. You finally avenged your people,* Darkmor thought. He smiled.

"Althar served his purpose too," he said. "Put this O'skaa in with your mounts. Send riders to every company. They must leave the valley, and go into the mountains. I'm going to cast a spell. Ensure that no-one is left behind, or they'll die. I'll begin in one hour."

"Yes, Master," chorused the riders.

Darkmor turned and raised his staff. He lifted off the ground, and flew to the top of the tower. He saw the O'skaa riders taking his message to the different companies that were camped in the valley. His gaze left them and swept over the stilled warriors. For over a thousand years that spell had held, but now it was time to undo it.

Darkmor put his hand into his robes and withdrew Willowen's pendant.

"Soon,' he said to himself. He put the pendant back in his robes.

He walked over to the door and let himself in with a wave of his hand. The door closed behind him with a thud.

On the ledge above the tower Silveron and Nomayon lay side by side. The Seer's eyes were vacant, and the Elf knew that Nomayon had seen and heard what Darkmor had said to the Schaaka. He had seen some of it himself in his mind, but he didn't dare to intrude in case Darkmor sensed his presence.

Why were Darkmor's forces breaking camp? Why were they leaving the valley? He watched and saw them marching away into the mountains. Why had they done this?

"Nomayon knows."

Silveron saw that Nomayon's eyes were clear.

They both backed away from the edge, and rejoined their companions, who had been waiting for them.

"Nomayon saw and heard the Dark One," The Seer said.

"What were his orders, Nomayon?" Silveron asked.

"The spider told him of a battle," Nomayon replied. "A group of his Schaaka were all slain by a force that had both Elves and Goblins in it."

"Ah," Brador said, "Lord Shin's chokhutai."

"Yes Brador, I agree," The wizard said. "That makes sense. Go on, Nomayon."

"Ervin was with them. He slew the traitor Althar in single combat."

"So he has finally avenged his people," Egon said. "That is good news."

"Where was this battle, Nomayon?" Yosh-en enquired.

"At Stonebridge in the mountains."

"Stonebridge?" Silveron echoed.

"That is what Men called Linador," K'Reel said. "It was once a meeting place for all of the races. The Schaaka must have used it to spy on our army."

"Mmm. Yes, remember Stonebridge, I do," the Dwarf said. Fine work was done there, by both Elf and Dwarf."

"Why did Darkmor's forces leave the valley?" Silveron asked.

"The Dark One is going to cast a spell," Nomayon said.

"What kind of spell?" Egon said.

"Nomayon does not know. But he goes now to the stone from the sky. He has Princess Willowen's pendant."

"Trying to unlock the Starstone's power, he must be," Brador said.

"Yes, but why?" Silveron said. "What can the spell be?"

"It must have something to do with his forces leaving the valley," Egon said.

"It makes no sense," Yosh-en said. "Why would they have to leave? There is nothing in the valley..." he trailed off.

"The warriors from a thousand years ago, there are," Brador said.

"Could he be going to release them from that spell?" K'Reel said.

"I do not know," the Elf said.

"Even if he did, can they be alive after all this time?" Egon said.

"We must assume that they could be," Silveron replied.

"If that's true," Egon said, "then the forces that faced him all those years ago would still be against him."

"Would they?" Silveron said. "Surely he would not free them from the spell, only to have them as his enemy again. I fear he would also be able to turn them into his allies."

"Makes sense, that does," Brador said. "Go and stop him before he casts this spell, we should."

"We do not know where in the tower he is," The wizard said. "We should wait here and make sure that he is going to lift the spell."

"But waste time that does," Brador argued. "Go now, we should."

"Silveron is right," Egon said, "we don't know how to find the Dark One. It's better that we stay here and watch and wait."

"I agree," Yosh-en said. "If it turns out that he does lift the spell, we will have to warn King Anarys."

"That is where I come in," K'Reel said.

"Good, K'Reel," Silveron said. "We will wait here and see what happens." He exchanged a glance with Brador. "But once we see what the result of his spell is, we will go down and enter the tower by the hidden door."

The Dwarf grinned.

"Acceptable that is." He lay down and closed his eyes.

The Elf smiled. He knew that Brador, as a seasoned campaigner, was taking his rest while he could.

"That is a good idea," he said. "All of you rest. Nomayon and I will keep watch, and wake you if necessary."

The group made themselves comfortable, and Silveron and Nomayon crept back to the edge.

Far below them Darkmor came to the door that led to the Starstone. The two Schaaka there bowed to him. He waved his hand, and the huge metal bolt pulled back with a screech. The door opened slowly, and a wave of heat gusted out. He entered, and the door closed behind him. He traversed the narrow bridge that led to the platform on the far side. The lake of fire grumbled and hissed in the depths below. He was half way across and his face was already shining with sweat.

The sorcerer stepped onto the platform. He strode purposefully up to the raised area where the Starstone sat. It shrieked at him, a metallic howl that echoed in the chamber. Hate and fury were in that cry. Darkmor knew that if the intelligence within the stone were released from the sorcerous bonds that he had bound it with, it would seek to destroy him.

He stood before it, his gaze sweeping the sigils that he had put in place.

They were all as they should be. Even so, he knew that the thing had been straining against its prison.

"So, you still don't accept me as your master."

A metallic wail answered his statement. It went on, changing pitch and timbre. The thing was trying to communicate with him. But there was only fury and detestation in the sounds. The sorcerer knew that it was venting its hatred for him in a tirade that he couldn't understand, but he felt its rage nonetheless.

He stepped closer, and the intensity of the sounds increased.

"You'd like to escape, wouldn't you?" He smiled. "You'd like to break out of your prison, and destroy me."

A harsh metal grinding was his only answer. It sounded like the frustrated sound a beast would make that couldn't reach its prey. It rose to a deafening pitch.

He pulled Willowen's amulet from his robe and dangled it in front of the Starstone. The howling shut off as though it had been cut with a knife.

"Ah. Good. I'm glad to see that I have your attention."

A whine came from the Starstone. It sounded like a whipped puppy.

"Now," Darkmor said. "I want you to give me your power."

He raised his staff and began to chant...

Two hours later Darkmor appeared upon the tower's top. He hadn't bothered with the hundreds of stairs that led to the chamber below. With the help of Willowen's amulet, he had unlocked the Starstone's power. It filled him. He felt like he was filled to the utmost part of himself with blazing energy. He walked to the edge and looked out over the valley.

The sorcerer raised his staff with both hands and closed his eyes. He formed in his mind the sigils that corresponded with the words of the incantation. The eyes of the serpent bracelet kindled, and a ball of black fire appeared at the staff's tip. Black flames ran down the staff.

"Chah!" Darkmor cried. A sigil formed before him made of black flame, as though an unseen hand was writing in the air.

"Mok!" Another sigil joined the first. The air around him began to shimmer, as if Darkmor were wreathed in a heat haze.

"Dahk!" A third sigil appeared and blazed alongside the others.

"Chekh!" A fourth sigil burned upon the air.

"Toh!" The fifth sigil was added.

"Ley!" The sixth sigil appeared.

"Dun!" The seventh sigil was added.

Darkmor opened his eyes and stared fixedly at the blazing sigils. Only one more remained, and the spell would be complete. He took a deep breath.

"Mahk!" He cried. The eighth and final sigil appeared.

Darkmor brought the staff down with both hands and slammed its base against the tower. The sigils vanished with a thunderclap. A shock wave radiated outwards.

Under the blood red light of the occluded sun, the wave of energy pulsed outwards from the tower. It flowed over the stilled warriors. A low humming accompanied it, making the walls of the valley vibrate. It went on for a few moments, and then the wave dissipated, and the sound stopped. There was stillness.

A vast groan went up. It came from the throats of the thousands of warriors who had been held in the Spell of Stasis. Here and there were small movements as they began to move. Slowly, these movements intensified, until it could be seen that all of the warriors had turned to face the tower.

"Come to me," Darkmor said.

Slowly, the host began to advance towards him. Like sleepwalkers, they came on, the sound of their tramping feet and the hooves of their mounts rumbled like thunder. Elf, Man, Cobran, Dwarf, Avianinn, Felininn, and all the nameless things that had made up the Army of Darkness came closer. They advanced right up to the tower's base and stopped.

"I am your master," Darkmor said. "Go into the mountains until I call for you. Do not interfere with my forces there. Go!"

As one, the immense horde began to move away. Darkmor watched them for a time, and then he lifted his staff and vanished.

Silveron and Nomayon had watched everything unfold. They hadn't had to wake their comrades; the sound of the shockwave and movement of the warriors crossing the valley had woken them. They lay upon the ledge, staring at the thousands moving below them. Thousands, that for centuries had remained locked in the sorcerer's spell.

"They are all under his spell," Egon said.

"Bad, this is," Brador said. "Even the Elves obey him."

"We must send word to King Anarys," Silveron said.

"I am ready," K'Reel said.

"Tell His Majesty what has happened," the wizard said. "We will wait here until you return."

"I obey." K'Reel leapt into the air, and with a sweep of his wings, hurtled away.

"Look, Silveron," Egon said, pointing.

Silveron saw a majestic figure upon an Elven horse. Her golden armour looked dull under the blood red light. Her cape was a dirty brown. Even her hair looked red, although Silveron knew it was a golden mane. She led a large group of Elves that were mounted, and behind them came Elven foot soldiers.

"Queen Nerolynn," He said.

"Loath King Anarys will be to face her in battle," Brador said.

"We must ensure that that never happens," Silveron said.

"How can we do that?" Yosh-en asked.

"I do not know. Perhaps if I can find and use the talisman to banish Darkmor, this spell will be broken."

"Will they not die if that happens?" Brador said.

"I do not know," Silveron replied.

"Better to die than be a slave of the Dark One," Egon said.

There was a murmur of assent at this statement. They all returned their attention to the host marching below.

"Why are the birdmen walking?" Egon said. "They should be flying."

The Avianinn walked along with the rest of the host. Their wings hung slackly.

"Lucky for us they do not," The Dwarf said. "Find us, they could."

"There are some Felininn amongst them too," Silveron said.

The feline warriors sat upon their giant birds. Hundreds of them rode along with the horde that was marching into the mountains.

"Yes," said Yosh-en. "Lord Tong-en was sent to answer the call of the Elf-King. But I do not see him. Perhaps he has fallen in battle."

"That would be an honourable death," Toran-en said. "But this, this is unnatural. I would rather die."

"No argument here," Brador said.

"Well, we must await word from King Anarys," Silveron said. "We should stay out of sight, even though we have seen no patrols."

They backed away from the edge. The tramp of marching feet and the sound of shod hooves upon stone continued on for a long time.


K'Reel saw the Army of Light advancing below him. He went lower, and landed in front of them. Captain Enriss called the army to a halt. King Anarys rode forward, accompanied by F'Leet and Vandaron. The wizard riding a horse, but F'Leet was on foot. He had just returned from scouting ahead.

"Your Majesty, My Lords," K'Reel said, and bowed with his wings opened behind him.

"K'Reel. Why have you come to us? Is something wrong?" Anarys regarded the Avianinn with trepidation. *Has Silveron failed?* He thought.

"There is, Sire. Silveron sent me to report to you."

"Have you met with resistance?" F'Leet said. "Do you have casualties?"

"No, My Lord," K'Reel replied. "But something – *strange* – has happened. Silveron thought it was imperative that I report it."

Captain Enriss rode up.

"What is your order, My Liege?"

"Captain. K'Reel has an important message from Silveron. Go and tell the section leaders the army may rest here for a while. Tell them to be ready to march again at a moment's notice."

"Yes, Your Majesty." He turned his horse and rode off to obey the order.

King Anarys dismounted. Vandaron followed suit.

"Well, K'Rell, please give me your report."

"Yes, Sire. We had found a hidden door at the back of the tower. Silveron had decided to see where it led. He wanted us to go inside to try and find both Princess Willowen and the talisman. But before we could do so, Darkmor appeared on top of the tower and cast a spell."

"I see," Anarys said. "And this spell, did it release the frozen warriors that were in the valley?"

"It did, Your Majesty. How did you know?"

"I thought Darkmor would do this if he could manage it. Go on."

"Many of the host were released. They all came to the tower at his bidding. He ordered them to go into the mountains." He stopped, unsure how to go on.

"These warriors, were they all from the Army of Darkness?" Vandaron asked.

"No, My Lord," the Avianinn answered. "Some were Elves, some Dwarves, and Men and Avianinn and Felininn too. All obeyed Darkmor."

"I know what you are hesitant to say, K'Reel," King Anarys said. "Queen Nerolynn was among them, was she not?"

"She was, Sire. She was on horseback, and led a vast group of Elves, both mounted and foot soldiers."

"What a cunning mind Darkmor has," Anarys said. "He will make us fight our own people. He knows that will take the fighting spirit out of our warriors."

"It would be a terrible thing for you to fight your Queen, Sire," Vandaron said.

"Indeed, Vandaron. That is just what Darkmor wishes us to think. K'Reel, where are Silveron and his companions now?"

"They await my return, My Liege."

"F'Leet, go and fetch Lord Nildoron and a dozen of your best wingmen."

"Yes, Sire." F'Leet leapt into the air.

"What do you have in mind, Your Majesty?" Vandaron asked.

"F'Leet and his wingmen will follow K'Reel back to Silveron and his friends and wait while they enter the tower. Nildoron will go with them. When Silveron has rescued Willowen and banished Darkmor, they will fly them back to join us."

"Do you still think Silveron will achieve this goal, Sire?" Vandaron said. "Remember how Darkmor struck him down, and took both Princess Willowen and the talisman."

"I have not forgotten, Vandaron. But I have faith that Silveron will be successful."

"Let us hope that your faith is justified, Sire. Perhaps I should go, and assist Silveron in this task."

"Do you expect him to fail, Vandaron?"

"No, Your Majesty. I hope he succeeds, but if he does not –"

"All will fall. I know you think he is not capable of achieving victory. I have watched you belittle him before us."

"Sire, I –"

King Anarys held up his hand. Vandaron's mouth shut like a trap.

"I will hear no more of this, do you understand? It is Silveron's task, and no other. Goldwen had faith in him, so do I. That is the end of the matter. Do I make myself clear?"

The wizard nodded.

"Yes, Your Majesty."

"Good. Ah, here comes Nildoron."

The Elf-lord reigned in his mount, and dismounted and bowed before Anarys.

"You sent for me, Sire?"

"Yes. I want you to go with F'Leet and his wingmen and wait for Silveron and his companions. When they have rescued Willowen and Silveron has banished Darkmor, you will fly them back to us."

"I understand, Sire."

As this exchange was taking place, F'Leet and his wingmen arrived. They landed and bowed before Anarys.

"What is your order, Your Majesty?" F'Leet asked.

"Take Lord Nildoron and follow K'Reel to where Silveron and his companions are. Lord Nildoron will enter the tower with them. Once they have rescued Princess Willowen and the sorcerer has been banished, you will fly them all back to join us."

"We obey, Sire." He walked over to Lord Nildoron. "My Lord, I will carry you myself." He went behind Nildoron, reached under the Elf's armpits, and wrapped his arms around Nildoron's chest. "Are you ready?"

"Yes," Nildoron said. He grabbed the Avianinn's arms, and held on for dear life.

F'Leet spread his wings. His wingmen followed suit. He nodded to Anarys.

"We go, Sire." All of the Avianinn hurled themselves into the air.

With K'Reel in the lead, they sped away.

Anarys and Vandaron watched until they had disappeared from view.

"Vandaron," the King said, "do not tell anyone about what Darkmor has done."

"But should we not tell them, Sire?"

"No. Many of us will have to face old friends in combat. That is bad enough."

"But would not the shock be lessened if they were forewarned?"

"Perhaps it would. But I believe our warriors would worry if the truth were known. They would wonder who of their old comrades were now under Darkmor's spell, and worse than that, they would wonder if they could slay them in battle."

Vandaron knew that Anarys was thinking of Queen Nerolynn. Surely it was torture for him to know that his own wife was under Darkmor's spell, and that he might have to fight and kill her on the battlefield? *If they could be killed,* Vandoron thought.

"As you wish, Your Majesty. I will not speak of this to anyone."

"Good. Here comes Enriss."

Captain Enriss reigned in his steed. He bowed to Anarys.

"What is your command, Your Majesty?"

"Captain. I believe we should be moving again. Please send a groom to take Lord Nildoron's horse."

"Yes, Sire." He turned his mount, and rode off to give the order to march.

King Anarys and Vandaron mounted their horses. A groom rode up and bowed to Anarys.

"I will lead Lord Nildoron's mount back to his troop, Your Majesty." He led the horse away.

Captain Enriss returned and bowed to the King.

"We are ready to march, Sire."

"Proceed," Anarys said.

Enriss held up his hand, and then waved it forward. The army started to move again.


Willowen awoke to the sound of the bolt of her prison cell drawing back. She rose from her sleeping pallet and stood. Who was it? Had Darkmor come to torment her again? He had the amulet. No doubt he had worked out how to use it. Perhaps he had used it on the Starstone?

The door opened wide, and Kalindra appeared in the doorway. She was carrying a tray that had a plate of food, eating utensils, and a bottle and two goblets.

She entered the room. One of the Schaaka who stood guard closed it behind her. The girl came over to Willowen and bowed.

"Your Highness."

Willowen smiled.

"I am glad it is you, and not Darkmor."

Kalindra returned her smile.

"Will you eat, Your Highness?"

She walked over to the table and placed the tray on it. Willowen came and joined her. The girl put a plate of food in front of Willowen and filled a goblet and placed it before her. Willowen sat down. The food smelt good. She picked up the goblet and tasted the drink.

"This is honey wine," she said, surprised.

Kalindra sat down.

"Darkmor said that you could have it now. Are you pleased? He said it would please you."

"It does indeed. As does your company." She raised her goblet and toasted the girl.

"Thank you, Your Highness."

"Has something happened? There was a sound like thunder, and I thought I heard many warriors on the march." Willowen took up the small knife and fork and used them to cut the meat. She popped some in her mouth and chewed. It was mouth-watering.

The girl nodded.

"Darkmor used a spell to free the warriors that were frozen in the valley. It was amazing. P'Kaani and I watched it from the window. They came to the tower. Darkmor ordered them into the mountains. We could hear his voice commanding them."

The Elf paused in the act of taking another mouthful.

"Were they all freed?"

"All except those who had been slain in battle."

"What happened to them?"

The girl went pale. Her freckles stood out. She licked her lips nervously.

"Oh, Your Highness," she said, her voice filled with horror, "it was awful."

"Tell me."

Kalindra took a deep breath, and then went on in a rush.

"They turned to dust! It was as if the centuries had finally caught up with them. They had been frozen in time for so long, and it seemed as if all of those years were laid upon them all at once. I turned away, but P'Kaani is a Plainswoman, and is made of sterner stuff. She watched it all. She described it in great detail. I wanted to stop up my ears, but she kept on."

"Is that what happened to the Army of Light and its allies?"

"Oh no, Your Highness. The ones who were – *summoned* – by Darkmor, came and marched with his own forces that he had freed. I saw a beautiful Elven Queen, mounted upon an Elven steed. She led many of your warriors."

Willowen put her knife and fork down. She gazed at the girl in shock.

"Your Highness? What is it?"

"The Queen you saw is my mother. She has been lost to us for a thousand years."

"Oh, Your Highness, how terrible for you." The girl reached across and put her hand over Willowen's.

"Thank you. I remember when my father came here to try and free them. He had with him Goldwen, who was the mightiest wizard of the time. But whatever they tried, they could not free them. They had to admit defeat, and leave them as they were. My mother was lost to us." She frowned. "Why would they not resume their fight with Darkmor once they were awakened? My mother hated the Black Circle. The enemy then was the Man Malkaar, and he was the last of that sorcerous group, but now his soul possesses Darkmor the Elf. Surely they would have continued the fight against him?"

"They seemed to be under a spell, Your Highness. They obeyed him as his own warriors did."

"What happened then?" Willowen asked.

"P'Kaani and I watched as the others marched away. It seemed to take a long time. There were thousands of warriors."

"I see." Willowen was lost in thought. Her mother lived! There must be some way to save her.

"Your Highness, I think I know what Darkmor wants to do."

"And what is that?"

"He came to us and used us as before. But afterwards, he was boasting. He said something about King Anarys and his warriors not being able to face their own people in battle. He thought it would take the fight out of them. And he said there was another force that no-one knew about."

Willowen took the girl's hands in her own.

"Kalindra, I must escape. I have to warn my father. Can you get the talisman for me?"

"I will try, Your Highness. Darkmor is tiring of me. I know he will get rid of me soon. Can I come with you?"

"Of course you can."

Willowen picked up the bottle and filled their goblets. She raised hers in a toast. Kalindra followed suit.

"To freedom," Willowen said.

"To freedom," Kalindra echoed.

The goblets clinked together, and they drank.


Meanwhile, F'Leet, Nildoron and the Avianinn came to the valley. Nildoron had had a brief moment of terror when they had first taken to the air, but now he found it exhilarating. He had spoken to F'Leet while they were flying, pointing out features of the landscape that they passed below.

"The valley, F'Leet, and Darkmor's tower," he said. He had needed to raise his voice to be heard above the wind that rushed by.

"I see them, My Lord."

"There is something different," Nildoron said, his voice puzzled.

"The warriors are gone," the Avianinn rumbled.

"You are right. It is completely empty. Are they now all under Darkmor's spell?"

"I do not know, My Lord."

As they entered the valley, Nildoron swept his gaze over the land below. Not one warrior remained. But there was a grey ash or dust that covered the valley floor. He wondered what it was.

Ahead of them K'Reel began to lose height. F'Leet and the others followed him. They came down and landed where Silveron and his companions were waiting.

F'Leet released Nildoron and stepped back.

"Thank you, F'Leet," Nildron said. "That was breathtaking. I now understand the love you have for flying."

"It is my honour to serve you, My Lord." He bowed.

"Greetings, My Lord," Silveron said. "I did not expect you to bring so many Avianinn with you."

"It was the King's idea. I am to join you in the search for Princess Willowen and the talisman. F'Leet and his wingmen will wait here for us. When we have rescued her and the talisman has been found and used, they will fly us back to the army."

"I must thank His Majesty for his confidence in my success."

"Tell me about this spell," Nildoron said.

"Darkmor came to the top of his tower. He spoke several Words of Power, and sigils appeared before him. There was a thunderclap, and then moments after, the warriors who had been frozen came to life and made their way to the tower. He spoke to them, and commanded them to go into the mountains."

"He sent them into the mountains? Why would he do that? Would he not have them form up in battle formation and prepare to meet our army?"

"Mayhap an ambush he prepares," Brador said. "Empty the valley is now. An inviting emptiness, it is."

The Elf-Lord nodded.

"You may be right, Brador. But King Anarys would not march across it without considering it a trap. Silveron, did all of the warriors leave the valley? Surely there had been some who had been cloven in two, or had lost limbs or head in the conflict. Would Darkmor's spell revive them and make them whole again?"

"No, My Lord, that did not happen. Did you see the dust on the ground in the valley?"

"I did. I wondered what it was."

"That is all that remains of the warriors you speak of."

"They turned to dust?" Nildoron said.

"Aye," the Dwarf said. "Freed from the spell they were, and all the years that they had stood there were finally laid upon them heavily."

"You saw this happen?"

"We did," Egon said. "Thousands of them crumbled to dust before our very eyes."

"What an awful thing to have been frozen for a thousand years and then just turn to dust." Nildoron shook his head.

"There is something else, My Lord."

"What is that, Silveron?"

"Queen Nerolynn was among the warriors that Darkmor released."

"The Queen?" Nildoron said.

"She went into the mountains with thousands of your people," Egon said.

"The Queen is under Darkmor's spell," the wizard said.

"I told His Majesty of this," K'Reel said.

"What was his reaction to this news?" Nildoron asked.

"He said that he would not inform the army that the Queen and so many of your own people were now under the Dark One's spell."

"He did not even inform me," Nildoron said. "Darkmor has done this so that she and all the others who were once our allies may now be turned against us."

"That is what I thought too," Silveron said.

"I cannot imagine how the King would react if he were to meet her on the field in battle," Nildoron said.

"Stay his hand, it would," Brador said. "Cunning, Darkmor is to make friends into foes."

"He is indeed cunning," Nildoron said. "We must not let that fight happen. Silveron, where is this door you found?"

"Come, I will show you."

Silveron walked over to the ledge and lay prone. The Elf-Lord came and joined him. The wizard pointed to the back of the tower.

"See there? The door is hidden among trees."

"Is it guarded?"

"Yes. There are eight guards. Four Schaaka, four Cobrans, and one of the Schaaka is an O'skaa rider. His spider is with him."

"That is all?"

"Yes."

"Then we should go. The army is getting closer every moment. If you can carry out your task before they arrive and are forced to fight Queen Nerolynn and her warriors, banishing Darkmor should negate his spell."

"What if negating the spell destroys them as the warriors in the valley were destroyed?" the wizard said.

"We must take that chance. If we wait until the army arrives, they will fight. It will be too late then."

"I agree."

The pair backed away from the ledge and rejoined the others.

"We are going now," Nildoron said. "F'Leet, you and your wingmen remain here until we return."

"What if you do not return?" the Avianinn rumbled.

"Then you are to join His Majesty and fight to the end."

"Yes, My Lord." He bowed.

"Come, Brador," Silveron said. "It is time to put your war hammer to work."

The Dwarf grinned.

They walked over to a path that they had found and began the descent to the door.

# CHAPTER XX

# THE END OF THE BEGINNING

Sardia smiled to herself. As she had thought, Anarys was holding himself back from the battle. She knew that he was loath to face his queen on the battlefield as the Master had planned. She watched as he and Sirlyk sat protected behind Candreen's shield. All around them the chaos of battle raged. She wished she could see his face, but he was too far away. Sardia imagined the turmoil that was going on in the Elven-King's mind.

*Now,* she thought, *This is the time...*

"Garduk."

"Yes, My Queen?"

"Send in the Bright Ones the Master enslaved."

Garduk grinned wickedly.

"Yes, My Queen."

"Let us see how they will face their own."

*Or if they will face them,* Oolikhorr sent.

The Queen of the Goblins stroked the hair on the monster's head.

"Yes, my sister," she said gleefully. "Now we will see how Anarys reacts."

*Perhapss he will refusse to fight?*

"If he does not fight, he will die."

Garduk had been sitting on his O'skaa listening to this exchange with relish. Now Sardia realised that he was still there.

*"Go!"* she cried.

Garduk bowed in his saddle.

"Yes, My Queen." He turned his mount and went off to relay her order.

*What of the birdmen and the catmen?* Oolikhorr sent. *Sshould we not ssend them in to fight?*

"I do not think that we will need them. Anarys and his army will not fight their kin. They are doomed."

The sound of an Elven horn pierced the air. Once it had been a clear sound, ringing out over the battlefield. But that had been a thousand years ago. Now it had a somewhat harsher sound. Sardia turned atop her mount, as Nerolynn and her mounted Elven troops rode past. The former Queen of the Elves drew her sword as the horn sounded again.

"Now we will see what Anarys does," Sardia said.

The Elven-King listened intently. Was that an Elven horn he heard? It sounded strange somehow. He listened for the sound again but there was nothing. Perhaps he had imagined it? The tumult of battle around him had made him think –

The strange horn was sounded again.

*There it is again,* he thought. *Where?*

"Anarys."

He turned to Sirlyk who was mounted by his side. The King of the Goblins pointed, and Anarys looked in the direction that he indicated. Coming towards them was a large force of mounted warriors. Elven warriors. At their head rode...

He gasped as he realised who the leading figure on horseback was. His heart fell. A tear formed in one eye, and then rolled unheeded down his cheek.

The horn sounded again. The weird tones echoed in the valley. Nerolynn cried out an order and held her sword aloft. Her mounted warriors drew their own blades, and they urged their mounts into a faster gait. The mounted warriors then broke into a headlong charge, and plunged towards them.

Anarys stared at them aghast as they came on.

*"Anarys!"* Sirlyk cried.

The Elven-King came out of his trance. He looked over at his friend confusedly.

"You must give the order to stop them," Sirlyk said firmly.

"Yes – yes," Anarys said dazedly. "I –" he faltered.

The Goblin reached out and grabbed his arm. He shook it roughly.

The Elf merely kept staring at him.

*Has his mind gone?* Sirlyk thought with horror. He released the Elven-King's arm and addressed the warriors around them, raising his voice to a stentorian bellow.

*"Warriors! Those who now come against us are ensorcelled by the Dark One. They are no longer the friends and loved ones that you once knew. Strike them down! Protect your King!"*

He ripped out his sword. "Lord Merys," he said, "you must take charge."

Lord Merys was staring at King Anarys in disbelief. He nodded once.

"You are right," he said bleakly. *"Warriors, make ready! Bowmays, target those riders!"*

All around them, Elven warriors and bowmays readied themselves for the onslaught. Sirlyk could see doubt on some of their faces. Even so, he sighed with relief.

"Master Candreen, Master Vandaron," Merys said quietly, "not one of them must reach the King." He drew his sword. "Especially not Queen Nerolynn herself."

"We understand, My Lord," the wizards chorused.

Vandaron raised his hands in front of himself, and concentrated. A whirling ball of destructive force spun into existence between his outstretched fingers.

Nerolynn and her warriors bore down upon them. Commander Lysanna raised her hand. The bowmays drew back on their bows.

"Wait," she said. "Let them come closer." She gauged the distance between them and the oncoming force. It was lessening rapidly.

"Wait," she said.

Nerolynn's mounted force pounded towards them. The combatants in front of them parted and gave ground, leaving a huge gap for the mounted warriors to charge through.

"Wait," Lysanna said.

The riders stormed up until they could see their blackened eyes, and the gray, dusty faces that showed how the passing of a thousand years had been wrought upon them. Scarcely a bowshot remained between the two forces.

Lysanna brought her hand down. *"Meht!"* she cried. A hurricane of arrows rushed towards the riders, and fully half of them fell.

But the others, Nerolynn at their head, came on.

"Your Majesty, Lysanna said, "we are out of arrows." She regarded the oncoming horde grimly. *"Swords!"* she cried. The bowmays dropped their bows, and drew their blades in one shimmering movement.

*"Forwards!"* Lord Merys cried, and the Elven, Goblin, and Dwarven warriors rushed out to meet the enemy. With a shout, Vandaron released the spinning sphere of energy, and it blasted a path through the ensorcelled warriors. He made to create another, but a spear hurtled out of the oncoming horde and pierced his chest. He looked down at it in shocked surprise for a moment, and then collapsed into the mud and blood that covered the valley floor.

Candreen hurriedly raised the shield, and the enemy smashed into it.

*"Fools!"* Darkmor hissed. "You have no power to defeat me."

"There is the talisman," Silveron said.

Darkmor's lips curled in a sardonic sneer. He reached into his robe, and brought out the talisman. He dangled it in front of them teasingly.

"It's a pity that you don't –"

Silveron's hand shot out, and the talisman snapped its chain, flew through the air, and came to rest in his grasp.

The sorcerer snarled incoherently. He made to step forwards, but Silveron raised the talisman, and Darkmor halted his advance.

"You know the power of this," Silveron said. "Good."

"That was a neat trick, *brother*," Darkmor said. "I'm impressed." He regarded him with grudging respect, and bowed mockingly.

"You are no brother to me," the Elf replied coldly.

"You wound me," the sorcerer said sardonically. "What happens now, Silveron? Do you banish me from this realm forever? Isn't that what your Council of Light wanted?"

The wizard nodded.

"It is. The task was given me by Goldwen, and I will carry it out."

Darkmor shrugged.

"If that's what you really want to do, do it." A crafty look appeared on his face. "But what a waste it would be."

"A waste?" Silveron echoed. "What do you mean?"

The sorcerer regarded him with a superior gaze.

"I mean that *I* am the only one in this realm who has the knowledge of the Dark Magick that has been forbidden to all Elves." He stared at Silveron. "Wouldn't *you* like to possess such knowledge? Think of it: with such secrets in your grasp, you could remake Erathyn into a paradise." He gestured behind himself. "I could show you how to use the limitless power of the Starstone. You could create your own world!"

"Don't listen to him, Silveron!" Egon cried.

With a hiss, Darkmor bent his furious stare upon the Man.

"Silence, dog! I'm not talking to you!"

Egon subsided, cowed beneath the gaze of those burning orbs.

"And what of you, Darkmor?" Silveron asked reasonably. "What happens to you once you give me this forbidden knowledge?"

The sorcerer spread his hands.

"I'll serve you, Silveron. I'll do anything you want me to." He lowered his head deferentially.

"Even die?" Brador said. He hefted his war hammer suggestively.

Darkmor's head came up quickly and he regarded him angrily, but said nothing.

"He merely bandies words with you, Silveron," Nildoron said. "You only have to complete your task, and he is gone forever."

"Aye," added Brador, "Nildoron speaks the truth, lad. Speak your spell, and rid of him forever, we are."

The sorcerer's eyes turned to slits. He was furious, but made no response. He regarded the wizard. He looked closely at Silveron, and saw uncertainty on the Elf's face. A realisation suddenly came to him. He laughed.

"You don't know how to cast the spell, do you?" he smirked.

The wizard stared back at him defiantly.

"That's it, isn't it?" Darkmor said. He laughed again. "You don't know how to do it!" He grinned and clapped his hands together in glee.

"I will find the spell," Silveron said grimly.

The sorcerer folded his arms nonchalantly.

"You'd better hurry, then. Every moment that passes sees more of your friends die." He unfolded his arms, and made a gesture. An image of the battle far above them resolved itself in the superheated air. They saw the overwhelming numbers that pressed the Army of Light. O'skaa riders were everywhere in their thousands. Many Elves and their allies lay dead in the mud under the blood-red sky. Anarys and his warriors were beset by...

"*Queen Nerolynn!*" Nildoron cried. He drew his sword, and made to rush at Darkmor.

The image winked out like a snuffed candle.

The sorcerer fixed Nildoron with a freezing gaze. The Elf-lord halted. Thinking he saw an opening, Egon drew his dagger, and hurled it at Darkmor. The sorcerer brushed it away with a negligent flick of his hand, and it skittered along the rocky floor.

"Fool," he hissed. "Your little toy can't harm me. Not even the energy that burns within the heart of a star can destroy me now." He raised his right hand, and the eyes on the serpent bracelet kindled into fire.

"Stop," Silveron said curtly. He raised the talisman.

Darkmor regarded him, and slowly lowered his hand. The fire in the serpent's eyes dimmed and went out.

"What now, Silveron?" he asked. "Do we stand here forever?"

"No. Let my companions go. Only you and I need do this."

"Go where, Silveron?" Egon said. "The bridge is out."

"Stairs there are over there," Brador said. He gestured with his hammer.

"Where do they lead, Darkmor?" Silveron asked.

"Out, eventually. They come out at the top of the valley behind the tower."

"All of you go, then," the wizard said.

"No, lad," Brador said. "To the finish we are with you."

"Yes, Silveron," Egon added, "we won't leave you now."

"You cannot help me. Take Willowen to safety."

The Seer picked the Princess up, and addressed them.

"Silveron is right. We must go. Only he can face the Dark One."

Darkmor's gaze lingered on Willowen's shapely form. Silveron knew what thoughts burned in the sorcerer's brain.

"Let them go," he said threateningly.

"Very well,' Darkmor said with a sneer. He waved his hand dismissively. "I can always hunt them down after I've dealt with you."

The companions still stood there, reluctant to leave.

*"Get out!"* Darkmor snarled. "Before I change my mind, and kill you all."

"Thank you, Silveron," Nildoron said. He bowed to the wizard.

"Goodbye, lad," Brador said. He raised his hammer to his heart.

"We won't forget your sacrifice," Egon said.

"It has been an honour to fight by your side," Toran-en said. He and Yosh-en bowed deeply.

"Yes, yes," Darkmor said impatiently, waving his hand dismissively. "This is all very touching. Go."

"Nomayon knows Silveron will know what to do," The Seer said meaningfully.

He began to carry Willowen towards the stairs. After a moment, the others followed him. They looked back at Silveron who smiled at them. Nildoron drew his sword and saluted the wizard. Then he sheathed the blade, and set his foot upon the first stair. He climbed, and the others went after him. Silveron watched them ascend until their forms shimmered in the heat and disappeared from his sight.

"It's just you and me now, brother," Darkmor said. "Let's finish this." He took a defensive stance, and his hands came up before him. The fire lit up in the eyes of the serpent bracelet.

Silveron raised his staff and desperately searched his mind for the spell that would activate the talisman.

*Father,* he thought frantically, *help me!*

Candreen was tiring. Sweat ran in rivulets down his face, and burned his eyes. He was exhausted by the effort of maintaining the shield, and with Vandaron slain, the enemy attacked it relentlessly. He knew it was only a matter of time before they broke through his defences. The wizard shivered with fatigue, and his mind was aching with the constant maintenance of their protection. He panted with exhaustion.

*Why did I not stay with Amberon?* He thought wretchedly.

Candreen stared out at the combatants that were beyond the shield. He gazed in horror at the O'skaa riders as they slaughtered the Elven warriors and bowmays. The wizard watched aghast as Lysanna was flung to the ground and trampled by O'skaa. He saw Lord Merys dragged from his horse and butchered by three Schaaka warriors. The Dwarven warriors vanished beneath the O'skaa. He stared horror-struck as the monstrous arachnids rushed up and climbed the shield. Candreen could feel the pressure of the multitude of hairy bodies, and dropped to his knees. The wall of energy that protected them began to give way under their weight. Behind the O'skaa riders came the ensorcelled Elves, Nerolynn among them.

He cried out.

*"Sire!! I cannot – hold..."*

The wizard's concentration failed, and the shield collapsed. Shrieking, the O'skaa riders fell upon the defenders. Jhara Shin and his scouts disappeared beneath the rush of hairy bodies. Vosh-en was struck by one of the monsters legs, and fell and lay still. Nerolynn cried out an order, and her warriors rushed to come to grips with Anarys and his guard. Candreen rose shakily to his feet. A Schaaka impaled him upon his reversed goad. The Elf fell, and was trampled by many arachnid feet as they pressed their assault.

Anarys came to his senses as an O'skaa rider attacked. He drew his sword, and parried the Schaaka's thrust. At his side, Sirlyk split an enemy's skull to the teeth, and as the rider fell from his mount, the Goblin-King skewered it with his blade. He turned to see how Anarys fared, and a riderless O'skaa smashed into his warbeetle, and knocked him flying. The monster sank its fangs into Chukdah, and then it turned and regarded Sirlyk with a hungry gaze.

The Goblin-King rose to his feet and stood his ground, and brandished his sword menacingly at the creature.

*"Come and take me!"* he cried.

With an evil scream, the arachnid charged.

"So, Silveron," Darkmor said. "Here we are. Any idea of the spell you need?" He smiled.

They were circling each other, watching warily for any sudden move. Darkmor's hands were raised, and the fire burned in the snake bracelets' eyes. Silveron had his staff in his right hand, and in his left was the talisman.

"I will find it."

"You'd better. Anarys and his friends are almost finished. Vandaron and Candreen are both dead, and now without their magical protection, my army can't be held back. The O'skaa will dine on their flesh."

The wizard didn't reply.

The sorcerer raised an eyebrow.

"Don't you care that they are all going to die?"

"Of course I care," Silveron said. "But Anarys himself told me that they were willing to sacrifice themselves to make an end of you."

"How noble," Darkmor sneered. The sneer turned into a sardonic smile.

"And now they will get their wish. My forces will slay them all. They will all have died for you." He glanced at the talisman held in Silveron's fist. "Died for you and your precious toy." He laughed jeeringly. "The toy that you don't know how to use."


Anarys had slain his opponent. He heard Sirlyk cry out his challenge, and made to turn his horse so he could assist him. Suddenly a mounted warrior was before him, and with a mighty swing of their sword, his horse's head was swept off. As his mount collapsed in a fountain of blood, he was thrown heavily to the ground. Anarys sat up and looked up at his enemy. He scrambled to his feet as he saw who had struck him down.

Nerolynn dismounted, and came in for the kill. He saw the blank face, and the white eyes that seemed not to know him. The Elven-King raised his sword, and their blades met with a metallic clang and gave off sparks. They traded blows, and stepped around each other, dodging slashes and thrusts. Around them the carnage went on.

With a shout, Darkmor cast a fireball at Silveron. The Elf went to block it with his staff, but the blazing ball of flame struck it from his hand. The wizard watched in dismay as the staff was turned to ash. He took up a defensive stance and held the amulet before him.

The sorcerer was standing and staring at him with a mocking look on his face.

"I'd say now would be a good time for you to think of that spell," he said sarcastically.

Silveron desperately searched his mind for the spell, but nothing came to him.

*Goldwen*, he thought, *please!*

Darkmor caught his thought.

"Goldwen is dead," he sneered. "He can't help you. You're all alone."

"As are you," Silveron replied.

The sorcerer laughed. "Are you forgetting something? My army –"

Silveron unleashed a blast of energy that flung Darkmor across the floor. The sorcerer lay prone for a moment, and then rose to one knee. He slowly got to his feet. He wiped some blood from the side of his mouth. Darkmor looked at it, and then regarded Silveron with a deadly gaze.

"That wasn't very sporting of you," He said. His voice was low and menacing. "Time to finish our little game." He raised his hands before himself, and between his palms a vortex of destructive energy began to form.

Silveron waited for him to strike.

The group of companions came to a door. They had climbed a long way in the heat. Silveron and Darkmor had vanished in the heat haze that lay behind them. Nildoron approached the door, and gingerly pushed it. It swung open. He drew his sword, and went through. The others followed.

They came out into an open space. No guards or O'skaa were present. Nildoron sheathed his blade. They looked about, and saw that they had come a fair distance from the tower.

Egon tore a strip of cloth from his cloak and went over to Brador.

"Let me see your arm, Brador," he said.

He made a sling, and eased the Dwarf's broken arm into it.

Brador winced.

"I thank you, lad. Much better, that is."

Willowen was regaining her senses. The Seer placed her lightly on the ground, and they gathered around and watched her return to consciousness.

She looked up at the ring of faces.

"Nildoron? Brador?" She said. "Egon? Nomayon? Yosh-en? Toran-en?" She smiled. "We have escaped?"

"Yes, Your Highness," Nildoron replied. He knelt at her side, and helped her to her feet.

She looked around at the faces that were smiling at her.

"Happy we are to see you safe, My Lady," Brador said.

They all bowed to her.

A frown wrote itself across her beautiful face.

"Where is Silveron?"

They all looked at each other, hesitant to make a reply.

"Where is he?" Willowen demanded.

"The sorcerer, Your Highness –" Nildoron began.

The Princess's face went white. She leapt to her feet and turned and rushed for the door.

Egon and Brador ran forward and took her arms, and held her struggling form. They dragged her away from the door.

"Release me!" she cried. "Silveron needs our help!"

Nildoron was suddenly in front of her.

"Lord Nildoron, I demand you unhand me, and let me go to him! Silveron _"

"Is doing what he was tasked to do, Your Highness. We cannot help him. None of us is a match for Darkmor."

She stared at him blindly, and then tears formed in her almond eyes. She sobbed, and then wept uncontrollably, heedless of those around her. The Man and the Dwarf relaxed their grip, and she hurled herself into Nildoron's arms. For a moment, he was shocked and taken aback by her actions, but then he put his arms around her and comforted her. He held her shaking body as she cried.

The others stood there and wept to see her distress.


Anarys blocked another of Nerolynn's swings. His arm felt like lead. Their armour was rent and torn and spattered with blood and mud, and their cloaks were mere rags that hung from their shoulders. Their blades were notched. The Elven-King defended himself, but made no move to strike his opponent down. He had attempted to speak to her, but no response had come, and her blank expression had never changed. Anarys knew that the Dark One's spell had robbed her of her reason, and it was obvious that she did not know him. Still, he hoped that he could break through that sorcery and make her recognise him. Perhaps it was a vain hope, but he knew he had to try.

"Nerolynn,' he said, "Do you not know me?"

He dodged another savage thrust.

Their blades met. They both stepped forward, and their faces were close. He peered into her white eyes, and saw only emptiness there.

"Nerolynn, it is I. Anarys."

With a mighty heave, she disengaged, and flung him away. They began to circle each other.

"I know you are still in there somewhere. Fight it! Come back to me."

Nerolynn rushed forward, and he was forced to block her attack in a flurry of sword strokes. He backed away, and raised his notched sword defensively. They circled each other again.

"Nerolynn, please. I do not wish to fight you." He lowered his weapon. "My love, come back."

She stepped towards him. Anarys tossed his sword to the bloody ground.

"I will not fight you." He spread his arms wide in a gesture of surrender.

Nerolynn rushed at him, and made to strike him down. Anarys stepped backwards involuntarily. He tripped over a corpse, and fell onto his back. He attempted to rise, but his fatigue and the weight of his armour kept him pinned to the ground. The Elven-King stared aghast at the apparition that had been his love as she advanced to deliver a killing blow. He raised his arm in a futile attempt to block her strike.

*"No!"* Sirlyk cried. Suddenly he was between them. Her blade fell. Sirlyk parried the blow, but Nerolynn's sword broke his blade, and her sword chopped into his shoulder. The Goblin-King dropped to his knees. His black blood ran freely down his battered breastplate. He fell backwards against Anarys.

*"Sirlyk!"* Anarys cried, and gathered him against his chest.

He cradled his mortally wounded friend and looked up at Nerolynn as she loomed over them like the spectre of doom. She raised her sword again.

*So,* Anarys thought, *this is how it ends.*

He bowed his head and waited for her to strike.


"The King!" K'reel cried, and leapt into the air. The Avianinn around him followed, except for F'leet, who looked on horrified.

"K'reel!" he boomed. "Stop! Come back!"

But K'reel and the others ignored his cry, and hurtled towards the battle and the helpless Anarys.

With a roar of rage, the Winglord hurled himself into the sky, and rushed after them.

Darkmor made to cast the ball of energy at Silveron. He smiled wickedly, but then his smile fell. He was looking at something that was behind the wizard. The spinning vortex between his hands collapsed, and he stood there in amazement. He slowly lowered his hands to his side.

*"Impossible,"* he whispered. His eyes were wide with disbelief.

"Do you think I would fall for such a simple trick?" Silveron asked. His gaze was fixed upon his enemy.

"Simple?" A voice said; a voice that the Elf knew. "No, I would not call it simple."

Warily keeping one eye on Darkmor, he glanced to the side. A figure stood there.

"Goldwen!" he gasped in astonishment.

Goldwen nodded to him, and came forwards.

"How can this be?" Silveron said. "You died." He stared amazed as Darkmor did.

The wizard smiled.

"Only my body died. This is my Self."

Sudden realisation came to Silveron.

"You put your Self into the talisman!"

"Yes. Now I have come to help you."

"Help him!" Darkmor scoffed. "You're only a phantom. You can't hurt me!"

Goldwen's Self raised its hand, and made a gesture. Darkmor rose into the air. He struggled, but he couldn't break the hold that the wizard's Self had upon him. He raged, crying out incoherently. The sorcerer's eyes blazed with impotent fury. His hands clenched and unclenched as he strived to free himself to no avail.

Keeping its eyes and attention focussed on Darkmor, Goldwen's Self communicated with Silveron using mindspeech.

*Here is the spell. Use it quickly.*

Alien words streamed into Silveron's mind through the link Goldwen's Self had established. Suddenly Silveron knew exactly what to do, and how to do it. It was easy. He raised the talisman, and gathered the energy in his mind as the Self was showing him. He began to speak the spell. A nimbus of glowing energy emanated from the talisman, and formed a beam of light which speared outwards to envelop the sorcerer.

Darkmor screamed in frustration as the spell began to work.


Anarys stared at Nerolynn as she stood over him as he lay cradling the dying Sirlyk. Fragments of memories rushed through his mind; of how they had first met, of the instant bond that they had both felt. She had stood by his side through many years of strife. Love there was there too.

He shook his head.

Love? No, that had fled along with her senses. Now she was just one of the Dark One's minions.

The Elven-King forced himself to look into her blank eyes.

"Do it," he said. "Slay me. All is lost. Silveron has failed. This world now belongs to the Dark One."


Darkmor twisted and turned like a fish on a hook, but nothing he did could release him from the magic. Silveron spoke the spell, and eldritch syllables not meant for Elven mouth to utter hung blasphemously in the heated air.

*Dark Magic!* Silveron thought in shock, even as he cast it.

The sorcerer's eyes blazed.

*"Hypocrite!"* he cried, his gaze fixed upon Goldwen's Self. "Now we see the *true* source of your power!" He gasped as he felt his body begin to slip away.

Malkaar's Self separated from Darkmor with a wrench that send needles of pain shooting throughout its form. Darkmor's body fell to the floor.

Silveron paused in his spellcast. He stared at his fallen brother.

"Hurry," Goldwen's Self said urgently.

Malkaar's Self stared at its nemesis, hate filling every atom of its substance. Its control of Darkmor's body lost, now it could sense other controlling spells being negated as the spell began to break it apart.

Nerolynn's sword was poised to deliver the final blow. It never fell. The blankness in her eyes slowly cleared, to reveal the blue eyes that Anarys knew and loved. She lowered her blade, confused. All around her, her own warriors ceased their fighting, as bewildered as she was. He watched in amazement as his Queen looked about in puzzlement. There was a pause in the battle as every ensorcelled Elf wondered where they were, what they were doing, and how they had got there. Why did they fight their own kind? How had the battle turned around?

*"What is this?"* she whispered, her voice dry and dusty.

"Nerolynn!" Anarys cried.

She looked down.

"Anarys! What is happening? We waited for you, but you did not come." She realised who lay across Anarys.

"Sirlyk! Oh no!" Nerolynn saw the Goblin-King's blood as it flowed down his armour, and then looked down at her sword in apprehension. The blade was fouled with his blood. She was suddenly filled with dread.

"How?" she said confusedly. "How could I –"

"*Silveron!*" Goldwen's Self cried. "You *must* complete the spell!"

Silveron stared down at Darkmor's lifeless body. He shook his head angrily, knowing he had allowed Darkmor's fall to interrupt him and continued speaking the alien words. A nimbus of powerful energy engulfed Malkaar's Self. The form began to ripple and break up. It screamed in agony as the force tore at it, shredding the very fabric of its being.

Sardia stared at the stilled battlefield. All of the ensorcelled combatants had ceased to fight. Her O'skaa riders had also paused in their attack, puzzled why their allies were standing and staring about themselves in confusion.

"What is this?" she said, baffled. "Why have they stopped –"

*It iss the Bright One,* Oolikhorr sent. *He fightss the Masster! Ssister, he iss loossing!*

The import of the arachnid's Sending exploded upon the Goblin Queen.

"*No!*" she cried. "We cannot let him be defeated!"

*We cannot reach him in time,* the monster sent. *The Bright One will sslay him.*

A wordless exclamation of fury answered this. Sardia fixed her gaze upon their former allies. Her eyes blazed with hatred.

"*Slay!*" she screamed. "*Slay them all!*"

She raised her goad and urged Oolikhorr forwards, and the thousands of O'skaa riders who were standing by behind them followed as they hurtled towards the battle. The O'skaa and Schaaka who had ceased fighting saw them coming, and resumed their attacks. The Elves who had fought by their sides under Darkmor's spell were now the enemy.

Malkaar's Self was fading swiftly, being torn apart by the spell that Silveron was casting. It knew that the end was near, and raged against Goldwen's Self's magic. But its hold over it was too strong. It suddenly sensed that its own hold over Nerloynn and her warriors had been broken. With an intense effort of will, it renewed the bond with her, hoping that when Silveron felt the magic, it would distract him. Then it would strike.

Anarys stared up at his beloved, and saw the empty whiteness return to her eyes. He heard Sardia and her O'skaa riders as they rampaged through the battlefield, striking down their former comrades.

The Elven-Queen raised her sword.

The image of Nerolynn standing over Anarys and Sirlyk suddenly burst upon Silveron.

*"Anarys!"* he cried out, and his concentration was lost for an instant. It was a fatal instant. As Malkaar's Self felt the loss of the magical assault, it gathered its fading energy, and sent a bolt of lightning at its enemies. Goldwen and Silveron were both flung to the rocky floor.

Willowen and Nildoron looked down into the valley. Their far-seeing Elven eyes showed them every detail of the combat. Their companions stood around them, listening as the pair described the battle to them. The Elves suddenly saw Queen Nerolynn standing over Anarys, ready to deal the death blow.

*"Father!"* Willowen screamed.

Silveron struggled to his feet. His head was ringing. The link with Goldwen's Self had been broken. How could he finish the spell now?

He did not need to. Goldwen's Self spoke the Word of Command that finished the spellcast. The energetic aura that surrounded Malkaar's Self ripped at it with an intensity that it had never felt before. It began to break up.

In desperation, it turned and flung out its right hand. A line of force came into being, and connected it to the Starstone. A metallic shriek went up into the superheated air. A shockwave pulsed outward from the Starstone, enveloping Malkaar's Self, Darkmor's body, Goldwen's Self, and Silveron. With a bright flash, all four vanished. The shockwave expanded in a brilliant sphere of multi-coloured light that grew larger and larger until it penetrated the rocky walls.

The sphere emerged out into the valley, and every Schaaka, O'skaa, Goblin, and Elf that it touched disappeared instantly. The Men that Darkmor had resurrected were contacted by the energy, and were instantly turned to dust. It continued to expand rapidly.

The Avianinn had covered half of the distance to the fallen Elven-King when the energy field reached them. K'reel and his wingmen plunged into it and disappeared. F'leet desperately tried to break his forward rush and back away from it with mighty sweeps of his wings, but in an instant, the sphere had touched him, and he also vanished.

Nerolynn brought her sword down. The sphere reached them before she could finish her stroke. All three, Nerolynn, Anarys, and Sirlyk vanished. Around them, most of the combatants disappeared with them. The ensorcelled Men stopped fighting, and turned to dust. Only the Dwarves remained. The shockwave continued to ray outwards. The moon, held in place for so long, began to move again. The sun suddenly shone out blindingly. A massive tremor shuddered through the ground.

Malor rushed towards Shelarindel. He could finally make her out. She and Neldriin were racing towards him, desperately trying to outrun the oncoming horde of Cobrans. The snake-men had hacked and chopped their way through almost half of the army, and were closing in on the two fleeing women. Chaos reigned about them as the two forces clashed. Shelarindel looked up and met Malor's eyes. Then his horse stumbled as the ground shook beneath it. He was thrown to the ground. He struggled to his feet, searching wildly for his love, but he could not see her due to the milling crowd of combatants. He threw several warriors aside as he staggered forwards.

"*Shelarindel!*" he cried desperately.

The battling warriors suddenly parted, and he saw her. Her energy must have been almost spent, for he could see Neldriin dragging her along. Close behind them came a group of Cobrans.

Malor tore his sword from its sheath. He ran towards them. "*Shelarindel!*" There was only a bowshot between them.

The healer heard him, and redoubled her efforts to reach him. She and Neldriin came on, with the Cobrans at their heels. Malor raised his sword, and rushed to come to grips with the enemy.

The wave of energy reached him, and he was gone. Shelarindel stared aghast, not comprehending what had just occurred.

She turned as the girl screamed. The Cobrans had reached them. Their blades were fouled with blood. She closed her eyes in resignation of their fate as Neldriin clutched her in terror. The Cobrans raised their swords.

The energy swept through the area, and they all disappeared.


Nildoron and the Princess stared at the expanding sphere of light. They could see its effect on the combatants. The wave of energy grew and grew. As it reached the sorcerer's tower, that massive edifice vanished. It began to approach the ledge upon which they stood. Nildoron addressed the others.

"This is your world now. Use it wisely. Use it well." He bowed to his companions.

Willowen put her hand over her heart.

"Nephana," she said.

Then the sphere had washed over them, and they had gone. Egon and Brador looked about themselves. They were alone. The Seer and the two

Felininn had vanished along with the two Elves.

Amberon and Narwen felt the unleashed energy of the Starstone. They saw the expanding wall of force as it took the battling warriors. They stared at the image horror-struck as it pulsed outwards in ever expanding movement. Another tremor shook the room, and they both fell to the shivering floor.

The sea heaved and rose in monstrous waves. As the moon continued to move, an earthquake of cataclysmic proportions raced through the entire world. Just a short distance inland was a mountain range. With a shattering roar, it crumbled and disintegrated into shards. A vast chasm opened up. The land dropped. The sea rushed towards the chasm. Beyond lay the Great Plain.

Egon and Brador had been flung to the ground. It rippled impossibly beneath them as though it were made of water. Both of them cried out in terror, but their voices were drowned out by the massive roar of quivering rock around them.

A wave a thousand feet high rushed towards the land, inundating everything in its path. Forests, villages, cities, all were smashed down before its incredible destructive power. The wave rampaged inland, and nothing could stand in its way.

Amberon and Narwen struggled to their feet. The image had disappeared from the wall. They staggered across the shaking floor to look out of the window. The sight of the orb of expanding energy rushing towards them met their horrified gaze.

Far below them in the dark chambers of the Tower of Sh'kaarl, The

Guardian sensed the oncoming wave of energy.

"So," he said, and bowed his head in acceptance.

The Elven wizards stared at the oncoming energy. All thoughts of conquest and mastery of Erathyn fled in the face of its overwhelming power. Both of them realised that they were helpless before such awesome force.

Amberon screamed.

In moments, the energetic sphere had reached them. It touched Algol, and with a flare of bright light, the City of the Wizards winked out of existence.

The wave thundered on. It reached the Great Plain, and the grasslands vanished beneath it. A large city of tents lay before it. The savage Plainsmen gaped in awe at the onrushing waters, and then all disappeared beneath the unstoppable wave.

The tremors began to subside. Egon slowly looked up, to see the sun shining clearly. The moon was moving away, returning to its natural orbit now that the magic that had held it in place had been broken.

"Egon," Brador said, his voice raw, "how is it with you?"

The Man slowly and painfully rose to his feet. He saw his comrade lying there, and went over to him. He helped the Dwarf to stand.

"I am alive," Egon said. "What happened? Did Silveron do this?"

"I know not," Brador replied.

They went to the ledge and looked down. Both armies had scattered. The remains of the Dwarven contingent were gathering together. But of Elf, Goblin, Schaaka, and O'skaa, there was no sign.

The water finally began to slow in its onward rush. It settled in its new position, and after whirling about for a few moments, became almost still. Where the Great Plain had been, now there was an inland sea. Many cities and villages had been engulfed by the deluge. Wreckage and debris floated on the water, and many bodies bobbed here and there amongst the flotsam. The smashed remains of trees were mixed with this wreckage also.

"It seems as if everything that was magical is gone," Egon said, wonder in his voice. He looked at Brador. "How –"

"No magic there is in me, lad," Brador said, "Only craft. But right I think you are. All that was of magic has been taken by that force."

"How did it happen?" Egon asked. "I thought only Darkmor was to be banished."

"Once again, I know not. Mayhap it worked too well, the spell did. Or mayhap even the Dark One's doing this is."

"Maybe the Elves underestimated the power of the thing," Egon said.

"True, that could be," Brador said. He looked down into the valley. "Help me down this path, lad. Let us be gone from this place."

They walked over to a path that led downward. Egon took the Dwarf's good arm, and helped him to descend the wide steps.

"What happens now?" the Man asked.

"Well, Lord Nildoron told you."

"What do you mean?"

"He said that your world Erathyn now is."

Egon regarded his companion confusedly.

"Surely not *all* the Elves are gone?"

"With your own eyes you saw the magic take them."

"Yes, and the Schaaka, O'skaa, Goblins..."

"Then Men and Dwarves are the only ones left, to be sure." He grinned at Egon.

"Learn to live well in this new world, you must, lad. Time it is for Men to make it their own. The magic is gone."

"What of you? What of the Dwarves? Will you not live amongst us in friendship?"

"Back to our underground kingdom we will go. But ever shall Men be welcome, as long as they remember us." A sad smile came to his face. "But it is the doom of Men to forget that which went before. Repeat the same mistakes, they do."

"I will never forget our friendship, Brador. I will tell my children of this day, and of the deeds that were done. I will tell them to tell their children, and the memory will never die."

Brador nodded.

"A good thing, that is. Songs my people will sing of the bravery of all here also."

"I will tell them of the courage of the Army of Light, and of how the Elves and Dwarves fought and died for Men. Sirlyk and his Goblins; the Felininn, the Avianinn, all will be remembered with honour." Egon paused, thinking. Then he went on.

"Above all, Silveron and his bravery will not be forgotten. He saved us all."

"He did that. Saved Erathyn, he did."

They stopped, as memories flooded into their minds of their companions. They stood at the top of the steps for a moment, reliving the past adventures that they all had shared.

"Come, lad," Brador finally said. "A new world awaits us. Let us go and see it."

They continued down the stairs into a new age.